call of the
highland moon

KENDRA LEIGH CASTLE

SOURCEBOOKS CASABLANCA™
AN IMPRINT OF SOURCEBOOKS, INC.®
NAPERVILLE, ILLINOIS

Published by Sourcebooks Casablanca, an imprint of Sourcebooks, Inc.
P.O. Box 4410, Naperville, Illinois 60567-4410
(630) 961-3900
FAX: (630) 961-2168
www.sourcebooks.com

Library of Congress Cataloging-in-Publication Data

Castle, Kendra Leigh.
   Call of the highland moon / Kendra Leigh Castle.
      p. cm.
   ISBN-13: 978-1-4022-1158-4
   ISBN-10: 1-4022-1158-9
   1. Werewolves--Fiction. 2. Supernatural--Fiction. I. Title.

PS3603.A878C36 2008
813'.6--dc22

                        2007049046

Printed and bound in Canada
OPM   10 9 8 7 6 5 4 3 2 1

For Brian
My Hero

Acknowledgments

It's been a long journey from the proudly scrawled poetry of my childhood to the publication of my first novel. I know I never would have made it this far without my parents, Keith and Karen Castle, whose unflagging enthusiasm for my work and absolute certainty of my success never ceased to brighten even my darkest days. I'm eternally grateful to my husband Brian, who refused to listen whenever I said "I can't," and to my children, who (almost) never used my writing time to destroy the house and/or one another. I'm also deeply indebted to my wonderful agent, Kevan Lyon, for her belief, support, and guidance, and to my editor, Deb Werksman, for loving my heroes as much as I do.

Chapter One

THE NIGHT WAS CALLING TO HIM.

Gideon MacInnes stood before the open window, inhaling the biting mid-December wind, savoring it as though it were the most intoxicating midsummer's breeze.

Run with me, it whispered.

But was it safe?

He closed his eyes and tilted his head back slightly, his shaggy fall of dark brown hair just grazing the tops of his shoulders with the motion, and scented the lay of this place. It was at once unfamiliar and yet not so very unlike the land, an ocean away, he called home.

Gideon's nostrils flared slightly. Pine. Wood smoke. The rich, earthy smell of decaying leaves. The temptation of a lone, foraging deer. And underneath it all, winding like a ribbon through each singular aroma, the unmistakable promise of snow. Judging by the heaviness of the air, there would likely be more than any of the locals would like by morning, even as accustomed as they were to spending close to half the year at winter's mercy. He really ought to go, Gideon knew, if he didn't want to find himself stranded for a few extra days. Especially when he'd just gotten off the phone after announcing his decision to return home at last. But then again …

Gideon opened his eyes, once more scanning the grounds of the small, luxurious inn he had selected specifically for its privacy. Then, satisfied, he trained his unnaturally golden gaze on the darkness of the woods that very nearly surrounded this place.

Alone.

Good.

Gideon shrugged off the simple button-down shirt already hanging open on his muscular frame, feeling his skin prickle at its contact with the open air. Already he could feel his blood rising with a kind of savage joy that he had not felt, had not allowed himself to feel, since fleeing Scotland some two months before as though the hounds of Hell were snapping at his heels.

What on earth had possessed him to think he needed the city? Gideon wondered as he slid his favorite pair of faded, weather-beaten jeans down over taut, sinewy muscle to the floor. He had tried them all, and fled them all just as quickly as he had run to them. Los Angeles. New York. Las Vegas. Chicago. All of them the same. He could admit, now that he was thousands of miles away from the man, that his father may have had a point when he'd accosted his resolute son on his way out the door.

"Go, then, you stubborn fool, and you'll see exactly what it is you're missing, what's in all of this 'life' you think is passing you by. Too much light. Smells to send you running for the bathroom. Sound so that it could deafen a normal man. And though you may hate it, Gideon, you aren't a normal man, and never will be. What they call 'civilization' was never intended for the

likes of us. Blessing and curse our lot may be, but you'll have to accept it. What's in you isn't about to give you a choice."

Gideon fought down a snap of temper as the image of Duncan MacInnes rose in his mind, glaring at him as though he were nothing but a petulant, stubborn child and all but wagging his finger at him as he gave his parting shot.

"Some things are more important than sowing your own bloody oats, lad. I might have expected this from your brother, but you … well, have your time, then. But if you even dare to think you're pushing this off on Gabriel, let that be followed quickly by the memory of who taught you to hunt. I'll haul your sorry carcass back by the scruff of your neck, make no mistake. Now. Come and give your da a hug, then."

So like Duncan, Gideon thought with a shake of his head as he straightened, fully nude in the biting air. The threat of a whipping, and then gruff affection. It had taken only a couple of rather painful lessons in Gideon's teenage years for him to understand that Duncan meant both. His brother, however … well, Gideon didn't think Gabriel had quite figured it out yet, which might explain why he was still intent on acting so consistently like a damned idiot. That, and the fact that Gabriel didn't want the Guardianship any more than Gideon had. Gideon might have been the accursedly firstborn, but Gabriel, knowing Gabriel, probably considered his continuing irresponsibility in any and all facets of life as just one more bit of insurance that it would never fall to him.

He also, thought Gideon with a grimace, got to have a great deal more fun, and would continue to if things continued on their present path.

"Ah, well," Gideon sighed softly as he lifted his eyes to the glowing silver of a moon not a week from reaching her fullness. "Might as well enjoy my taste of freedom, then, while I have it."

He'd been brooding ever since he'd gotten to the States, trying to decide what was best to be done when, in his heart of hearts, he'd known all along he was fighting a losing battle. In city after city, his heart had done nothing but ache for the wild places, the things he had been so eager to leave behind. The great sights Gideon had dreamed of seeing had not moved him. The novelty of having multitudes of women from which to choose, rather than a handful, had not enticed him as he'd thought they would, plentiful and willing though they were. And in truth, he thought with a rueful twist of his mouth, skulking about public parks when the Change came upon him, in fear of being shot by some well-meaning officer with a tranquilizer gun and waking up in a local zoo, had been a rather humbling experience.

The fact that he had finally gravitated to this little town on the edge of Lake Ontario in rural Northern New York, a place both beautiful and forbidding due to the harshness of its climate, was most telling of all. And so it had finally prompted his decision, and the call. After all, it was the place that reminded him most of home.

And there was a sort of peace in accepting that, Gideon decided as he relaxed his muscles. His golden gaze sharpened, becoming oddly predatory before he dropped his lids, thick black lashes twining together, and willed the beast within to the surface. It wasn't as though the idea of running herd on a pack of Highland werewolves really bothered him, nor even the weight of the responsibility of guarding the Stone. For if he, who had been groomed for the task his entire life, declined, then to whom would it fall? Gabriel had declared himself unfit whether or not it was true, and the thought of Malachi taking over would chill the blood of any sane person. No, Gideon thought, it wasn't as though his lot was really so objectionable. The only question was, then, could he learn to live permanently with the restlessness that had been gnawing at him steadily for the past few years?

Since the one thing that might assuage it was looking less and less likely to ever materialize, Gideon supposed he would have to accept it, make his peace with it, and find contentment where he could.

He'd start tonight—right now.

Running had always been his freedom, and his peace … as was the wolf.

After years of practice, Gideon's inner beast came quickly when it was bidden. Despite humankind's multitude of amusing misconceptions about his kind, the truth was that while the Change was unavoidable at the full moon, he could shift by force of will at any of her phases. Although his powers wouldn't be at their full strength at this time of month, Gideon was still, and always, a formidable adversary, so there was little fear of being overtaken by humans. Most of his pack Changed fairly often, really, if only for a quick run, or simply for the sheer joy of it. He had been no different.

Was still no different, it would seem.

There was a burning pleasure as flesh stretched and shifted, as bone shortened and changed. Claw and tail, fur and fang sprouted as Gideon dropped to the floor, pain blending with the pleasure of release, just as always when he opened himself to his true nature. Within moments, the figure that had been a dark, brawny Scotsman had been replaced by that of a large and powerful wolf with fur the color of midnight and uncanny amber eyes that seemed to give off a preternatural glow. Its muscles bunched. With one single, powerful leap, the massive beast was through the second-story window and racing across the hard-packed snow into the embracing shadows of the forest.

Gideon's thoughts became simpler, more directed, his emotions clearer as what he always thought of as his wolf-sense took over. He was all lean grace and strength as he bounded into the welcoming trees, his senses sharpening, almost frightening in their acuity. When Gideon ran through the forest, he *became* the forest.

The creatures of the wood scattered from his path and then stilled, not wanting to betray their locations with a sound. This was an ancient beast that ran among them now, and while they had never encountered one of his kind, their blood knew his. It should have been, had always been, glorious. And yet …

There was a strange and sinister current slithering through this darkness. Some odd, bitter tang he had never tasted in every breath of arctic air. It enveloped Gideon as he pushed himself forward, spurring him on even as the night thickened around him. His father's voice whispered through his mind, words that had been spoken in warm invitation. Now, with Gideon's blood rising until it thundered in his ears, those same words became a sly taunt.

Or a plea.

"That's a good lad, Gideon. Hurry home, then."

Hurry home …

Hurry home …

It was a cadence in his mind as he ran, loping through the underbrush with the snap of dried branches and the velvety crush of snow beneath his paws as the only other music in the muffled quiet of the winter night.

A picture formed in his mind of the bright orb of the full moon scattering her light across the gentle waves of Loch Aline, the sheltering darkness of the Highlands behind him, the Sound of Mull beyond him, her islands cradling the ancients and their secrets still. Both sides of him, human and wolf, reached toward home in that moment. In his mind's eye, the pine canopy above him vanished to reveal nothing but the millions of stars above as he imagined running along a distant water's edge.

It was an image that had always brought him joy. But tonight, the thought of home made his heart swell with an almost frantic grief. It made no sense. He had lost nothing. But the ache intensified until Gideon finally sought the only release he knew. Upon reaching a small clearing in the trees, he skidded to a stop, threw back his majestic head, and howled. And for the first time in his life, his song was one of purest desolation. Purest pain.

It was what he had needed. There was finally a bit of relief from the inexplicable despair, the smothering sensation of the forest darkness. Until the last sound he would have expected here, in these woods, reached his ears.

As the ululating rise and fall of three more voices engaged in wolfsong answered him, Gideon's ears pricked, and the fur bristled along his back. Ordinarily, he would have welcomed the company of a native wolf-pack, beasts that had always shown his kind loyalty and respect and often enjoyed joining in for a romp or a hunt. What sang to Gideon were no forest wolves, though.

Although none of his kind roamed this part of the world, Gideon knew the call of his people. And the intent expressed in that howl, difficult as it was for him to believe, was as clear as the night sky above.

Attack.

Gideon crouched low to the ground, paws spread, and growled a warning low in his throat. He cursed himself silently for his distraction earlier.

Followed. But why?

His pack was his family, all differences aside. And yet he was in an enviable position, especially to those who found what he had to be only slightly out of their grasp. The image of a familiar but unwelcome face swam quickly to the forefront of his mind as Gideon reached for some sort of explanation.

Jealousy, yes. Hunger, certainly. But ambush? Murder?

He wouldn't have believed it until now.

Yet there was only one possible explanation.

Malachi.

The thought was staggering, and not only because the justice visited upon his cousin by the Pack would be both swift and brutal once this was discovered. Malachi, if this truly was his doing, would be breaking one of the Sacred Dictates, the cardinal rules that had governed their Pack since the time of Saint Columba. They were ancient things, handed down in oral tradition from generation to generation, but the years had made them no less venerated, and no less adhered to. Pack community—loyalty, trust, and solidarity—was the only thing that kept safe the Stone. Without those things, they were nothing but a bunch of vicious natural oddities, dangerous and unpredictable … even to one another. Hence, the first dictate, most sacred of all: *First, no harm against thy brother Wolf.*

Traitor, Gideon thought, baring his teeth as he moved silently back toward the trees, eyes never leaving the direction from which the voices had come. That his cousin would be so bold as to plot this sort of coup spoke of his supreme confidence that he would succeed.

Overconfidence. It was Malachi's biggest flaw, and it was going to prove fatal. Gideon would live to see his cousin pay.

Gideon turned at the edge of the clearing and streaked swiftly off into the sheltering woods, melting noiselessly into the shadows and trees. He was miles from the inn at this point. It wasn't in his nature to shy from a fight, but Gideon instinctively understood his vulnerability in this situation. He was alone, in unfamiliar territory, facing at least two adversaries stalking him with the intent to kill. Best to draw them into the open, take the advantage. He would not take the blood of another Wolf if he had a choice. It was how he had been raised, how he had been trained. No, the most important thing now was to alert the Pack, to let them know what wheels had been set in motion. Gideon might be the biggest obstacle to a change in power, but he was not the only one.

Speed, stealth before strength.

Keep safe the Stone.

Protect the Pack.

He flew silently over the snow, sensing, rather than hearing, that he was being pursued. His nose told him that he wasn't far from civilization—only a mile or two. He pushed himself harder, though he was already moving at a speed that could only be called supernatural. The smell of humans grew stronger, and faint lights began to flicker through the trees in the distance. He was going to make it out.

Hurry home …

Hurry home …

The first blow forced the breath from his lungs, knocking his feet from under him in mid-lope with unexpected force. Gideon skidded a short ways on his side, then scrambled quickly to his feet. He whipped around to face his adversary, hackles raised, a vicious snarl tearing from his throat. The smaller, stockier gray wolf faced him, yellow eyes seeming to taunt him, growling low in response. Gideon narrowed his eyes, claws lengthening, digging into the snow. This was no Wolf he'd ever seen, but a Wolf just the same.

No, not the same, Gideon thought, bristling. There was something off, something not right about this creature. He was smaller, but somehow radiated the sort of power only seen in the purest bloodline, a supernatural strength that threatened violence in the smallest flicker of movement. Gideon sensed this, and the oddity of it had him struggling to maintain his focus. But what was worse, what roiled his insides and screamed at him to *retreat,* to *run,* was the smell. It poured off of the Gray, befouling the air of the forest, burning Gideon's nostrils. It seemed to radiate from within him, from the strange collar that glinted from around the beast's neck, stinking of some unfamiliar and horrifying madness. It was an assault to his senses such as he'd never endured before.

He was suddenly determined to eradicate it at the source.

Gideon's muscles tensed, ready to spring, to rip, to tear. Then, suddenly, the growling grew louder, and louder again as two more Wolves padded menacingly out of the darkness. Gideon stilled, drawing himself up, staring down his would-be attackers. These were unfamiliar Wolves as well, and again, not Pack. Weaker. And yet their scent marked them as not entirely unfamiliar, either.

It seemed that his cousin had decided to break more than one sacred rule.

And, as usual, he had sent others to do his dirty work.

The jagged scar that crossed Gideon's right eye twinged a bit at the memory of Malachi's *last* deception, the wound inflicted by a Pack male who had been poisoned with tales of Gideon wooing his mate. It had been a painful lesson, but Gideon had tried to be thankful that he had at least kept his eye in the learning of it.

First, no harm against thy brother Wolf.

He'd always thought that Malachi had merely intended him maimed, a crime bad enough. Now, in this circle of Wolves with malice hanging heavy in the air, he was no longer so sure. From the ravenous look in these new werewolves' eyes, maiming was kind compared to what they intended.

Traitors.

The Wolves began to circle him, teeth bared, eyes fixed upon Gideon. For his part, Gideon remained immobile, head high, letting his disdain for them show. In this form, he was magnificent, very obviously of the Alpha bloodline with his broad, powerful chest, long, muscular limbs, and more than that, the fact that he stood a head taller than the others. He was calm, focused. He had been trained to fight. It was in his blood. If he had no choice but to use that skill against his own kind, then so it was. These were not of his Pack, and they were no brother Wolves of his.

But he had never imagined that he would have to stand for his Pack, and for the Stone, so far from either one.

When it happened, it was fast. The Gray, who seemed to be the leader, uttered a short, sharp bark, and all three set upon Gideon at once. All the years of sparring with Duncan and his two lieutenants, Ian and Malcolm, came rushing back as he fought them off. Rolling, slashing at vulnerable flesh, sinking his fangs past fur and into skin. For a time, there seemed to be nothing to Gideon's world but a snarling, snapping mass of claws and teeth, shot through with bright flashes of pain and brief moments of triumph when he caused more than he had received.

Impressions flickered, vanished, raced through Gideon's consciousness as he fought to stay alive.

Hind claws finding purchase in a soft underbelly. A shriek of pain at the snap of his teeth. Vicious, tearing pain across his shoulder. And always, through the haze of blood and pain, the mocking gleam of yellow eyes like, and so very unlike, his own.

At last, Gideon managed to throw one of them off balance long enough to sink his fangs into the ragged brown fur at its throat. With no regret, he tasted blood as he found the jugular. The world finally seemed to still and right itself as Gideon gave the limp carcass a final shake and then tossed it from his jaws to land at the feet of the Gray, whose bloodied, battered sides were heaving as much as Gideon's own.

Gideon snorted out a hot mist of breath in the frigid air, hunching for attack, ready to finish it. It appeared that this Wolf was no more invincible than any other, after all. They regarded one another for a moment that spun out into an eternity, the only sound the soft moan of the wind picking up as the first flakes of snow began to fall, in slow motion, through the canopy of trees from the endless blackness above.

The stillness was finally shattered when the Gray bared his teeth at Gideon, then limped slowly backward into the shadowy trees. In seconds, first he, then the angry violet glow of the chunk of stone dangling from his collar, disappeared from sight. His one remaining companion was decidedly worse off. Ginger fur matted with blood, it followed as quickly as it could, dragging a broken hind leg as it went. Gideon remained immobile as he watched them go, sensing their message as clearly as if it had been spoken aloud.

This isn't over.

No, Gideon though, curling his lip. It sure as hell wasn't. And damned if he was going to let them go without finishing it. But it wasn't until he took a step forward—and the trees in front of him blurred and swam—that he realized the extent of his own injuries. He might have given better than he got, but it had still been three sets of fangs and claws to his one, and all of those had done some damage despite his best efforts. As Gideon stood there, swaying slightly, he licked the foam from his muzzle and tasted blood. As dread formed a leaden ball in his stomach, he looked down only to see more blood dripping from his chest, his legs, and his underbelly, slowly turning the snow beneath him crimson.

Hell.

He took another tentative step forward, and his vision rimmed with black. *A draw after all,* he thought ruefully. He'd lost too much blood. If it had been anything but other werewolves, he could have rested, assured that he'd heal quickly enough to stanch the lifeblood slowly exiting from his wounds. But it was different among his own kind. It was why they were forbidden from harming one another, why he still carried the scar of that surprising attack so many years ago when the rest of his body carried not a mark. Their healing powers worked much more slowly when the wounds were inflicted by one of their own, and sometimes, as in the case of Gideon's scar, not quite as well.

Or not at all.

Gideon knew that if he didn't want to die there in the snow, he was going to have to find help, and fast.

Keep safe the Stone.

Protect the Pack.

It took a Herculean effort to start forward, toward the lights in the distance. And as he half-walked, half-dragged himself in their direction, it became harder and harder to keep at bay the blackness that wanted to consume him.

Hurry home, the voice in his mind whispered, mocking his efforts.

Later, Gideon would think that he must have blacked out and somehow still kept moving. It seemed as though one moment he was still deep in the pine trees, and the very next, he was lurching through the tidy backyards of a small town, trying desperately to stay clear of the bright glow of windows, of barking dogs who smelled wounded animal and blood. He raised his head as much as he could and scented the air for what seemed like the hundredth time, confused in his weakened state. He was unsure whether he should attempt a Change, whether he even had the strength to make it through one, unsure of where to look for help in this unfamiliar place. He whined softly, his once glossy black fur now clumped and matted, exhausted from making it even this far. Despite his best efforts, he was going to have to lie down; and out here, with the storm coming in, Gideon was fairly sure that once that happened, he wouldn't be getting back up.

Then, just as his legs began to buckle for the last time, Gideon caught the faintest scent of … *something*. It was barely there, carried on a breath of arctic wind, but it was compelling enough to bring the great head up again, his nose searching the air greedily for another trace of it. What was it? So familiar … like berries and cream, with a hint of vanilla … and perhaps a dash of spice, something almost exotic.

And just like that, Gideon's pain faded around him as he concentrated on that wonderful, delicious smell, a scent both familiar and unknown, yet holding some mysterious promise of coming home. Instinct took over—propelling him, driving him. He put one paw in front of another, then again, and then slowly, deliberately, he was moving again, the intense need to find out the source of the intoxicating aroma overriding his body's every command to shut down.

Left, through a darkened churchyard.

There, a hint of cinnamon!

Now right, down a wide alleyway.

So much stronger, and impossibly, irresistibly sweet!

At last, all reserves of strength drained, Gideon got as close as he could to the source: a small red door, on which hung a simple holly berry wreath, that led into an old brick building from the alley. The door filled his vision. Its cheery color was a beacon that seemed, at that moment, made solely for the purpose of leading him out of the cold. In his delirium, Gideon lost all sense of time and place, hanging onto the promise carried on a whiff of arctic breeze.

Home?

He paused there, on the soft rubber mat, and willed everything he had left into raising one shredded paw to scratch feebly at the door. Once. He heard a voice from within, but it stayed distant. Twice, and then once more Gideon scratched, now whining pitifully as he sank to the ground, defeated.

Guard ... Protect ... Home ...

Gideon's mind struggled, but he felt unconsciousness barreling toward him like a freight train. In those seconds before the blackness claimed him, Gideon rolled his eyes heavenward and said a silent prayer for a mangy, flea-bitten cur such as himself to be taken Home.

God, however, apparently had His own ideas. At that moment the red door swung open, bathing Gideon's broken form in soft, warm light as a feminine gasp of shock reached his ears. Hope kindled in Gideon briefly before he finally floated away on a dark and distant sea. His last conscious impression was that of being wrapped, head to toe, in that no-longer-elusive scent, rich with caramel and cocoa and so, so many of his favorite things. He moaned again faintly, this time with pleasure.

A small, graceful hand touched the side of his face gently, light as the brush of a butterfly's wing.

"Oh, you poor thing," sighed a voice like music.

Gideon turned his muzzle into the hand, seeking comfort, and then he knew no more.

Chapter Two

"Celestine has a point, you know. I think you have to at least allow for the possibility that it exists."

"Please. Please tell me you're not serious about this."

"I don't know. Why *couldn't* there be such a thing as tear-inducing sex?"

Carly Silver, proprietor of Bodice Rippers and Baubles, rearranged herself in the faded elegance of her overstuffed wing chair, tucked her feet back up beneath her, and sipped at her glass of chardonnay to hide her grin. It had been her idea of a perfect evening: another successful book club meeting, enough chocolate to put lesser women in a coma, and a fascinating discussion about Dana Bellamy's latest trilogy. And, now that the shop was nearly empty, the fun of playing devil's advocate while her best friend tried to get a rise out of Celestine on her way out the door.

True to form, Regan O'Meara just couldn't resist taking the bait.

"Oh, come *on*, you two," Regan laughed from where she was curled gracefully on the chaise, her dark eyes dancing with mischief. "I mean, have either of *you* ever even thought about crying after sex just because you're so overwhelmed by the"—and here she fluttered her long, dark eyelashes—"*beauty* of it all?"

"What a cynic you are," Celestine clucked from where she stood by the door, barely sparing Regan a glance. She seemed to be completely involved in the process of draping an impossibly long *something* around her neck that might have once been envisioned as a scarf. Now, however, it was just as unidentifiable as the rest of the things Celestine knitted. Carly had to give the classy, sixty-ish British expat her due, though. She might be a lousy knitter, but she was as unflappable as they came. It was a character trait that often came in handy during discussions of the book club's steamier selections.

Not to mention one that drove Regan completely, eternally nuts.

"I suppose it would be safe to say that *you've* never been driven to passionate tears, in any case."

"Untrue," replied Regan, obviously relishing the raised eyebrows this statement provoked. She looked around at her companions with studied casualness before elaborating. "Dumbass ripped my new seventy-dollar bra. I cried like a baby."

Carly rolled her eyes as Celestine burst into delighted laughter. "I'm so glad you save these little gems for *after* the meetings, Regan," she informed her.

Regan merely arched a slim black brow and grinned unrepentantly. "I bring the joy of realism to your mushy little hearts. You wouldn't know what to do without me."

"Eat store-bought cupcakes, then mope about it."

But she had a point, Carly conceded. No meeting would ever be complete without her best friend. That she also happened to be the owner of Decadence, a neighboring bakery famous for its sinful treats, was just a bonus. An extremely *big* bonus, Carly amended as she contemplated the remains of Regan's truly excellent chocolate torte and considered just another few bites of pure, sugary sin. And even when she wanted to hate her for being tall, dark, and fascinating—as opposed to her own short, fair, and relatively boring—Carly couldn't imagine a more perfectly imperfect being than Regan.

Of course, she was pretty sure Regan couldn't either. Fortunately, that was part of her charm.

Instead of further inflating her friend's already-considerable ego, Carly just shook her head and forked one of the few slices of Regan's torte that remained intact onto her plate. As the first bite all but melted on her tongue, Carly felt the last little bit of tension from the day melt away right along with it. When all was said and done, she decided as she closed her eyes in pleasure, there was nothing like unwinding with friends in your own little temple of femininity. And really, it didn't get much more feminine than a bookshop solely dedicated to the genre of romance. Bodice Rippers was exactly what she'd wanted even before she discovered the money her Great-Aunt Apollonia had left her just a little over three years ago. That final kindness had given her the seed money for building this place, her dream place. A chance to finally make something of her own.

So when she'd done it, she'd done it right.

And Carly could honestly say that all the agonizing, the sleepless nights, and the blood, sweat, and tears she'd poured into making the dream a reality had been worth it. Everything was just as she'd envisioned it. There were the rich fabrics and textures of the central sitting area surrounding the brick fireplace in the middle of the shop, the walls lined with built-in bookshelves that were crammed full of any sort of romance your heart could desire. More, there were the artfully scattered displays of hand-worked jewelry, deliciously scented candles, unusual glassware and serving pieces, and other lovely bits and pieces, all glinting and peeking out from places both expected and unexpected. It was Carly's own little slice of heaven, and she'd made it herself.

And things were looking good, Carly decided, savoring the last bite of the torte and brushing the crumbs off of the pale blue cashmere twinset she wore. Kinnik's Harbor had gone upscale the last few years. The quaint lakeside town, best known for a small but victorious battle against the British during the War of 1812, had revitalized the cobblestoned Main Street, turned the old stone barracks into lavish apartments and eclectic eateries, and begun advertising itself as a scenic getaway from the hustle and bustle of city life. And, miracle of miracles, it was working. After years of being run-down and dormant, the Harbor was coming back to life.

There were some who already thought the Harbor was getting too big, too commercial. Carly just wasn't one of them. That shift had brought Celestine Periwether and many like her to her door. Not just customers, but friends. And she wouldn't trade them for all the tea in China (or in Celestine's pantry, for that matter … Carly wasn't sure, but she strongly suspected that her friend might very well have more tea squirreled away than most of the Asian countries put together).

For now, the woman in question turned in the doorway, the first flakes from the reportedly impending storm swirling in around her as she wagged a finger at Regan.

"There's a mushy little heart of your own in there somewhere, my dear. I'll uncover it yet."

"Idle threats," Regan called after her as the door shut, taking a moment to uncoil into a long, feline stretch. "Anyway," she yawned, "she'd need a jackhammer."

"Celestine's right," Carly remarked with a small smirk, getting up and walking to the front window to look out. "You are a cynic."

"The hell you say." After a moment, Regan appeared at her side. Together, they studied the dimly lit street in front of the shop, their breath fogging up the chilled glass.

"Hmm. Weather's moving in."

"Think we'll be able to open tomorrow?" Carly asked her, watching the thickening curtain of snow falling from the sky. It was wrong, she knew, since it was her livelihood that would be taking a hit. But the thought of sleeping in and then staying in her PJs all day, reading and drinking hot cocoa (and on a Wednesday, no less), sounded just about perfect.

Except for the part where she was still waking up alone.

Carly bit back a sigh, tired of fighting off the same old mope. She could try to blame work, but it wasn't like she'd had such a stunning social life before she opened the shop, either. She'd never been much of a party girl, and having two overzealously protective older brothers hadn't helped. But the fact remained that being here six days a week, from nine in the morning until whenever she got done—even *with* two employees—had eaten up whatever was left of her social life. Regan usually managed to drag her out a few times a month, but she was hard-pressed to find any of the drunk and idiotic men she usually met appealing. If only she could manage to turn a shade less red than her usual "volcanic" whenever a reasonably attractive male approached her, then, maybe.

Well, Carly sighed inwardly, no need to have a pity party about it. Her life was fulfilling enough, even with the occasional bout of the lonelies. Hopefully one day a handsome bookworm would wander in to sweep her off her feet. Until then, she'd take the PJs and the cocoa as an acceptable alternative.

"We'll be stuck at home if it does what it's supposed to, but who can ever tell?" Regan eyed her friend, tuned in as usual to how she was feeling. "You okay tonight? Want to go down to the brew pub and bitch a little? I'm up for it."

Carly managed a half-smile, but shook her head. She was sure Regan really was up for it, and would also probably join her in a good wallow. It always amazed her, but despite all of the attention she got, Regan had about the worst luck with men of anyone she had ever known. She claimed it had ceased to bother her long ago, but Carly often wondered.

"We're quite a pair, huh?"

Regan simply shrugged and slung an arm around Carly's slim shoulders.

"At least we can be scary old cat ladies together someday."

"Only if I can bring the doilies." Carly laughed softly, allowing her mood to brighten a little. She might well be on the scary old cat lady track, but Regan was not going to let her drive herself crazy, at least.

They watched the snow in companionable silence for a few minutes, until Regan could no longer fight the need to fill it.

"So … what's on the docket for next month, anyway?" she asked. "Naked pirates?"

Carly turned to fix her with an innocent smile. "You wish. No, I think you're really going to like this one. Jeanette Gleason's new one, *Stroke of Midnight*. It's a modern take on Cinderella with a disgustingly happy ending. And now that you mention it, I've got your copy right behind the counter."

Regan winced. "You're just lucky I love you."

"Yeah," Carly laughed as she patted her friend's head. "Same goes."

Half an hour later, Carly lay sprawled out on the camelback loveseat, one arm thrown over her eyes, basking in the comforting silence of the place where she felt most at home. The cups, glasses, and plates had been washed and put away, the crumbs had been vacuumed up. The contents of the cash register that sat atop the richly colored, slightly distressed mahogany cabinet that she used for a front counter had been tallied and readied for deposit.

It had been a fun evening, she thought with a faint smile, as usual. Still, she'd felt an overwhelming sense of relief when Regan had finally gone after helping her

clean up and then rambling on about ... well, something ... before finally heading out the door about five
minutes previous (while still carrying on some sort of
conversation—presumably, at that point, with herself).
Regan liked to talk, but fortunately, you could get by
when you were seriously tired by just smiling and
nodding periodically.

Tired. More like exhausted, Carly thought. She enjoyed
her book club, making small talk with her customers and
friends, even the occasional night out when Regan gave her
no room to decline. Still, the company she tended to enjoy
best was her own.

Carly removed her arm from over her eyes, rose up on
her elbows, and turned her head to look through the
wide, floor-length picture window at the front of the
shop. Framed as it was by the crushed red velvet curtains
drawn back on either side, the snowy winter scene could
have been an atmospheric moment in a holiday movie,
pretty as a postcard. The old-fashioned streetlights lent a
faint glow to the thick curtain of snow now obscuring all
but the faintest image of the wide front porch of the Boat
House, the restaurant across the street.

Too bad this was real life, which in Carly's case
included a fun little car with bad traction and an
obstacle course of snowbanks that seemed to have all
the malicious gravitational pull of Charlie Brown's
kite-eating tree.

"*Ugh.*" Carly groaned loudly and flopped back down,
lying splay-legged for a moment as she contemplated the
possibility of planting herself in a giant pile of snow on
her short drive home. Sometimes, the appeal of living in

a place so famous for its lake effect that it had everything from streets to beer named after it wore a little thin.

And she had just about convinced herself to head out into it when the phone erupted into nerve-jangling rings.

"Christ!" Carly barely managed to avoid jumping out of her own skin. She looked at the wrought-iron hands of the large clock that hung on the wall, saw that it was about ten of ten, and wondered if Regan had changed her mind about trying to get her to go for that drink. It was either that, or one of her brothers trying to play hero to the helpless female. *Again.* Against her better judgment, she padded, barefoot, across the thick Oriental rug to the source of the annoying sound and picked up the phone.

"I'm fine," she said firmly into the receiver, hazarding a guess that she was about to find a family member on the other end of the line. After all, it was snowing. And God knew that, left to her own devices, any number of things might happen to her during the two-mile trip home. She could die of hypothermia! Be attacked by a mob of starving squirrels! Hell, she could pull a *Ripley's Believe It or Not* and spontaneously combust!

"Don't shoot the messenger, okay? Mom's having a spaz."

Carly closed her eyes in a silent prayer for patience, placed a hand on one cocked hip, and started tapping one finger against her hipbone. Luigi, naturally. The Lackey.

"Weege, I'm just closing up and heading home. Tell mom I'll be *fine.*"

"Aw, come on, Carly," her brother pressed, "I can be down there in the new Tahoe in two minutes, mom won't give me the lecture on how I'm a horrible brother and have probably sentenced you to a snowy death … *again* … and you and me can play Playstation and eat Doritos until we pass out! It'll be *awesome*."

Ah yes, Carly mused, the new Tahoe, made possible by the fact that her grown brother, who had graduated college but preferred to spend his time playing at line chef at the Boat House (part-time, of course) and emceeing on weekends at the Main Street Comedy Shoppe, still lived comfortably and rent-free in her parents' house. Whereas her other brother had somehow become a reasonably responsible dentist. Genetics was an infinite mystery.

"Weege," she sighed, hating that she always came out of their conversations sounding like the world's youngest old fart, "you know I love you, but some of us, especially those of us who are not thirty-year-old men whose mommies still cook for them and do their laundry, are tired after a long day at work and just want to go home and have a hot bath."

"And some of us are getting a little tired of being threatened with a wooden spoon," Luigi grumbled. "Have a heart, will ya?" And Carly knew just how he'd look in that moment: a husky, hairy man-boy wearing ancient track pants, rolling his eyes, and keeping close his open (and mostly empty) bag of the aforementioned Doritos on the couch beside him. That was Weege, though, Carly acknowledged as a reluctant smile tugged at the corners of her mouth. He was like an annoying yet lovable kindergartner.

"I do have a heart, Luigi. My fatigue is just stronger right now."

"You are a royal pain in the ass, *Carlotta*. Have it your way, see who gets his butt chewed for this." And with the invocation of the forbidden name, he was gone with an irritable *click*.

Carly glared at the receiver for a moment before replacing it in the base. One of these days, she was going to get in the last word, even if she had to tie him to his beloved recliner to do it.

"Okay," she sighed to the empty store. "Time to pack it in." As long as her butt had finally moved from Point A—the hard part, as far as Carly was concerned—she might as well get it moving toward Point B: a steaming bath, and bed. She slipped her feet into the pair of big, furry boots she kept by the front door, pulled on her long, dark blue wool coat, and was headed back to the counter to grab her purse when a noise, so soft that at first she wasn't sure whether or not she was imagining it, reached Carly's ears.

Scratch.

She paused, cocking her head toward the back of the store. She'd almost decided she had imagined it when it came again, so faint she almost missed it.

Scratch.

Then there was a soft noise which, while it might have been the wind, sounded like the whimper of an animal. A dog, maybe. And it sounded like it was coming from her back door.

Carly's brows drew together in concern as she left her purse where it was sitting and strode quickly back to the stockroom. She hoped to God it wasn't a stray, half-frozen to death from hunger and the cold. If that was the case, she'd probably end up taking it home for the night and playing nurse until she could get it to the vet's tomorrow, and that was really going to trash her plans for the rest of the evening. Well, she consoled herself as she headed for the back door that opened out into the alley, it wouldn't be the first time. And it was a matter of pride that, as famous as she was for being the local bleeding heart when it came to the befurred and in need, she hadn't lost one yet.

Regan, Carly knew, couldn't understand why her best friend had such a soft spot for strays. But it was well known that Bodice Rippers' back stoop always had fresh bowls of food and water for all things feline or canine. It was a compulsion for Carly, always had been, and she'd seen every stray that had come to her doorstep down to the local SPCA and, eventually, adopted. Still, she knew it wasn't quite as much fun as having one of your own. That was why she'd decided that this year, for a Christmas present to herself, she was going to go back down to the SPCA and *leave* with an animal for once. Not a baby, no matter which flavor she chose, but something a little more mature that could handle hanging out with her at work without shredding the stock or terrorizing the customers.

Maybe, she thought as she unlocked the door and pulled it cautiously open, she was going to get her Christmas present early.

Then again, maybe not.

"Oh my Jesus frigging holy mother of …" She heard herself gasp as she got her first look at the ruined beast that lay sprawled across her mat. *What had gotten at this poor animal?* Carly tried to push past her initial shock and take in the whole picture, not just flashes of blood and fur. It looked like it might be a … dog? If so, it was one hell of a big one. There was blood, so much blood … She couldn't even begin to tell where it was coming from, and there was so much area on this thing! The chest was pretty bad, she saw, crisscrossed with long, evil-looking gashes. The haunches looked like they'd been munched on pretty good. There was a long, white scar across its one eye that looked old, but everything else was fresh. And if the spreading red stain beneath it was any indication, she didn't want to see its underbelly. The thought stabbed at her again. *What could take down something this big and do so much damage? A Mack truck? Maybe, if trucks had teeth.*

Carly chewed at her lower lip, uncertain of how to proceed. If only it could have been a friendly, slightly frozen golden retriever! Even an ornery, hungry little Chihuahua!

But no, not for her, she thought miserably. All she got was a very big, very dead mutant dog. "Well, merry freakin' Christmas," she muttered, ignoring the petulant tone she heard in her voice and focusing instead on the great black lump of shredded fur before her. She noticed two things almost immediately. One, it wasn't dead … yet. Its sides were still moving faintly. Two, the more she looked at it, the less it looked like a dog and the more it looked like a …

But they didn't have wolves around here, did they? Maybe this was some kind of weird Great Dane/wolf crossbreed? Because she had never heard of a wolf that looked as though you might be able to ride on it.

Her thoughts scattered as the great beast moved its shaggy head slightly and moaned deep in its throat. Carly made a soft, pained sound in response. She knew what was going to happen, and she was powerless to stop it. She swore she could almost hear the music as every last one of her damned heartstrings was plucked at once. Carly crouched beside it, pity welling up inside her, and reached out her hand.

Don't touch it don't touch it you're going to get your stupid arm chewed off don't TOUCH IT, her little voice of reason beseeched her, sounding more and more horrified the closer her hand got. She paused, inches away from ink-black fur, knowing how utterly dumb it was to go anywhere near wounded animals with your bare hands. But then, did that really apply when they seemed to have sought you out specifically just to throw their sad, broken selves at your mercy?

Oh, hell, you're going to touch it anyway, aren't you?

Carly felt a moment of shock, an odd little spark of connection as she reached the rest of the way and slid her fingers into thick, soft fur. Instantly, inexplicably, all of her misgivings were put to rest as she stroked the wolf-dog's cheek. She didn't know how or why, but somehow Carly was sure that she was in no danger here. "Oh, you poor thing," she sighed, melting the rest of the way when, rather than baring its teeth at her, the animal simply turned its muzzle into her hand, seeming to seek comfort, and then sighed deeply and went limp as it lost consciousness.

Carly continued stroking the beast, lapsing into an almost trancelike state as one hand, then both, moved over the velvet ears, the silken flank, the massive paws, stroking over both bloodied, matted areas and those that had escaped damage. She had never felt fur like this, so warm and soft she could hardly keep from burying her face in it. She wanted to curl up against the massive chest, draw from the warmth, the softness, and sleep ...

It was only the sight of the slow but continuous bleeding still oozing from beneath the animal that finally snapped Carly to, and by then both of them were covered in a thin blanket of snow.

"Shit," she hissed, shaking her head to clear it. What the hell had come over her? She was a big-time animal lover, sure, but she couldn't remember ever totally losing it over something as simple as a quick pet. She'd just worked too late, she told herself as she stood, brushing the snow off of her coat. Worked too late, for a whole bunch of nights, and then had a giant dog decide to bleed out all over her back stoop. It was the perfect recipe for a little bit of goofiness on her part, Carly consoled herself, even as she made a mental note to let Jemma and Chris take on a little more responsibility around the shop, much as it pained her to give over any control. Bodice Rippers was her baby, but she wasn't prepared to work herself into the nuthouse just on some stupid principle. She needed more rest. She needed, maybe, a day off once in a while.

She needed to figure out what to do with Barkley, here.

It took her exactly three minutes to decide on a course of action. She just hoped her back was up to it. Her nice new chenille throw would have to do as a makeshift stretcher, Carly decided with a defeated sigh. And if she didn't want animal control or the cops called, outside help was pretty well out of the question. She didn't know how far the two of them were going to get, but there was no way she could leave this thing out in the cold to die; that was for sure.

"Well, big guy," she said softly, looking down at the dog's still form, "it's up to you. Think you can fit in the backseat of a Mini?"

One large, amber eye opened slightly to regard her, the unnerving gaze holding a lot more understanding than Carly cared to think about right then. All she knew was, if it was going to come to and still be as lovey with her as it had been initially, maybe she wouldn't have to do all the work. She'd concentrate on that and worry about dog eyes that looked more human than canine later, once she had it bandaged up and resting comfortably in front of the fire. *Her* fire.

Looked like maybe she wouldn't have to go all the way to the SPCA for company after all, she thought a little ruefully as she hurried off to get the throw. And maybe, just maybe, she'd go ahead and name it after the monstrously huge dog on *Sesame Street.* God knew it was going to have to be that or Clifford.

You are such a sucker, her common sense whispered to her before apparently giving up and going to bed for the night.

"Okay, Barkley," Carly said when she returned, taking a deep breath before kneeling and getting to work. "Let's get you home."

Chapter Three

"INTERSTATE 81, NORTHBOUND AND SOUTHBOUND, IS currently closed from Syracuse to Watertown as this stalled-out weather system hasn't budged since last night. Below-zero temps, high winds, and lots and lots of blowing snow are gonna make this a good day to stay in, folks. State troopers have declared no unnecessary travel..."

Carly groaned softly as she slapped at her alarm clock until she hit pay dirt and the morning radio deejay abruptly shut up. Seven a.m., and the wind outside was moaning, making more noise than her little clock radio could ever have aspired to.

And by some miracle, the power wasn't out.

Not that it counted as a reason to actually get out of bed or anything.

Staying curled into a tight ball beneath the cozy fluff of her down comforter, she opened one eye just a crack, noting the gray cast of the light faintly illuminating her small bedroom. Then, going with instincts finely honed from years of living in the North Country, Carly shut it again in preparation for at least two more hours of sleep. It looked like she had her excuse to play hooky. Now all she had to do was sleep late, laze around in her pajamas, relax, and dig into a good book.

Well, that and figure out what to do with the abnormally large wolf-dog that might or might not still be sleeping and/or breathing out in the other room.

Carly frowned and burrowed more deeply beneath her covers. It could wait. She didn't want to think about it right now. Which, of course, meant that it was *all* she could think about right now. Not to mention last night. She wasn't normally prone to nightmares, excepting the occasional oh-my-God-I'm-naked-at-the-mall anxiety dream, but it seemed like she'd passed the entire night caught in a jumble of hazy, disturbing images. Glowing eyes. Hulking, menacing, inhuman shadows. Some weird, nasty-looking mountains beset with funky violet lightning. And padding through all of it, just ahead of her, had been a giant black wolf, her tour guide on what had seemed like a field trip through Hell.

Naturally, that particular wolf had borne a striking resemblance to a certain something she'd decided to bring home with her. Something that might almost be a full-blooded dog … if you squinted at it hard enough.

Carly bit back a groan at the memories of touching … petting … *cooing,* for Christ's sake. Since when had she gotten so damned *dumb?* Most people would have gotten either animal control or a gun. Or both, for that matter. But not her, Carly thought ruefully. Oh no. She looked at blood and claws and teeth the size of a great white's and just *melted.*

She shifted slightly in the old iron bed and sighed gustily. She'd been known to have her moments of stupidity, yes. But last night had been bad, even for her. Bad enough that she'd be lucky if she didn't end up winning a Darwin award for it, posthumously of course, for dumbest method of proving the theory of natural selection. Had she really imagined that the animal had sought her out specifically? That they'd had some sort of weird *connection?* God, she must be losing it. It was obviously time to either up her caffeine intake—again—or cut back on her hours. To think she'd been determined to try and *pick it up.* Carly shuddered slightly, remembering the details of every vicious dog attack she'd ever seen reported on the news.

At least she hadn't actually done it. Not that coaxing a staggering, bleeding canine train wreck into her car (and then her *house*) had been any better. He'd followed her willingly, Carly remembered. Determinedly, even. But maybe he hadn't come to and dragged himself after her because he'd wanted help, she thought with a grimace. Maybe he'd just been hungry. And hadn't she just recently heard about some pit bull actually eating someone?

But it was too late now, damn it. She'd gotten Barkley the Possibly-Man-Eating Dog settled in front of her nice new gas fireplace on a pile of old blankets. She'd brought home and fussed over an overgrown carnivore of indeterminate appetite, not to mention temperament. And eventually, she was going to have to call either the vet or the pound. Or, if things really went to hell, the local SWAT team.

Carly hunkered down further for a good session of stewing. Then a sudden, lusty snore from directly behind her had her thoughts scattering to the wailing wind outside. Her eyes flew open, full of disbelief.

Following her home was one thing. But had that massive, ripped-up animal actually followed her to *bed?*

After spending a frozen moment torn between flattered surprise and outright horror, Carly steeled herself and rolled slowly over. What else was left to do? It wasn't like she could talk him into giving her a break on her snow day. *No sudden movements,* she reminded herself. Just in case.

Please let him still be friendly, she prayed silently, remembering nothing of big pleading eyes and everything about huge, dagger-sharp teeth. *Please let him be …* The thought ended abruptly as Carly got her first look at what had curled up with her in the night. She closed her eyes, hard. Opened them. Tried it again when the first time had produced less-than-satisfactory results. But no matter how many times she blinked, it absolutely refused to turn into a dog. And it stubbornly refused to *stop* being a big, buck-naked man.

Carly felt all the blood drain from her face as her widening eyes took in well over six feet of definitely-not-a-dog. Her mind, still sluggish from sleep, tried desperately to wrap itself around what she was seeing. In her bed. Sprawled out on his stomach. And snoring, no doubt dreaming of what he had planned for her.

I should run. I should go for the phone. And a knife. What kind of sicko snuggled up with you all night, then did God-knows-what to you in the morning?

Adrenaline flooded her veins like ice water. Her muscles tensed, heartbeat accelerating until she was sure her unwanted bedmate would hear it. And then … and then he'd …

Carly forced herself to focus. If she didn't want to complete that thought, she was going to have to be smart. Careful. And very, very quiet. She maneuvered herself slowly up onto her elbows, then, ever so slightly, nearer to the edge of the bed. *Inches,* she told herself. *Only inches.* Even if it felt like miles.

She glanced quickly at the door, gauging distance and laying plans, and then back. At *him.* Jesus, he was huge. Carly drew in a shaky breath as silently as she could manage. She moved again, inching along, then waited to make sure her shifting weight wasn't disturbing his sleep. A pause, and then another snore had her exhaling with relief.

Almost there ... almost there ...

Why had she been sleeping so close to him? Carly wondered miserably as she inched along in slow motion. How could she not have realized he was there? But then she reached the edge, freedom finally within her reach, and pushed those thoughts back. Nothing was going to do her any good now but silence and speed. As long as he didn't wake up.

Please, God, don't let him wake up.

She angled her head just a little to peek through the thick fall of wavy dark brown hair that mostly obscured the side of her unwanted guest's face. *Just to make sure. Just to be certain.*

It was then, when her scream of terror welled up and then froze mid-throat and her limbs turned to unresponsive jelly, that Carly realized she'd waited too long to run.

"Morning, darling," rumbled a deep, velvety voice still thick with sleep as one amber eye opened to meet her gaze. "Enjoying the view?"

Her mind raced, frantically searching for something, anything she could do to immobilize him. Sic her new dog on him, maybe? And then it dawned on her: *Oh, God, the dog!* Her eyes flicked to the angry red slashes crisscrossing his back, obvious evidence of a vicious fight, and she knew: the dog, or whatever it had been, was gone. Carly felt tears sting her eyes as she realized that this asshole had probably killed the poor creature so she wouldn't be alerted to his presence. All her former thoughts about having brought home nothing short of Cujo were instantly forgotten. Whatever that animal had been, he hadn't deserved this.

Fear turned to furious loathing as a red haze descended over Carly's vision and years of training from her two belligerent older brothers flashed quickly through her mind. This guy thought he could just sneak in here, kill an innocent animal, take what he wanted from her, and then leave? Jackass should never have messed with a Silver, then, because boy did he have another thing coming.

"Bastard," she hissed, and punched him in the head as hard as she could.

Then she ran.

He'd obviously lost his touch, Gideon thought as pain exploded in his temple. He really should have kept his comment to himself, and he knew it, but when he'd awakened under her intense (and, so it had seemed to him, appreciative) scrutiny, he'd forgotten himself for a moment. After all, he'd never had a woman use her fists on him after spending the night with him.

Then again, he thought as he grunted at the surprising pain such a small thing had managed to inflict on him—but then he *was* still feeling a bit under the weather, he excused himself—he had never before gotten into a woman's bed by pretending to be a pet. Not that he'd ever thought he looked much like a pet in wolf form … it was a bit insulting, really … and oh, hell, there she went to find something to stab him with. Gideon supposed his wounded pride would simply have to wait.

Gideon rose like lightning from the bed and had her in four long strides, moving so fast that she barely had time to let out a quick squeak before he'd silenced her. He pressed her back against the wall of the hallway, pinning her slight form with his massive one and keeping her mouth covered with one hand. He could feel her against him, every inch of her vibrating with fear. Gideon cursed himself for making her feel that way after all she'd done for him last night, though he knew for certain that there was nothing he could have done about Changing in his sleep. When his body had healed enough to do so, it simply had, and he was wise enough not to bother blaming himself for it. No, what he blamed himself for, at the moment, was getting into the woman's bed in the first place. What the bloody hell had he been thinking? *Had* he been thinking? Looking into a pair of wide eyes the deep, true blue of the evening sky, Gideon hardly knew.

It wasn't like him not to remember. Then again, Gideon thought, it wasn't like him to get very nearly ripped to pieces by a trio of renegade werewolves and then stagger into the arms of a woman to heal him. He frowned slightly, trying to ignore the effect his expression had on his captive. If only he could *remember.* He recalled the fight, yes, with perfect clarity. And then he'd dragged himself, and there'd been some kind of a scent in the air he'd been nearly frantic to find the source of.

Just then, as though he'd summoned it with a thought, Gideon caught another whiff of the intoxicating scent that had found him his safety last night. It was crumb cake and fresh berries, he thought, inhaling a bit more deeply as his eyes dropped to half-mast in a rush of sheer, unexpected pleasure. It was whipped cream. It was knickerbocker glory. It was …

It was her. Gideon's gaze refocused in surprise, his eyes locking with hers, even as the delicious smell thickened and enveloped him so that he had to struggle not to start rubbing his stupid head against her and rolling around like a damned cat in heat. Gideon gave her a quick up and down, as much as he could, and his frown deepened. She was just a tiny bit of a thing! She looked like, any moment now, she was either going to vomit or pass out from fear! And his instincts were telling him, no, *screaming* at him, that this was his mate?

He'd been mistaken, Gideon thought with a soft, defeated groan. He hadn't come to America. He'd gone to Hell. And wouldn't you know it, he thought with a dark sort of amusement, it was cold.

A muffled noise against his hand brought him back to the reality of his current situation. Gideon's mind moved quickly, brushing aside his irrational reaction to this woman for the moment and focusing on how best to explain his situation and bring her over to his side. It was true, by the cold gray light of morning this didn't look like the world's best idea. But Gideon wasn't really seeing that he had many options except to convince her to let him stay until the storm had passed, both literally and figuratively. He could try to get out and find another place to hole up while he healed, but he saw two big problems with that right off the bat; one, he didn't have a stitch of clothing either on or with him, and two, if he left this woman now, she'd send the police right along after him.

No, Gideon decided, best to try and get her to believe the unbelievable. It was probably a long shot, but considerably better than being tossed on his bare ass out into the snow. As she was quiet now, he took a chance and slowly removed his hand from her mouth, expecting and dreading that she would begin by whimpering and pleading for her life. She was obviously horrified. Gideon opened his mouth to reassure her, but was shocked by how she cut him off.

"What did you do to my dog, you asshole?" she spat, rendering Gideon momentarily speechless. Of all the things he'd been anticipating, this wasn't even on the list. His brows shot upwards, even as he quickly moved his leg to block a nasty little assault she tried to execute on a rather sensitive place. Fear, had he thought? There was some of that, yes, but Gideon was now pretty sure that the far greater part of her emotions right now was bloodthirsty rage. He fought back an amused smirk, which he could instantly see had not helped his cause.

"Oh, you think this is funny? To murder people's pets, and then … then …" Gideon saw that she didn't seem to want to say what she was thinking, lest she give him any ideas. Fortunately for him, she was unaware that she didn't need to provide him with any more food for thought than she already had. For he was looking at her now, *really* looking at her, and he would have had to be a dead man not to appreciate what he saw.

Her hair was a long mass of pale blond waves that reached well past her shoulders in a cloud of morning tangles, framing a small, heart-shaped face. The mouth that was pulled taut with anger was a pale pink rosebud, and her fair cheeks were flushed attractively, though Gideon doubted she'd appreciate his observation right then. Her nose was adorable, small and straight but with an interesting, pointy little uptilt at the end. A stubborn nose, his father would have called it. Large, long-lashed eyes glared up at him from stormy depths of endless blue, and though she only came up to the middle of his chest, Gideon had gotten a good look at her figure as she'd bounded away from him, and … well, he'd just label her "well proportioned" and leave it at that, as more in-depth visualization of her supple, bouncy little curves would make them both very uncomfortable before long.

Lovely, Gideon thought, surprised anew at the strength of his reaction to her. He tended to be too busy to let himself be taken by the beauty of women. He enjoyed their company occasionally, to be sure, but he hadn't the wit or the will of his lothario brother to keep himself surrounded by them. Women were an endlessly

changing puzzle, it seemed to him, and Gideon considered himself a basic, simple man. He liked his life
equally basic and simple—or at least he'd thought he
did, until recently. Still, even knowing what was nagging
at him, accepting it as natural, he hadn't looked to fall.
His kind did that only once, and actively looking for
such a thing had made him nervous. Besides, when it
happened, it would happen, or it wouldn't, but if it was
for someone like … someone like …

Gideon stared hard at his captive before deliberately
looking away.

Christ Almighty, what a bloody mess.

She'd started off terrified.

Now, damn it, she was mostly insulted.

Carly couldn't believe herself, but she'd moved from
terror to fury to some sort of stupid annoyance all in the
last two minutes, and at this point in the insanity, she
figured she might as well just give up wondering why
and go with it. When he'd come out of nowhere (*like a
damned cat,* she'd thought in the instant before he'd so
nicely smashed her into the wall), Carly had figured that
this was it, that this was the part where he hurt her. She
was prepared to fight, even though her chances against
someone so much bigger than she was were pretty poor.
She'd even braced herself as much as she could for the
pain of that first blow, even though she knew she was
shaking like a leaf. She'd waited, and *waited.* But then
he'd just stood there, looking at her like he was trying to

figure out some really complex puzzle, and the silence in the rest of her house had both given her time to think and confirmed her worst fears.

He'd done away with her dog.

That's when the famous Delfiore temper her mother had gifted her with had kicked in (as usual, at the most inopportune time available) and she'd stopped keeping her mouth shut. Well, and also tried to knee him.

Intelligence, Carly ruefully acknowledged, was not now and to her knowledge never had been acquainted with the Delfiore temper.

And now, just when she'd decided to bite a finger off the next time his hand got too close to her mouth, her attacker had to go and start looking like one of the most miserable people on the planet. Misery, she noted with an unpleasant jolt, looked entirely too beautiful on him to be tolerated.

He was truly mesmerizing, she realized. Which made it doubly unfortunate that she was going to have to maim him and then make sure he was locked away forever. Weren't scumbags like this supposed to look like what they were? Wasn't she supposed to be utterly repulsed? Though she was trying like hell not to notice, that shoulder-length hair, slightly wavy and the color of chocolate, was no longer covering his features.

And this man, whoever he was, was a sculptor's dream come true.

He wasn't soft enough to be pretty, Carly decided as she stared at him, but rather angular and rough. Thick stubble covered his square jaw, and the lips of a mouth that looked as though it could be generous when he was in a better mood were firm and perfectly sculpted, set in a line that was just as hard as the rest of him. His nose was strong but not overpowering, regal in a way. It was his eyes, though, that caught Carly and held her when he finally came back from wherever his mind had been and focused solely on her. They were deep-set, framed by dark, downward-slashing brows, and an improbable burning amber in color, a shade Carly didn't think she'd ever seen before. When those eyes locked on hers, she immediately felt as though all of the wind had been punched out of her at once. How was she supposed to concentrate on this guy's demise when all she wanted to do when he looked at her was melt into a puddle at his feet? And why, after giving her a thorough once-over— even, she could almost swear, *sniffing* at her—did he look even more miserable than before? Yes, it was morning, but seriously, she doubted it was *that* bad. And what was he expecting? Marilyn Monroe? Jessica Alba? What?

He was probably some nutcase druggie, Carly thought, increasingly irritated at being pinned while not being told what was going to happen to her. It was a shame, she thought, and a bigger waste than she'd ever seen. But maybe, if that was the case, she could try to talk him down. After, of course, she found out what he'd done with poor, unfortunate Barkley. The bastard.

"Did you kill him?" she tried again, and those amazing eyes returned to her. He had a long, interesting scar that slashed across his right eye, she noted. It was bizarrely, distractingly, annoyingly hot. He was probably lucky he still had the eye. Of course, that was what she'd thought about the dog's scar.

Carly frowned. *Well, that was weird.* Her rescue project and her new bed buddy had matching scars. Weird, but then, maybe not too surprising. Big, beastly guys like this were usually brawlers, from what she'd seen. A strange coincidence, maybe, she decided firmly, but that was all.

She had enough problems at the moment without trying to make connections that weren't even there. Beastly, though, she thought as she eyed him. That was one word that suited him to a T. But then, she supposed whatever substance he'd recently been messing with hadn't much helped that.

"Did I kill who?" He sounded dazed. Yeah, Carly decided, definitely a druggie. She was obviously going to have to speak slowly and use small words. That should be easy, since he also sounded Scottish, of all the worst possible things he could be when she needed her wits about her. Was there a woman alive who didn't have a thing for delicious men in kilts? But this guy was *not* wearing a kilt, Carly reminded herself. Nor was he remotely delicious.

Mostly.

Even though he wasn't just not wearing a kilt. He wasn't wearing *anything.*

"My big, huge dog," she said with determined focus, trying to enunciate each syllable. "You couldn't have missed him."

"Ah, that." He paused, briefly, as though unsure how to proceed, and then plunged on ahead. "Yes, well, I think we need to talk about that." He furrowed his brow, looking away for a moment, and Carly knew, she could just *tell,* that he was about to break the bad news. Despite her best efforts, her eyes were filling up all over again when she thought of what that poor baby must have gone through at the hands of this … this … well, sometimes, there just weren't enough curse words. *Stop being such a big baby,* she chided herself, even as she felt her lip quiver. For God's sake, why did she always have to ruin everything by being such a girl?

"Never mind." She cringed inwardly as she heard her voice tremble, but she'd be damned if she was going to look away. "I guess you've already answered my question."

The man's eyes widened slightly, and for some reason he looked surprised, as well as a bit mortified. "Oh … killed, you mean … *oh,* good Lord, no, you've got it all wrong. I haven't done a thing …"

In a futile attempt not to hear him, Carly kept right on talking over him. She would have plugged her ears with her fingers and started humming, but she was *so* not stooping to his level. Also, her hands were still pinned at her sides. "I hope you know that I've got a big Italian family, and I have a lot of cousins in the mafia …"

"No, you see, I haven't done anything to your dog. I mean, well, yes, I suppose *technically* …"

"… and you can do whatever you want to me, I can't stop you, but I just think you should know that they *will* hunt you down …"

"… but then it couldn't really be helped. You see, I was attacked, and then …"

"... and honestly, I think my cousin Vinnie has pulled out more than his share of fingernails to get people to talk ..."

"... Christ, what are you *talking* about, woman?" Completely flustered as Carly's words finally registered, he heaved a gusty sigh, seemed to brace himself, and then, one hand on each of Carly's shoulders, stooped down to look her directly in the face. "I haven't killed your bloody dog. I have never laid a finger on your dog, which, I must tell you, is ... tell me something," he demanded suddenly. "*Why* for the love of God would you ever decide that creature was a dog? Did it *not* seem to warrant some other kind of classification than, say, some sort of bloody retriever?"

Carly opened her mouth once, then shut it, then opened it again, surprised into answering. If she hadn't known better, she would have thought she'd just insulted him somehow. "I, um, well, I know he was kind of big."

"You're damn right he's big!"

She eyed him cautiously before continuing. "And, it did cross my mind that he might actually have a lot of wolf in him, although he certainly acted pretty tame."

"Oh, for the love of—I was *dying!* What did you expect me to do, ask for help and then maul you to death? What do you take me for?" Carly's eyes widened. He was practically snarling, and did he even realize what he'd just said? Whatever he'd been smoking, she decided, it must have been really something.

"When was this that you were dying?" she asked, hoping that if she stayed calm, he'd lose that wild look in his eye. "Are you hurt somehow? Do you need help?

Because if you'll just let me go, I promise, I'll do whatever I can to get it for you."

He seemed to catch himself then, shaking that gloriously shaggy mane of hair and looking disgusted—with himself, mainly, which struck her as kind of odd—before interrupting her in a quiet, determined voice. "Look at me," he breathed. "Does nothing about me look familiar to you? Look into my eyes and tell me you don't remember. Look at me. And see."

Carly's breath caught in the back of her throat as she struggled to resist the power of that deep, seductive brogue. His voice was chocolate for the ears, was the thought that flitted through her floundering mind. And that sexy burr … mmm, definitely Scottish. The improbability of her home being invaded by a Scottish sex god wandered briefly through her sluggish mind, then ceased to matter entirely as her eyes locked on his and her breathing slowed, then steadied. Soon, there was nowhere she could look but into those two pools of liquid amber, not even if she'd tried.

Not even if she'd wanted to.

Carly felt her breathing become deep and rhythmic, and begin to match her captor's as she looked, searching, not sure of what she was looking for or what he wanted her to find. But then there was something, a feeling that began as an odd sense of déjà vu, telling her that she'd looked into eyes like these, so singular, so beautiful, just once before. And along with that, she began to realize, there was more. It was as though her whole body was awakening to his, Carly thought dazedly, the wonder of the sensation rushing up from her toes like a molten river

to make her aware of each and every place his body
touched hers. Her legs trapped between his. Her breasts
pressed against his broad expanse of chest, rising and
falling in time with hers. The long, graceful fingers,
strong but hardly using that strength, wrapped around
her wrists.

The mouth just inches away from her own.

Her eyes dropped. She couldn't help it. All she could
think of was the sensuous curve of his lips, the way they
were parted, ever so slightly, almost like an invitation.
She could imagine how they would feel against her
own, like warm silk, firm but not entirely unyielding. A
lover's mouth.

Oh, Jesus.

Carly dragged her eyes back up, some faintly functioning part of her brain sounding the *This Is Not A Good
Idea* alarm loudly enough that it registered. Sort of. How
long had she been staring at his mouth? God. Maybe he
hadn't noticed.

No, he'd noticed. Had she thought his eyes looked
like they were on fire before? Carly wondered dazedly.
Because looking into them now was to look into
glowing, liquid gold. She bit her lip in anticipation as he
kept his gaze fixed on hers, as something about it
changed, became wild. Became inhuman. He dipped his
head toward her, those amazing eyes becoming heavy-
lidded, but no less fierce, in anticipation. There was
something about them, still pulling at her. *Something.*

Beastly, her mind whispered, casting her earlier
thoughts about him in an entirely different, and infinitely
more disturbing, light. And then suddenly, she knew.

"Oh my God," she whispered. Hearing her, he stopped a breath away from the kiss, his hesitation an unspoken question. "You're … you're a …" She couldn't quite get it out yet, couldn't believe the word was even going to fall, in all seriousness, from her lips. But the man who had just turned her notions of reality completely upside down, seeing her distress, exhaled softly, released her wrists, and took a step back from her. Carly had to bite back a soft, pleading moan as that lovely, lingering heat they'd seemed to generate together flooded out of her like so much water. When he spoke, although she couldn't imagine why, Carly thought she heard something like regret.

"My name is Gideon MacInnes. I'm a werewolf from the Highlands of Scotland. And I need your help."

Chapter Four

THE PHONE HIT THE WALL JUST AS HIS MOTHER WALKED IN.

That, by itself, wouldn't have been anything out of the ordinary. It was the ten-thousand-dollar vase that hit the wall after it that indicated Malachi MacInnes might just be in a fouler mood than usual, if such a thing were possible.

As far as Malachi was concerned, until today, it hadn't been.

Moriah, sensing trouble, paused in the middle of the room and got right to the point. "Is it done, then?"

Malachi was uninterested in playing the polite son. Not bothering to dignify her question with an answer, he only spared his mother a quick glance and a disgusted snort before getting up to fix himself a glass of single malt whiskey, the finest Scotland had to offer.

"I'll assume that's a 'no,'" Moriah said after a moment of watching her son's broad back tense and bunch over the wet bar. She marched purposefully over to the two Louis XIV chairs positioned in front of the miles of cherry wood Malachi called a desk, a small, whipcord-thin woman dressed in a stylish D&G suit and sharp, needle-thin Jimmy Choo heels. Moriah was fifty but looked ten years younger, although her sharp, foxlike face and oddly colored eyes would never have been called beautiful. Interesting, yes, and striking, but never beautiful. With time and a bit of wisdom, she'd finally found that she preferred it that way.

And Malachi heard her every move; he knew her so well that he could sense what she would do almost before she did it. He felt her regard him, his obvious tension, and then heard her *tap tap tap* over to the chairs on those damned ridiculous shoes she'd insisted he buy for her. Then came the rustle of fabric as she sat, primly, of course, and smoothed her skirt once before waiting patiently for her only child's attention.

And get it she would, Malachi thought ruefully as he knocked back the whiskey in one gulp and poured himself another. No one denied Moriah MacInnes— wealthy Scottish socialite, mother of one of the top antique dealers in the entire UK, and, lest anyone forget it, sister to the great Duncan MacInnes, Pack Alpha and Guardian of the Stone—anything. Least of all her baby boy. She was fresh from shopping on Princes Street, no doubt. *Again.* Not that he'd say a word, despite the money that flowed in a steady stream from his accounts each month. After all, there were certain things, important things, that she expected of him. Always had been, always would be. And now, as in all things, even as some small part of him still railed against it, Malachi would find a way to give her what she wanted.

Malachi straightened, strode back behind his desk, and flung himself into his chair. He looked (he knew, as it was an effect he had cultivated over the years) for all the world like some petulant tyrant king, brown-black locks falling forward over his angular, almost gaunt face while his glittering slate eyes gave away no emotion at all. This, he knew, was how she liked him best: calculating, capable, and so, so cold.

But then, Moriah had taught her boy well. She wasn't the only one who knew how to get what she wanted. And what Malachi needed right now, more than anything else, was just a bit more time. He hated her, oh, with an intensity he had learned to keep hidden over the years even as his enmity grew. He had even thought about killing her, with increasing regularity of late. But as her luck would have it, however much he despised the woman who had given birth to him, Malachi hated Gideon MacInnes more.

And so he would give Moriah what she wanted this one last time.

Moriah faced him, as usual, he noted, the picture of perfection. Idly, he wondered how much he'd paid for that suit, the nails, the perfectly coiffed red hair expertly rid of any trace of gray, before he turned his attention fully to the matter at hand. She stared at him intently, her expression never changing except for the slight arching of one eyebrow. *All right, then,* he thought to himself, *let's get this over and done with.*

"Obviously," he snapped, "it isn't done. They took him in the woods, as we planned, but Gideon was more willing to turn on a fellow Wolf than we'd thought." Not to mention better matched against a Drakkyn than he was entirely comfortable with, despite the Andrakkar's assurances. But such matters were not, would never be, for his wretched, unworthy mother. "Jonas and Morgan need at least a day to heal. Jamie, stupid bastard, managed to get his throat ripped out."

He watched Moriah closely, seeing the rage that was always so close to the surface in her begin to bubble up as she leaned forward to grip the edge of the desk, her long, red nails lengthening ever so slightly as they dug into the wood. "Careful," Malachi chided softly, his eyes never leaving hers. "I won't be giving you money to replace that."

"I should have sent Marcus," she hissed, her lip curling up over gleaming white teeth that always looked ready to bite. "We obviously needed the strength of one *I* made for this task. Weakness," she growled, staring fixedly, viciously at her son as her large golden eyes went even more yellow, "is carried through the bite, you know."

Malachi could only stare back dispassionately. It was nothing he hadn't heard ten times a day for most of his life, after all, and whether or not there was anything to it, he found that about this, as with most things anymore, he just didn't give a damn. *Weak. Just like his father.* As the years had passed, though, Malachi had reassessed his view of the man who had given him life and then stolen away without a word. Weak he may have been, though all in their circle were forbidden to speak of him and so he couldn't truly say. On one count, though, the count of having had the balls to turn his back on Moriah … well, Malachi supposed that was a braver man than he'd ever be.

But then, if the whispers he'd heard were true, it was entirely possible that Benjamin Douglas hadn't left of his own free will at all.

He thought of this, the hate twisting just a bit deeper into his gut, before answering in a voice just as dead as his mother's eyes. "You haven't let me finish, Mother. Unlikely as it would seem, we still have the advantage. There's been a storm. Gideon won't be going anywhere just yet."

He watched Moriah digest this, watched her eyes slowly return to what passed for normal as she released her grip on the desk and relaxed back into her chair. Splaying her fingers out before her, she studied them a moment, then responded.

"And are you certain that we can finish this effectively? Because you *know* he'll be warning his good-for-nothing brother and his pathetic sap of a father. They'll be looking within to find the culprit."

Malachi laughed softly, a thin, cold sound. "You know as well as I that Jonas, Morgan, Jamie, even your beloved Marcus," he sneered, not bothering to hide his feelings for the lover his mother had made, and then made such a fool of herself over, "do not exist in the eyes of the Pack. No one even knows of their existence. And you know that no one would suspect, given the, mmm, *difficulty* of the process. Gideon might, but he also knows well that without proof, nothing can be done." Malachi smiled, a true one now, as a rare spark of real pleasure kindled within him at the memory of Gideon nearly having his eye removed.

He would have finished the job, of course, but in Pack matters, one did have to have a bit of discretion.

Malachi's smile earned him one from his mother, although there was something about hers that made one want to crawl away screaming. He always got the feeling that there was madness there, behind the bared teeth, waiting for the right time to bloom.

Her eyes shone now with one of her favorite memories. "I'll never forget the night Laura died. She'd wanted Duncan's bite so badly, begging and begging, and then died writhing in pain when her body rejected the Change." Moriah practically purred with pleasure when she added, "I really don't know how Duncan lives with the guilt, seeing that he told me not two days before that he'd never try to convert his poor little wife, that he knew she'd never make it because she didn't have enough of the wolf in her nature to survive it. Poor, poor Duncan. I'm sure, deep down, that he wishes someone would simply put him out of his misery."

"How fortunate, then, that he has such a caring sister," Malachi replied sarcastically, although, with Moriah lost in her usual delusions of grandeur, his comment fell on deaf ears. He sighed. Truly, he would have had the old bitch either locked up or hunted down long ago were it not for the fact that he needed her help, once his cousins were out of the way, to cement his position as Alpha. Simply because he would then be the last of the Guardianship blood didn't, he knew, guarantee his ascension to power. He'd been suspected of too much, been tied to too many schemes in his stupid youth to be at all popular with the Pack now. But Moriah, he knew, had the ties to pave the way.

And oh, how he longed for it, Malachi thought with a glance out the window at the city that surrounded him. He had chosen the Old Town of Edinburgh because the close streets and medieval buildings satisfied his longing for tradition, for the darker days before humanity had forgotten how to fear his kind. Before his kind had utterly forgotten themselves.

But his dreams were haunted by the Hunting Grounds, the land of his people. His days might have been spent constrained by duty, by business, by millions of tiny demands that shackled him to this office. But at night he ran wild across meadows full of long grass and the tightly furled buds of wildflowers whose scent lingered in the soft Highland air, padding beneath the gnarled branches of the oaks of the forest, silent as the trees themselves, as he stalked a lone red deer.

He'd had to exile himself, Malachi tried to remember. Had to leave what he loved to get it back. But the knowledge didn't prevent his well-manicured fingernails from slicing into his palms as he clenched his fists, creating perfect crescents that welled with blood.

To calm himself, Malachi riffled idly through some papers, breathing deeply. Letting the sting of the wounds he had given himself bury the violent anger he had to work ever harder to control. But no matter how he tried, his mind was already turning back to the increasingly irritating problem of Gideon. Soon his own claws would grip the source of power his clan had protected for well over a thousand years. And while that was going to happen, infuriating cousins or no, it would help a great deal to not have to kill the very Pack he was set to lead.

At least not many of them.

Malachi felt the bloodlust, the creeping madness he had to work harder and harder of late to keep at bay, rise in his blood. *Focus,* he commanded himself. *Breathe.*

The Stone of Destiny, the fabled *Lia Fáil,* would be his, and with it all the magic it contained. Brought to Ireland, then to Scotland from Egypt, where it had been Jacob's pillow on the night he'd dreamed of his ladder, the Stone was a mystical thing, its origins shrouded in mystery. Even from those who Saint Columba had sworn to protect it.

Had it truly been the pedestal of the Ark of the Covenant? The stone from which Excalibur had been pulled? He hardly knew, nor did he especially care. What he *did* know, Malachi thought with deep satisfaction, was that the famous symbol of Scotland's sovereignty did not rest in Edinburgh Castle, returned by the benevolent English (on loan, of course) who had stolen it. No, the Stone upon which the Scottish kings had been crowned since time immemorial rested in an entirely different place. And soon … soon he would have the key to unlock the power that was not even whispered about in legend. His Pack had done their job well.

Old Edward I, Hammer of the Scots, had never bothered to wonder why the Stone's keepers had given it up so easily. And now it would never matter again. Even most of the Pack didn't know what that Stone was truly capable of—which was, Malachi had recently discovered, a hell of a lot more than just symbolically making someone king. Once he had the Stone of Destiny, he would be in possession of a power great enough to rule more than just a pack of pacifist werewolves that had long since outlived its purpose. *Shadows,* Malachi thought with disgust. The lot of them, pale shadows of what they had once been, their leaders too mired in archaic and useless concepts to wield what power they had even if they'd known.

Honor. Duty. Responsibility.

Utter bullshit.

With an army of beasts at his back, Malachi MacInnes would be a king such as none had seen before.

And he would have allies that even his clawing, striving mother would never have imagined ... though they might be the last things she'd ever see. How he dreamed of the day he would finally stand before the Andrakkar, the Drakkyn lord who had promised him all that could be had in the darkness from which his foolish clan had fled so, so long ago. He would relearn the ways his people had turned from, had forgotten. And he would remind them of what it was to serve a worthy master. His entire future would open up along with a single door.

Such a small thing, really, to turn the key.

The thought warmed his dark, cold heart.

Moriah stood and gathered up her purse and coat. Apparently, Malachi decided, she'd had enough fun gracing him with her presence for one morning. When she looked at him again, her gaze was piercing.

"Finish it tonight," she instructed. "He's not our only obstacle, but he *is* the key. When he falls, we can act quickly. And if your *boys* can't handle it, well, I can always send a man." Her lips curved cruelly.

Malachi had to fight back his grimace. To let his mother see it would only have increased her pleasure. She knew, of course, how he felt about Marcus, a simpering, sniveling sex toy she'd found God-knows-where going on three years ago now. The man apparently had the fortitude to withstand his first Change, true, but other than that, Malachi had always found him to be more weasel than wolf. With his long blond hair and a body he spent most of his time perfecting (when he wasn't pleasuring Moriah, that was), anyone could see that he fancied himself some sort of supernatural god of lust. But to Malachi, Marcus was by far the most emasculated creature he'd ever seen, existing only by the leave of a woman who had always paraded her lovers before her son and who would, at some point, devour this one whole and find another pretty toy to play with.

And recalling the feast Moriah had, literally, made out of her last conquest did make it quite a bit easier to keep from retching each time Malachi had tales of Marcus's virility shoved down his throat.

"It will be done," Malachi replied, "when the time is right, and not before. But it *will* be done, and soon." Malachi turned away from Moriah's outraged expression deliberately, his patience for her orders nearly at an end. As he always did these days, when just the sight of her threatened to throw him into a snarling rage, he concentrated on the thought that one day, very, very soon, when her usefulness was at an end, he would allow himself the singular and indescribable pleasure of hunting her down and tearing her throat out with his own fangs. Hers … and then, if he was still around polluting the Hunting Grounds with his stench, that of the ass she was keeping in her bed.

As Malachi pictured his fondest dream, his tension flowed from him like water. Moriah, on the other hand, now looked as though she might erupt in flames and go shooting through the roof. He knew she was unaccustomed to this new defiance in her son, whom she had always been able to bend to her will, and the hint of fear that showed in her furious eyes pleased him more than he had anticipated. *Good,* he thought, the image of her mangled body still dancing in his mind like a treat held just out of reach. *I'll let you worry about whether your days are numbered.*

Malachi watched placidly as Moriah opened her mouth to speak, but then, unable to give proper voice to her fury, simply bared her teeth at her son, growled angrily, and then spun on one highly overpriced heel to *tap tap tap* back to whatever sick hell she existed in when she wasn't bothering him.

Once the door was slammed, however, Malachi gave in to his instincts, if only for a moment. His face contorted into a mask of rage as he stared at the door, his teeth lengthening and becoming wickedly sharp, his clenched hands beginning to drip blood as claws emerged to slice deep into his palms.

"You'll soon learn," he snarled in a deep, raspy voice that was almost completely inhuman, "not to turn your back on me, *Mother.*"

Much, much later, when the setting sun had turned the December sky to fire, Malachi turned from watching well-bundled humans scurry up and down High Street four stories below him and reached beneath his desk. He slid one long finger into a groove invisible to the naked eye, unlocking one of several secret compartments he'd ordered incorporated into the design, and withdrew the ill-fated cell phone from earlier. Aside from being a little dented, it seemed to be in working order, and that was a relief. After all, this was his only way of communicating with Jonas and Morgan, the only sure way he had of contacting them that couldn't be traced back to him. He knew his men would answer only calls placed from this number.

It was just a damned good thing the phone was still operable.

He really was going to have to try to rein in his temper, Malachi decided as he thought for a moment, then punched in several digits and hit Send. Assassination was proving to be a tricky and frustrating business, but it would, he was sure, prove valuable education for the future, if only he could keep his cool and focus. A bit of good news would certainly go a long way toward achieving that. All he could do now was wait for an answer, and hope. There was a click as someone answered on the other end.

"Tell me."

Jonas's rough, low voice, like the rustling of field grass as some unknown predator passed through it, answered him without hesitation. "It's still snowing. Most of the roads are closed, and the ones that aren't are basically impassable. He's not going anywhere."

Malachi began to toy with a small sculpture on his desk, something priceless even by human standards, and even more so because of what it represented to him. "How soon, then?" He wasn't about to throw a screeching fit like his mother surely would have, but any further delay really was unacceptable. He would hate to have to kill Jonas while he still had so much use for him. Jonas's answer, however, was not at all what he'd been expecting.

"That may depend, sir. Our target has chosen an interesting sanctuary." Jonas's tone held something Malachi rarely heard from his loyal servant, a sort of black glee that seemed to precede only his bloodiest and most satisfying kills. He leaned forward, tense with anticipation, his eyes emanating a faint glow. Jonas was his prized possession, a wanted criminal who had killed far more than the authorities could begin to suspect or fathom. Malachi had been patient, tracking him, watching him, waiting for the right moment, then stealing away with Jonas's bullet-riddled body, so nearly dead, once the police had found him.

He'd given Jonas a new life that night, and in so doing had gained a soldier both fiercely loyal and utterly ruthless. And he had, it turned out, unwittingly done what no Wolf before him had ever even dreamed of.

He had turned a being that had never even been human to begin with. A being with secrets, with *connections*. Most importantly, with a master sympathetic to Malachi's cause. A master with the key to the *Lia Fáil*. He reached up to draw a small violet chunk of crystal, hung on a thin silver chain, from where it was hidden beneath his shirt. Jonas hadn't been pleased when he'd discovered the piece missing from his own crystal. But he'd needed Malachi's help too badly to retaliate. Jonas's collar was cursed, impossible to remove. But through it, the great Andrakkar could see, could hear.

Could whisper, and redeem.

Jonas's master. *His* master, he thought as he toyed with the crystal, feeling the current of power that flowed just beneath the smooth, cold surface of it. Here, he was expected to serve the good of the many and gain nothing. But when one served a High Drakkyn well and faithfully, the rewards were endless. As was the pain that came with betrayal. Jonas had discovered that the hard way. And in his fervor to regain the trust of the Drakkyn lord, he had provided Malachi with the purpose he had sought all his life.

Gideon had no idea what sort of beast had been unleashed on him, Malachi thought with a tight, hungry grin. And now that he'd drawn Jonas's blood, no idea what sort of an enemy he'd gained.

"Where is he? A church? After meeting *you,* does he really think you'll respect the sanctity of hallowed ground?"

"He's given himself into the care of a woman," rasped Jonas, a dark smile in his voice. And for a moment, Malachi could say nothing at all. In all the years he'd spent watching and loathing Gideon, this was only the second time he'd ever done anything that surprised him. When the stoic, fearless Gideon, ever the dutiful son, had gone running off to America, it had been a shock. It had also been a gift, as far as Malachi was concerned, because all at once his problem of isolating his cousin for an attack had been solved. But this ... "gift" did not even begin to describe what this was.

"What have you seen?"

"I've tracked them to a small cottage. That won't

pose a problem, of course. We could take him tomorrow night, once Morgan's leg has finished healing."

Malachi tapped a long, dagger-like nail on his sculpture, a rectangular piece of obsidian engraved with golden Aramaic characters which had disappeared from the National Museum under mysterious circumstances several years ago. It was said to be an accurate representation of the Stone of Destiny from the seventh century, although the slab of sandstone the British had recently "loaned" back to the Scots to display at Edinburgh looked nothing like this beautiful, magical thing. Malachi smirked as he toyed with the piece. He couldn't wait for the bloody English to finally discover exactly what they'd been crowning their kings and queen on for the last seven hundred years. As he rubbed his slim fingers over the carvings, soothed by the smoothness of the stone, Malachi considered how he could best turn the situation to his advantage.

"Have you gotten a look at the woman?" he finally asked.

"Mmm," Jonas confirmed. "A delicious little morsel."

"And he gave himself into her care, she didn't just drag him off, you're *certain*?" Malachi knew he was probably being overcautious, but so much was riding on this.

"I watched. I'm certain."

Malachi lapsed into thoughtful silence. Relief mixed with adrenaline and flowed like quicksilver through his veins. He leaned back into the soft leather of his chair, a faint smile on his lips. A beautiful distraction. He would never have dared to hope. And now he needed to be careful, so careful, in deciding just how this should be played. Should be used. The possibilities, after all, were myriad. Endless. And so, so appealing.

"This may change things," Malachi finally said. "Until I've decided, do what you do best. Watch. Wait. And keep me informed." There was another click as Jonas hung up on his end, but Malachi was too adrift in his own thoughts to hear it. *Well, well ... our boy may have found himself a mate.* It was almost too good to be true. Almost. But as long as the snow held, as long as Gideon stayed put, he would watch, and evaluate. In the woods last night, Malachi had simply meant to have Gideon killed. Now, presented with the possibility of destroying him mentally and emotionally first, well ... it was something one wanted to consider, in any case.

"Really, Gideon, after all this. A *woman*," Malachi murmured softly to the empty room. "How very cliché of you. But you won't find me complaining." He rubbed the small black stone again, this time for luck. "Thanks for the weapon, Cousin," he continued, a far-off look in eyes as gray as the Atlantic on a cloudy day. "I only need to learn how best to wield it. But when I do," and he smiled, a terrible thing full of sharp, biting teeth, "I promise you'll be the first to know."

In his mind, the velvet darkness of the Hunting Grounds called to him, at last within his reach.

Delicious, Jonas had called her.

He could only hope that Gideon would take the time to find out.

Chapter Five

"I THINK I NEED A MINUTE."

"Is there anything I can, um … I'm sorry, I don't even know your name."

Carly moved the hand she'd placed over her eyes slightly to look at him. Gideon. Her wounded *werewolf.* He actually looked apologetic, like he really wanted to help but couldn't figure out how. Her eyes dropped, then slammed shut as she covered them back up, hoping that her hand would also cover most of the red flush she now felt spreading across her cheeks like wildfire.

"Carly. Silver. And if we're going to have an adult conversation, pants would be a good start."

"Oh." There was a pause as her words sunk in. "*Oh.* Right."

Good. Now at least she wasn't the only one who was mortified. He started to move, then stopped, his uncertainty actually audible. Carly took pity on him.

"Spare bedroom, second drawer down. There should be some sweats of my brothers' in there. They'll be a little short, but they'll work."

"Thanks. Be right back." When the sound of his bare feet padding across the rug faded off in the direction of the bedroom, Carly finally felt safe enough to open her eyes again. She blinked twice, looked around. No, she finally decided after a quick once-over of the short hallway that connected her bedroom, another smaller bedroom, and a decent-sized bath to the living area and the rest of the house. Pale yellow paint, the photographs of her shop, downtown, the lake in their thin silver frames still hanging straight and tastefully on the walls. She hadn't gone to Oz after all, it seemed. Crazy, maybe, but not Oz. Was it wrong, she wondered, that she was starting to wish her body had simply wandered off to pick up a man last night, instead of this? Whatever "this" turned out to be.

Carly kept her mind carefully blank until Gideon meandered back around the corner. It struck her again, the grace and ease with which he moved despite his size. Except some of that effortless animal grace with which he'd hunted her down in the hallway seemed to have slipped. Gideon was obviously favoring his left side a little and now, funny as it seemed to Carly after the way he'd moved to catch her, looking very, very sore.

He also looked very, very uncomfortable in a snug-fitting tee-shirt of Mario's that advertised Torre's Auto Mall, and an old pair of Luigi's sweats that, on Gideon, looked more like extremely unfashionable capri pants. And God help her, she was going to giggle. Could she *be* any more inappropriate? Then again, Carly reminded herself, she was going nuts anyway. She should probably just enjoy this part before she was compelled to run naked through the streets singing show tunes. Carly pursed her lips, trying to stop them from twisting into a smile, but Gideon looked down at himself, shrugged, and then gave her an adorably lopsided grin.

"Short must run in your family, eh?"

Great, she thought. A hot Scottish werewolf with a sense of humor, and he was all hers. In her wilder fantasies, this sort of thing had always been a lot less complicated. Then again, in her wilder fantasies, he wouldn't have been wearing the world's highest high-waters, and she sure as hell wouldn't have been standing here in comfy old flannel pajamas with her hair sticking up in various directions.

Reality, she decided, could be extremely overrated.

Carly curved one corner of her mouth up at him; she was willing to consent to a friendly conversation before figuring out what exactly he was doing here, but she did arch one pale brow at him before heading for the kitchen. "Lots of things run in my family. Be happy I only got short." His grin didn't fade, but Carly could have sworn she heard a faint snort of amusement. "Hey," she informed him, "never underestimate the vertically challenged. Remember Napoleon? Now come on," she sighed with a resigned shake of her head and one final, disbelieving glance at him. "I need coffee."

Ten minutes later, they faced one another across the small table in Carly's kitchen, each with a steaming mug of freshly brewed coffee in hand, sizing one another up.

She was dealing with the situation remarkably well, Gideon thought, enjoying the way she sat in her over-sized pajama pants and shirt, her knees tucked up in front of her to keep her feet off the cold ceramic tile floor. She gripped her coffee cup with both small, graceful hands, sipping occasionally while she looked at him with a mixture of curiosity, apprehension, and a sort of charming embarrassment. For which of them, he wasn't sure, but he was eternally grateful he was at least now wearing pants, even if the woman did appear to come from a family of midgets.

No rings, he saw. Thank God for that. He'd nearly kissed her, and it wasn't like him to move in on another man's woman, or even, if he was being honest, to move so quickly on an available one, no matter how beautiful she was. Or desirable. Or completely delicious. Not that his relief went any deeper than that, Gideon told himself, even as he quickly buried the memory of his body's unsettling reaction to her. He had only meant to calm her, as his kind were capable of inducing what amounted to a light hypnosis when need be. He hadn't meant for the kind of physical connection that had occurred to enter into it, and yet he'd been unable to ignore her body's heated response to him … or, he thought with no small amount of shame as he remembered how close he'd come to taking complete advantage of the situation, to control his own.

Your mate, his instincts insisted.

Over his dead body. Silver bullets wouldn't kill him any more than real ones, but her last name was an omen if Gideon had ever seen one. Carly Silver could end up being delightful in every other respect, but as a werewolf … Gideon thought of the way she'd trembled against him, the way her wrists felt like fine porcelain with his hands wrapped around them. Her inherent human frailty, her incontrovertible weakness.

Breakable, he'd sensed, even as he'd leaned in for just a small taste. He had learned about breakable women. They were better left alone.

Unfortunately, this one and he were going to have to work out a way to coexist for just a bit longer.

Gideon nodded his head to indicate the window behind Carly, the glass providing a view of nothing in the outside world but a thick, almost solid curtain of snow. "I think it's worse than last night, really."

She turned, looked for a moment, then turned back to him, apparently unimpressed. She shrugged, a delicate lift of the shoulders. "You live up here long enough, snow all starts to look the same. Still, a snow day is a snow day." She sipped, considered him. "So. You said you needed my help. Assuming I can overlook the fact that you crawled into my bed last night as a dog, that is."

"Wolf," he corrected her, frowning. Was the woman ever going to quit talking about him as though he shifted into a pet?

"Whatever." She waved her hand dismissively, and Gideon could appreciate the fact that she was trying to be businesslike about all this, bizarre though the situation was, especially for her. Carly Silver was already revealing herself to be a woman of contradictions, though Gideon doubted she knew it. Calm and capable, but a bit shy and unsure all the same. He could see it in the way her eyes kept dropping away from him onto the table, in the faint pink flush that crept into her cheeks whenever he spoke or looked at her for too long.

"Assuming I can overlook that, and that you were a naked *guy* when I woke up this morning, and scared the bejeezus out of me, chased me down the hall, and let me think you were going to kill me."

Gideon arched a brow. "Not to mention had the audacity to apologize at least three times for all of that already."

Carly stopped, looked at him, seemingly nonplussed, at least for the moment. "Well. Fine." She frowned into her coffee cup, then sipped, lapsing into thoughtful silence. *Regrouping,* he decided, and that was fine. As long as it led to him getting the rest and shelter he, at present, desperately needed, she could take all the time she wanted. Meanwhile, Gideon, who felt fortunate in that he didn't tend to find silence uncomfortable, relaxed in the honey-colored pressback chair he was occupying and looked around as he enjoyed the coffee Carly had brewed.

It was a bit more frilly than the way he usually took his—vanilla-flavored, but still good. Just feminine. Much like the little house she lived in, he thought as he took in the cozy kitchen with the copper fixtures and the warm-toned granite countertops, the interesting mix of teapots she obviously collected and had placed atop her cabinets. There didn't seem to be much space to spare, from what he'd seen in his short time there, but she'd somehow managed to make her home cozy without being cluttered.

In the kitchen, just as in the living room it opened up into, the colors were earthy and warm, the furniture plump, the fabrics sink-into-me soft. The things Carly had chosen to decorate with were a mixed bag of styles that nonetheless, at least to his eyes, worked together, from a bright Van Gogh print above the fireplace to the apothecary chest she used as a coffee table. And then there were the books.

Gideon wondered if they could be considered an addiction, because if so, Carly Silver was in need of at least one twelve-step program, and probably two or three. The small bookcase Gideon could see from the table had apparently long ago reached capacity, and its refugees were scattered about, from a small stack on the counter to one or two on end tables, with what looked like at least two more tucked beneath the corner of the richly colored blanket she'd draped over the edge of her couch.

They may, in fact, have counted as clutter. But even her books seemed to fit seamlessly into this little universe she'd created, Gideon thought, surprised to find himself suddenly fighting off a wave of homesickness. He liked to think his place, his own small cottage of wood and stone, not really much bigger than this, suited him as well as he imagined this place suited her.

It was the mark of naturally solitary creatures, he thought, that they crafted their caves so carefully and well, and made them the kind of places that silently entreated you to stay, sit a while, abandon your plans, and simply relax. Was his erstwhile savior a bit like him, then? He shouldn't want to know. Of course, Gideon thought with a touch of resignation, he shouldn't want to finish that little moment they'd had in the hallway, either, but damned if he didn't. He looked out the window again, and then back at the woman who sat opposite him, considering him once more with her fathomless blue eyes.

Then he made the mistake of looking at her mouth, and Gideon could actually feel his common sense deserting him, like a rat leaping off a sinking ship. If Carly hadn't been so definitely all-human, he would have wondered if she didn't have a heritage that gave her some hypnotic ability of her own. Such plump, inviting lips, he thought, imagining how they might taste, perhaps a bit like how she smelled to him if there was any justice in the world. He watched them move, mesmerized. There was a pause, and then they moved again. He was so sure she'd be delicious. If only he could have one small taste and be done with it, he knew he could be satisfied.

"Gideon."

"Mmm." He liked seeing the shape of his name on her lips. He wondered how it would be to nip at them, to run his tongue along them …

"Gideon!"

His head snapped up, and he found himself looking into a face that had taken on a great deal more irritation and suspicion in the minutes (and suddenly he knew, with a sinking certainty, that it had indeed been minutes) he'd been daydreaming. She folded her hands deliberately in front of her, although, with her knees still tucked up, the gesture didn't even come close to being intimidating. Still, it was a sign that she meant business.

He wondered if she was aware that the top buttons of her pajama shirt had come unbuttoned. At the sight of the barest hint of what Gideon was maddeningly certain were two perfect breasts now peeking out at him from her gaping neckline, Gideon bit back a groan of frustration. Christ, this was shaping up to be one hell of a vacation.

"I'm only asking for a place to stay until the weather breaks and I can travel," he said, figuring that he might as well be open about what he needed most badly. "I have a room at an inn about thirty miles from here, but I can't ask you to drive me in this, if the roads are even open, and also," hell, he hated to admit it, "I'm needing some rest after last night. As you might imagine, I'm not feeling exactly a hundred percent."

She looked at him so thoroughly and thoughtfully that, oddly enough, Gideon felt he was going to start squirming under the scrutiny. For such a small bit of a thing, this Carly was almost intimidating, he noted with something like wonder. And, he thought as his skin burned in the places where it was still healing from last night's assault, he badly needed her to give him sanctuary. She took her time considering, looking out the window onto a day that was nothing but frigid shades of gray and swirling white. Finally, she spoke. It was a funny thing, though. She seemed fairly amazed at herself as she fumbled out an answer, even shaking her head a bit in disbelief.

"Well, Gideon … I guess, all things considered … I mean, with the weather and all, I suppose I don't actually have a problem with that." Gideon started to smile, opened his mouth to thank her, but she held up her hand. "If, that is, you can give me satisfactory answers to a few questions I have."

Relief flooded him anyway. Carly Silver knew nothing about him or his people. How difficult could her questions be to answer? Certainly, there were a great many things he wasn't at liberty to tell most of his Pack, much less a woman he'd met only hours before, and a good number of other things he simply didn't think she needed to know. Still, it shouldn't be hard to keep his information general and simple. Of course, he was going to have to twist the facts just a little, Gideon rationalized as he considered just what he would tell her. It was safer for her, and it would make it easier for the both of them.

No matter how much his conscience was already stinging.

A Wolf will not keep secrets from his mate.

Except she wasn't his mate, his conscious mind insisted, and never would be. His father had let his love make him selfish, and he'd paid for that mistake ever since. Duncan would be the last MacInnes man that tried to make a mate of one who he knew could not bear the gift, Gideon vowed. Then he gathered himself, pushing the dark and nonsensical thoughts from his mind as he straightened and tried to look as honest as possible.

"Ask away."

"Great," she said with some obvious relief of her own. "So," Carly took a deep breath, charming Gideon inadvertently with her determination not to be intimidated by all of this, even though it must have gone against all her instincts, "here's what I know so far. You're a werewolf. You're Scottish. You showed up on my doorstep last night mostly dead. This morning, not so dead, but definitely naked, not quite healed, and also snoring away in my bed." She ticked off these items on slim, manicured fingers, a look of intense seriousness on her face. Gideon bit back a smile, again struck by the impression that Carly Silver, whatever else she was, appeared to be a businesswoman through and through. He idly wondered what she did for a living. The memories of her rescue of him the night before were fuzzy at best, but wherever he'd turned up had obviously been where she worked. It had, he reasoned, probably been an office of some sort. He could certainly see her in tailored little suits, bringing an incredibly sexy touch to a cold, clinical profession. An accountant, maybe? Lawyer? He had to be close.

Idly, Gideon wondered which of the myriad things Carly was sure to be curious about she'd decide to question him on first. The one she picked, however, startled him.

"So I guess what I really need to know is ... is whoever or whatever tried to kill you last night going to be coming back?"

Gideon could only stare at her, surprised into silence. Finally he managed to get out words, although they weren't much good to him. "I. Um. Well." *Genius,* he thought with a mental slap to the forehead. He had assumed she'd start with something easy, something born out of curiosity. After all, how many bloody werewolves could she have met? He'd never thought she'd get to the heart of the matter so quickly. He'd thought she'd be intrigued, maybe even fawn over his wounds a bit with some of the gentleness she'd shown him when she'd thought he wasn't human.

Obviously, he'd been wrong.

Carly gave him a hard look, frowning slightly. "Yeah. That's about what I thought. Don't know, do you?" She rose, moved to the counter to refill her cup. "More?" she asked without looking at him. Gideon fumbled through his thoughts, searching for an appropriate response.

"No, thanks. Why are you so sure someone was trying to kill me?" Ah, lovely. Defensive, not to mention stupid. Gideon gritted his teeth. Why couldn't charm have been his strong suit, as it was for his brother? Gabriel never seemed to have a problem keeping his rotating harem completely enthralled with him, no matter what manner of asinine stunt he'd just pulled. At this rate, his effect on *one* woman was going to find him either arrested or camping nude in the nearest snow bank. Apparently, the silver tongue only hit once in a generation.

Carly turned, gave him a long-suffering look that plainly asked what sort of an idiot he took her for, and sat back down. She tucked one foot beneath her, and dumped what to Gideon appeared to be a small truckload of sugar into her steaming mug.

"Got enough coffee in your sugar?" he asked, indicating the dark liquid that she was now stirring furiously. She simply stared back, obviously troubled. *Damn.*

"Ha. Look, Gideon, you've been pretty straight-forward so far, no matter how bizarre this all is, so I'll return the favor. I found you ripped halfway open last night. You could barely move." The pain Gideon saw reflected in her eyes both surprised and moved him. "I was going to do what I could, but I honestly figured you were just going to bleed out right there in the alley. And all I kept thinking was, what does this to an animal this big?" Her face was pale, her expression strained. She'd been really worried about him, Gideon realized with a strange jolt. Was, in fact, worried still. And damned if he knew what to do with that.

"Obviously, whatever you are heals pretty quickly, but I," she spread her hands in front of her as though making a plea, "am just human. If I get torn up like that, I will, in all likelihood, stay torn up. I have a life I love, a family I need to protect. And if you want to stay, even for five minutes, you'd better tell me what exactly I'm getting myself into."

He looked at her then, a small, delicate beauty in too-large pajamas worrying over a lot more than just whether the big, bad wolf was going to end up blowing her house down, and he knew what he was going to have to do. Quickly, Gideon calculated. Barring a complete natural disaster, he'd be here a day, two at the outside. While he knew his cousin would have made sure that none of this could be traced back to him, the fact was that one of his minions was dead, the other two wounded badly enough that they'd need to lay low for at least another full day to heal. Neither of them would be in the sort of shape required for trekking through a storm in Wolf form, any more than Gideon himself would in the immediate future. By the time they were able to try again, Gideon figured, he could and would be long gone. Back to the source, to settle this the way it ought to be settled: with Pack justice. This time, he would find a way to ensure Malachi got what he deserved, even if it meant the last resort of an Honor Battle, a fight to the death.

He might have underestimated Malachi, but Malachi had also underestimated him. It would be the last mistake, Gideon vowed, his cousin would ever be able to make. And as for other mistakes …

Gideon turned his attention back to Carly, pushed off the regret that wanted to creep in. He couldn't have her. Lying to her to set her mind at ease was all for the good, and she'd never know any different. All that mattered was that she wasn't going to get hurt, and that in a few days, she was going to be able to forget all about him.

And he, for his part, could try like hell to forget about her.

He looked her dead in the eye. "There was another Wolf in the woods last night," he told her. "I wasn't expecting it. I didn't provoke it. But I'm the only one who came out alive."

She must have caught a flash of something in his face, because for just a moment, she hesitated. "Are you sure?"

"I'm sure." And something he couldn't name twisted in his gut, even as he sealed it with words he was no longer certain were true. Just not in the way she might expect. "You're in no danger from me. I promise."

Carly faced some serious problems, not the least of which was that she seemed to have completely lost her mind in the past hour. *Werewolf in the bed? Sure, why not! What, you need to stay awhile? Hey, make yourself comfortable! And while you're at it, why don't you get naked again so I can climb your hot body like a tree? No problem? Great!*

"Oh, God," Carly groaned, her head resting on the table. After his vehement reassurances that she wasn't in any danger, her new houseguest had been nothing but a perfect gentleman. He'd gamely answered several of her random werewolf-related questions (yes, it was a hereditary issue; yes, there were more of them; no, he hadn't ever had a blood lust/dismemberment problem), and while he didn't strike her as the world's biggest chatterbox, he'd done just fine making small talk, even offering to whip up something morning-appropriate on the stove. He'd done nothing since they'd properly introduced themselves to invite anything like the kind of animal lust she was now fixating on him with.

She peeked up, saw nothing but Gideon's firm, completely grabbable ass sticking out of her fridge as he looked for the makings of the breakfast he was so insistent on making for both of them, and dropped her eyes back down. Actually, what she really wanted to do with her head was just to go soak it for a while. Of course, the steam rising from it afterwards would have been a dead giveaway.

Regan was right. She had been celibate for too long, and now, as punishment from her neglected libido, she was going to burst, literally, into flames. What the hell was wrong with her? Had any guy, ever, caused her to have even one iota of the lust-drenched torrent of feelings she was currently grappling with? She was racking her brain, but sadly, there didn't seem to be much left to rack. Gideon shut the refrigerator door and looked curiously at her with those intense honey-gold eyes.

"Headache?"

"Mmm," was all she could manage. At that moment, Carly was afraid that if she tried to say anything else, all that would come out would be X-rated. It was so wrong, she thought miserably. All she'd wanted was a pet, to care for a wounded animal and make it her own. Instead, she had the hottest mythological creature she'd ever imagined making her breakfast. Not that it would have been quite so bad, she decided, if he were the kind of man that ever might have been interested in her. But there was just no way, and she knew it. Guys who looked like wanton gods of sex did not lust after shy bookworms. Oh, she was okay to look at, Carly knew. But she wasn't a dark, irresistible gypsy like Regan. She was, she decided, sort of like Tinkerbell without the attitude. Short, curvy, and unfortunately, more apt to be reading about her ideal Peter Pan than chasing after the real one. How exciting.

"I'm not surprised your head hurts if this is all you have to eat." Carly looked up again at the sound of Gideon's rich brogue, seeing that he held her ancient jar of mayonnaise in one hand and a pathetic-looking orange in the other.

Glad for the distraction, she blew a lock of hair out of her face as she tried to remember where the latter had come from. "Oh, yeah. I remember." She pointed to the orange. "Last month I decided I was finally going to start eating healthy. Then Regan invented this new cheesecake that works surprisingly well for breakfast and I fell off the health food wagon."

"Last month." He looked at the unfortunate fruit, looked back at Carly, his face serious but laughter playing around the corners of his mouth. "Somehow I doubt you were ever actually on the health food wagon. I'm thinking you just looked at it a moment as the junk food wagon passed it."

"I have cereal," she offered.

"No doubt something full of marshmallows?" He sighed when she just smiled. Her smile faded a little, though, when she noticed that he was still favoring the one leg pretty badly as he moved to forage in the cupboards. That one had been shredded worse, she remembered. Not that much of him had actually escaped injury. *One* other werewolf had done that to him? It was hard to believe, but it wasn't like she was an expert on that subject. All she had to go by was Gideon, with whom she was strangely comfortable at some level, even as he was fraying all of her nerve endings at another. It was a weird mix. Kind of like him, she supposed. But just because he could no longer be mistaken for a wounded animal didn't mean he wasn't a wounded *man* who still needed some tending to, even though he looked like the type who would probably be difficult about it. She was just going to have to shrug off this attraction and do what her *other* instincts told her to, tucking his image away for some serious fantasizing once he was gone.

And he *was* going, probably soon, Carly reminded herself. No reason why he shouldn't. But in the meantime, she could spare him trying to put together something decent from the meager supplies she kept in her kitchen.

She stood, moved to Gideon's side as he pushed around a half-empty box of Cheez-Its and a bag of Flamin' Hot Cheetos. "Christ, woman," he muttered without looking at her. "It's a medical miracle you're living and breathing, if this is all you eat."

He looked absurdly right standing there, big and male and confused by the mysterious habits of the single woman, causing yet another little twist of both longing and lust deep in her belly. *Not for me,* she told herself firmly, and put her hand on the rock-hard muscle of his arm, sucking in a soft breath at the unexpected jolt of electricity she felt at the connection. What *was* that? *Not for me,* she insisted to herself again, but this time it was weaker, almost a question. She forced humor, even as Gideon stilled at her touch as though she'd struck him, turning his unusual and heated eyes on her full force.

It was all she could do not to puddle at his feet.

"Don't worry," she managed with a shaky laugh. "I live because of the nutritional wonder that is takeout." When he didn't answer, but merely dropped his gaze to her mouth (and oh, God, she was chewing her bottom lip again, she realized, even as she forced herself to stop it), Carly reluctantly moved her hand, breaking the connection, and took a step back, making a mental note not to touch him again unless absolutely necessary. What was she doing, letting him stay here, she asked herself frantically, fighting against her body's natural instincts to run from that predatory gaze. He was at least half beast; she could see that from the silent, graceful way he moved his massive form, the hint of danger that flickered in the way he looked at her, warning her. If she ran, Carly wondered, would he chase her? And more importantly … would she let him catch her? The thought that she very well might nearly had her fleeing the house as fast as her feet would take her.

"I, um," she fumbled, then drew in a deep breath, straightened. She was going to have to stop being such a shrinking violet, she chided herself. Gideon was intimidating, on a lot of levels, but damn it, this was her house, her life he'd crashed into, and if she didn't take the reins back now, God only knew what kind of shape she'd be in by the time he crashed back out of it. She cleared her throat, tried again, and fought back a flash of irritation as what looked like amusement flickered across Gideon's face. She'd just thought of a perfect, completely practical escape hatch so that she could clear her head. She was going to use it.

"Look, I'm going to save you some trouble here. There is nothing fit to eat in this house. However, my best friend runs a bakery and, as luck would have it, lives just two houses away. I'll go forage for food. You rest. You look like you need it."

To Carly's relief, he seemed to have managed to shut his prey drive off. He looked normal again. Or as normal as he probably got, anyway. Gideon shut the cupboard, leaned back against the counter, and raised his dark brows at her. He didn't have to say anything. His disbelief was obvious.

Carly felt her temper trying to bubble up again and reminded herself that there was no reason for Gideon to trust her not to sneak off and have him hauled out of her house. He didn't know her, after all, she told herself. Although it might have been nice if he'd given her a *little* more credit, all things considered.

"I'm walking there. In a blizzard," she pointed out flatly. "Also, I don't usually save people's lives just so I can have them tossed in jail. If you don't believe me, however, you're more than welcome to find another place to stay."

Gideon's look of chagrin was a perfectly adequate balm for her wounded pride.

"Sorry," he muttered, shoving a hand through his hair, and Carly saw that, despite his casual demeanor, he found the entire situation just as awkward and uncomfortable as she did. Against her will, she felt another warm little twist in her belly. Getting all friendly-warm-and-cozy with Gideon MacInnes would be nothing but trouble. If only he wasn't proving to be so damned likeable.

"I don't mean to imply," he started, raising his eyes to her a little before moving them back to the floor. "That is, you've been more accommodating than … and it's not as though I don't appreciate … oh, hell."

"Apology accepted," Carly offered, throwing him a line. If saving Gideon was a trend, she might as well continue it.

He blew out a breath, nodded. "Well then. A baker for a friend," Gideon, obviously relieved, collected himself and gave her a curt nod. "That should do nicely. And despite your, er, flattering assessment of my condition, I am going to need to sleep. I'll heal more quickly. Normally I'd be fine by now, but when my kind go after one another, the damage tends to be a bit longer-lasting." Gideon paused, and Carly couldn't help but wonder if he was thinking of his eye. Had another werewolf done that to him? And *why?* So many questions, and she had no idea when or if to even begin asking them.

"And of course," he continued slowly, his gaze direct, "the more quickly I heal, the faster I'll be out of your hair."

"Then by all means, sleep," Carly laughed, even though she didn't even want to imagine him leaving yet. Which was, she chastised herself, so utterly dumb, it was frightening. "Take the guest bed this time, though." Gideon just chuckled, a throaty rumble that made Carly's knees feel slightly watery.

"I'll do that. But do you mind if I use your phone first?"

"Oh. Um, Scotland?" She'd sort of forgotten he'd be making international calls. Silly, because that deep, growly brogue of his had already ruined her for all other accents, forever and ever, amen.

Gideon looked at her apologetically. "I was supposed to be flying home today. My brother and father will be wondering where I am. I'll make it quick."

Carly rolled her eyes and gave an exaggerated sigh, happy to be back on some sort of even footing. Teasing she could do. Having two older brothers, she was a master. It was the migraine-inducing sexual tension that made her want to run screaming. *Keep it light and simple,* she instructed herself. Banter was good. Though she wasn't about to tell him that even if he felt the need to call Japan, it was no big deal because her phone had seen even less action than she had lately, which was really saying something.

"Okaaaaaay," she drawled, then narrowed her eyes. "But you owe me."

His expression turned unexpectedly solemn. "I know I do. You saved my life. I'll be forever in your debt for that."

And so much, Carly thought, *for light and simple.*

"Oh," she stammered, feeling the heat flood her face immediately, "that's okay." She searched for something, anything to say that would cut the crackling tension arcing, once again, between them. She tried for a smirk, hoping against hope that it didn't simply look pained. "You're just lucky I'm not squeamish. You were kind of an ugly dog."

He grinned easily. "And you were a bit rough when you were dragging me around. Fortunately I'm not picky any more than I'm a *dog.* So I guess we're both lucky."

Some of us more than others, Carly thought, still wondering exactly how she'd ended up with tall, dark, and preternaturally gorgeous hanging out in her kitchen and planning on staying for a visit. Maybe she shouldn't look gift horses in the mouth. Maybe she should just enjoy and quit overanalyzing.

And maybe, she thought as her stomach rumbled, she should just get her ass in gear and go beg for food at Regan's door. Now *that* was going to be an interesting visit. "I'll be back in a few. Make yourself comfortable." She headed to the front door, yanked her ski jacket off of the coat tree, and pulled it on while shoving her bare feet into her big, clunky winter boots. Gideon came around the corner of the breakfast bar, studying what she was doing.

"You're going out in your pajamas? I don't need food that badly. I think I can wait if you want to dress first."

"Nah." He might not need food that badly, but she needed some space, and immediately. Carly pulled on her hat and mittens and wrapped an enormous fluffy pink-and-white-striped scarf around her neck until she had to push it down to speak clearly. "It's eight in the morning on a snow day, Gideon. I'm not even officially up yet."

He eyed her scarf with a mixture of horror and amusement. "I think there might be a bit of that left to wrap around your head, instead of bothering with a hat. Though from the looks of that thing, I'm not sure you'd come out alive."

Carly frowned at him, though she doubted there was an expression on earth that wouldn't have looked silly surrounded by all that pink fluff. "For your information, a good friend of mine knit this for me. And it happens to be very …" she searched frantically for an adjective that was not a synonym for *ugly* and finally came up with " … warm." Which it was. And she'd be damned if Celestine, sweetie that she'd been for making it for her, would ever hear any more about it than that. Not that she would probably ever get Regan to stop referring to it as "The Pink Nightmare" on a regular basis.

Gideon considered her for a moment as though he could read her mind, giving her a wicked smirk while he studied her with eyes warmer than ten of Celestine's scarves. Carly was suddenly thinking about removing layers to cool back down. "Well. I suppose it does match your pajamas, in any case. And there won't be any losing you in the snow."

Carly pursed her lips wryly as she stared back at him. A smartass. It figured, she thought resignedly. If there was one thing she couldn't resist, it was a man who could verbally fence with her. Even, she thought as she made a point of examining the length of his sweatpants, if he was currently dressed like a refugee from *Revenge of the Nerds.*

"Not that you could come looking for me. I'd hate to be responsible for causing, however indirectly, frostbite of the calves."

Gideon's grin widened as he relaxed against the wall. "Maybe I should ring up your brother, complain about the length of his inseam."

Carly growled, both in playful defeat and in frustrated reaction to the coil of heat that seemed to wind itself tighter at each upward curve of Gideon's lips. She threw up her mittened hands and opened the door.

"I give. I'm going. Be good, as in, don't break my stuff, throw a party, and/or leave all the toilet seats up in the house."

Gideon looked slightly incredulous. "Have these things been problems before?"

"Hey, I have older brothers, remember?" Carly turned, and a gust of wind sent snow spraying onto her wood floor. A quick look at the sky confirmed what that weather report snippet she'd heard this morning had said. Nothing but dark gray as far as the eye could see, nasty wind, and lots and lots of blowing white. She wondered whether she shouldn't have gotten dressed first, when another gust of wind sent slivers of cold straight through her worn flannel pants; but the prospect of getting this over with, coming back, and then covertly staring at Gideon in that tight shirt for the rest of the day got her putting one foot in front of the other and moving out into the snow.

Be good, she'd instructed him. Not that she really wanted him to, even though she was pretty sure he would be. Not that she knew how to be anything but, no matter how much she wished it were otherwise.

But hey, a girl had to dream.

She'd looked ridiculously adorable in her pile of winter clothes, telling him to behave himself. Gideon stood at the window, watching Carly make her way through snow that was now well above her knees until her small form faded into white.

And now that she was gone, he had to know.

Gideon opened the door, stepped out into the frozen waste that was now Kinnik's Harbor without so much as a care for either shoes or a coat. The tough skin of his feet was barely chilled as he paused, gauging the direction of the wind, and then headed to his right, around the side of the house sheltered from the wind. Serpentines of snow hissed across the ground in front of him as he crouched slightly while he moved, scenting for the faintest hint of what he was looking for, his eyes changing, sharpening as they scanned.

The ground was nearly bare right along the side of the house, what he could now (between vicious gusts of wind, at least) see was a quaint little New England cottage, white with dark blue trim and flowerboxes that held nothing but miniature snow banks to match the ones piling up alongside the road, or what was left of it. It truly was awful weather, as the plows obviously hadn't even been able to venture out yet. He'd picked a hell of a time to come for a visit, Gideon thought as he moved, slowly placing one foot before the other, trying to ignore the stinging slaps of snow. He almost wished he'd just stayed home.

Almost.

He straightened, satisfied, as he neared the back corner. Nothing. If they'd been here, they would have had to come around this way because the snow was up to the windowsill around the other side. And wounded as they were, it was so unlikely as to be ludicrous anyway. But something about the Gray niggled at him, though he couldn't put his finger on just what had disturbed him so. Something, something about the odd collar he'd been wearing. And his behavior, his ability, hadn't been like anything he'd ever seen before. Nothing, Gideon decided, could be discounted. Because he wanted, needed, to make sure that the woman who had so trustingly taken him in would be safe, just as he'd promised. For reasons he didn't care to think about, keeping his word to her was important to him for more than just his own personal sense of honor. Now it looked as if that was going to be much easier to accomplish.

And then he saw it, at the back corner of the house where the snow began its steep, wavelike ascent; familiar grooves dragged into the white wood. Claw marks. Territory markings. And within the impressions, faint streaks of crimson.

Shit.

A low, menacing growl poured unbidden from his throat as he glared first at the print that had just ruined his morning, then at the stormy sky which threatened to ruin a lot more if it remained as it was. He would have to be on his guard.

Against all odds, it appeared they were being watched.

And any animal who could keep hunting after the injuries the Gray had sustained last night demanded a great deal of caution, and even more concern.

Gideon stalked back through the snow, ignoring the chill that was beginning to prick at his bare arms, and stepped back through the doorway into the comfortable warmth of Carly's house. Immediately his nostrils flooded with her scent, nearly knocking him back with the intensity of longing and fierce protectiveness it provoked in him. He needed to go. He needed to keep her safe. He needed … he *needed.*

Be good, her voice whispered in his head. Except the look in her eyes told him something different, although her shyness would never permit her saying so if the frequency of her blushes was any indication. *Be good.* Except that if he was still here when night fell and the wolf within grew stronger, he wasn't sure he'd be able to. Or if he even wanted to.

Gideon stomped over to the breakfast bar, picked up the portable phone, and began to dial a number he knew by heart. He needed to speak to someone else who had a Y chromosome for a while, clear his head.

He needed to figure out what the bloody hell he was going to do about getting back as soon as possible, and in one piece. He needed to decide how to turn the tables on Malachi and his unexpectedly resilient henchman. And he really needed to talk to someone who had a way of putting relations with the opposite sex in sharp, unflattering perspective.

There was a click as someone picked up on the other end, the sound of a merry, chattering crowd in the background.

"Wolf at the Door pub, Gabriel MacInnes at your service."

Gideon closed his eyes, relieved.

It was a lucky thing he happened to be related to just the man for the job.

Chapter Six

"So let me make sure I have all this. You're somewhere in remote upstate New York, our idiot cousin has sent some non-Pack werewolves to kill you, one of whom is too stupid to know he should just go home and bleed for a bit, and meanwhile a blizzard has rolled in, trapping you with some succulent little blond who saved your sorry hide and is currently off getting you breakfast. Have I missed anything?"

Gideon relaxed on Carly's bed, figuring what she didn't know wouldn't hurt her, and gave into temptation, rubbing his head against her sweet-smelling pillow. "Did I mention exactly how succulent she was?"

Gabriel groaned. "I know it may shock you to hear me say this, Gid, but I think there are more pressing things we need to deal with right now than your little conquest." He paused thoughtfully. "Not that I don't approve. I've often said you could do with a good …"

"I doubt it would be the curative you're hoping for. And in any case, I don't think it would be a good idea."

"Always the martyr. When are you going to allow yourself a bit of pleasure, eh? I know you're the mighty and self-sacrificing future Alpha, but I don't think that being no bloody fun has ever been an official part of the job description."

"Gabriel, I rest secure in the knowledge that you have more than enough fun for the both of us," Gideon sighed, enjoying having his brother to banter with but wishing he didn't have to hear the "you're no fun" lecture for the umpteenth time. After all, it wasn't as though Gabriel had ever been expected to do anything but exactly what he'd wanted to. Despite having been raised in the same household, the two of them had had decidedly different upbringings. Gabriel had been the baby, the handsome clown, always ready with a joke or his charm to get him out of trouble (which they always had). He'd learned to fight, as all Pack males did, to control his power and wield it as best he could. But when it came to the bits he'd considered optional, the rigorous training Gideon had gone through, the added responsibility meant to toughen up those in line for Guardianship, well, Gabriel had always opted out. And their father had indulged him, Gideon thought with just a hint of that old jealousy, never pushing too hard, sending him off with his blessing when Gabriel had announced he was running off to Tobermory to open a pub, be back sometime, fare thee well.

Naturally, it had been a success. Everything Gabriel had ever touched had turned to gold.

It was just a damned shame he'd never bothered to do much with it. But then, what did he know, Gideon thought, shaking off the mood that always threatened to settle on him when he and Gabriel had this particular conversation. He'd always pushed himself, always taken on more than perhaps he ought to have. So busy training for the future that he'd forgotten to enjoy the present.

And wasn't that some of what this little last hurrah of a trip had been about?

A lot of good that had done. Gideon snorted softly, shaking his head. Obviously, some people were simply not meant to indulge themselves. And others, like Gabriel, soaked up all the indulgence for them. It might have been an unfair balance, but a balance it was, and he and his brother had long ago accepted that they were opposite sides of the same coin.

It helped them to continue loving one another when they wanted to kill each other.

"Do you want me to tell Dad?" When Gabriel turned the topic, the concern in his voice was evident. Say what you like about him, thought Gideon, but Gabriel's loyalty, once given, was as solid and true as the *Lia Fáil* itself.

"You'd better." Gideon switched the phone to his other ear, listened again for any sound of Carly's return. He had no idea how he'd explain lolling about in her bed, and he doubted she'd join him at this point, so he was keeping his ears pricked, just in case. "I know Malachi's always hated me, but those beasts he sent to off me weren't right. Wouldn't surprise me if he's been turning the worst sort of criminals to work for him, and if that's the case, you know he's not going to stop at me. The rules he's breaking are too big to mean anything but. Dad needs to be watching his back. He's going to make a play for Alpha."

"And Moriah will finally have her little dynasty. God knows she probably still thinks she can make some sort of king out of her baby boy once she gets her paws on the Stone. You'd think she might have bothered to learn a bit about the nature of what we protect with our damned lives, wouldn't you? Not that Dad ever told us much, but he did always laugh whenever we suggested crowning ourselves on it."

"You mean *you* always wanted to crown yourself on it. And if she was always as frightening a hag as she is now, then no, not really." Gideon tucked his arm behind his head, realizing that he was finally beginning to relax. "Wonder if she's still dyeing her hair that color that makes her head look like it's on fire?"

"I guess I'll be finding out, since I'm going to have to pay our stupid cousin a visit, and you know mummy's never far off. Listen, I'll poke at him, see what I can get, have a go at warning him off. But all of this … be careful, Gid. If he really is trying to kill you, and truly, it's so outrageous I can barely get the words out, then he's finally gone *completely* off his rocker. Once Malachi knows that we're onto him, he may move more quickly, especially since his little friends have made it clear they're keeping an eye on you. And you know it's going to be near impossible to turn everyone on him without some kind of proof. Malachi can be a charming bastard when he likes, although I have to say, he doesn't hold a candle to me. Can't see how everyone doesn't see right through it."

"Always so modest," Gideon chuckled. "No, you're right. He's far from loved, but then again, everyone knows he and I have history." He stroked his finger down the line of his scar. "And to come out flinging wild accusations when I've just done the only crazy thing I've ever done and gone running off to America … they'll be *asking* him to take on the Guardianship."

"No." Gabriel's tone was firm. "You needed this. If ever a man needed a vacation, it was you, Gid. I know I'm a broken record, but you need to try and think a little less of the Pack once in a while, and a little more of yourself."

Gideon's laugh was short, humorless. "Tried that, and look what a mess I'm in."

"Oh yes," Gabriel replied, and Gideon could actually hear his brother's eyes rolling. "It's all terrible. Especially the part about you being snowed in with some pretty thing who wants to save you. Not to mention I've never heard you say more than two consecutively nice things about any girl you ever dated, and suddenly you're wanting to gobble up the one you're with. Careful, you," he chided, "because if I didn't know better, I'd think you'd found your mate."

Gideon heard his voice harden, but his back was up now and he couldn't help it. What the hell was *this?* Gabriel was supposed to be warning him off, telling him horror stories about people he knew who'd gotten themselves tied down, dismissing his attraction as a meaningless nothing easily cured by a quick shag and an even quicker exit. But if Gideon wasn't mistaken, what he was hearing in his brother's voice was *encouragement.* And just what was he supposed to do with that?

"You know damned well that would never work," he growled. "She isn't strong enough to take the bite. There's no natural wolf in her. She's too soft. Too *human.*" Just like his mother had been, he thought, and it was one more drop of sorrow into the endless well he'd built on the faint memories of a woman whose softness and warmth he had never truly stopped feeling the loss of.

Gabriel sounded unfazed by his brother's snap of temper. "So, you *have* thought about it. Well, Dad always said, when it happens, it happens fast."

"Like you'd know."

"Gideon, in case you haven't noticed, I'm making a concerted effort *not* to know."

"Hence the merry-go-round of unsuitable women?"

He heard the satisfied smile in Gabriel's voice. "Exactly." Gideon just shook his head, pitying the woman who would eventually catch his brother's heart as well as his eye. He had a feeling neither one of them was going to be all that happy about it. He could only hope he'd be around to grab a bowl of popcorn and watch the show.

"You know, it's not as though you'd *have* to try and turn her. You're a good boy, you could keep your teeth to yourself."

Gideon pulled the phone from his ear, glared at it, and returned it to his ear, wishing his brother would just let the subject drop. It was the most utterly upside-down conversation he'd ever had with him, and as a wave of fatigue washed over him, he found he was quite ready to go back through the looking glass into the real world now, thank you very much. He was sore, he was exhausted, he wasn't even going to begin to think about the sexual frustration, and he was ready to have a nap.

"What woman could *possibly* be happy living like that?" He'd closed his eyes now, but the frown was still firmly in place. He gritted his teeth when, instead of blackness, he kept envisioning Carly in the one place every shred of sense he had insisted she shouldn't be: his home. But the harder Gideon tried to block it, the better he could see it; Carly, her blond waves flying behind her, laughing as she ran ahead of him over the rolling lawns and gardens that surrounded his cottage. Whether he was man or Wolf, she would run with him, daring him to catch her before she disappeared into the embrace of the silent, sheltering trees. The sky above them would be pale with evening, and all around them, the singular, endless green of Morvern would fairly shimmer.

Gabriel's voice, when it came crashing through the daydream, was annoyingly cheerful. "Ah, back to being a martyr again. That's comforting. Well, you have a point, Gideon, I sure as hell can't see anyone wanting to live with you. Not with all the pissing and moaning you do. But maybe your girl's going for sainthood, being that she hasn't tossed you out on your ass yet."

Gideon growled in response.

"Temper, temper," Gabriel sighed breezily. "Well, on that note, I'll be off. I've got a blonde lovely here who can't wait to have her paws all over me. I'll sniff around our dear cousin, see if I can get his back up. Now that I've got your number there, I'll call and let you know how it goes. I'll be talking to Dad about it, too. Not that he'll give a damn, stubborn old goat that he is." Gabriel chuckled, but Gideon knew he was right. Which only made getting to the bottom of things quickly even more imperative.

"Until then, take care of yourself, brother."

"Watch your back too, Gabriel. Once we can prove it's Malachi, he'll have to be dealt with. And it looks like he's wanting to deal with us first."

There was a soft click as Gabriel broke the connection, and Gideon hung up on his end as well, tossing the phone to the floor. His mind was suddenly fuzzy, his body feeling as though it were made of lead. The morning had taken a lot out of him during a time when he really should have been resting, healing. Now, his body didn't just need it, it was demanding it, and Gideon realized with dawning horror that he was never going to make it back to his assigned room, much less out of Carly's bed. He was going to sleep, whether he liked it or not.

"Hell," he growled weakly, even as he shifted slightly to wrap his arms around one of Carly's pillows and bury his nose in it. He inhaled deeply, his tired mind awash in images of a small blond pixie bearing sweets.

Moments later, his snore reverberating through the quiet house, Gideon was peacefully, thoroughly asleep.

"Tell me something, Carly. Does this look like the Sav-Mart to you?"

Carly barely paused to look at her friend before returning her attention to Regan's enormous fridge, a good portion of the contents of which she was busy emptying into the biggest paper bag she'd been able to find. She knew from experience that Regan's tone was more intrigued than disgruntled, so she felt no compunction about raiding her kitchen whatsoever.

And as for Regan's intrigue … well, she was just going to have to stay that way for the time being, because as close as they were, there was no way she could spill all of the details about what was going on without sounding like she needed to be heavily medicated. And maybe she did, Carly thought as she dropped a package of bacon into the bag along with the rest of her ill-gotten goods. God knew even she hadn't quite wrapped her brain around the situation yet, and the werewolf in question was currently holed up in *her* house.

Werewolf. At her house. Carly stopped for a moment, shook her head, then reached for one of Regan's multiple cartons of eggs. If her house was empty when she got back, she decided, she was taking herself directly to the nearest psych ward. Even if she had to walk.

"You have enough food to feed a damn army, Regan," Carly pointed out from the depths of the refrigerator. "And I'll pay you back anyway, which you know." Regan's heavy sigh had her pulling her head out to look at her. "What?"

Regan—maddeningly put together even at this early hour in loose jeans, a tunic-length sweater in vibrant purple, and, Carly had already noted with little surprise, bare toenails painted exactly the same shade—frowned at her from where she relaxed against part of the vast expanse of granite countertop that encircled her kitchen. Some half-stirred concoction that would probably, at some point in the future, make Regan a pretty profit sat forgotten beside her, and Carly knew with certainty that she'd already been up for hours puttering around her kitchen. Regan was an excellent baker, and never had been able to sit very well. It seemed to work, as most things did, to her advantage.

"I'm not worried about the food," she began, "although the word *blizzard* often sends people out to the store a couple of days prior for extra supplies. You *do* know the meaning of the word, right? Lots of snow, high winds, no unnecessary *leaving your damn house.* This system is stalled out over half the state, messing things up to one degree or another. No one knows what it's going to do anymore."

She hadn't known *that,* actually, but Carly wasn't about to admit it. "I had … a few things."

Regan snorted. "Tell me you've at least gotten rid of that pathetic orange and given it a decent burial. *Please.*"

Carly pretended to be extremely interested in a container of yogurt. "Mmm."

Regan sighed dramatically. "As I suspected. You're still living off of takeout and air. And flat soda, probably, but I can't handle thinking about that right now. Still," she continued, sauntering over to peer with interest into the nearly full bag at Carly's feet and plucking something from it with long, thin fingers painted the exact shade of her toes, "I have never known you to get so hungry that you suddenly decided you needed an economy-sized package of chicken breast."

Carly straightened, huffed an errant strand of hair out of her face, and tried to project indignation. Of course, she decided with a sinking feeling, that might be easier if she didn't always have to look *up* at Regan.

And if she hadn't been one of the world's worst liars to begin with.

"What are you trying to insinuate here, huh?"

Regan was immediately triumphant. "Aha!" she crowed. "You *are* hiding something!"

Shit, thought Carly, she really should have known better. Somehow, on her face, righteous indignation always looked a lot more like guilt. Resigned now, she watched Regan close the refrigerator, nudge the bag aside with her foot, and waggle her index finger at the table and chairs tucked into the breakfast nook.

"I'm afraid it'll be details for food this morning. Have a seat, Miss Silver."

Carly made a face, but she did as instructed and took a seat. She'd been around long enough to know that where Regan O'Meara was concerned, resistance was futile. "I don't have to wear a dunce cap, do I?"

"Oh," Regan said as she slid gracefully into the seat opposite her, "I don't think that will be necessary." Once she was situated, her gaze sharpened. "Now come on, Carlotta. You're never secretive about anything."

"Watch it with the name-calling," Carly returned with a warning look. "And I'm never secretive, due to a reason I like to call My Life Is Boring."

Regan only waved the comment away with her hand. "More like you have an aversion to adventure. And we can argue about that later."

"We usually do."

Regan paused long enough to give Carly a pointed glare, then leaned forward intently. "Something is up. The question you get to answer is, what? And *please* don't tell me it's something boring, even if you have to make it up, because my life really *is* about as exciting as watching paint dry right now."

Carly laughed reluctantly and shook her head. Regan was nothing if not predictable as the Queen of Drama. "If you're going for vicarious thrills from me, you *are* desperate." When Regan simply continued to stare at her, waiting, Carly groaned and thought quickly. Lying, she sucked at. Some doctoring, however … that she could probably do.

"Fine. I seem to have gotten myself an, um, unexpected houseguest." She tossed the statement out there and watched, with more than a little apprehension, as Regan's eyes narrowed thoughtfully while she absorbed this.

"Unexpected."

"Mmm." Carly fought not to fidget. "Tourist. His car broke down last night as the storm was coming in. He came knocking on my door and, well, stayed." She pursed her lips in frustration as she watched Regan's eyebrows lift until they were just shy of her hairline. "Honestly, Regan! Remove brain from gutter, okay? He slept in the *other* bedroom. *Alone.*"

"Oh." And leave it to Regan, Carly thought, completely exasperated, to look disappointed about that. "But he is *male,*" Regan finally said hopefully.

Carly sighed. "Unless I'm missing something."

"Hot?"

"*Regan.*"

"Oh, come on!" cried Regan, tossing her hands up. "I'll be so sad if you're just putting up some big ugly fat guy!"

Carly gave her a long-suffering look, beginning to suspect that Regan's membership in the Bodice Ripper Book Babes was not all due to loyalty to her. Somewhere in the romantic cynic, there appeared to lurk a lover's heart. Or some reasonable facsimile, anyway, Carly amended. Something that could also encompass a great deal of soft porn.

"Gideon is … attractive," she finally allowed. Regan's eyes lit up immediately.

"Gideon? Ooh. Nice."

You have no idea, Carly thought, but out loud she tried to be more pragmatic. "Yes, nice. And also on his way back to Scotland as soon as the weather breaks."

"Hot and *Scottish?*"

Carly winced as Regan leaped from her seat. "Regan. Babe. You're yelling now. I think my ear is bleeding."

"I can't believe this!" Regan howled, ignoring her. The internal switch had obviously flipped right to over-drive, Carly saw. Her friend was just about vibrating.

"You," Regan continued, pointing an accusatory finger, "you came over to get food for some gorgeous, stranded, *Scottish* … and you weren't even going to tell me?"

"Regan," Carly said evenly, wanting to nip the hurt feelings she saw starting in the bud, "it really isn't any big deal. And I would have told you at some point."

"Only because you can't lie for shit," Regan sniffed.

"But I just didn't want you to get all worked up about it. Which, I might point out, is exactly what you're doing."

"Maybe because the gods have finally seen fit to drop a big, handsome gift in your lap and you're doing what *you* always do! Jesus, Carly." Regan ran an agitated hand through her hair, making the short black crop stand up in spikes. "How can you always be so calm? This is not business as usual, for God's sake! Live a little!"

Carly's jaw tightened. "Your definition of 'living a little' always seems to involve me having sex with random men on my kitchen floor."

Regan glared at her. "It probably wouldn't hurt you to emerge from the fantasy once in a while, you know. It's not like you haven't done enough research, considering what you do for a living."

"That's not me, and you know it. I wish you would just accept it." Carly stood, shoving her chair back a little more abruptly than she'd wanted to. She wanted, in that moment, nothing more than to get back out into the stupid snowstorm that had caused her all of these problems in the first place and cool off. She needed comfort, not criticism, and the last thing she needed at this point was a fight with her best friend. Before this became one, she needed to go. Because her nerves, Carly knew, were already shot. Futile though it was, Carly wished for a nice warm hole to crawl into and hide until she was fully functional again.

As she bent to pick up her bag, Carly felt Regan come up behind her. She kept moving, but more slowly. She didn't want to leave angry unless she had to.

"You know I don't *really* want you to have sex with strangers on your kitchen floor."

Carly turned, sighed resignedly. It was, for Regan, somewhere in the vicinity of an apology. Generally, that had to work for "as good as."

"Often," Regan finished after a beat, and then Carly couldn't help but answer Regan's smile with a reluctant one of her own.

"Idiot."

Regan put up her hands, talking as much with them as she did with her mouth. She always did so when she was trying to extract her foot from the latter. "I just … I know I get a little carried away sometimes. I *know*. But sometimes I think you forget that you no longer have to answer to your overbearing, dorky brothers when it comes to your love life. You know? I know you think you're too shy, but guys *like* shy. Shy is cute. Just don't *hide*."

Carly bit back the impulse to voice her opinion that she wasn't the *only* one who knew how to hide from things. She knew it would just keep them at loggerheads, and so instead made a concession. "Maybe your kitchen floor idea *would* do me some good," she acknowledged, a little appalled to find she was only half-joking when she put Gideon in that picture, "but Regan, cute shyness notwithstanding, you forget. You and I do not attract men in the same league. And Gideon is way out of mine, even if I were looking for some kind of fling. Which I'm not." *I don't think.*

"Hm." Regan studied her. "The only difference I see is your comfort level in your own skin. You are *beautiful*, Carly. I have never understood why you can't see what's right in the mirror."

"I looked before I came over here. It was not good."

"And I wish you would. Because methinks you're interested in this guy."

112 KENDRA LEIGH CASTLE

"And *me*thinks you have an overactive imagination," Carly returned. "He is *leaving*."

Regan just grinned and touched a finger to the tip of Carly's nose. "And it is still *snowing*. Just do me a favor. Consider, at least consider, the possibilities."

Carly gave her a knowing look. "You're thinking about my kitchen floor again, aren't you?"

"Okay," Regan conceded, turning Carly by the shoulders and steering her towards the door. "I give up. Do what you will about the mystery man. But just so you know, I'll be over here doing the Snow Dance in support of your best interests. You could use an adventure."

Carly turned her head to smirk at her friend as she pulled on her coat and boots. "I should get some sort of talisman to ward you off, then, because I seem to remember *your* last adventure involved me posting bail…"

Regan was now all but shoving her out the door. "Go!"

"… at some ungodly hour …"

"It wasn't my idea, which we have *discussed* …"

"… and weren't you dressed as a pirate?"

With that, one bare foot was planted firmly against Carly's backside as she was pushed, unceremoniously, out onto Regan's snow-covered wrap-around porch. Regan stuck her head out the storm door, however, to have the final word.

"The charges were dropped, you know. It hardly counts."

"I'll keep that in mind," Carly laughed as she turned away, clutching the overstuffed bag to her chest and praying it didn't rip. She peered through the blowing snow in the direction of her house, which was hidden in impenetrable whiteness, and felt something unfamiliar shiver through her veins in tiny, icy-hot explosions.

Possibilities, maybe?

"Call me!" Regan yelled to her over the wind. "And seriously, Carly. Next time I'm at your house, we are burning those pajamas!"

Carly gave a wave back over her shoulder and started down the steps. She also made a mental note to hide the pajamas. *Possibilities.* She turned the word over in her mind as she ducked her head against the wind and waded into the snow. *I'm considering, Regan,* she thought, *but man, if you only knew the half of it.*

She would love it. And Carly knew it. Things to think about, she decided as her cheeks tingled from the cold even beneath her scarf. Later. For now, there was only breakfast, Gideon … and possibilities, up to and including the floor of a certain room of her house.

"I am in so much trouble," she sighed, and headed home.

Ten minutes later she stood in her doorway, watching Gideon breathe deeply as he clung to her pillow as though it were the only thing anchoring him in her little house, in the storm.

She should wake him. She should probably kick him out, at least out of her bed, and in all likelihood out of her house. And maybe she would … after watching him sleep for just a while longer.

What was *wrong* with her? It wasn't as though she'd never seen a hot guy before. And simple attraction, she could deal with. But Gideon … he just slammed into her every time she looked at him—had done so, in fact, from the moment she'd laid eyes on him as a big, gorgeous human. All she could seem to think of was getting closer to him, his heat, his strength.

God, it was all she could do not to try and crawl inside his skin just standing there looking at him, Carly realized with dawning horror. She wanted him on levels that she shouldn't be thinking about until after months, much less just a few hours, and yet there didn't seem to be any controlling the bizarre physical and emotional reaction she was having to him. It was *not* normal. Then again, Carly thought with a frustrated sigh, what about any of this *was?*

Gideon frowned in his sleep, a small crease appearing between the strong arches of his brows, and made a soft noise in the back of his throat. It tugged at her, made her want to know what was upsetting him so she could fix it, chase it away. Carly bit her lip, taking in his massive form sprawled across her bed, making it look no bigger than a child's, the way his large, coarse hands cradled her pillow to his chest, his face. *I don't know you,* she had told him. And yet she found, to her misery, that it made absolutely no difference.

She had always wanted impossible things; the conquering yet tender hero, the rescue from the tower, the declarations of undying love. The happily ever after. Her dreams had been safe, in a way, because she knew they'd never happen. No swaggering warrior had ever, to her knowledge, come within a mile of her, and that had been okay. She couldn't ache as badly for someone she'd never seen.

Except that now she'd seen him. And she had a feeling that "ache" could very well be an understatement for her feelings once he went back to whatever life he'd had before he'd come here if she wasn't very, very careful.

Gideon stirred then, as though he sensed her presence. Carly stepped back, ready to make a run for it, but he didn't wake. Instead, she watched, wide-eyed, as he nuzzled her pillow. And softly, barely audibly, breathed her name.

"Carly ..."

And as she forced herself to leave him there, to close the door and walk away, Carly wondered with a growing terror just exactly what she'd done. She was beginning to suspect that when your fantasy finally showed up at your door, in that one moment, everything changed. Possibly forever. And there wasn't a damn thing you could do about it.

Chapter Seven

SHE'D LET HIM SLEEP.

He must have slept for the better part of the day, Gideon realized, groggy as he noted that the light through the blinds, still gray, was deeper. He raised his head a little, sniffed, and found his senses immediately flooded with some delicious aroma wafting from the kitchen. His stomach growled loudly, reminding him that he hadn't eaten all day and had likely missed out on whatever confections Carly had returned with that morning. He yawned, stretched, looked casually around.

He was in her bed.

Christ.

Gideon sat up quickly, swung his legs over the side of the bed and scrubbed at the sides of his head, trying to get his brain working so he could come up with an explanation. Or an apology. Or something. Sleeping all day had left him muddled, uncertain. Was she cooking for him? Did that mean she wasn't angry? Would she simply throw him out when she saw him, or had she decided to poison him?

Gideon stood, stared at the closed door of the bedroom for a moment while he worked himself up, and then opened it to head out into the house and see for himself what he'd done with his carelessness. He was a powerful, supernatural creature, he reminded himself as he moved. He would lead his people one day. He'd never been afraid of much, and he sure as hell wasn't afraid of a tiny human woman. His intense desire to head back into the bedroom and shut the door was obviously just a natural reaction to his weakened state.

Just before he rounded the corner out of the hallway, he stopped short, hearing voices. It took him a moment to figure out that it was just Carly, checking her machine, but there was a nasty second where he thought perhaps she'd decided to bring in the police after all. And that would be his own damned fault for curling up in her things when he'd been asked not to, like an ill-disciplined pup. God only knew what she was thinking he'd do to her.

He certainly hoped she'd never find out just what he *was* thinking about doing to her, Gideon thought as pieces of his fevered dreams came rushing back to him. And he had to stop again, just out of her sight, as he fought to calm his immediate physical reaction to just the thought of her.

He'd healed. And unlike any other time he'd had to, instead of dreaming of home and the unbridled joy of running beneath the moon, he'd dreamed of Carly's creamy skin, of licking the tiny droplets of moisture from her skin as she moved beneath him, the sheen of her pale hair his only moonlight as it fell in a wave behind her arched neck.

He barely knew the woman, he reminded himself. No matter the signs, no matter what she was already doing to him, he did not need a frail human woman, and he did not know her.

Now if only he could find a way to convince himself he didn't want to.

Seeking distraction, Gideon cocked his head, listening to the multitude of messages that Carly seemed not to even be bothering to listen to as she went through them, erasing them one by one.

"Carlotta, this is your mother. Don't tell me you're still sleeping … your father and I were thinking …"

"This message has been deleted."

"Carly. Mario. You up yet? Mom's been bugging us to call you …"

"Deleted."

"Carlotta Teresa Silver, I know you're up now. This weather is awful, honey, we have lots of food and I really think you should come stay …"

"Deleted."

"Carly, it's Weege. Hey, do you think you could call Sheriff Neubaker's wife, see if maybe she can talk him out of the ticket I got last night? I know you're not supposed to do donuts, okay? But it was just in the parking lot, for chrissakes …"

"Deleted."

"Carly, it's Dad. Your mother thinks …"

"Carly, Mario again. You even alive over there?"

"Carly, got any extra sauce stuff you could bring over tonight? You know you're gonna break and come, mama's having a fit …"

"Carly, we need …"

"Carly …"

Gideon finally composed himself enough to round the corner, and found his hostess punching the delete button on her little answering machine with such force that he wasn't sure it was going to make it to the end of her messages. She must have had the ringer off today, he guessed. Otherwise, from the sound of things, he never would have gotten to sleep in the first place.

"Sounds like you have an involved family."

She must have been really concentrated, because at the sound of his voice Carly jumped about a foot in the air, then clutched her chest as she looked at him. He should have been prepared for it, but Gideon just hadn't expected the sight of her to crash into him all over again. She'd pulled her hair back so that it fell in an elegant tail down her back, he saw, and she'd switched from the morning's pajamas to a thin V-necked sweater that picked up the deep blue of her eyes and a pair of fitted jeans that showcased every curve he'd felt curled against him in the night, that had pressed up against him that morning. He flexed his hands, resisting the impulse to just grab her and fill his palms with those curves. Gideon kept his stance deliberately casual, hoping that none of the beast snapping at the end of its tether showed in his eyes.

Her flush, the small step back she took, told him he hadn't been altogether successful.

"God, you scared me!" Her laugh was nervous, and she steadied herself with a hand on the corner of the breakfast bar where the answering machine now sat silent.

"Sorry. About that, and about the, er … well, you see, I was on the phone, and I must have nodded off …" Inwardly, Gideon winced as he heard whatever pathetic excuse was currently coming out of his mouth. And just what had he been doing on the phone in her room, then? Brilliant.

"Well, I know you were tired." Carly's eyes had dropped to the floor in discomfort. Her lack of anger, her refusal to meet his eyes had Gideon suddenly wondering just what she'd thought when she'd seen him. And somehow, within five seconds, he was picturing her naked again.

Damn it.

"Just, you know, next time …"

Gideon nodded, relieved that this was all the reprimand he was going to get. "Won't happen again, I promise you."

She looked up again, returned his nod. He watched her straighten herself, making a concerted effort not to cower in front of him, and he had to admire her for that. Gone was the bravery of the morning, he saw, probably a result of having had time to think about the situation and wonder exactly what she'd gotten herself into. Tentative interest had been replaced by wariness, and that something he couldn't decipher.

He never had been able to read women well, had never sought out their company to try and get better at it, and no amount of wishing it were otherwise at this moment would change it. Still, he knew he was intimidating, whether he wanted to be or not, even around his own kind. It had to have taken a great deal of courage to let him stay, Gideon knew, and he was grateful for that, more than he knew how to express. The least he could do was to try and set her at ease for as long as she had to put up with his presence.

So, as the uncomfortable silence spun out, he tried again.

"I'm used to having a lot of people poking at me, as well." He inclined his head toward the machine. "It can get frustrating."

It took a few seconds for his words to sink in, but when they did, he was gratified to see they'd earned him a tentative smile. "Oh. Yeah, I guess I should be used to it. Big Italian family and all. And I love them. But sometimes …"

"You wish they'd just let you be for a while?"

"Exactly."

They faced one another across the small living room which now seemed to Gideon a vast expanse, their uncertainty about what to do with one another a palpable thing. One of them was going to have to cross it. Gideon searched for something to say, something to further break the ice, but to his surprise, it was Carly who jumped into the breach.

"So … are you hungry? Because the foraging was a success. I've got dinner going."

"Thank God," Gideon sighed, and that earned him her soft, sparkling laughter. He felt the tension between them begin to ease almost immediately.

Carly gestured to the plush couch. "Well, good. If it's one thing my mother taught me to do, it's cook enough dinner for a small army. And lucky for you, I stole a few things suitable to cook that were neither freeze-dried nor chemically preserved. Sit."

Gideon smirked. "Stay?"

"Good boy. You still look tired." She looked at him closely, and her natural concern for him caused his stomach to do an odd little dance. "Are you sure you're going to be okay? I can always call a doctor. Or a vet."

"Funny." Gideon threw himself onto the couch, sighing as he sank into the cushions. "No, I'm mending. I'll be fine by tomorrow, really." Please, God, and away from this maddening infatuation. "But thanks."

She stood uncertainly in the middle of the room, playing with the small ring, coils of white gold set with glittering circles of pink sapphire, she wore on her right hand. "It's going to be a few minutes. There are some sugary, fattening leftovers from this morning, if you'd like something to tide you over. I mean, just because you haven't actually eaten anything today."

Gideon shifted uncomfortably. He was perfectly capable of taking care of himself, and he wasn't about to be treated like a helpless infant. Carly obviously felt obligated, but it was wholly unnecessary. He'd never needed a nursemaid before. He wasn't about to start looking now. "No, I'll wait."

"Would you like a drink, then?"

He felt himself bristle, tried to hide it behind a smile. "You don't have to wait on me, Carly."

She flushed. "Oh. Well, I'll just, um, go back to cooking, then." Gideon closed his eyes. Somehow, some way, he'd just managed to injure her feelings. The loud slamming of a cupboard seconds later confirmed it. Reluctantly, he dragged himself off the couch and headed into the kitchen to try and fix whatever the hell he'd just broken.

Maybe she was being a bitch, but just now, she didn't really care. Her blood had been on a low simmer all damned day, and at this point, she was almost grateful it had finally shot up to full boil. It might not be quite the release her knotted-up body had in mind, but hey, it was at least something.

Carly opened a cupboard, took out glasses, slammed it shut. How *dare* he? Just dismiss her, in her own house, as though he was brushing off an annoying little insect. She banged the salad bowl on the counter, just for the hell of it, and went hunting for silverware. He'd better hope she didn't find any sharp knives.

She felt, rather than heard, Gideon come into the kitchen behind her. Did he have to be so damned quiet all the time? She didn't turn around, wouldn't give him the satisfaction of acknowledging his presence. He sighed, loudly. It only pissed her off worse.

"Carly."

"Just for your information, I'm not trying to *wait* on you, oh master. Maybe you're some big deal back in Scotland and have women falling all over themselves to serve you, but around here, it's just called common courtesy." She stalked to the refrigerator, flung it open, and stared at the still-mostly-empty shelves. Maybe there was something good to throw. She considered a carton of milk a day past its sell-by date and a semi-flat liter bottle of soda.

"Carly, I …"

"And another thing," she snapped, cutting him off smartly as she slammed the fridge shut again. She might have ruled out physical violence, but God, she needed to vent. "When someone saves your stupid life, then agrees to take you in out of a nasty storm, *despite,* I might add, your extreme weirdness, which would put almost everyone else completely off, you don't treat them like some pathetic little girl making goo-goo eyes at you."

She advanced on him, in full-blown rant mode now. Carly was gratified to see Gideon's eyes widen slightly, and the small step back he took. "So I made you dinner. So what? You don't want me to *wait* on you? Good. Go outside and make yourself a goddamned snow cone for all I care." She ignored the confusion written so clearly across Gideon's beautiful features, determined not to feel sorry for him. He'd hurt her feelings, damn it! He'd just wandered into her life and started to mess it up and didn't even care what he was doing to her, getting her all churned up, and …

…and she didn't even care why she was angry anymore. Still ignoring him, she went to another cupboard to find salad bowls. Naturally, being that they were used for healthy food, she'd put them way up out of her limited reach. Well, there was no way she was asking *him* for help, that was for sure. Carly blew a long blond strand of hair that had slipped free of her elastic out of her face and rose up on her tiptoes, willing herself to stretch another inch, possibly two or three, while she scrabbled uselessly at the edge of the shelf with her nails.

When his broad chest connected with her back, she stopped breathing. Quietly, deliberately, he reached above her head and extracted two salad bowls from the shelf, then, just as deliberately, set them down in front of her. Every place she felt him, every nerve ending brushed seemed to sing with the contact. Carly could actually feel all rational thought seeping out of her the longer Gideon stayed connected with her, leaving her with nothing but the insane urge to turn around, climb him like a tree, wrap her legs around his waist and *bite*.

She shuddered in a single breath as Gideon finally stepped back, then hung her head as she realized exactly what she'd been doing. She'd been acting like a lovesick teenager who's just discovered the boy she likes doesn't like her. God, what was *wrong* with her? No matter what Regan had been trying to talk her into, it certainly wasn't Gideon's job to lust after her just because she'd been kind. She really needed to get it together, Carly decided. It wasn't Gideon's fault that the very sight of him made her feel so… so…

"I'm sorry," she said softly. "It's been kind of a weird day. I shouldn't have taken it out on you." She turned to find Gideon not two feet away, studying her with those intense amber eyes that made her feel like melting at his feet every time she looked into them. *Keep breathing,* she reminded herself, even as her heart stumbled along in her chest.

"No," he murmured in his dark, silken voice. "You've been wonderful. You barely know a thing about me, except that I wasn't exactly human when you found me … and you're right, that *would* have put most people off, to say the least … and yet you've opened your home, gone out of your way to keep me comfortable, when I've done nothing to earn it. And I am, I have heard on occasion, a bit of a grouch when

I'm feeling under the weather, though it's unintentional. Usually. So *I'm* sorry."

Whatever wind had been left in her sails disappeared. There he stood, her wildest fantasy made flesh, taking up most of her kitchen and looking for all the world like he wanted to be anywhere but there at that moment. Gideon hadn't asked for this any more than she had, she realized, nor had he asked for her to babysit him during his stay there. Despite her best intentions, she had to admit, Gideon MacInnes didn't look like the kind of man who would ever want or need coddling. This was one-hundred percent pure alpha male. It wouldn't kill her to try to remember that, and respect it. After all, she wouldn't be in half as much unrequited lust with him if he were any other way.

"Tell you what." Carly stood her ground and held Gideon's golden gaze no matter how much she wanted to look away, determined to find some sort of workable middle ground for them to meet on. All those years refereeing fights between Mario and Luigi couldn't have been for nothing, right? "I'll agree not to hover, flutter, or be intolerably concerned if you agree to be respectful of the fact that you *are* here by the grace of a habitually worrying, concerned female. Truce?"

She stuck out her hand, watched Gideon consider it before he smiled that slow, lopsided grin of his that Carly found so ridiculously sexy. She watched as he reached out and closed his big, calloused hand around hers, swallowing it almost into invisibility.

"As I don't fancy being stabbed in my sleep with the cutlery," he said as he shook her hand once, twice, "a truce, then."

When he let go, her hand still tingled. Still, she managed to force a casual smile, determined, desperate, in fact, to keep it light. "Then let's start over. I think conversation over way too much chicken Parmesan is a decent beginning, don't you?"

"My appetite is *always* a decent beginning."

But her smile faded just a little as he turned from her to grab a plate. It didn't matter how hard she ignored it, it seemed, as her eyes caressed his broad shoulders, the way the thin cotton tee-shirt showcased every taut muscle. But Gideon wasn't the only one who was hungry.

And no amount of chicken Parm was going to fix that.

She'd fed him. She'd plied him with a decent bottle of red wine. And after a while, Carly had had to concede something.

On this one subject, Maria Silver's advice had been right on the money. Apparently, a man's stomach was indeed the magical portal into his good graces. And although it didn't look like it on the outside, she thought as she watched him start on his fourth helping, in Gideon's case, that was one hell of a big opening.

She sipped at the cabernet, her lips curved as she watched him over the rim of her glass. Despite her earlier impression, it turned out that under the right circumstances, Gideon MacInnes was pretty engaging company. Granted, the fact that the bottle of wine was now empty might have had something to do with that. Well, at least, it had something to do with her current state of relaxation. Carly thought back, tried to remember how much she'd had, versus how much Gideon had imbibed, and winced.

She actually didn't want to think about how much of that bottle of relaxation she was currently owning.

"So tell me again," Gideon asked after he'd swallowed another mouthful, "why your parents named your brothers after a Nintendo game?"

She shook her head, laughed. "Well, Mario and Weege actually predate the game, so you can't really pin that on them. But no matter how much they protest, they get a big huge kick out of the coincidence, believe me."

"Mario, Luigi, and Carlotta. I have to say, your ethnicity is awfully ambiguous."

"It's only Carlotta if you want your butt kicked. And actually, I'm only half Italian, despite my mother's best efforts to eradicate the other side of our ancestry."

He raised his eyebrows, sipped his wine. "Which is?"

"British, mostly. A little Dutch thrown in for flavor. Jonathan Silver, however, is one whipped puppy, no matter how much I love him. I keep expecting to show up there one day and find him in a velour tracksuit and some gold chains."

"Ah. I wondered, you know. About the blond, and whether it was some sort of genetic fluke."

"You'd think. No, lucky combo of some way-back blond Northern Italians and my dad's family. My brothers, though … you'd never know we were related. Luigi thinks he's DeNiro." Carly paused, considered. "Actually, he's not that far off. In, you know, the least flattering way you could possibly imagine that."

She enjoyed it, Gideon's easy smile, his throaty laughter. How nice it was to see him finally relaxed. An odd thought occurred to her, that maybe he wasn't so different from her, just cautious with people until he got comfortable. It was strange to think of a big, strapping *werewolf* having anything in common with an introvert like herself, but stranger things had happened.

At least he liked her cooking, Carly thought as she watched him finish up the rest of what was on his plate. She wasn't sure she could swing it right now, but maybe, eventually, once she stopped having palpitations every time he was anywhere near her, Gideon MacInnes would make a fascinating friend. And as a lover …

But no, damn it. She wasn't going to torture herself with that right now. She leaned back in the chair, toying with her glass. She'd been talking a blue streak, but her guest had been remarkably quiet on the subject of himself. It was time, to her way of thinking, to turn that around.

"So what about you? Your family? Apart from the obvious, I mean."

Gideon pushed his plate away from him and propped his elbows on the table. "Hmm. I was hoping you'd let me slide on that and eat more of your truly excellent dinner while you talk about … let's see … what you do for a living. We haven't made it that far yet."

She was having none of it. "I own a business. So do they all have extra heads or something? Embarrassing jobs? Poor hygiene? They can't be any worse than mine. Spill it, Gideon, I'm all aflutter."

He sighed, looked intently at the ceiling. "Well. Let's see. My father's actually Pack leader, or Alpha, as we call it. He's sixty, looks forty, and is a holy terror when you cross him. He takes care of the family estate, which would be about sixty acres of Highland wilderness, plus a massive, drafty old house and a bunch of cottages, one of which is mine. The main house he runs as a sort of bed and breakfast, and the cottages are rented out to people on holiday. Does quite well at it, actually. And my brother lives across the Sound, little more than a ferry ride away, not that he crosses it any more often than he has to. Runs a pub, chases women. Not necessarily in that order. And as for me …"

Carly leaned in, interested. "You hang out and be heir apparent to the werewolf dynasty? Do you have official duties or anything? Sit on a throne? What?"

When he smiled, the corners of his eyes crinkled up. "Actually, I help my dad run the place most of the time, along with a passel of cousins. Most of the land is just let be. It hardly needed any improvement from people. But the bit we use still requires quite a lot of work. So I fix things, play tour guide, keep the books, do odd jobs. It's all mine one day, if I want it. And no, no throne." His shaggy hair fell across his eyes as he shook his head, laughing. "My Pack has gatherings, but a lot of them don't live on the Hunting Grounds anymore. We're a little remote, you know, near Lochaline in the Western Highlands. It's a ferry ride to get there no matter what you do."

"And yet you all manage to make a living by being visited?" Carly asked politely, trying to figure out exactly how Gideon's family was not all dirt poor and living in shacks. The place sounded like a monstrosity in the middle of nowhere, probably the genius purchase of an ancestor who liked his ale a little too much.

Gideon simply raised a superior brow. "Although *some* people prefer their vacations to be full of hermetically sealed hotels and overexposed giant rodents, it just so happens that the world is full of enlightened individuals who would rather explore the untouched corners of the earth on their own two feet. We get bikers, hikers, hunters, photographers, naturalists …"

Carly held up her hands in surrender. "Okay, okay, point taken. Although there's a lot to be said for oversized singing mice, I have to tell you." When Gideon merely wrinkled his nose in distaste, she shrugged and smiled at him.

"Just saying." But she was intrigued, despite never having been the outdoorsy type. She'd certainly read enough about the Highlands, though she'd always assumed the breathless descriptions had been exaggerations. Now, however, listening to Gideon, she began to wonder.

"There's nothing like it, not that I've ever seen," Gideon said softly, looking pensive. "And I've been traveling enough lately to know. Old seat of the Clan MacInnes, and my people never left. Except now, a lot have scattered to the cities. Glasgow, Edinburgh, London. But they always come back, if only for short periods of time. It's beautiful country, peaceful, wild. Quiet." Gideon paused a moment to study her. "Actually, you know, I think you'd like it."

He was looking at her that way again, the way that made her flush all the way down to her toes, and Carly quickly sought to turn the subject. If she didn't, she was pretty sure she'd spontaneously combust. "Um. So. Hunting Grounds. Like stomping grounds, I guess?"

"Yeah, sorry. Just what we've always called where we make our home."

"And home is an estate you putter around at." Carly pushed the last few pieces of chicken around on her plate without really paying attention, focused on Gideon. How, she wondered, had she come to have him sprawled in a chair at her little table at all? She knew she was a little sheltered, but even *she* could never have imagined something like this. Life in Podunk, New York, had never seemed blander than when Gideon talked about his own little corner of the world. A corner apparently populated by a large pack of werewolves. Wild. *There are more things in Heaven and Earth,* she reminded herself.

"Mmm," he agreed, nodding as he chewed the last bite of his dinner. "The land's been in our family … well, as you can imagine, quite a long time. The current main house is blended with what was left of the original castle. The guest cottages we rent out have existed, in some form or other, for a couple hundred years."

Carly nearly choked on her wine. "Your family has a *castle?* Is it, like, picturesque Scottish or more, I don't know … Frankenstein?" Sadly, the thought of Gideon skulking around a dark, mysterious ruin (and she was trying so, so hard to at least remove the flowing cape from this image) was attractive. Really attractive. Carly barely managed to fight off the impulse to start fanning herself with her napkin and inwardly cursed the now-empty bottle of wine.

She cursed it harder when Gideon's deep, rolling laugh nearly got him a full-body tackle. "Ah, picturesque, I'm afraid. And it's more a manor house now than a castle. A lot of the original structure had crumbled away—that'll happen after eight hundred years or so—by the time my great-great-grandfather decided something had to be done. Opening the place up to guests has worked out well for us, and because of … I mean, there's always been money. The Alphas have all tended that legacy well." That probably wasn't the half of it; Carly knew it from the way he'd caught himself. But what he *was* telling her was just too intriguing to allow her to really care. The Highlands had always seemed like a mystical place to her, almost unreal. Magical.

She had to admit, having Gideon suddenly appear from there hadn't done much to dispel that impression.

"*Iargail,* we call it."

"*Iargail,*" Carly repeated, liking the foreign, exotic feel of the word on her tongue. "What does it mean?"

"Twilight." Gideon paused, lost in thought for a moment, then drank deeply from the nearly full glass of Cabernet Sauvignon in front of him. "A fitting tribute, I think, to where my kind exists."

"Beautiful," she sighed. He looked sad, now, Carly thought. Possibly he was homesick, though something told her there was more to it than just that. She wished it were otherwise, but instinctively, Carly knew that whatever it was, Gideon was going to keep it to himself. Quickly, she tried to lighten the mood. It was all she could think to do.

"So do you? Want it someday, I mean?" She thought of Gideon in ragged old jeans playing Mr. Fix-It, tanned and windblown and relaxing in a place that was his own, maybe stopping to chat up the occasional guest or friend, and felt another tug at the knot of desire she seemed to be carrying all the time now in her lower belly. He would be perfect in the setting she imagined. She wished—futilely, she knew—that she could see him in his natural element.

"You know, it's funny," he said, standing and taking his plate to the sink. "I wasn't sure for a while, but now … yes, actually. I think I do. Wandering a bit has had its purpose, but," he inclined his head toward the window over her sink, and the snow that continued to fall, white against the darkness, "turns out I like what I was running away from best."

"I hear you," Carly said as she stood as well and began to collect things from the table. "I ran too. College, first. Not too far, but far enough to get my feet wet. And all I ever thought about was coming home, starting my business here. So as it turns out, I ran exactly two blocks away from my parents' house. But I can't complain."

Gideon turned, cocking his head at her. "And there's that. I know I was there, but I wasn't exactly looking around. What sort of business do you run, Miss Silver? I've got you figured for a lawyer or an accountant."

An *accountant?* How did you look like an accountant? If her hotness level was actually that low, she was going to have to seriously reevaluate her wardrobe and makeup choices. Carly sensed a shopping trip with Regan coming on, and as soon as possible. Not, she thought as her heart sank a little, that Gideon would be around to appreciate the results. But there was always some future guy, she guessed. If she could ever get past the mere fact of Gideon's existence long enough to let there be a future guy, that was. Encountering perfection was probably going to damn her.

Carly wrinkled her nose at him. "'Miss Silver' is a little better than 'Carlotta,' but you're pushing it. Makes me sound like an old cat lady, which, I must tell you, I am still a few well-placed doilies and floral housecoats shy of, thank you very much."

Gideon paused before the sink and gave her a casual, thorough inspection that warmed her from the top of her head to the tips of her toes. Carly could swear those amber eyes took on a faint, nearly imperceptible glow before he tore his gaze away from her. When he spoke, it was with something like reluctant admiration. "You're a bit farther away from it than that, I think."

"Oh. Well. Thanks." Blushing again, damn it. She should probably just accept it as a permanent thing, at least for as long as Gideon was around, but *why* did she have to get the Pink Gene? And just like that, the two of them had rocketed straight back to awkward, do not pass go, do not collect two hundred dollars. Carly struggled to collect herself, to pick up their completely unraveled thread of polite, interesting conversation.

"Actually," she said, her tone sounding a little overly bright to her, "I own a bookstore."

Gideon surprised her with a laugh, shaking his head as he rinsed off the dishes. "Of course you do. I should have known." When Carly just looked at him quizzically, he elaborated. "The books," he explained. "You've got them tucked into every little space. I thought it might just be an addiction. Instead it's your job. It's perfect, really."

He turned back away from her, busy loading his things into the dishwasher while Carly tried to work up the nerve to get as close to him as she would need to in order to finish cleaning up. She'd been doing okay. That was, right up until she had to get close enough to Gideon to actually possibly brush against him. Now, Carly could feel every thudding beat of her heart as her lungs threatened to seize up completely.

Carly chewed her lip, staring at Gideon's broad back while she worked up her nerve. It shouldn't be this hard, she told herself. She was a little on the shy side with men, sure, but nothing ridiculous. And the fact that this particular man had a genetic predisposition to turning into an animal occasionally wasn't even what was putting her off so badly. It was almost impossible to put her finger on exactly what had her so jumpy. But there was something about Gideon that had Carly less worried about what he might do than about what *she* was having a harder and harder time *not* doing.

She huffed out a soft, frustrated sigh. The effect Gideon had on her was decidedly unsettling. Even across from him at the table, Carly had felt Gideon's presence in every cell, a helpless planet caught in his orbit. In fact, Carly wouldn't have been surprised to find out that werewolves actually exuded some sort of gravitational pull. That would explain why all she wanted to do was get closer to him, to the probable point of crawling directly into his lap. It certainly didn't help that the closer she got to him, the lovelier she felt. And then there was the way her skin still shimmered with heat in each place his eyes had touched, however briefly. Silently, she cursed her hormones.

"So what do you call it?" The rumble of his voice jerked her out of her thoughts.

"What?" Carly was glad he was turned around, because she was pretty sure she'd been standing there with her mouth open.

"Your bookshop. What do you call it?"

"Oh." *Bookshop? Did she have a bookshop? Where was she again?* "Bodice Rippers and Baubles. Ah, because we sell some jewelry too, you see. Curios. Pretty things."

When Gideon turned to look at her this time, the expression on his face said it all. "Bodice *what?*"

Steeling herself, Carly grabbed as much as she could carry and headed towards him. "I sell books with a *romantic* theme, thank you." Her nose was in the air. She knew it, she couldn't help it. But she really didn't want to hear Gideon make fun of her life's work and shatter her little fantasy of him as the perfect man. Or, well, almost-man. He surprised her, though, as he stepped aside to allow her better access to the sink.

"That's an interesting idea, actually. I've never seen anything quite like that. I'd imagine you do quite well."

"I don't think," she began, already launching into her standard defense, when what he'd actually said sank in. "I mean … oh. Well. Yes, I do. Thank you." She placed her dishes in the sink, letting the water run over them, and glanced up to smile at Gideon. Maybe he was just flattering her because he was sort of there at her mercy, but she appreciated it nonetheless. He didn't look insincere, though, Carly saw with a jolt as her eyes met his. He looked deadly serious.

Did he have to stand so close? Carly's breath caught a little when she realized exactly how few inches separated the two of them. And Gideon showed no interest in moving, just kept looking at her with that singular intensity she'd never seen in any other man's gaze … especially when they were looking at her. She swallowed, licked her lips, thinking she would just say something to lighten the air around the two of them, since it seemed to have thickened, charged, in a matter of moments. When those golden eyes dropped to her mouth, however, any thoughts she might have had deserted her completely.

"Is it," she finally rasped, then stopped to clear her throat. "Just out of curiosity, but it's, um, not the full moon yet, is it?" Because the predatory vibe Gideon was giving off right now was making her as skittish as a stalked animal. And despite his assurances that she was in no danger, Carly wasn't at all sure she wanted to be around when he stopped being human again. Although, she thought dazedly as Gideon's eyes returned to hers, being devoured by this particular beast might be kind of … wonderful.

"No," Gideon finally replied, his voice so soft and low it was barely recognizable. His eyes never moved from her face. "No, we've a few days yet. I won't *have* to turn until then, but … it pulls at me."

"Pulls at you?" she asked dazedly, helplessly ensnared, unable to tear her gaze away from him. His pupils had expanded, she noted with wonder, the color of his already unusual eyes going brighter, almost glowing. And then, in one quick, fluid movement, he was facing her directly, trapping her with her back to the sink, a hand braced against the counter on either side of her.

"The moon," he almost sighed, and Carly, even through her haze, could sense that she was seeing another part of Gideon, the one that was much closer to the beast she'd rescued than the man she'd had dinner with. And she wondered, with that odd chemical reaction to him setting off fireworks in her blood, what it would be like to be with a man like this, who was human and animal so thoroughly entwined.

It was almost as though he read her mind. "You'll have to forgive me," he murmured as his breath fanned her face, making the final move that would close the space between them.

"Forgive you?"

"For this." And then there was nothing for Carly but that glorious shock of connection with him as he dipped his head toward her. He brushed her lips once, twice with his own sinfully soft ones. Testing, it seemed to her, giving her one last chance to run before he crushed her to him. Before he claimed her fully.

But she'd been lost before he'd ever laid a hand on her, and now, as his tongue slipped into her mouth to mate with hers, Carly knew it, accepted it. Embraced it.

Yes.

All the blood in her veins seemed to surge and sing in the instant of that first, hesitant touch. One light touch. And then Gideon plunged. Carly slid into him like water, savoring the way every inch of her molded perfectly against him. The softness of her breasts pressed against the hard expanse of his chest while he slanted his mouth over hers again and again, nipping, licking at her lips until she gasped. *This* was what she'd wanted, needed, what the nameless thing that drew them together had been promising. This … and so much more. Carly arched up, winding her fingers in his thick, dark hair and tugging at him until he deepened the kiss again. She felt dizzy with the pleasure of it, drowning in the rich scents he seemed to carry with him of earth and the spice of dark, moonlit forests.

She moved restlessly against him, wanting to get closer, to crawl inside his skin, if need be. Gideon's hands cruised over her arms, her back, his fingers slid into her hair, all in restless, perpetual movement, as though he wanted to touch all of her, every part of her, at once. Carly sighed against his mouth, taking his lower lip in to suckle at it briefly, an action that only seemed to intensify Gideon's need. To her delight, he responded with a low, sexy growl.

He was at once so utterly foreign and so achingly familiar, Carly thought as the two of them moved rhythmically against each other, finding some hidden beat in the pulse of their kiss. She had always thought a kiss was nothing more, really, than a meeting of lips, a physical expression of a measure of attraction. She had never imagined it could be this, this falling into some warm and decadent abyss, rising and falling on a dark ocean of pure, liquid sensation.

Gideon's mouth became rougher, more urgent as Carly felt herself being lifted to sit on the edge of the sink, allowing him better access to her ... and her to him, she thought as she slid back against him, allowing Gideon to nudge his way between her thighs until he was hard against the very heat of her. *More,* she thought hazily, wrapping her legs around Gideon's waist, shocked, on some level, that she was enjoying, even encouraging, his roughness.

He couldn't seem to get his fill of her, plundering her mouth over and over again, dragging a strangled cry from Carly as he moved his hands beneath her sweater. Gideon's warm, calloused palms created delicious friction with her own soft skin. She arched as he filled them with her breasts, then squeezed, *hard.* Carly wrapped her legs tighter around him, some unfamiliar thing within her rising up to urge her on, to take more, harder, faster, and above all, *now.*

"Gideon," she hissed against his lips, her own deliciously bruised. Then, obeying an inner instinct she had never before known, she hooked her fingers into claws beneath his shirt, against the hot iron of his bare back, and dragged them slowly, excruciatingly, downward as she let her head drop back in invitation.

I submit, she thought madly as Gideon snarled, a sound at once wholly inhuman and utterly sexual. He scraped his teeth, sharper now and dangerous, down her jaw, across her neck, pausing to dip his tongue into the pulsing hollow at the base of it.

Yes, oh yes, I submit …

Gideon locked his hands beneath her, pulling Carly up against him, turning to carry her back into the dark, she knew, of her room, and her bed, though at this moment, she knew he could take her anywhere and she wouldn't give a damn as long as he just *took* her. A darkly amusing thought of her earlier comments about her kitchen floor flitted through her mind as she tossed her hair back. She caught a glimpse of burning gold before she took his mouth again, moved to his ear to bite and lick. The throbbing between her legs was becoming unbearable as Gideon held her tight against him, and she dropped her mouth to his shoulder as he carried her, about to do the unthinkable, knowing he wanted it.

Bite you, she thought. *I want to taste …*

And then she caught something, the slightest flicker at the edge of her vision as they moved away, something that her eyes moved past at first but then returned to as though pulled by some unseen force. And as her own blue eyes, now wide and terrified, locked with the glittering yellow ones peering in at her from the darkness outside her window, Carly heard a strangled noise that sounded like a wounded, terrified animal.

With reality crashing down around her, it was precious seconds before Carly realized that the sound came from her.

"Gideon," she finally managed.

"Yes, love," he growled against her neck, oblivious to the sudden change in her, still wrapped up fully in what they'd had only a moment ago.

"G-Gideon," Carly stammered again, unable to take her eyes from the window, feeling the malice from that other creature pouring through her. "The window. God."

And he knew. Carly felt him tense against her, coiling to spring. Still, he managed to lower her with surprising gentleness to the ground before turning to see what she had seen.

"Bloody *hell*," he snarled. And as the yellow eyes, mocking, they almost seemed, vanished into the darkness outside, a vicious, terrifying growl tore from Gideon's lips. He was through the back door and gone, slamming out into the night, before Carly could move, much less collect herself enough to figure out what was happening.

Then, at last, it began to sink in. And amazingly, that was worse.

She curled into a ball where she was sitting, drawing her knees up against her chest, and held herself tightly to keep from shaking apart. Whatever wild thing had gotten into her only minutes ago had left her just as abruptly as it had come, leaving her cold, empty. And for the first time, truly afraid of the creature she'd let in.

He'd known. She was sure of it. Hadn't been expecting it, necessarily, but then, hadn't been entirely surprised, either. And that could mean only one thing. Gideon had lied to her, and in doing so, from the look of those burning eyes in the night, he had put her and everything she held dear in mortal danger. *Why?*

Lying Bastard.

She hated him.

And God, she hoped he was all right.

As a chilling howl rent the darkness somewhere in the distance, Carly dropped her head and wept, bitterly. *What had she done?*

Chapter Eight

SHE WAS A PRETTY LITTLE BITCH, HE'D GIVE GIDEON that much.

Jonas hulked in the darkness, just beyond the small circle of light cast by the glow from the woman's kitchen, and watched, and waited … to see what he would see. And oh, he had seen, Jonas thought with a grim pleasure.

Malachi would be well pleased, of course. But more importantly, Master would be pleased. And then, he would be allowed the one thing that drove him, all that sustained him. He would be allowed the kill … and the feed. A thin rivulet of saliva slid from his mouth and hung, suspended, for a moment before falling to the snow. It was the only movement in a form that otherwise might have been mistaken for a statue. The whirling snow caught in his fur, collected on his back. Jonas hardly noticed, all of his attention fixed on the woman Gideon was pleasuring. Such a small, weak creature. Delicate. He was surprised, given what Malachi had told him about Gideon's mother, that he would have chosen such a one to make his own.

Then again, it shouldn't really have surprised him. In his short time in this world, Jonas had learned that these earthly shape-shifters had moved rather drastically away from their exalted roots and taken on some of the less desirable traits of their human charges. Weakness. A tendency toward an almost maudlin sentimentality. *Love.* Jonas wrinkled his nose in disgust. Master would be appalled at the little scene unfolding before him right now.

Not that Jonas would ever complain. The darker gods had blessed him the night Malachi MacInnes had found him, strengthened him with the ancient power of his bite. This *arukh* form, this *wolf,* was not quite what he desired. But in time, he knew he could make the great Andrakkar see that he could best serve with his abilities restored. He had misbehaved, oh yes, had let the fire he could rend the night with rule him instead of his loyalty to the Master. And had anyone ever been punished as much as he? Had he not sworn he would redeem himself even as his great wings were being torn from his back, as he was cast into the whirling vortex of the Tunnels?

"Serve me," whispered the faintly glowing crystal at his throat. *"Open the door … let me in … redemption …"*

Jonas growled in acknowledgment. He would embrace the abilities now given him, abilities once feared by all but the High Drakkyn until they were lost from his world long ago. And he would not fail.

In one night, he had gone from wretched outcast to favored one, elevated in Master's eyes because he could provide the key to reclaiming this lost place in the exalted name of Drakkyn. He would not waste the favor that Narr, god of blackest night, had surely seen fit to bestow upon him in giving him this one last chance.

He had been promised much that he had told no one, even Malachi, with whom he felt an odd sort of kinship even though he knew it would pain him little when he eventually took his life. Malachi thought he now had the Andrakkar's ear, that he could steal the Master's favor.

Jonas's muzzle peeled back in a grotesque parody of a smile. *He was wrong. He would soon see.*

Still, for now, he could only be gladdened by the weaknesses of these creatures, Jonas knew. For this woman he now watched opened the way to endless avenues of pain, and for Jonas, pain was God. Gideon MacInnes was doomed anyway, but now, Jonas thought as he allowed himself to feel the wounds not yet fully healed, the burning in his shoulder, the deep ache in his abdomen, he would make sure that death came slowly. Excruciatingly.

Deliciously.

Jonas licked his muzzle as the woman wound herself around his prey, no doubt enthralled by this first taste of the pleasure his kind could give her. And still, she had no idea. Perhaps, before he tore her throat out, he would instruct her personally. But for now, he would give her a gift, the only one he had been born with and the only one he had been allowed to take with him into this new, blood-bathed life.

Fear.

He had found that it could make the taste so much sweeter.

Jonas moved forward slightly, padding up the ever-deepening ocean of snow that rose and undulated in waves across this barren landscape. The cloudy purple jewel that hung from a thick chain around his neck glinted dully in the shifting light. Its weight was reassuring, reminding him that the Andrakkar was watching, listening, always. It was the piece of his world, of Master, that was with him always. The connection. The key. And despite his banishment, he had used it well.

Oh, how he hated it here, the openness of it, the freshness of the air. He much preferred to wallow in the stench of humans and their filth, to take them in the dark, cramped spaces while the endless possibilities of lives left to take buzzed about him, adding danger, adding pleasure. Still, the one thing about *here* was that it came with so many places to hide what was left of his prey when he was done.

Not that there was ever much. Waste not, want not, after all.

Such a pretty thing, Jonas mused as he came closer. *A lovely bauble to toy with for a while.* Her glory of pale hair had come unbound, framing her face to turn her into a painted angel. It was time to let her see the demon that lurked in the shadows.

Look at me, he willed her. *See me.* And he knew the exact moment she had, the widening of her eyes, the stiffening of her lush little body. The rush of her fear flew to him through the darkness, and nearly took his legs from under him. *Yes,* Jonas decided as he gathered himself in the split second before the MacInnes bastard rushed out after him. *Remember me, pretty. I'll be seeing you again soon.*

With the promise of fresh blood singing through his veins, Jonas turned and melted back into the churning night.

And howled his impending triumph.

Gideon searched as long as he could, but in the end, he knew he'd have to concede this round to the ghost who hunted him.

It was infuriating … and deeply disturbing. He'd thought he understood the minds of his fellow Wolves, the way things worked. Couldn't, in fact, imagine any other way. And then had come this gray beast that came and went like a wisp of smoke in the night, fighting when he should have been dead, hunting when he should have been writhing in pain.

Disappearing when he should have been easy for one such as Gideon to find. And yet here he was, empty-handed, chilled to the bone, returning in disgrace to the woman who had protected him, and who it now seemed he would have to protect. That he had endangered her tore at him, but as before, there was only one way to remove the threat. Only the urgency had changed.

And none of this was bound to make Carly feel any better when the time came to tell her. At least the storm seemed to be ebbing, finally, but it was small comfort. Tonight had not gone at all how he'd planned. Gideon padded slowly back through the sleeping town, his paws, though tough, nearly frozen from hours of searching. The sky had begun to take on a faint gray cast, an indication that the night was nearly spent. It was time to head back, although the thought of what would be waiting for him had formed a leaden ball of dread in his stomach. He was going to have a lot of explaining to do.

And what had he been thinking, to just fall upon her like that in her kitchen like some ravenous animal? Gideon had imagined a pleasant evening, with enough conversation to make Carly comfortable with his presence. He knew she felt their connection, was drawn to him as he was to her. And he'd wanted her to feel reassured that he had no intention of acting on it.

Then night had fallen, and he'd proven completely unable to control himself. Just the way she'd stood there, he remembered … so innocent, so pure, and so unaware that he could read every naked emotion that crossed her lovely face. He couldn't recall it ever happening before, but one look at her obvious desire for him, combined with the endlessly hungering pull of the moon, had been his undoing.

But then, Gideon thought as he reached Carly's street and turned to run silently past darkened houses, he couldn't recall any other woman who had filled his head so insistently, so completely. Still, he wasn't a fool. He'd paid attention to the elder males of the Pack, and he knew what it meant. When a werewolf found its mate, the bond was immediate and intense. And, for better or for worse, singular. That there were so few humans who could survive the bite often turned that mating instinct into a cruel joke, so his people tended to be careful in their associations, moving in small circles, surrounding themselves with one another, and with humans of strength, to lessen the possibility of that drive kicking in in an impossible situation.

Just like the one Gideon found himself in now.

It appeared that the next Pack Alpha would be another lone male. And though he would never forget her, it was best that when he walked out of Carly's life, he did so for good. The only question now was when that would be possible, because if the yellow eyes in the darkness had seen all there was to see through the window, her position in all of this had just become infinitely more complicated.

And, he thought with a burning shame for bearing the responsibility for it, dangerous.

Carly's cottage was dark, Gideon saw, a little surprised that not one light was burning even though he was fully expecting her wrath the moment he walked in the door. After a quick look around to make sure he was alone, Gideon moved to the back door, and the pile of clothes he'd thrown off as he'd rushed through it earlier. He Changed, his desire to get inside to try to win back Carly's trust making the shift almost instantaneous. Gideon stooped to gather the clothes, his weariness allowing the cold to affect him quickly. They were snow-covered and frozen, and he decided to just go on in and rummage for some other ill-fitting things rather than have them against his skin.

Anticipating the small thrill a blast of warmth was sure to give him, Gideon reached for the handle, turned it … and found it refused to give. He frowned, needing a moment to let it sink it. She'd locked him out? Gideon jiggled it again.

It was definitely locked.

But then, it did make sense. She'd been frightened. She wouldn't have left the doors wide open. He was sure she'd let him in if he knocked. If there was one thing he'd learned about Carly Silver, it was that she didn't have the heart to leave any creature to freeze to death out in the cold, and tonight it was well below zero.

Gideon rapped quietly on the door. "Carly," he whispered, just loudly enough to be heard inside. "It's Gideon. Let me in, we need to talk." He cocked his head, waited, but from inside came nothing but silence. Shivering a little, he rapped again, a bit louder this time.

"Carly!" It was as loud as he could manage without starting to wake up the neighbors, and still, no response. Gideon's frown deepened as he looked down at the frozen clothes he held in his hands. It was beginning to look as though he would have to put them on, after all. *Hell.* Gideon gritted his teeth and managed to get into the stiff, damp clothes, even though putting them on only made the shivering worse.

Maybe she was sleeping? After the night she'd had, the thought of Carly sleeping that deeply sounded more than a little naive, but still, it was worth a shot. He pushed through thigh-deep drifts of snow until he got to her bedroom window, dark behind the drawn blinds. He tried as hard as he could to peer through any cracks, but there were none. He knocked lightly on the window.

"Carly? Carly, it's Gideon. I'm sorry, all right? I know I should have explained better, but I didn't think I'd have to. I'll make this right. Look, please let me in so we can talk." He stopped, listening. Still, the only sound he could hear was his breathing. Gideon stood there, stock still, as he realized that locking him out was *exactly* what Carly had done. No thought for his safety, no thought for frostbite ... Christ, he knew he'd fouled up, but had it really been that bad? Gideon raked a hand through his hair, thinking.

It took him exactly sixty seconds to recognize that yes, he really had screwed things up that badly.

But that didn't mean he ought to have to sacrifice fingers and toes for it, did it?

Gideon made his way back to the door, rubbing his arms for warmth while he tried to decide what to do next. Obviously, Carly had no intention of letting him back in. He could rip the door off the hinges, he supposed, or bash in a window, but he doubted that would make her interested in having the conversation he needed to have with her. No, he needed to get inside, get warm, possibly get into some clothes that fit, and then wait until he could catch her in a place where she'd have to talk to him.

Gideon growled. It would be best if the roads were open, but as the snow was just beginning to lighten up, he doubted it. Returning to his room at the inn was out. He might get the one way on four feet, but cutting and running was no longer an option. He closed his eyes in frustration, sighed loudly. Then he caught it on a breath of frigid air: the faintest hint of something sweet, something baking.

Her friend.

Hadn't Carly said her baker friend lived just two houses over? He opened his eyes again and studied the sky. It was somewhere between four and five in the morning, he guessed. He knew bakers often rose before the sun, but could she really be up at this hour? Gideon shivered once, violently, and decided it certainly couldn't hurt to find out.

Regan O'Meara lived in a rambling old Victorian, one of the crown jewels of Kinnik's Harbor and her family's most precious heirloom. Her great-great-great-grandfather had built it for her great-great-great-grandmother, and the love involved in the giving of it had made it priceless to her and hers. That he had been the famous Admiral Kinnik and she his mistress (not to mention the mother of several of his illegitimate children) made the house a fascinating, if slightly tawdry, landmark for everyone else.

And for Regan, the fact that Lizziebeth Kinnik-Monroe, town matriarch and all-around pain in the ass, still refused to walk by it made it most valuable of all.

She was just sliding her first batch of chocolate chip muffins out of the oven when the knock at the door came. Regan looked up at the clock, puzzled. Had that much time gone by? Because she really needed to have some appetizing product for people to buy first thing, and it wasn't going to happen if she made like a slug around her kitchen.

She could have gone in to the shop, she guessed, and maybe she should have … she'd heard a plow out earlier, meaning that things were lighter. Still, the weatherman had used the most dreaded words in the North Country vocabulary, *lake effect,* in the context of today's weather when she'd flicked on the television earlier. And truth be told, she'd been secretly hoping Carly would call with some at least semi-juicy details of her night with the Sexy Scot. But in any case, it was just as easy to start up for the day in her kitchen here as it was at Decadence.

Coming from a wealthy family had its perks, which she appreciated every time she looked around her sleek modern kitchen with its commercial-grade oven, the sub-zero fridge, the acres of black granite countertop flecked with copper, the gleaming cherry wood cabinets and table. It had always been the heart of the house, but in remodeling, Regan had made it her own.

She was certain her grandmother, who'd left it all to her, would have approved.

And now her cozy, quiet early morning, the time of day that was always just for her, was being invaded. The clock read four-thirty. Regan sucked in a breath. Visits at hours like this were never good. Had her mother finally gone off the deep end and thrown herself under a train after her latest Mr. Wonderful had done a disappearing act? Since Regan still didn't quite have a handle on exactly who her own father was, she hoped to hell not. And Carly … well, Regan thought with a hint of a smile, Carly was probably, hopefully, still snuggled up in postcoital bliss, if she'd done any listening at all yesterday morning.

Well, shit. She was just going to have to go see. She wiped floury hands on her comfy cotton track pants as she headed into the hallway, through the darkened house and toward the front door. She could make out a lone, very large figure through the stained glass of the window, and stopped in mid-stride. The Harbor was a small place, and the local weirdos were all sort of quaint and charming, but that didn't mean the occasional homicidal maniac wouldn't wander through. Then again, would a real homicidal maniac knock?

Regan slid her long, thin fingers up into her hair and tugged at it, annoyed. She could bake on autopilot this early, but actual deductive reasoning, decision-making … *thinking* … not her thing, not at this hour. She got moving again, right up to the glass on the door, which she pressed her nose against. Civility, she decided, was optional at this hour.

"This had better be good," she announced, even as she got her first look at her visitor. And really, it couldn't have been much better than the towering hunk shivering on her front porch wearing minimal clothing. Had it started snowing men?

"Sorry to bother you," came a deep, husky male voice through the door, its timbre so rife with pure animal sensuality that Regan felt a lovely chill work its way down her spine, "but I know you're Carly's friend, and as she and I seem to have had a bit of a …" The voice paused, and then started again, this time with a definite chatter in it. "I've put her in a bit of a position, which she didn't exactly, er …" He gave his arms a brisk rub, stomped his feet. *Bare,* Regan noted with a natural curiosity that was quickly displacing any fear she might have had. *Interesting.*

Sadly, her visitor didn't seem to be in much of a mood to let her consider him from behind the glass.

"Oh hell, I'm freezing my ass off out here. Do you think I might explain *inside* so I don't die of exposure?"

Good Lord, and was that a *Scottish* accent? Regan peered more closely at her visitor through the glass, and she couldn't help but lick her lips. So *this* was Carly's conquest. *Damn.* Well, Regan thought with a sigh, this at least explained why her friend had herself all tied up in knots. She probably would have done the same thing herself in pretty short order if he'd shown up on *her* doorstep looking for a place to stay. Not that she had that kind of luck. Although considering that this particular specimen of pure male beauty was camped in front of her door at four-thirty in the morning *without* her so-called lucky best friend, there might be less luck involved on Carly's part than it had appeared.

But there was always the appeal of watching him grovel.

"Why don't you give me a quick summary before I decide?" she asked sweetly. "Because there's always the possibility that you *deserve* to be out there freezing."

At that point, he did what people rarely managed to do. He surprised her.

"I may, at that," he growled, obviously impatient. "But I'd like the opportunity to fix it, which will be a bit more difficult if I'm dead."

"Mmm, true. Which is why if I were you, I'd summarize quickly." Yep, Regan decided as she watched his jaw tighten while he gave his arms another quick, angry rub. Definitely a lot to be said for having the power. And from the looks of this one, he wasn't used to anyone having that but himself. Well, he was going to have to learn, if he wanted to be allowed in, much less anywhere near Carly again.

"You two being friends, and women, I expect she's told you about me."

"Yeah, yeah, tourist, Scottish, busted car. Blizzard. Old news. Continue."

He gave her a strange look, but after a moment he continued, albeit with gritted teeth. "Yes, well, she agreed to let me stay with her until the storm passed, once I assured her that she would be in no danger from making that decision. And I didn't," he shoved his fingers through the shaggy hair that was falling in his face, "truly didn't think she would be. How was I to know there was going to be a bloody snowstorm? And that they'd heal quickly enough to track me? And now she's gone and locked me out, and I've no way to explain, to protect her."

"Whoa, whoa, slow down there, buddy." Regan was beginning not to like the sound of this at all. And the fact that she'd been pushing her best friend to sleep with this guy … Regan grimaced. The guilt, when it landed, was not going to be good. "Let me get this straight. You lied to Carly, and in doing so, somehow put her in danger." Through the glass, she saw a grim nod. Regan blew out a breath, completely nonplussed. Where Carly was concerned, this was all a new one on her. "No wonder she's pissed."

And really, the thought of Carly locking *this* guy out in the cold? Not only was he gorgeous beyond words, but he had a deliciously dangerous *something* about him. She must have been cataclysmically pissed, Regan thought with a touch of wonder. She hadn't known that mild-mannered Carly Silver had it in her. *Go Carly.*

He sighed. "It sounds bad, but I didn't feel that she needed to get mixed up in it. My intentions were good."

"Yeah, well. You know what they say about the road to Hell and what it's paved with. So what is this? Are you in trouble with the cops? A gang? Jesus, did you *murder* someone?" Regan could feel herself winding up with quickly deepening horror. Carly often accused her of having an overdeveloped imagination, which she vehemently denied. This *would* have to be the one time she proved Carly wrong.

The stranger's hands flew up, as if to ward off her accusations. "No! No, good Christ no, slow down, woman! I'm an upstanding citizen. I don't kill people. This is more of a ... family problem. Directed at me and unprovoked."

Regan eyed him suspiciously through the glass. "Family. La Cosa Nostra?"

He went stock still then, and the glare he fixed her with had an unnerving yellowish cast to it even in the relative darkness. Must have been the tint of the glass, Regan decided. Although she felt suddenly, oddly lightheaded. That rich, dreamy voice seemed to fill her head when it spoke again, and as it did, Regan could feel all of her misgivings and apprehension simply evaporating into thin air.

"I'm sorry to impose upon you. I won't harm you. But I need to come in. *Now.*"

And just like that, her hand was heading for the deadbolt. Everything was lovely, everything was fine. Everything was ... well, no, Regan thought foggily, her hand pausing at the lock. Not quite right, though she couldn't put her finger on just why. She was suddenly convinced of her visitor's sincerity, but that didn't mean she should just fling the door open in welcome. Did it?

Regan peered back out the glass, doubts creeping slowly back in. "It doesn't really sound like I should let you anywhere near either of us, though."

Gideon's voice was strained, and the note of bone weariness Regan now heard in his voice tugged at her, though she tried not to let it. "She's my responsibility now, whether or not she wants to be. Your friend has no idea what these ... people ... are capable of, what they might do. I need to protect her. I *will* finish this, but until then, I have to be with her. I need to talk with her."

Then he said, so softly she could barely hear it, "I need to tell her how sorry I am."

That did it. Regan turned the deadbolt and unlocked the door, although, as a matter of principle, she held out her hand to stop him when he stepped forward. Her head was clearing, thank God. Even if she was still feeling sort of warm and fuzzy. Which was so not like her. Well, she would just have to fight the power.

"For the record, I think what you did sucks. And the only reason I'm letting you in is because you need to stay alive to fix whatever the hell it is that you've done." *And because what I just heard in your voice when you talked about Carly is something she's needed her whole life,* Regan added silently, although whether or not he was worthy was something she had yet to decide. "And if you don't, I will make sure that you pay for it for a long, long time."

His eyes, strange and solemn in the dim light (were people even *supposed* to have eyes that color, she wondered?) met hers, and he nodded once, his mouth set in a grim line. "Understood."

Regan put her hand down, stood aside to usher him in. She gave him a critical up-and-down as he hulked in, taking in the undersized sweats and tee-shirt. Property of Carly's brothers, no doubt. That was never going to work if loverboy here needed to be taken seriously. Lucky for him, she had a repository of clothing left behind by past jerks that she'd never gotten around to getting rid of, and as a general rule, she liked tall. Plus, in for a penny, she supposed. But for the moment, first things first.

"Since it looks like we're going to be working together," she stuck out a hand, "Regan O'Meara." And now, a ghost of a smile played about the corners of his mouth. A shame, Regan thought admiringly. He really was something to look at. But if anybody deserved a living centerfold, it was Carly. She couldn't help but smile. If this worked out, the illustrious Super Mario Brothers' heads were going to explode.

Gideon returned the gesture and shook her hand, firmly. "Irish, eh? I'll be certain to stay on your good side, then. Gideon MacInnes."

"That's assuming I have a good side," Regan snorted, turning to lead him back down the hallway whence she'd come. Still, she had to give him points for stroking her ego in one of its most susceptible spots. Her ancestry was a point of pride with her, famous Irish temper and all. And she had to admit, her temper, particularly, she reveled in.

"So. How about I bake, you talk, and we'll see where we end up at."

"I thought you were going to help me."

Regan's grin was wicked when she looked back into Gideon's wide, pleading eyes. "I am going to help you. But to what extent … now, that depends on you."

"I'll warn you, it's a rather long story."

"I've got time."

"You likely won't believe it."

She glanced sharply back at him then, her curiosity piqued. He still looked nothing but deadly serious. Maybe she'd wished a little *too* hard for Carly to have herself an adventure. Not that that made her any less intrigued. "Try me."

Stepping into the secure kingdom of her kitchen, Regan inhaled deeply, basking in the scent of freshly baked goodies and the sound of one big, mouth-watering male tossing himself into one of her chairs. Life in the Harbor could get maddeningly stagnant sometimes, it was true.

But it was shaping up to be one hell of an interesting day.

Gabriel MacInnes paused just inside the elegant, etched glass doors of Solstice, swallowing his nervousness that he'd be recognized as a pretender to this sort of society and tossed out on his ear, and finding, almost too quickly, exactly who he was looking for. The latter, as expected, caused much more of a visible grimace than the prospect of the former.

Damn you, Gideon, he thought, which made him feel better even though he knew that none of this was his brother's fault. He normally enjoyed Edinburgh, wandering Old Town with its singular mix of the modern and the medieval, watching the street performers in the summer, having a pint or two in one of the many pubs while he chatted up some local beauty or other in any season. But there weren't enough pints in the world to make this outing enjoyable. And neither his cousin nor his aunt qualified as a beauty by any man's definition.

Didn't it just figure they'd be lunching together? Double the pleasure, indeed, he thought morosely. Still, there was nothing for it now. If he was going to do this, it was best done quickly.

Gabriel breezed past the maître d' and strode towards the cozy corner table currently occupied by his apparently homicidal cousin and his unquestionably psychotic mother, keeping his demeanor cool, casual even as his insides roiled. He'd arrived in Edinburgh about an hour ago and staked out a position across the street from MacInnes's, Malachi's antique brokerage. Gabriel had been certain that his cousin would be heading off to lunch at some insufferable, overpriced restaurant at some point. Visibility, the appearance of prestige … truly, looking at his own last name affixed in huge gold letters to the front of the imposing façade of the brokerage told Gabriel all there was to know about his cousin's priorities. He'd listened to enough of Malachi's blathering over the years to know he'd want to be in the public eye as much as possible, and was not the sort of creature who'd be slaving away at his desk over a limp sandwich during the noon hour.

Now, faced with the prospect of, at best, a severe case of indigestion, at worst having his aunt try to claw his eyes out, Gabriel tried to be happy he'd been right.

It was, of course, Moriah who spotted him first. Some ugly emotion flashed across her fine features for a split second before she composed herself and smiled, showing very straight, very white teeth. Malachi turned as well, but seemed to have decided against manners for today and kept right on glowering.

Figured.

"Well, if it isn't my favorite nephew!" Moriah's voice was as smooth as cream when she spoke, although Gabriel had been around long enough to hear the river of poison that ran just beneath the surface. She offered one rouged cheek to him, and Gabriel, through sheer determination, managed to kiss it without biting her. If Malachi was, against all manner of sane judgment, after Gideon, it was a sure bet Moriah was somewhere pulling the strings. "I had no idea you were in town. When did you get in?"

Gabriel settled his tall, lanky frame into one of the two empty chairs, enjoying the pained expression on Malachi's face when he did so. "Had some business this morning and thought I'd grab a bite before I headed back." He grinned. "Thought I'd go upscale today, and lucky I did, since now I have some company."

Moriah's face twisted into some interesting imitation of regret. "Ah, I'm afraid not for long, darling. I actually just popped in to tell Malachi I was going to have to break our lunch date today. Things do tend to crop up when you run in the circles we do. Not that you'll ever have to trouble yourself about it, dear. Although I must say, you're looking nearly civilized today."

And that was Aunt Moriah, Gabriel thought as he graced her with an artificial smile of his own. Niceties and knives, all wrapped up in a pretty bow. And funny, but he could've sworn he'd seen her ordering as he'd walked into the restaurant. Must be the "circles" she and her exalted son ran in were telepathic as well as busy. He had to give her points for noticing his nod to polite society, though, in that he'd actually bothered to sleek his generally unruly hair back so that it didn't fall into his eyes. He might keep his hair shorter than his brother's, but it was no less wild without the pricey pomade Tori, his latest conquest, had picked up for him, and damned if he'd ever be putting that goo into his hair again after today. The rest of the package, though, worn jeans, dark green Henley, scuffed brown shoes, and broken-in leather jacket, were all, he was afraid, standard-issue.

And as for civility, he really didn't give a damn past not getting booted out before he'd managed to get to the table. Of course, that was mission accomplished, so …

Gabriel winked at his aunt, shoved his fingers back into his hair, and scrubbed until it fell as it usually did, longish on top and brushing his cheekbones on the sides. Just a bit wild. Just like him. "Well, then, Auntie Mo, recognize me better now?"

Her lips, painted blood red, thinned as she stood and regarded him with glittering eyes that were never truly anything but yellow, no matter what exotic color name she'd come up with for the moment. A mark of her distance from humanity, Gabriel supposed, and wondered how she ever managed to lure in her little boy toys with eyes like that, eyes that held nothing but death. There was a cold allure about her, he supposed. If you liked worrying whether or not you were going to be ripped open from neck to nether region from one moment to the next. At least she seemed to have settled on a shade of red that made it look a little less like her head required the immediate services of a fire extinguisher.

She stood, spread her hands on the table like claws, and leaned forward. "Oh, I've always recognized you for what you are, *dear*. A self-centered, undisciplined, weak-ling half-blood brat. How could you be anything else, with the blood that runs in your veins? I knew her blood would out in you," she hissed in a ragged whisper, "knew it the moment you were born. And you've never disap-pointed me."

It was a struggle, but Gabriel managed to keep his voice even, his gaze steady when he responded. "Nice to see you too, Auntie Mo," he said softly, landing another childish but satisfying blow with the use of her hated nickname. "Enjoy your prior engagement. And by the way, if you ever mention my mother again, I'll tear your bloody throat out."

Moriah's mouth turned down into a grimace that changed her entire face into something hideous. Some-thing, Gabriel thought, quite a bit closer to the truth. She looked like she wanted to bite him. God help him, he'd like to see her try.

"You'll pay, soon enough, for that." She straightened, turned on one dagger-sharp heel, and tapped angrily out the front door, nearly toppling two servers carrying large and laden trays as she charged through. Well, that had gone about as well as could be expected, Gabriel decided as he turned his attention to his cousin, sitting silently across from him. Moriah had never felt much need to hide her distaste for either him or Gideon ... at least not when no one she considered important was around. And it was a trait she'd been very careful to cultivate in her only son.

Malachi MacInnes. Gabriel hadn't seen him in close to a year, now that he thought of it. Been avoiding the Hunting Grounds, which he'd just chalked up to intense dislike of the rest of his family and, probably, disdain for the Pack in general. And no matter what, he probably hadn't been too far off the mark with that. Trying to kill off your closest cousins indicated more than a bit of dislike, after all. And still, he looked about as he remembered him: a bit too thin, a bit too pale, and with a sort of hungry anger, more intense than he remembered, in his eyes. Eyes which were now fixed on him.

"Lovely woman, your mum," Gabriel said, jerking his head toward the door which Moriah had just stormed through. "Don't know why we don't see more of one another."

Malachi, however, didn't appear to be in the mood for small talk. "What do you want, Gabriel? Whatever it is, I'd appreciate it if you'd just get it out and get going, since looking at you for too long is bound to ruin my appetite."

"Still no sense of humor," Gabriel sighed, enjoying his cousin's irritation. "I thought I might grab a bite, actually, since I'm here. Food good, is it?"

"I don't recall inviting you to lunch, *Cousin*."

"Ah, come on, Malachi. I know you're always happy for the company. So few others can tolerate it, after all. You should be grateful I arrived when I did, since you've been deprived of your mother's sparkling company."

Malachi rolled his gray eyes back into his head. "I doubt I would have been, if you hadn't wandered in."

Gabriel placed his hand against his heart in mock horror. "My God, man! You don't mean you think *I've* run her off, do you?"

Malachi smiled, albeit thinly. "Still the clown, then, are you? Well, I suppose some things never change." A waiter arrived with a small salad of field greens, placed it in front of him. Gabriel eyed it suspiciously.

"You haven't gone veg, have you? Because that all looks a bit … green."

"There's more to life than meat, Gabriel. If you'd ever come out of the damned wilderness, you might discover a thing or two." Malachi forked up a bit of the salad, which looked to be coated in a light vinaigrette, and placed it in his mouth, chewing contemplatively, never taking his eyes off his cousin. Gabriel, for his part, worked very hard at not pulling a face as he watched him eat. Apart from the occasional potato- or tomato-based product, he remained, as he had always been, deeply suspicious of anything overtly vegetable.

"Something for you, sir?" The server, polished in a crisp dress shirt and tie, regarded Gabriel with polite interest.

"Just a pint of Guinness for me, thanks. Not enough time for much but a meal in a glass today." He caught the beginning of the server's amused smirk before he turned away, which was a great deal better than the expression Malachi had on his face, with closed eyes and a pained frown.

"I have yet to comprehend," he managed in a strained voice, "how on earth you manage to run a successful business. I would imagine the clientele must be a lot like you, which means it pleases me to no end that I haven't been back in some time."

"Mmm. You know, it might have made us curious, if we'd bothered to notice."

Malachi opened his eyes, glared daggers at him. "What do you *want*, Gabriel?"

"Ah, well, that's the thing, isn't it?" Gabriel picked up the pint glass that was set quietly in front of him, leaned back in his chair, and took a long, restorative swallow. A meal in a glass, indeed, he thought as he held it up and studied it with a grin, realizing that he was generally his own best audience, but still … if you didn't nurture your sense of humor, you'd end up a sour old witch like his aunt, or a bitter, violent mama's boy like the one sitting at the table with him, to his way of thinking.

"I notice you haven't asked about Gideon."

Malachi raised a brow sharply. "Shocking, since the crown prince and I are such close friends."

"Ah, but you see, what I want pertains to him." Gabriel set down the glass, propped his elbows on the table, and folded his hands before him. And his cousin's demeanor remained cool, indifferent … but still, there it was, just a hint, the faintest whiff, of uneasiness. "Strangely enough, I don't really like it when people try to kill my brother."

Malachi snorted, began to fork through his salad again, although this time he did little more than toy with it. "Puzzling, that, as he is a bit of an ass. But I'm afraid you still haven't mentioned what you want from *me*. I'm not terribly interested in some paranoid fantasy, so if this is all, I'm going to hope that you have some small shred of dignity that'll make you leave before I have you removed."

"Fortunately for you, that tactic hasn't worked on Gideon thus far."

Malachi's lips peeled back in a snarl. "And what exactly is *that* supposed to mean?"

Pleased it had been this easy to get a rise out of his cousin, Gabriel switched tracks quickly, sighing and shaking his head gently back and forth. He'd see more, he figured, if he could keep him off balance. "Tsk, tsk, Cousin. Shame on you for listening to your deluded mum. Do you really think that if you just sweep us all away that planting your sorry ass on the Stone will make you more than the pathetic, grasping little beast you are? Not that you'd ever get to it, in any case. The Pack will never have you." He leaned forward, eyes filled with an angry, unnatural light. Well, he thought. Perhaps he wasn't going to be quite as even-tempered about this as he'd thought. "And neither will we."

Malachi's pallid skin flushed with anger, and his voice, when he spoke, shook slightly with the effort to keep it down, keep up the outward appearance of a normal conversation.

"*If* someone, somehow, managed to get rid of the bloody ruling MacInneses, that wouldn't be for you to decide, now, would it? But, sadly for you, you're wasting all that hot air you carry about with you. If someone's trying to kill your irritating brother, you'd best look elsewhere for the source. And as for the *Lia Fáil* … I don't think a damned one of you has any idea where it even came from, much less what it can do. Now if you'll excuse me," he snapped, shoving away from the table and standing, eyes flashing, "I'd best get back to work before you manage to ruin any more of my day." He tossed a few bills on the table for his mostly uneaten salad and strode off, leaving Gabriel to sip at his beer and watch him go.

Normally, he would have been congratulating himself on managing to run off two of his least favorite family members in under fifteen minutes. But something was off, and badly. He'd felt all that nervous tension coiled about Moriah and Malachi, noted too that their tempers, though infamous, had gone from having only a short fuse to practically none. And most importantly, through all of the smoke and anger pouring in his direction, he'd smelled fear. Now, though he and Gideon would have a definitive answer as to who was behind this little coup attempt, Gabriel was left to wonder if, in getting that answer, he'd done more harm than good. He still had no proof, but he'd doubtless just added some desperation to the mix. It might make them sloppy, he reasoned. Then again, it might just make them faster, more deadly.

He needed to call Gideon. He needed to head back to *Iargail* to have a chat with his father as well.

And damn that bloody snowstorm Gideon had gotten himself stuck in, because the three of them really needed to take a united stand on this. But for now, he was going to have to concentrate on actions instead of what-ifs, and see what he would see. He set the empty glass aside, placed large, calloused hands over his eyes, and rubbed, his only concession to the weariness and worry that was hovering at the back of his mind.

And he decided that after this, he was due for a damned vacation himself.

Malachi slammed into his office in a rage. How dare he? *How dare he?* To walk into his life, disturb and unsettle him in front of people, influential people, people who would *talk.*

Bastard.

He should have gone for Gabriel and his insufferable, smug mouth, his embarrassing lack of anything even resembling class, first. Should have known that Jonas's incompetence the other night would set off the alarm. Should have known that it would point, because Gideon was the initial target, right in his direction. *Stupid,* hissed his mother's voice, always the first to berate him in his mind when he made a misstep, when what he did threatened to dishonor the one branch of the family that was still fit to guard, to lead. To *rule.*

"I'm sorry, Mother," he muttered, not even realizing he spoke aloud as he moved quickly through the opulent

CALL OF THE HIGHLAND MOON   173

office he knew he didn't deserve, to the locked desk drawer that contained his only hope of salvation. "I'll make it better ... I'll make it right."

He managed, with shaking hands, to spring the locking mechanism on the third try. He ran a caressing hand over his salvation, the destiny hung on a chain around his neck that whispered to him even now.

"Destroy him ... clear the way ... I shall reward your loyalty ..."

"I will do as you ask, my Master. Only a little more time, I swear it." Malachi picked up the cell phone, hurriedly punching in the numbers. The Andrakkar's patience would not last forever ... and even the hints Malachi had seen of his displeasure had been nothing short of terrifying.

Answer, he thought, his stomach roiling and burning with both temper and a terrible, sick fear. *Answer, you incompetent bastard, or I swear on all that is sacred I will come to kill you myself.*

On the third ring, he picked up.

"Tell me," Malachi growled, willing himself not to grip the phone so tightly that he would crush it.

"You're going to be pleased. They're lovers, or near enough. And now he knows I've seen her, that I'll take her. She's his mate, though he fights it. And when he discovers he can't stop me ... it's going to break him."

Malachi braced himself against the desk, tears of relief filling his eyes. A gift. Salvation. If nothing else, didn't this prove what his mother had always taught him? That St. Columcille, that God Himself was on their side, the side of the strongest, the fittest?

"There is suspicion," he said, more evenly now, more steadily. "You know what needs to be done. This is the key to them all, but it must be finished by the full moon."

"I'll be in contact. Soon."

Malachi broke the connection and sank into the plush leather of his chair, shaking with the release of all of the pent-up nervousness. The stress. He needed to focus, he told himself. To center. Tomorrow, the next day at the latest, this would all be over. And the luxury he was now surrounded with would be nothing, *nothing* compared with what was to come, what had been promised. He was smarter, stronger, quicker. He had been *born* to rule, and over more than just a ragtag pack of indifferent werewolves. He would create his empire. He would fulfill his destiny, and the destiny of that magic piece of rock so carefully hidden all these hundreds of years.

Even now, with the moon coming into her fullness in just days, he could feel his strength gathering, readying for the rush he would make on this last barrier. And at last, he would be what he was meant to be. He would be a king among Wolves, a god among men. Fit to be called Drakkyn once again. And finally, finally, he would make his mother proud.

"A king," he whispered raggedly, serene even as he felt something within him begin to crack. "A god. I'm ready."

And his smile, when it came, was madness.

Chapter Nine

HER CAR WAS SNOWED IN, STUCK IN HER DRIVEWAY, SO she'd hiked down to work.

She'd been that desperate.

Carly perched atop her little stool behind the counter and stared out into the dimly lit street beyond her window, now plowed as well as it could be but, in general, a mess. And she was brooding. She knew she was brooding. But damn it, who did this stuff happen to, outside of those dumb, busty blonds in the horror movies her brothers always used to force her to watch? At least she'd avoided the part where said busty blond was impaled, decapitated, or generally killed in some disgusting way or other.

So far.

But Gideon had lied to her, and from the looks of those eyes outside her window last night, and his reaction to them, it had been a big one. She shouldn't be hurt, Carly told herself firmly, even as something inside her ached persistently. She barely knew him. It wasn't as though he was some kind of fixture in her life, someone she'd allowed into her heart as well as her life.

Except that wasn't exactly true, was it? Carly toyed with a pen, doodled little circles and spirals on the corner of a Post-it. Something about Gideon pulled at her, had from the beginning. She ought to be a big enough girl to admit that to herself. It wasn't just that he was amazing to look at, although no one could ever dispute that he most certainly was. No, she decided, it was the air of lonely nobility he seemed to carry with him, something that had called *take care of me* to her when she'd looked into his beautiful, golden eyes.

Not that he'd like it if she told him that, she supposed, now stabbing angrily at the paper. Small, indented dots of displeasure marked it as she imagined Gideon's reaction to her perception of some vulnerability on his part. Because aside from that strange sense of need Carly felt from him, there was nothing but big, tough alpha male. And big, tough alpha males didn't, as far as she knew, enjoy anything resembling emotion unless it was somehow anger or lust related. Hadn't he even said that the position he was going to inherit was *called* "Alpha"?

Figured.

Well, they'd certainly covered the "lust" area of the program, Carly thought, even as she fought off images of what they'd been doing in her kitchen when everything had suddenly gone to hell in a handbasket. What she'd *wanted* him to do. What they hadn't quite gotten to.

Stupid. It had been stupid of her to invent some weird connection between them, stupid to imagine Gideon MacInnes as some mystical hero who'd ridden in on a white charger to sweep her off her feet. Who would be some manifestation of her dreams of romance. Well, he was out of her life now, Carly thought, burying the pang that accompanied it. Gone, and his libidinous mind-fuzzing abilities along with it. She could breathe again, think straight again. Clearer heads could finally prevail.

Now, she just needed to work on being happy about that.

Carly frowned, rose, and moved to the door to flip the sign to OPEN, even though it was just eight-thirty. She was twenty-seven years old. Young yet, yeah, but too old for fairy tales. Carly looked around her as she reached for the sign, at the rich wood, the gleaming spines of the books, the glimmer of beautiful things peeking out from unexpected places. Her sanctuary. But it was time, she realized with an embarrassed flush, to remember that stories were only stories. If she was ever going to find a man she could be happy with, a healthy dose of realistic expectations was in order.

Not that anything about this entire situation was either realistic or expected. More like a sexual fantasy wrapped up in a nightmare. Gideon MacInnes was a lesson in "be careful what you wish for" if she'd ever seen one, and oh, she'd learned it. She was just lucky, she supposed, that nothing more had been hurt than her feelings.

Then the vision of those intense, somehow malevolent eyes resurfaced in her mind, and she wondered if she should be breathing a sigh of relief on that score just yet.

God, she thought with a shudder. She hoped so. But then, there was no real way to know, being that she'd stayed huddled in her bed, trying desperately to ignore Gideon's pleas to be let in, to explain. Worried that if she let him in, he'd get to her, and she would crumble under the weight of her reaction to him ... and she would let him keep *taking*. Wasn't it pathetic, she chastised herself, that even now she had to slap away the worry for him that wanted to creep into her thoughts? The guilt? He'd *used* her, after all. Even if he had sounded so tired ... and sad ... and somehow sincere.

And she wasn't going to get a damned thing done today if she spent the whole day feeling sorry for herself and analyzing her stupid mistake half to death. Even if the weather moved back in as predicted, she still had the morning to freshen up her displays, order more stock. She had a business to run, a real, concrete business.

It had been enough for her before. It was going to have to continue to be.

Carly moved back to the counter, slid back up onto the stool, and began working up a list of things she had to get done. There was a small stack of special orders that needed to be taken care of, a book signing with a local, popular author that needed to be organized, ordering decisions to be made, her mother's fifty thousand phone messages to return ...

After a half hour at it, she was so deeply absorbed that the silvery ring of the bell above her door sent her nearly jumping out of her skin. After she'd caught her breath and swallowed the scream that had nearly escaped her throat, it took her a good minute of squinting to even identify what, at first glance, appeared to be a sentient pile of winter clothing as female.

"Good morning. Can I help you?"

The blue wool coat raised its arm to the fat pink knit hat and scarf, which revealed only a few tufts of light-colored hair and the impression of bright, twinkling eyes, and pulled down the scarf. "You most certainly can. If I have to spend one more moment in that house with Reg, much as I adore him, I'm going to have to bludgeon him to death with the tea kettle."

"Celestine!" Carly burst out laughing. Thank God, she thought. Celestine was just the thing to lighten her mood this morning. She'd thought Regan would be the one for that job, but she'd been a little odd on the phone when she'd spoken to her earlier. Granted, the roads weren't really fit to drive on, and there was nowhere to park downtown that wasn't covered in at least a couple of feet of snow, but Carly would have liked to delay herself for a while to help Regan move goodies from home to store just the same. They'd done it together before, after all. But though Regan had operated under the guise of friendly concern once Carly let it drop that she'd kicked her visitor out on his ass, still, Carly had gotten the distinct impression that she was being brushed off. Sweetly, and minus any malice, but definitely brushed off.

It was something she had every intention of poking into later. But for now, all she wanted to do was forget her pissy mood for a few minutes and enjoy the company of one of her favorite people.

"Honestly, Celestine, the way you talk about that cat, you'd think he was your husband. How bad can a fat old housecat be?"

"I hope you never have to find out," she sighed as she unwound yards of scarf from around her neck, draped it on a branch of the coat tree, and then plucked off her mittens and hat. "That animal is a menace. Two of my favorite pairs of shoes, chewed to pieces, along with a cozy mystery I was reading. And I know you won't believe me, but I am *determined* he's been raiding my potato chips." She smoothed down her hair with a few quick, graceful strokes of her hands and in moments was looking as crisp as she always did. It was a skill Carly had always envied, and watching it always left her tugging self-consciously at her simple tail of hair, just as it did now.

"Well, I was kind of leaning toward a dog anyway." Although, she supposed, her last experience with anything canine might have been some kind of omen … and damn it, could she *please* not think about that man for five minutes? "Although a cat is always a possibility."

"Well, caveat emptor, as they say, dear." Celestine unbuttoned the coat partway and scuffed off what she could of the melting snow on the mat in front of the door before she started towards the bookshelves. "I thought I was getting a quiet, self-sufficient, and most importantly, low-maintenance companion. Instead I got a miniature cow masquerading as a feline who specializes in property destruction." She shook her head. "And yet I do adore him, which is why I haven't had a hat made out of him. Who needs a husband? I have enough aggravation between Reg and the occasional boy toy."

Now it was Carly's turn to shake her head, albeit with a smile. Celestine's last "boy toy" had been short, sixty-ish, and balding. He had also been smitten and very, very rich, lavishing her with gifts and taking her on one globe-trotting adventure after another until the two of them had burned one another out and parted, as most often happened in her case, amicably, continuing on as friends.

Carly didn't know how she did it, but she was beginning to think Celestine had the right idea after all. It had to be better than feeling like you'd just been run over by the dump truck of love. Not that she knew him well enough to actually *love* him or anything. Not that there was anything like love at first sight ... or touch ... or semi-mauling ... that existed outside of her beloved books. And anyway, no love at first sight that she'd ever heard of had involved nausea, even though that's what she felt every time she thought of Gideon's face. The desire to throw up in no way equaled any sort of love. That, at least, she was sure of.

Almost.

"Now then," Celestine continued, wandering over to the new releases and pulling a pair of cat's-eye glasses, framed in small, glittering red rhinestones, from her inside pocket to slide on so that she could peruse the titles, "why don't you tell me about your man troubles while I decide what to take home with me?"

Carly opened her mouth to speak. Shut it. Opened it again. "I ... why would you think I was having man troubles?" God, did she have it written across her forehead in marker or something?

"Carly, dear, you look tired, slightly ill, and you have opened your shop nearly two hours early on a day when you would have been well within your rights not to open at all. Add to it that I have been around that particular block quite enough times to know, and the answer is rather obvious. So," she looked back at Carly with a sympathetic smile before turning back to ponder the covers, "who is he, what has he done, and do I or do I not hate him eternally on your behalf?"

"God, that's sweet, Celestine," Carly sighed, grateful for the offer of a shoulder even though she was still too stuck in the "mortification" part of the program to even begin to know what to start with. "But since I'm not sure how to answer any of the above, I don't even know what to tell you."

Celestine turned again to Carly, her interest obviously piqued. "A man of mystery, hmm? How intriguing!"

Visions of Gideon in a tight velvet suit driving a garishly painted Mini Cooper danced unbidden through Carly's mind at that, and she didn't know whether to laugh or wince. As a compromise, she did both. "He's not Austin Powers, Celestine. He's …" A dangerous creature of the night? A lying Scottish sex god? Was there any sort of answer to this that wasn't going to make her sound like a complete idiot? A quick inventory of her possibilities gave her the answer to *that* soon enough. Well, then, she supposed she'd have to settle for semi-idiot and be done with it. "He's sort of indefinable."

All that earned Carly was an eye roll. Oh God. She was going to be spilling her guts within minutes, and she knew it. Why, Carly asked herself, weren't there self-help books on the art of understatement, fabrication, and general avoidance of stuff you didn't want to get into? Of course, she'd probably need a shelf full of them before she got any benefits, but still.

"Carly Silver," Celestine admonished, shaking Angela Garrity's newest Georgian masterpiece at her (and she should know, Carly thought, because she'd practically devoured the damned thing last weekend … lavish parties, tight breeches, and clandestine affairs were all right up her alley, and no way was she acknowledging the fascination as part of her general problem), "I'll have you know that I have been married five times and dated half the eligible male population of the world, and never in my life have I encountered a specimen who was absolutely, indescribably …"

The bell above the door rang again, but Carly's attention remained focused on Celestine, whose mouth was now hanging oddly agape. Carly figured she hadn't meant to spill about the ex-husbands, since that was news to her, and would have been, she knew, to anyone in town. Who would have thought that their Celestine was working on becoming the next Liz Taylor? She wasn't going to blab, but she sure as hell was going to press for the juicy details. After Celestine got herself back together, that was. Which she still hadn't quite managed to do.

"Um. Celestine?" Carly frowned, concerned, and slid off the stool to go to her.

"Indescribable," murmured Celestine, her eyes faintly glazed and fixed on a point over Carly's shoulder. Carly wondered if she was having some kind of spell, or if she ought to just go ahead and call an ambulance, because she'd never seen her friend just shut down, knocked on her ass like this. She turned, though, to see what had so captured her attention, and

stopped dead in her tracks herself. She thought she
made a noise. Some sort of stupid, female yummy
noise. But she couldn't be sure, because the mere sight
of him had melted her brain into mush.

He'd gotten clothes that fit him somewhere, some
small, still-functioning part of her mind noted. Fit. Yep.
They sure did. Her eyes skimmed slowly up Gideon's
massive frame, from the new-looking boots to the faded
blue jeans that hung loose on the leg and were just tight
enough everywhere else, to the long-sleeved tee beneath
what looked like a new ski jacket, and then just a bit
further up to his face. Carly didn't want to look. She was
already in enough trouble. But her good sense was over-
ridden by the rest of her with unfortunate ease.

He still hadn't shaved, she saw. His angular jaw was
covered in rough stubble. The loose waves of his hair
were pushed back from his face and tucked behind his
ears, not that that was doing much to contain it. And as
for the rest of it … Carly's belly tightened into a hot ball
of lust as his gaze connected with hers, slamming into
her with unexpected force. He looked tired, she thought
with unintentional sympathy. Tired and unhappy. There
were smudges beneath his eyes. Had he even slept? Her
guilt tried once again to rear its ugly head, and this time
she was less successful at shoving it back.

The moment they stood there staring at one another—
he seeming to take up her entire doorway, she pausing in
mid-stride on her way to her still-catatonic friend—
seemed to spin out for an eternity. There was an
unnerving sense of relief at the sight of Gideon, although
her heart constricted almost painfully. Her senses were

suddenly full of him, the sound of his breathing, the faint, slightly exotic and spicy scent of him.

Oh no, Carly thought, unnerved by the full-body reaction she was having. Hadn't she already decided there was no such thing as love at first sight? And hadn't she also just decided that Gideon MacInnes was exactly wrong for her on just about every possible level? *Oh no no no no no.*

She managed, somehow, to tear her gaze away from him and felt that awful pressure in her chest ease just a little. *Breathe,* she instructed herself. Celestine looked like she could have used a little instruction in that area herself, Carly saw. "Celestine," she said softly, ignoring the tingling sensation that ran up her back as Gideon moved up behind her. No response, just more open-mouthed adoration. Carly rolled her eyes heavenward, put a hand on each shoulder, and shook lightly. "*Celestine,*" she repeated, more forcefully this time, and the glaze cleared a little.

"This is my, um … this is … Gideon. MacInnes." Carly groaned inwardly. Well, that would tell Celestine just about everything she needed to know, she guessed. That was, if Celestine were still capable of any sort of rational thought, which at this moment was pretty debatable.

"Oh. My." Her friend raised a fluttering hand to pat at her already perfect hair, then extended it toward Gideon, who, Carly saw, now that she felt she could chance a look, had his eyebrows raised and was wearing an amused smile.

It was infuriatingly sexy.

"Celestine Periwether," she cooed as her hand was enveloped by his. "My," she murmured again as her eyes swept the length of him. "You are *big,* aren't you?"

"I've been told my family's rather tall," he rumbled, a hint of humor in his voice. Celestine simply giggled, which was just about enough for Carly. It was one thing to hear about the five husbands and innumerable boyfriends. It was quite another to watch how she'd landed them.

Carly stepped back and shot Gideon the look that had served as a warning shot to her brothers for years. Celestine, she'd forgive. Gideon was, after all, a little overwhelming at first. Gideon, however, should understand how he affected people. Women, specifically. Carly felt the first flames of temper begin to lick at her mood, and she welcomed them. It was a lot more comfortable than helpless misery and pointless lust. Couldn't Gideon have tried to tone down his ridiculous sex appeal just a *little* before he'd invaded her space this morning?

"Well, you two enjoy your chat," she bit out. "I have work to do." She shot her nose in the air and glided with quite a bit of grace, she thought, back to the stockroom. That was, until she managed to trip over her own foot about three steps from the door. Damn it. Carly pushed aside the red velvet curtain she'd draped across the doorway and slid around the corner, sagging against the shelves that lined the walls, which were interrupted only by a small, neatly organized desk tucked into the far corner. He would leave now, right? She put the heels of her palms to her eyes and pressed down, utterly flustered. She'd made it clear how she felt, and now he'd just … go?

Oh, God, she was doomed.

"Carly." Her name sounded like a caress.

So, so doomed.

"Mmm?" Her hands stayed where they were. Maybe, she reasoned, if she didn't look at him, he would simply disappear.

"Carly, I'm so sorry about last night. I understand you're upset, but we really need to talk."

No such luck, then. Damn. She removed her hands from her eyes, looked at him, and sighed. "Why don't you just go talk to Celestine? Because I'm not really in the mood." It was irritating, she decided, that she couldn't even sustain a decent mad at him. All she really felt was a simmering stew of hopeless attraction, hurt feelings, and general mistrust, all of which together made for a basic and unflinching misery.

Gideon didn't move from the doorway, just stood there watching her with unnerving intensity. The surface was calm, but Carly had a sneaking suspicion that she couldn't even begin to guess at half of what ran beneath it. At this moment, she wasn't particularly sure she even wanted to. Still, despite everything, Gideon managed to quirk a half smile at her.

"I'd rather talk to you, if it's all the same. Her, I've had to pat on her head and send on her way, although I'm not quite sure she knew where she was going. Not to be rude, and she seems a lovely woman, but your friend seems a bit … medicated."

Carly snorted. "Yeah, right. With the elixir of *looove*. As though you don't know."

Now he just laughed, a rich, deep roll that had Carly's belly clenching with an unwanted wave of lust.

But she'd be damned if she'd let him know. It was going to take a hell of a lot more than a great laugh to get back into her good graces at this point. Even if the way his butt looked in those jeans *was* giving him a slight advantage.

"Christ, woman. You do have a way with words. Not that I shouldn't have expected it." He swept his hand around to indicate the shelves full of boxes of books. "Words seem to be what you do."

Carly gave him a tight smile. "Did you come in here to impress the customers and flatter me? Because I was under the impression you wanted something worthwhile. Otherwise, I have work to do." She bet that was all it took with the other girls, Carly thought irritably as she watched his smile fade. And of course he had other girls. Probably enough to populate a small country. She'd been a pathetically easy target, she was sure. And with that, Carly noted with a sort of dull satisfaction, she had made *herself* nauseous. What a barrel of fun she was this morning.

Gideon pushed a hand back through his hair, which she was starting to notice he did whenever he was uncomfortable. *Good.* She was all about sharing.

"Look, Carly, what I came to say was, I know … last night. I didn't mean to … and I know I said …"

Carly leaned a hip against the shelving unit beside her and said nothing, simply raising an eyebrow. She couldn't think of a single earthly reason why this should be easy for him.

Gideon seemed to sense it. He stopped, took a deep breath, and started again. "Someone is trying to kill me."

Hearing it, the truth of it, rattled her more than she'd thought. Still, she managed to keep her tone carefully even. "It would have been nice if you'd mentioned it to start with."

"I know it isn't much of an excuse, but I couldn't take the chance that you'd tell me to go. I needed to heal, to rest. And I truly, truly thought I would be gone before anything else happened. I wasn't counting on a bloody snowstorm. You have to at least believe that."

Carly sighed, looked away. Chewed a little at her bottom lip. He was right, she supposed, even if she didn't agree with the rest of it. If he'd known her, though, he'd have known she'd never have tossed him out in the condition he was in. She would have at least found him somewhere else to stay. But then, that was the point, wasn't it? He didn't know. Just as she knew so little about him. And if they were going to get on any kind of an even footing, get to a decent place to start over, that was going to have to change. Starting now.

"I think you'd better tell me everything, Gideon. And not just the condensed, government-approved BS version this time. I deserve at least that."

He looked a little grim, but he nodded. And he was keeping his distance, not moving from the doorway, as though he wasn't at all sure she'd ever want him near her again. But it couldn't possibly be that bad. Could it?

"I suppose the best place to start is with my family."

"Which is a pack of Scottish werewolves, right?" Carly was still amazed she could get that out in a serious tone of voice, but there it was.

A ghost of a smile played around Gideon's lips, as though despite its truth, it still sounded a bit odd to him too. "To put it bluntly. It's a small group, perhaps two hundred of us at any given time, and scattered at that. Our traditional home, what we call the Hunting Grounds, is an estate called *Iargail*, near the village of Lochaline on the Sound of Mull. It's perfect for a bunch of werewolves, I suppose. There's room to run, tucked away from the rest of the world. Most of the Pack left, eventually. But the Guardians never did. And we never will."

Nor did he want to. Carly could hear it in his voice, see it in the way his eyes went far off when he spoke of home. "*Twilight,* right?"

Gideon nodded. "Which is where we seem to exist, as far as general humanity is concerned. And that's fine. We have to, really, because of what we are. And what we do."

"It sounds so lonely. I guess. You're young. Not that you'd necessarily want to live in party central, but I wonder why you'd deliberately choose that kind of isolation." And for the first time, Carly began to feel just how great the distance between their worlds actually was.

Gideon, for his part, leaned against the doorway looking pensive. "Exactly the reason most of the others only come for gatherings and visits. The reason, as a matter of fact, I'm here now. And oddly enough, at least part of the reason why I'm going back." He laughed, though there was little humor in it. "It seems I'm not a party central kind of guy."

"Well, I get *that,* believe it or not." And she did. Knew that some of it was what drew her to him. Like often sought like, Carly had always heard, and this estate of his, what was undoubtedly a lonely, windswept, altogether lovely place, sounded like a little slice of heaven to her, and only partly because her image of the place included Gideon.

"So what is it, then? What do your, um, people do, what's so important that you need to go back and be alone? Because I'm guessing that this is what you really came here to tell me." Enough, already, Carly thought. She hated herself for it, but she couldn't stand to see Gideon looking so damned miserable. It was time to rip the band-aid off, and all at once. Then, maybe, they could go on from there. Because seeing him again like this, if nothing else, had convinced her that no matter what her common sense said, that was exactly what she wanted to do.

His gaze returned to her from where it had wandered, across the room to her tidy little desk. It was sharp, alert, the scar that slashed across his one eye making it that much more predatory, like a scratch in the thin veneer of civilization that had been placed over something much more dangerous. Much more wild. Carly felt her skin chill.

"It's more what I'm in line to do that seems to be the problem. My father is, as I've mentioned to you, what we call the Pack Alpha. It is, for better or for worse, a hereditary position."

Alpha. Cute, she thought. Apt. But she doubted he'd appreciate the reaction. "And you're the firstborn."

"Exactly. The Alpha oversees the upholding of our laws, our traditions. He administers justice, when necessary, with his Guard. And, most importantly, he himself is the guardian and guard of an ancient secret. One that has been in our possession since Saint Columba brought us out of the wilds of our land, gave us a clan, law, our faith ... and one sacred thing to keep until the time came when it could be used again." He paused, and Carly found herself holding her breath, feeling the importance, the weight, of what he had decided to tell her. And despite her curiosity, she was compelled to stop him.

"Gideon, if you're going to get in trouble for telling me this ..."

His laugh was a frustrated bark. "I'm already in trouble. A bit more won't hurt. And I owe you the truth, I think, since I went and involved you." He shoved his hair back again, sighed. "Tell me, have you ever heard of the *Lia Fáil?* The Stone of Destiny?"

It rang a bell. Carly frowned. She'd run across it somewhere, although she read so much, things tended to get either lost or smashed together only semi-recognizably in her memory. It took a moment of digging, but finally, she thought she had at least a bit of it. "Wasn't that the stone they used to crown the kings of Scotland on? The one the British stole? Although I thought I read in the paper that they gave it back, or loaned it back, or some stupid thing recently." She raised her eyebrows at him, waiting for confirmation, and he did nod, although this time, the laugh that went with it was genuinely amused.

"Saint Columba crowned the very first Scottish king atop it back in the sixth century, and all after that until the end of the thirteenth, when Edward the First took it." Gideon gave a smug-sounding snort. "As though we would ever have given it up that easily. Never did occur to bloody idiots why, with all of our fierce and proud warriors, we gave up our treasure without so much as a fight. Or why, when in all the legends it was described as either a black or white ornately carved stone, we had supposedly been crowning ourselves all that time on a plain chunk of native limestone with a simple cross hacked into the top." He shook his head, chuckling.

Carly cocked her head, intrigued. "So what, may I ask, have the British been crowning *themselves* on all these years? Because I do remember now that they still use it for that, to show their sovereignty over the Scots. Which was why they just *loaned* it back to be displayed at Edinburgh Castle. Sweet, considering they stole it in the first place."

"Well," his grin was wicked, "we used what came quickly to hand, of course. And as the cesspits were, in fact, close at hand, and as they were covered with chunks of stone roughly the correct size ..." He trailed off, and Carly couldn't help but burst into incredulous laughter.

"Are you telling me that all of the British kings and queens since 1300 have made a point of being crowned on the top of what basically amounts to a medieval toilet seat cover?"

Gideon shrugged. "Draw your own conclusions."

"And you, your people ... you have the real one?" Amazing, she thought, that such a thing could get lost in history. Because from what she understood, everybody figured that what the British had given back was the real deal, including the Scots.

"We were charged with the care of it from the time it arrived on our shores, then charged with the keeping of it when it had to disappear. It's become legend; Jacob's Pillow, where he dreamed of his ladder to heaven, a magical thing with more power than any mortal can understand. Some say it has healing powers, others that it will sing when the rightful king of Scotland again sits upon it. Some say that it disappeared for a time, to Wales, where it had a famous sword pulled from it. All part of its purpose in being among mankind at all, such a sacred, powerful thing it is. And then," his face darkened suddenly, and Carly found herself fighting the urge to take a step back, for there, right beneath the surface, was the wolf, "there are those who think it holds the secret to rule not just Scotland, should her sovereignty ever be restored, but the world. Deluded, evil thinking, but the myth, and its believers, exist just the same."

"And is it true?" Carly knew her mouth had dropped open, but she couldn't help it. To know that things like that actually *existed* in the world and were guarded by, of all things, werewolves hired by a saint. What else was hiding out there, just out of plain sight? "Is any of that actually true?"

Gideon smirked a little, then gave her a sidelong glance and shook his head. And she knew, at that point, she'd gotten all she was going to. "I know a little. Less, I think, than I will when I take my father's place. But even then, so much has been lost with time. And remember, the Clan MacInnes, and its Wolves, were only charged to keep it safe, keep it hidden. Not to use it for any grand purpose of our own. But it appears at least one of our number has forgotten that."

She straightened, took a tentative step towards Gideon. It was so overwhelming, all of this. Two days ago, she'd been this normal, harried, boring business-woman who worried about things like whether her twinset looked stupid with her pants and whether the latest shipment of new releases was going to pique enough interest in her clientele. Now, she was all wrapped up in werewolves and ancient relics with magic powers and murder ... *murder.* She stopped short.

"Is that what ... who that thing was outside last night? Do you think it was just watching you?"

"I think," Gideon said flatly, "that I have a spineless, cowardly cousin with delusions of grandeur and a few homicidally inclined friends he didn't bother to tell anyone about. And I also think," he continued, his voice softening just a little with regret, "that I may have put you in a great deal of danger until I can nail the bastard, and his helpers, to the wall."

Carly's hand rose to her throat, then lowered. No, damn it. She was *not* going to get all weepy and hysterical, just because she was probably being hunted by some blood-thirsty monster ... even though that probably wouldn't have happened if *someone* hadn't decided to play "placate the little woman" instead of just being honest.

"And you ... you just thought it would be *okay* to ..." She gritted her teeth, bit off the scream that wanted to rip from her throat at the man who stood silently, watching her as though he were expecting, and ready to

accept, her rage, disgust, denial. All of it. And all it did
was make her angrier. "I have a *life,* goddamn it,
Gideon! I have a family here, people I care about! And
how dare you … *how dare you* just brush all that aside
like it doesn't matter!" She saw him open his mouth to
speak then, but she just rolled right over him. "No, I
know what you're going to say. You didn't know that
psycho-wolf or whatever that was last night was going
to find you so fast. You didn't know about the damned
snowstorm. But none of that changes the fact that you
lied to someone who went out of her way to save you,
who probably would have helped you anyway if you'd
just been *honest.*"

And she enjoyed it, seeing the shock that her statement caused, but it was true. She wasn't the kind of
person who ignored the pleas of those in need. But being
tricked into helping without being aware of the possible
consequences, that was what she couldn't stomach.
Being treated like a little girl who didn't need to know
any better, like a means to an end. She'd had plenty of
being the baby girl growing up.

But damn it, she was a woman now, and she was done
taking shit from men.

"Well," she snapped, crossing her arms over her chest,
"seeing as how I don't actually have a choice anymore, I
suppose you *have* to stick around to make sure that I and
my loved ones are still breathing when you get your little
problem sorted out. But I'm telling you right now,
Gideon MacInnes: don't ever lie to me again. Don't treat
me like you know what's best for me again." His brows
drew together, and now she could see the temper,

dangerous, rising to the surface. Good. Let him lift a finger to her and she'd have his ass thrown in jail.

"And finally," she hissed, cruising on the wave of her righteous fury, "don't you dare lay a finger on me again. I'm not a perk, I'm not a fun diversion for your personal amusement, and I am no longer interested. Got it?" She stood there, slightly out of breath, glaring daggers at Gideon while he simply stared back. But when he finally spoke, it was neither the apology she'd wanted nor the anger she'd almost hoped for.

"Are you finished?"

"Excuse me?"

"Because if you're quite done, I have a few things I'd like to say in response to all those lovely accusations you've just flung at me." He tilted his head, considering her for a moment, his stance making him appear almost relaxed until one got a look at the storm brewing in those *eyes.*

"Actually, I believe I've only got one thing, after all."

He moved through the doorway, still looking way too big, way too *male,* an invader in her little kingdom. The hair on the back of her neck rose at his approach, and no amount of willpower could dampen that crackling tension between them, that sizzling awareness of his nearness. She couldn't move. She could barely breathe. Carly tried, desperately, not to think of what had happened between them last night, the way his hands had stroked her as though they'd always known her, as if the two of them belonged that way, pressed together.

She felt a fierce blush rise to her face, but she kept her eyes locked with his, defiant. He was in the wrong here.

She'd be damned if she'd cede any more of her territory to him.

And he *knew*. He knew what he was doing to her. She could see it in the way the color of his eyes deepened to rich honey. And even as he closed the distance between them, even as Carly started to feel her knees go weak, she thought, *damn you*.

If only it hadn't been accompanied by the thought, *please*.

"I do owe you a huge apology, Carly," Gideon murmured as he slid his arms around her. "And I will protect you, and yours, with my life if I have to. But I will be touching you. And you will be wanting me to. And I'll be damned if I'm going to apologize for that."

And then Carly had only herself to curse, because she went from not being able to struggle to not wanting to. He lifted her against him, lowered his head so that his mouth was only a breath away from hers, and then did the thing that proved to be her undoing. He closed his eyes as she watched, helpless, twining those long lashes together. Then he slowly inhaled, taking in all of her, her scent, her breath, and the look on his face was pure ecstasy.

Carly watched him drink her in, felt something within her rise, then fall. And she knew that whoever he was, whatever he was, whatever he'd done, she wouldn't be sending him away again. The implications, the *feelings,* she was going to have to take some serious time and sort through later. But for now, feeling every fiber of her being cry out in a kind of joy just to be connected with his again, and knowing, seeing, that Gideon was just as affected, was enough.

Oh, God help me, was her last coherent thought.
And she moved to close the distance.

He hadn't intended to kiss her.

He'd intended to find Carly, corner her, apologize as much as it took, and then make her listen to reason. Kissing, particularly the sort that normally led to the removal of any and all bits of clothing, had not featured anywhere in his genius plan. Of course, having her skin him alive with her words and her hurt and anger hadn't featured either, but she'd done one hell of a job at that. And he could have taken it, taken all of it and let it be … until she told him he couldn't touch her, that she didn't want him, even if every inch of that tight, angry, delicious little body was screaming otherwise loudly enough for him to hear.

Next time, he might do well to remember how the woman affected him. Except he'd tried, and the sight of her, the scent of her, had still taken him down like a ton of bricks. So much for subtlety, Gideon decided as he pulled her into his arms. At least she wasn't yelling any longer. And despite all of her protestations, Carly didn't seem to mind.

That was something, at least. And it could be that a kiss, that even the oddly raw sort of passion he felt for her was an acceptable addition to the strategy. But when he'd brought her to him, he felt something inside himself take that last little nudge towards the edge.

And take the fall.

Her eyes, like the sea before a storm, seemed to expand enough to envelop him, and he felt his heart quicken its pace to match hers. He watched the soft pout of her lips part in anticipation, and as that delicious combination of vanilla and ripe, fresh berry, of everything he couldn't resist flowed off of her and through him, Gideon closed his eyes and stopped fighting what he'd known since the first moment he'd laid eyes on Carly.

My one. My only.

If only ...

And then her mouth met his, and he couldn't think at all. There was only Carly, the sensation of her, and for now, it was enough.

The crush of their lips against one another wasn't remotely gentle, and yet there was a sweetness to it as he felt Carly's hand thread up through his hair, as she dragged him down to her. Her small hand curled in his hair as she gave in to him, making a sexy little whimper in the back of her throat as she opened her mouth to his, willingly giving herself to him, asking without words for more. And Gideon was more than happy to oblige. He angled his head to deepen the kiss, sliding his hands down to cup her backside and bring her up even closer against him, letting her feel how she affected him, how hard he always seemed to be for her. She strained against him while he nipped at her lips, matched the wild rhythm of her tongue as it rubbed against his.

She wasn't quite through being angry yet. He could feel it, and oh, he knew even better than she did that she was well within her rights, even though he knew he'd never be as sorry as he ought to be. If things had been different, after all, he might not be here with this beautiful woman in his arms, enjoying the benefits of her decision to channel all of her anger into sexual energy that he could reap the benefits of.

"Gideon," she sighed as she moved her head to kiss along his jawline, to nibble at his ear. And some dim, still active part of his common sense told him that if they didn't stop, *now,* he was going to have her on the floor in a matter of minutes. *Calm down,* he commanded himself. Carly nipped at his neck and slid her legs around him, immediately negating any effect that might have had. A few more minutes of this could hardly be a bad thing, after all.

Gideon was just lowering her to the floor when he heard the bell above the door jingle out in the shop, and a female voice call Carly's name. *Damn.* And she'd just about convinced him to postpone their talk for a bit, too. Bloody commerce. Didn't people here look out the window at that much snow and figure staying in was better than going out? Well, he supposed, there was nothing for it now.

"Carly," he said softly as he straightened. He nuzzled her neck, trailed kisses down it even as he told her to stop. "Carly, love. I'm afraid we've got company."

"Mmm." She continued her tender assault on his ear. "That's nice."

She had no idea, he thought as he bit back a groan. "Unless you want to put on a show for them, which you've nearly convinced me to do at this point, you might want to think about saving this for later."

"Later. Customer." She breathed against his neck, but then some part of what he'd said seemed to get through. Carly raised her head to look at him, and he had to smile. She was delightfully mussed, her lips full and rosy from his kisses. Her eyes were slightly glazed, and all of that blond hair he wanted so desperately to get his hands in was coming loose from the elastic she'd pulled it back with.

Ravished, she looked. Gideon liked knowing he was responsible for it. It certainly suited her. He'd never met a woman who could surprise him so with her moods. Carly Silver was shy and proper one moment, cool and collected the next, and then a fiery little tigress who'd just as likely claw your eyes out as tear your clothes off and devour you. He had underestimated her, he saw now, and was sorry for it. How much, he didn't know. But he would certainly file that revelation away for future reference.

"Customer. Oh. God." Her eyes cleared. "Um. Do you think you could put me down?"

And just like that, she was back to shy and proper. Gideon grinned.

"Then you've decided not to throw me out?"

She just sighed, but there was a twinkle in her eye. "Could you have been any more persuasive?"

The woman's voice called again, a note of concern in it this time. Going against what he wanted to do, Gideon lowered Carly back to her feet.

"Go on, then. We can continue this very, mmm, *stimulating* conversation when you're through."

"When *I'm* through?" Carly smiled now, but there was a hint of something in it Gideon wasn't sure he liked. "Oh no, pal. You might have convinced me to let you stay, but my benevolence doesn't come for free. And if you're going to be protecting me, I see no reason why you can't make yourself useful."

Gideon felt himself wince as he caught her meaning. He'd been impressed, from what he'd seen, with her whimsical little hobbit hole of a shop, full of books he'd never dream of opening and lovely, sparkling things he'd likely never buy. Too *female,* although he got the appeal. Sort of. But spending the day there would be like living on another planet. And that, he saw, was exactly what she was intending.

"Slave labor?"

Her smile deepened, and Gideon was helpless in the face of Carly's winking dimples.

"Exactly."

Resistance, he could see, was futile. And so, trying not to drag his feet so that she'd notice, Gideon followed her out into the store … and onto Venus.

Chapter Ten

ONE OF THE THINGS ABOUT LIVING IN A SMALL TOWN that could be both a blessing and a curse was the tendency for news to travel at roughly the speed of sound. As Carly stood at the door of Bodice Rippers, watching the slow, swirling fall of snowflakes in the fading half-light and feeling the ache in the arches of her feet that always meant a productive day, she had to concede that today was one of the ones where it leaned decidedly toward blessing.

She flipped the sign to CLOSED, braced her palms in the small of her back, and stretched. Who would have thought that word she had somehow found a cover-hunk-quality Highlander to work in the store for the day would have brought out the entire female (and, truth be told, a little of the male) population of a town that was still, for all practical purposes, snowed in? The predicted rotten weather, however, hadn't returned, and apparently everyone was tired of being cooped up. The plows had been out in force, and although the snow banks were piled several feet high in some places, Jamison Winslow, who owned the sporting goods shop just down the street, had been busy with his extremely large snowblower clearing the sidewalks all morning.

Kinnik's Harbor was waking back up, and apparently, in desperate need of entertainment. Well, Carly thought with a smile, they wouldn't be hearing any complaints from her. And Celestine and her mouth, she decided, were deserving of some freebies the next time they came in. Because it had been the best day, profit-wise, since the weather had turned cold, gray, and snowy almost a month ago. Fall-That-Was-Really-Winter was an old tradition in this part of New York, and this year had been no exception. The problem was, when it happened, it was always a crapshoot as to whether people were actually going to work up the energy to get off their rear ends and leave their houses.

Apparently, Carly mused as she heard the scrape of a box across the floor and an irritable sigh behind her, she'd found the secret for making them do it. All she had to do was have a muscular hunk in the shop bending and lifting all day, every day, and she'd be a millionaire inside of a year.

Six months if she got him to wear a kilt, she thought, picturing it with a wicked grin.

Of course, she would also be hot, bothered, and continually, annoyingly jealous of the masses of eye-batting, tight-shirt wearing females who flocked in to hang all over this particular hunk all day. She pursed her lips, turned her head towards her grumpy, unwilling volunteer. It was entirely possible, she decided, that the ulcers she was bound to get wouldn't be worth it.

She had to bite back her smile when she looked at Gideon. Judging by the sour expression on his face, the rumpled, slightly sweaty appearance of him, and the large, book-filled box at his feet that he looked very close to drop-kicking, he wouldn't see the humor in anything right about now.

"You wanted these *where,* Highness?"

Ouch, Carly thought with a small wince. It *was* possible she'd worked him a little hard today, she supposed. Not that he hadn't deserved it. But her stockroom really had needed reorganizing. And the new historicals really *had* needed their own display. And an awful lot of the customers *had* seemed to want Gideon's help, specifically, in finding titles, even though everything was clearly marked and alphabetized by author.

Well. It was probably time to end his torment.

"You know, I can get that myself tomorrow. Just leave it."

He looked at her darkly. "With pleasure." And then he did kick the box, sending it skidding across the floor to stop beside the counter.

"Hey," Carly complained, even though instinct told her to leave it be. "I have to sell those, Gideon." And then she had to make herself stand her ground, because Gideon, looking more than a little mutinous, stalked over to stand only inches away from her, plucking a book from the box and dangling it before him like something unpleasantly smelly and dead on his way.

"I'm aware of that, Carly," he growled, and there was more than a hint of wolf in it. "I have, in fact, been up to my bloody ears in what you sell all day. I have learned the subtle and fascinating differences between subgenres, been lectured on what does and does not constitute a decent sex scene, and stood in the middle of the most bloodydamn boring debate in history about romantic cover art. I have also," he continued as Carly found herself taking an involuntary step back from the force of his onslaught, "had my ass pinched, patted, grabbed, and otherwise fondled every time I turned around, all in the name of making you happy. And so, Miss Silver," he finished, his voice dropping even further towards possibly violent, "I must ask: *are* you happy?"

She honestly didn't know whether to giggle or run screaming. He was kind of sexy when he was pissed off, though. Even if he looked just about ready to bite her. She finally managed a response that to her sounded like nothing more than a high-pitched squeak.

"Uh-huh." She nodded, and she knew her lips were quivering with that unwanted giggle. To his credit, when he noticed, Gideon simply glared at her, spun on his heel, and stalked back into the stockroom. When the thumping and banging started, Carly gave up, pressing her hands to her mouth and laughing so hard she had tears in her eyes. It really was sweet that he'd stayed and been her slave for the day. Not that she'd meant to torture him … at least, not quite so much. And who had been grabbing his ass all day?

She was still giggling intermittently and wiping at her eyes when a familiar face appeared at her door. Carly tried for a frown, but it didn't seem to be working.

Sensing a favorable atmosphere, Regan opened the door and stepped in. Her eyebrows rose at Carly's appearance, which, Carly figured, was probably slightly deranged.

"Oh no," Carly managed, pointing at her. "Uh-uh. You're banished."

Regan winced. "He told you it was me, huh?"

"No, I recognized the clothes, eventually. Dave, right? I used to think he slept in that shirt. And for the record, it is *so* weird that you have a closet full of ex-boyfriend clothes at your house."

Regan shrugged and looked unrepentant. "I always mean to burn them. I just never seem to get around to it."

"Pack rat. You're lucky you have that huge house to squirrel stuff away in. Now begone. You have no power here." Carly knew her stern face was failing miserably. She also knew she was defeated utterly when Regan held out the familiar brown box tied with pink ribbon, *Decadence* stamped across the top in pink foil.

"Damn. Does German chocolate cheesecake still have power here, then?"

Carly tried to resist. For roughly three seconds. She looked balefully at Regan and sighed, holding out her hand. "Do I have to writhe around and howl that I'm melting, or can I just eat the cake and shut up about it?"

Regan grinned, walked over, and handed the box to Carly. "I'm on board with the latter if you are. So," she craned her head over Carly's shoulder, obviously canvassing the shop, "should I not have bothered taking pity on him, or was I right, as usual?"

Carly snorted as she lifted the top of the box and inhaled. "Ahh, chocolate. Regan, you're neither comatose nor stupid, and you would have to be one or the other not to know he was here all day. Which doesn't make you 'right as usual.' It makes you 'possibly not completely wrong,' and also a pain in my ass. And that *is* as usual."

"And you know you love me." She leaned against the counter while Carly drooled over the cheesecake.

"Actually, I just use you for baked goods." Carly glanced up, smiled sweetly. "I'm surprised you haven't figured that out yet." Regan just laughed, stopping abruptly when the sound of something large and heavy hitting the floor erupted from the back room.

"Jesus, did you chain him up back there or something?"

Carly turned her head, studied the curtained doorway intently for a moment, and shook her head. "I think he might be reorganizing my stockroom. Onto the floor. I'm not sure working at a romantic bookshop agrees with him."

Regan frowned in the same direction. "Get felt up, did he?"

"Apparently. And Lizziebeth was in here driving him crazy for at least half an hour. I'm pretty sure she was one of the main culprits."

"That bitch!" Regan was plainly delighted. "Someone should have gotten it on video, sent it to that fish-lipped husband of hers. Then again, I think continuing to have to crawl into bed with *that* every night is probably punishment enough." She made an icky face and stuck out her tongue. Then her look turned serious.

"So listen. When I said you needed some adventure in your life, I didn't mean you should, you know, go all out and find a werewolf with a homicidal maniac after him to sleep with."

Carly eyed her as she straightened up the counter, surprised. "Well. Someone got awfully chatty this morning. FYI, I'm not sleeping with him. And are you trying to absolve yourself of guilt for telling me I should?"

"No," sighed Regan. "No, I have lots of guilt. There are plenty more German chocolate cheesecakes coming to you in the future. But honestly, Carly … what were the chances?"

"Zero, unless you're me, probably," Carly replied with a mirthless little laugh. Regan just continued to look unhappy. "Oh, Regan, babe," she consoled her, patting her shoulder, "this is *so* not your fault, cosmically or otherwise. I let him in. I let him stay after I knew what he was. I own it."

"I still think maybe I caused this by wishing for you too hard. God got drunk. My wishes exploded on you. That would be my luck."

"Nah," Carly replied, inhaling the promising aroma of her Guilt Cheesecake. "Actually, as things stand, I'm glad you helped him out. Apparently I'm going to be needing a bodyguard."

"Bastard," grumbled Regan, although it was, in Carly's opinion, a little half-hearted. "Getting you into this. I told him, if you get hurt, I'm going to kill him. I don't care how much he annoys you, Carly. You let him stick to you until he sorts this weird family issue out."

"Don't worry about that part of it. I'm a little freaked out … hell, who am I kidding, I'm *terrified* … so I want nothing more than Gideon MacInnes, twenty-four-seven, until this is over." And oh, you don't even know the half of *that,* she added mentally. "Anyway," Carly murmured quietly, "he doesn't really annoy me all that much."

"Uh-huh." Regan's tone indicated she had a lot of thoughts on that, which she would, out of deference to the urgency of the situation, save to air out later. Carly was grateful. She'd had enough introspection for one day.

"He said he'll protect me until this is over. I actually think I believe him. Not that I've got a lot of reason to, I suppose. But then I can't see that I have a lot of choice." Which could be said about a lot of things that had happened to her in the last twenty-four hours, Carly thought with a tiny twinge of resentment, but she fought it back. What she had told Regan was true, after all. She had taken him in. She'd let him stay. And good, bad, or indifferent, she was in a mess of her own making.

"Well, I wouldn't mess with him." Regan's smile turned wicked. "*That* way, anyway. In the other, more preferable ways, I'm not lucky enough to have the choice. Unlike some other people I know."

"And back to the gutter we go. Regan," Carly sighed as she began taking the money out of the register for the night, "I appreciate the obsession with my sex life. I think, anyway. But honestly, if I come out of this in one piece, I will be completely satisfied."

Almost.

Before Regan could open her mouth to argue, there was another loud thump from the stockroom, accompanied by a curse that was just slightly louder. Both heads swiveled back in that direction, and Carly wondered exactly how much fun he was going to be on the walk home. If she talked to him, would he toss her into a snow bank? Regan straightened, and Carly knew immediately she was being deserted.

"Well," she said as she started to back toward the door, "I can see my work here is done. You two enjoy your evening. Call me if you need anything."

"Oh, uh-uh. You just wait a damn minute." Carly put her hands on her hips and faced her. "Considering," she began, to the sound of another muttered oath from the back, "that the renewal of this little partnership is mostly your doing, I would think *at least* a ride home is in order."

There was a twist of her lips, a narrowing of her eyes. "I hope, if I agree, that you'll consider transporting you and your charming werewolf friend full payment of my debt. Because I don't care what kind of a mood he's in, I'm not going to be happy if he chews up my leather."

"Done." She looked around, decided there was nothing left that couldn't wait until tomorrow morning. Which was, at the moment, too bad. Being able to stall a little longer might make her at least a little less apprehensive about going back to get Gideon, much less taking him home for the night.

"All right, then. I'll go warm up the van, wait for you out there." Regan started for the door, then stopped, shook her head, and turned back. "Look, I know this is only marginally my business, but would you please take a little advice from the expert on failed relationships?"

Carly sealed the deposit bag, locked up the cash register. "If you tell me to jump in bed with him one more time, I'm going to smack you."

"Nope, not this time. I think I've said my piece on that." She smiled, but the look in her dark eyes was serious. "And minus the Dr. Drew stuff, all I've got for you is this: chances are, in a few days, tops, he's out of here. You just might want to let him know how you feel about him before it's too late." She held up her hands.

"Just my not-so-humble opinion, for what it's worth. I'll be out in the car."

And, Regan being Regan, she was out the door before Carly could even begin to formulate a reply, leaving her to stew in her own juices. Naturally, she'd hummed the appropriate ABBA song as the door shut behind her: "Take a Chance on Me." With Regan, it was always disco.

Carly shook her head a little. They were from totally different worlds. They lived thousands of miles apart. They weren't even exactly the same species, for God's sake!

And she knew, as she sighed softly and moved around the counter to grab her coat, that she wouldn't be able to get it out of her head. Regan was right about a couple of things, after all. She wanted him. He wanted her. Maybe, despite everything else, it was just that simple.

And maybe, whether it was or not, it was time for her to quit tiptoeing around it, to go against her instincts. Sometimes, it felt as though she'd been waiting her whole life for something to happen. But if she was really falling as hard and fast for Gideon as she suspected, waiting around wasn't going to do it, not if the fates had decided to pair up Mr. Stubborn with Miss Inertia. So she would give it a push, or possibly, because this was Gideon she was dealing with, a massive shove, and see how things looked when the dust cleared.

It could, Carly knew, be the biggest mistake of her life. She was no psychic. But she did know one thing.

Stirring up that dust was going to be an experience she'd never forget.

Somewhere between rearranging the boxes on the
shelves in Carly's stockroom (he refused to call it
tossing them around, as he'd been accused of when
Carly had discovered what he'd been up to, although he
was almost certain nothing in those boxes had been
breakable) and arriving back at her dark, warm little
house, Gideon's temper had cooled off. Some of it may
have been due to the subzero temperature of Regan's van
on the short drive home, but Gideon suspected most of it
was because he'd finally figured out who he was really
angry at, and it wasn't Carly.

Had he ever made such an ass out of himself for a
woman? Oh, he could blame her all he liked, Gideon
thought irritably as he followed his unusually quiet
hostess into the house, watched her flip on the lights as
she avoided looking at him, speaking to him, or otherwise acknowledging his presence. But he'd been a
willing participant in the daylong debacle at her little
shop, lifting things for women who pretended to be helpless, indulging them when they flirted with him,
ignoring it when they were ogling him and giving
running commentary on his physique to one another in
stage whispers.

And it might have been amusing, really ... he didn't
think he'd ever had so many females tripping over themselves for his company, and any man would have been
hard-pressed to mind. Except that no matter how much
he tried to convince himself otherwise, her wanting him
to stay and help her for the day hadn't contained one

single expectation that he would dash about at her heels like an eager puppy for the better part of it, trying to please her customers and friends just so he could see a hint of those lovely dimples winking at him from across the room. No, he had done the latter part himself, after he'd sworn he'd never make a fool out of himself for any woman. Ever. And the fact that the whole thing had been preceded by his nearly mauling her only made the whole thing worse, in his mind.

Gideon hung back and watched her click into the kitchen on her sexy little kitten heels, fixated on the way her simple, wide-legged gray slacks and emerald sweater clung to the ripe curve of her bottom, the swell of her breasts with every move she made. Even now he could only feel like a predator whenever he was near her, his nostrils full of her scent, his fingers curled into his palms so that they couldn't reach, grab, caress the way they wanted to. He was a man who valued his control, and it was rapidly deserting him where Carly Silver was concerned.

She knew he was watching her, he saw from the way she nibbled at her full bottom lip, the way she always did when she was nervous. Still, he knew she wasn't about to give him the satisfaction of telling him to stop. Which was good, because Gideon had no intention of stopping in any case. Still, it wouldn't hurt to twist her tail just a bit, particularly since she'd agreed they should be together at all times … well, outside her place of employment, Gideon amended. He'd had just about enough of *that* to last ten lifetimes, and truly, the hordes of chatty women milling about that place would frighten off the most determined attacker even in blackest midnight.

But still, the rest of the time, she was his. That made locking him out again a bit difficult, didn't it? And a good thing, too, Gideon decided, because he was finding out that beneath her collected exterior there was quite a bit of fire, if you knew where to poke to bring it out. Gideon smiled to himself at the memory of her with her finger poking into his chest, chastising him for "manhandling her inventory," as she put it, while the big, innocent blue eyes that had so ensnared him blazed so brightly they did everything but turn red and shoot flames. He'd never had a woman give him hell like that before.

It bothered him a bit that he seemed to like it.

"If the weather clears off the rest of the way and they reopen the highway tomorrow, I'd like to go over to the inn, pick up my things and bring them back here."

She lifted one pale eyebrow, glanced quickly at him before continuing to rummage through the cupboard she'd opened. "It's not like you need my permission to go places. I'll be safe at work. Go for it."

"Ah, but it's a bit out of the way. A bit far for me to leave you here unattended." He tried to look serious as her eyes shot back up, still spitting sparks from earlier.

"Well, I have to work. If you want me to come, I guess you're going to have to wait."

Gideon bent to unlace his boots so that he could toe them off, moving slowly and unconcernedly. "That's not very convenient, though, as there are some things I need, considering. Why don't you just go in a bit late?"

Gideon hid his smile when he heard the cupboard slam. "You know, it isn't actually very *convenient* for me to have one big, smelly werewolf imposing on me at home while I'm being stalked by another one … who, as we both know, wouldn't even be anywhere near my personal space if it weren't for big, smelly werewolf number one … so no, I think you can wait until *after* I'm done working. You know, at that place with the books that now probably all have footprints on them."

Gideon cocked his head, considered her for a moment. Her lips were pursed, her hands were on her hips, her hair was starting to come loose from its tie again. She looked like a very angry, very sexy schoolteacher.

Mission accomplished.

"You should be happy I want to go. I'll smell much better once I get my things."

"I should be happy." She inhaled with a soft hiss, then slapped her hands down on the counter and glared at him over the breakfast bar. "You know what? I am happy. I'm so frigging overjoyed, in fact, that to show my gratitude for what you have brought into my life, I am letting *you* make us dinner. I, on the other hand, am going to go enjoy a shower." She glared at him, tossed her head, and swept her arm across the kitchen. "Have fun."

Carly stalked off past him down the hallway, and after a moment, he heard the bathroom door slam. He started chuckling, even as he shook his head. He really shouldn't have pushed her after the way she'd gone after him about her books, but she was so damned beautiful when she was worked up. And, he could admit to himself as he wandered into the small kitchen, it seemed that working her up this way was a lot safer than working her up the way he had initially done that morning.

Though he supposed he did owe her dinner.

Gideon opened one neatly organized cupboard, staring at the small bottles of spices blankly. The kitchen had never been his natural habitat. *Iargail* had its own cook, his cousin Harriet, and the only thing he'd ever spent much time doing in their kitchen was quietly hunting for Harriet's carefully hidden sweets, or pilfering the leftovers. He'd been good at that. Actually making something on his own, however, was another story.

On a hunch, he went to the refrigerator, felt on top of it. When his hand closed on the paper-clipped sheaf of papers, Gideon knew he'd hit the jackpot. As he pulled down the small stack of take-out menus and began to thumb through them, he listened to the water running in the bathroom and imagined Carly in there, the water running over the curves he couldn't seem to be able to keep his mind off of. He had a problem, and he knew it. He ought to be working on the Malachi situation, ought to be actively hunting for his would-be assassins, trying to either find them or draw them out ... something proactive. Which reminded him, he also needed to check Carly's messages for anything from Gabriel. But he'd spent his day staring at Carly instead, and he was still having a difficult time working up any remorse about it.

Some of it might be overconfidence on his part, he supposed. Being ripped apart by his hunters never entered his mind as a possibility. He was strong, he was well trained. Next time, they wouldn't even be able to limp away. He would be ready. And it was true, it was better for Carly to be watched, to be near him, at all times until they showed themselves so he could get rid of them. But there was more.

"Ah, Chinese. Good choice." He plucked out the long, numbered menu, smiled at the small circles she'd made around her favorites, tidy, organized soul that she was. He could see her sitting at her little table, carefully marking the things she liked best on the menus, just in case she wasn't doing the ordering. It was a pretty picture. But then, how could it not be? She was in it.

And he was completely crazy about her.

Gideon froze as it hit him fully, his heart expanding painfully at the realization. He barely noticed as the menu crumpled in his hand, then fell to the floor.

The fact that he'd clicked with her on some primal level, well, he could almost deal with that. Almost. Even though it meant that as far as finding a permanent partner went, it was either Carly or no one. That was his biology. He wasn't the first MacInnes Wolf to bond with an unsuitable partner, and he wouldn't be the last. But he hadn't expected to feel so much beyond the expected desire for her, or to feel even that desire on so many levels. At every turn Carly Silver had surprised him, charmed him, intrigued him. Until he knew she was a woman he could happily spend a lifetime discovering.

Gideon slid his hands into his hair, tugged to try and get his brain functioning again. Coming here, it seemed, was the mistake that kept on giving, and he was starting to feel like he was more than a little in over his head. Two days with Carly, and everything was hearts and flowers. He was being stalked, and all he could seem to think of was playing house! The elders had always warned him it would be fast, but this was madness. And the distinct possibility, hell, the *probability* that Carly was feeling it too … he needed to finish this and leave. He needed time and space to sort out what to do about Carly, if anything, once Malachi and his friends had been dealt with. Because the longer he stayed, the harder it was going to be to just walk away and not look back, which was what he was going to need to do. Probably. He thought.

Christ.

Gideon picked up the menu to smooth it, then called in the order to the little Chinese place just off of Main he'd seen on their way back this evening. Thanks to the plows and the fact that the snow was only falling lightly and intermittently, they were, thank God, delivering. Carly also had a tab with them, which was fortunate since he didn't really want to have to beg her for money as well as her car. He had plenty of money, just not on him. But this way, he could stop and pay tomorrow.

In about twenty minutes, dinner would be served. Problem solved.

If only all of his problems were that easy, Gideon thought ruefully. He opened the fridge, grabbed one of the three beers he'd found tucked way in the back that had probably been there since she'd moved in, and wandered back out into the living room to sink onto Carly's couch, stare out the window, and wait.

What he was waiting for, he only wished he knew.

Carly wished she could hide in the shower, definitely for the night, possibly forever. Yes, it was unrealistic, but considering that was the bent her life had taken anyway, it might not hurt to try. She stood in the hot spray, lifted her hands to study them.

Pruney. Well, that wasn't going to work, either.

Hell with it.

She twisted the knob to shut off the water, reached around the curtain to grab her giant, fluffy bath towel, and stood in the residual warmth as long as she could, toweling off her skin and then scrubbing at her hair. She was thinking, a habit which she was seriously considering giving up after her life got back to some semblance of normal. Because thus far, thinking hadn't done anything for her but give her the beginnings of a nice tension headache.

To seduce or not to seduce. That was the question. Well, besides the question of whether or not she was even capable of a full-on seduction, but Carly really wanted to give herself the benefit of the doubt on that one. She'd talked herself into giving it a go, until she saw the disarray Gideon had put her stockroom into. Then she'd just wanted to take one of those boxes and … well, actually, she was pretty sure that somewhere in her fit of temper she'd told him exactly where she'd like to shove one of them. Not that he'd been repentant.

And not that she hadn't spent the whole time wanting to jump him, which just made her angrier. Carly pumped some vanilla-scented lotion into her palm and began to smooth it over her skin, frowning while she mulled over what to do with Mr. High-Handed, who seemed to have decided to make himself comfortable in her space, up to and including *telling* her that he was going to be taking her car for a bit, thank you very much, and you'll need to come so be a good girl, won't you? She bit her lip, counted slowly to ten so as not to punch anything and ruin her nails. God, being with Gideon was worse than PMS as far as her mood swings were concerned. She knew what Regan would say … it was time for a healthy release of tension. Which was all well and good, except Carly still wasn't sure that there was anything healthy about this fixation on Gideon. How could she be so crazy about someone she barely knew? And earlier, when he'd managed to knock her socks off yet again, the way he'd held her …

Love. The word formed in her mind immediately before she could put up any defense against it, promising to send her down the road to Migraine City if she didn't knock it the hell off. This was not about deep inner feelings. This was about finally having the guts to take something she wanted, just on a purely physical level.

And oh, horrifying. So, no thinking. Or as little as she could manage, Carly decided as she combed through her hair, eyeing herself critically in the oval mirror she'd hung above the pedestal sink. Not bad. Little tired, maybe. She wasn't big on a lot of makeup, but she had adequate emergency supplies for special occasions.

The possibility of sex, no matter how remote, definitely counted. In this case, as both an emergency and as a special occasion.

She dried her hair until it fell in loose, shining waves around her shoulders, slid on the simple black satin bra and thong that made up the entirety of what Regan had decided was her "sex collection" (how two items of underwear could possibly merit the term "collection" was something she'd brought up, but it hadn't seemed to matter, as usual) and pulled on her favorite jeans, the ones that shaped her butt somewhere between ScarJo's and J. Lo's. With that and the tight black scoop-neck tee-shirt she'd dug out, all she needed, Carly decided as she examined all her angles in the mirror, was a little eye shadow, gloss, and probably mascara since her lashes were pretty blond. Nothing major. Then, she'd just saunter on out, she guessed, and … something. Something possibly good, and possibly naked. She and Gideon. Naked. Oh, God.

No thinking, she commanded herself again. Otherwise, she really was going to live in the bathroom forever. She got her small pink makeup bag out of the tall, slim cabinet against the wall, rummaged until she found what she needed, and went to work. A smudge of gold across her eyelids, a hint of pale pink shimmer across her lips (flavored, just in case, she told herself, and thank God for Philosophy's nearly edible lip gloss). All easy enough, until she got to her nemesis, the tube of mascara. Carly leaned close to the mirror, brandishing the wand like a foreign and potentially dangerous object. Her tongue was out as she concentrated, a habit that didn't bother her nearly as much as the thought of stabbing her eye out.

She brushed lightly against her top lashes, cursing the evil genius who'd invented the stuff. She was usually at least semi-coordinated, but she always seemed to klutz up when it got to the really fine detail work. Probably, Carly decided, gingerly going after the lower lashes now, she should get rich enough to hire a makeup artist to follow her around all the time. A nice Lotto win would probably do it. Or a super-rich husband. But then…

"Ow! Shit!" She yelped, dropping the wand on the floor and clapping her hand over her eye, the one into which she'd just smooshed a nice glob of viscous black goo. She fumbled for a washcloth, wet it, and scrubbed at her watering eye. Years of exposure to her foul-mouthed brothers came pouring out all at once. "Piece of shit god damn son of a bitch!"

Well, that was nice, Carly thought, still muttering every obscenity she could think of as she glared at her reflection. Now she had a slightly swollen, non-mascaraed, violently red eye. And one pretty one. Very nice.

"Carly? Everything all right in there?" Gideon's concerned voice was right outside the door. Even better.

"I'm fine. It's nothing." *Go away,* she silently added as she gave in to temptation and rubbed the itchy eye again before dropping to her knees to pick up the mascara wand where it had rolled beneath the sink. So much for alluring beauty, she decided. She hoped to God some Visine would at least tone down the red.

"Are you sure?" Carly closed her eyes as she grabbed the wand and started to rise. Would it hurt him, just once, to do what she wanted and shut up about it?

"If I wasn't sure," she snapped, "I wouldn't have said … *ow shitshitshitshitshit!*"

She dropped the wand again to clutch the top of her head, which she'd just slammed against the underside of the sink. It hurt, enough to bring tears to her eyes, and she dropped back to sit on the floor and cradle her head, completely defeated. "Ow. And don't you dare open that door."

Naturally, he opened the door. She didn't even want to know what he thought when he got his first look at her sprawled on the floor with a bump on her head and a puffy eye, and to his credit, she only saw his lips twitch once as he took it all in. It was more than she could say for herself, unfortunately. At that moment, it was suddenly too much for her, too much seriousness, too much everything. Carly felt the giggles bubbling up her throat, felt her shoulders start to shake with them even before they were out. Some seduction. It would have taken all three stooges, but she ... she had talent. Gideon raised his eyebrows at her, and for some reason, that just finished her. She hid her head and burst out laughing.

"Dare I ask what all this is about?"

"I was attacked by beauty products," she managed between giggles. "I lost."

"Never would have guessed. Did you stab yourself in the eye?" Gideon crouched, angling his head to try and get a better look. "You can still see out of it, can't you? Come on, now let me see." He reached for her chin, but she scooted back, still gasping for air.

"No, just leave it. I'll recover." She waved him off, but he was determined.

"If you've managed to poke your eye out, you'd better let me see."

She smacked his hand away again and rolled her eyes. "I didn't poke my eye out. I just got makeup in it. And I bumped my head. Now *stop,* I'm fine." She swept her hair out of her face and wiped at her eyes again, the laughter subsiding but leaving her with a smile and a kind of amused humiliation. If Gideon still wanted her, she guessed he might as well know what he was getting. Super Spaz. She was certainly in all her glory tonight.

Gideon moved his hand but didn't rise, just sat looking at her as though she'd grown an extra head. "Why were you fiddling with your eyes? They were fine before."

"I ... well, I wanted to look pretty. Damn it." The defiance was totally ruined by the fact that she couldn't get the grin off her face, but she tried.

The corner of his mouth twisted just slightly. "And this would be achieved by murdering yourself in the bathroom?"

Carly could only laugh as a fresh wave of amusement hit her and shake her head. Men were so clueless sometimes, and Gideon, a testament to his sex, did indeed look confused.

"You didn't need to do anything to yourself. You looked fine before you did ... whatever it was you were trying to do in here."

Carly just gave him the most beleaguered look she could manage and sighed, loudly. Obviously, this was going to require spelling out. "No, genius. I wanted *you* to think I looked pretty. Not 'fine.' I was shooting for several degrees above fine."

"Ah." Carly swore she actually saw the light go on then, right before those suddenly less confused eyes dropped to take in her clothes and the cleavage that was, at least, as well displayed as she'd intended. "Why should it matter what I think?"

If only she had an uncomplicated answer to that one, her life would be a hell of a lot simpler. She wished. "Because. I ... like you." She winced as soon as the words were out of her mouth. She *liked* him? Yes, this was why she kept making out with him at every available opportunity. Could she *be* any more high school cheesy? She probably should have just passed him one of those old "do you like me check yes or no" notes and been done with it. It would have at least saved her an eye injury and a big lump on the top of her head.

"Oh, that's awful, just forget it." She plunked her face into her hands again and played ostrich.

"I like you too. I'm sorry you're unhappy about that." Gideon's voice was all rich amusement. "Is this related to your 'big, smelly werewolf' comment from earlier? Because I'm going to have to protest; I have been showering regularly."

She looked up again. Yep, he was smiling. She might have been too, if the whole thing hadn't been quite so humiliating. As it was, trying to explain herself was bound to only make things worse, but she had to give it a try. Even if he was, as she strongly suspected, about two seconds away from bursting into hysterical laughter, possibly while pointing.

"You know what I mean, Gideon. I think you're ..."

"Pretty?"

"Oh, for the love of ..." She reached for the nearest object to her hand, which turned out to be a box of tissues, and tossed it at him. He caught it, all his amusement showing in the deep crinkles at the corners of his eyes. "Forget it." She struggled to her feet, slapping away the hand he put out to help her up. "I'm not interested in making any more of an ass out of myself right now. I don't think I'd live through it."

The size of him, the way his presence seemed to fill the small room had Carly suddenly shooting into sensory hyperawareness. And just like that, none of this was funny anymore. None of it seemed quite so much like a meaningless game. She was going to need some air, some space, and soon. Because being so close to Gideon without touching him was starting to actually hurt.

Still, she managed a strained smile. "Just leave me in peace, because the mortification is starting to sink in, and you're not going to want to see this."

And then there was even less space, because he moved in on her, closing the gap between them to mere inches. When she looked away, his large, rough hand slipped gently beneath her chin to tip her gaze back up to him. "Carly?"

"Mmm?"

"You're not an ass."

"That is *definitely* a matter of personal opinion right now."

"But I'm afraid I don't think you're pretty."

"Ah." She could feel the heat flooding her cheeks while she wished she could just sink through the floor and disappear.

Gideon moved his hand, tucked some of the heavy fall of her hair behind her ear with a tenderness that stole Carly's breath. "I think you're beautiful," he murmured.

"Oh. I mean, oh," she stammered, now completely flustered. She'd never had a man look at her quite like this, never heard quite so much meaning implied in that simple statement. "I didn't mean … I hope you don't feel like you have to …"

He continued as though he hadn't heard her, which she was grateful for. Her brain and mouth seemed to have gotten out of sync somewhere along the way. "You are, in fact, the loveliest thing I've ever seen." And she couldn't look away from him, from the shimmering glow that filled his eyes. She couldn't, and she wasn't sure she ever wanted to again.

"Oh," she said again. Then she cocked her head at him, unable to help herself. "All things considered, I think you may have a pretty low bar for that."

Gideon chuckled, low and deep, and Carly felt a familiar liquid heat settle into the core of her, tightening her belly while she looked at him. "Does this mean you're through being pissed off at me for all of the egregious ass-pinching you got today?"

"Only if you're through sulking about those bloody boxes."

"I'll think about it."

He laughed again, lowering his head until he was only a breath away from her, and when he spoke again his soft burr had become the ragged growl that never ceased to send delicious shivers coursing through her body. "You're enough to drive a man mad, Carly. Your smile, with those bloody adorable dimples, your laugh." He rubbed his lips against her forehead, her cheek. "That delicious wee round bottom. And God in heaven, the way you *smell* …"

"Hey," she protested with what breath she had left, "I though we were done with the cheap shots about hygiene!"

"No," he laughed softly as he nuzzled the sensitive spot behind her ear, "no, it's like vanilla, and fresh cream, and berries."

She drew back then, her eyebrows raised. "I smell like *dessert* to you?"

"Mmm, yes," he breathed, and when he smiled, it was what Carly could only think of as wolfish. And to her surprise, she felt that wildness stirring within her to meet whatever lurked just beneath his skin. It promised, in a whisper, to melt away what inhibitions and misgivings she had left, until there was just the two of them. And intense, indisputable need.

"You *are* dessert, Carly Silver. And all I can seem to think about is taking a bite."

It was now or never, Carly knew. Time to run away, or to run to. And she realized, in that moment, that there had never really been a decision to make.

She took the final step, pressing herself up against him, biting back the moan that wanted to escape when that connection was made. She heard the hiss when he drew in his breath, saw what she wanted awaken behind the intense glow of his gaze.

No matter what came after, it was time to welcome the beast … and embrace her own.

"Only," she purred softly, "if I can bite you back."

He felt as though he were being led into some decadent dream by a wanton, fallen angel. Gideon had
expected her to want what he wanted, to feel what he
felt. To grant his silent wish and wrap herself around
him, immediately, giving in to the intense heat that was
now arcing between them like lightning and let him take
her right there, with slight variations. The floor. Against
the wall. Bent over the sink.

Expected. Hell, he was all but ready to *demand* it as
Carly moved in on him, the sight of her parted lips, the
hard little buds of her nipples straining against the thin
material of the tight little shirt she was wearing pushing
him to the outer limits of his restraint.

But she'd surprised him, shocked him into immobilized silence when she paused, only a breath away from
that lovely fantasy, and smiled with a promise hot
enough to turn what he hadn't thought could get any
harder into living stone.

"Not so fast. Not this time." Her dimples, his downfall,
flashed, just for a moment. "And no more sinks, thanks."

"What did you have in mind?" His voice sounded
distant, strained to him. Not surprising, Gideon
supposed, since the moon was nearly full and his more
animalistic tendencies were on a very short, increasingly weak tether. And if he hadn't known better, he
would have sworn that Carly was tugging at it
purposely.

"Something … softer." And he followed her, helpless
to do anything else, charmed when she took his hand in

hers and led him into the hallway, then left, toward her bedroom. "Sit," she instructed, pointing at her bed.

"We're back to that again, are we?"

She grinned, the inhibited creature she'd seemed before gone off to who-knows-where to be replaced by a being wholly, completely physical. Gideon didn't know whether to shout his thanks to the heavens or throw her on the bed ... or both. "Exactly."

So he sat. What else was he to do, he asked himself? If she'd instructed him to wait on the roof in the freezing cold while she took her clothes off, he would have. As long as he got to have his hands on her. And the look in Carly's eyes, the soft pant of her breath as she came to stand before him, just out of arms' reach, told him that having his hands on her was part of both of their agendas.

"I have wanted you," she said softly, gripping the bottom of her shirt with both hands and pulling it up just enough to expose a line of smooth, creamy skin, "since I woke up with you in my bed. I've had some time to think about this, what I'd like to do to you. What I want you to do to me. I want to make this last."

"I have some ideas on that as well," Gideon murmured, unable to tear his eyes from that small expanse of taut, flat belly, amused that they were having what sounded like a polite conversation about having sex. She might be acting bolder, he decided, but she was still Carly. And thank God for that.

"Well, then."

He watched her fight off her nerves, watched her flush only faintly as, keeping her gaze locked with his, she drew the shirt the rest of the way off, exposing the sexy little indent of her navel, breasts pushed up invitingly by her bra. Still, he sat, forcing himself to let her set the pace. He wanted Carly to enjoy this as much as he knew he was going to, wanted her to understand the power she had over him. There was so much fire in her, whether or not she saw it. Gideon intended to tease it out of her, to watch it consume her. Even if it took all night.

God willing.

She sucked her lower lip into her mouth for a moment, making him want to suck on it himself. Then he watched her small hands move down, unsnap her jeans, lower the zipper, and slide them down to her feet.

She was wearing a thong. God in heaven.

Gideon knew he'd made some small noise in the back of his throat. He couldn't help it. And he knew Carly had heard him when one side of her mouth curved up while she stepped out of the jeans completely and kicked them aside.

And then reached up behind her to unsnap her bra.

"Come here. Now." The wolf snapped again at the end of its leash, and he knew he *would* take her, hard and fast and rough, nothing to be done about it, if she didn't give him just a little to tide him over. Carly slid the bra off, exposing full, perfectly rounded breasts. And she seemed to sense how far she was pushing him, because she stepped toward him then, hooking her thumbs in the sides of her thong to pull it off as well.

"No," he managed to get out. "Leave it on. And come here." It was a picture he wanted to keep in his mind always, his golden angel, eyes gone to blue smoke with desire, wearing nothing but that little strip of silky fabric. And then she came to him, stepping between his spread legs, hissing in a soft breath when he grabbed her hips to drag her even nearer.

"Is this close enough for you?" The question was teasing, but Carly's voice was breathless. His silent answer was to pull her down onto his lap to straddle him, so that her full, swollen breasts were just in the right position.

"*Oh,*" she gasped as Gideon lowered his head to take one taut nipple into his mouth, flicking and swirling his tongue against it, then giving it a long, hard pull. Savoring her soft moans, Gideon gave the other nipple the same treatment as Carly sank down to settle firmly against him, arching back with pleasure when her hips moved against him in that first tentative rub. Then it was Gideon's turn to moan as she pushed against him again, the rough denim of Gideon's jeans against the silk of her thong creating hot friction for both of them. Gideon gritted his teeth, the need to be inside her threatening to consume every part of him.

"Not yet, not nearly." He began to grind a slow rhythm against her, drinking in the way Carly's eyes went blurry, the gasping moan she gave as her head tipped back. Submission. He felt it in every fiber of his being, felt his incisors lengthening for the bite he'd sworn not to give her. He couldn't have her that way, but he could take her every other way he knew how. And he would make it be enough.

Carly's nails raked up his sides as she dragged his shirt off, her hips still moving restlessly against him, trying to quicken the pace even as Gideon forced her to climb in excruciating slowness. "I need to feel you," she hissed. "God, Gideon, I need …"

"Not yet," he gritted out, in one smooth motion flipping her onto the bed to lie before him, legs spread, an irresistible invitation. She arched, her voice pleading, those perfect breasts thrusting toward him.

"I want you inside me. *Now.*" It wasn't a request; it was a demand. One he would be happy to oblige … soon.

"And I want to taste you. Now." He moved between her legs, lowering his head to kiss a hot path down her stomach, pausing to flick his tongue into the tiny cup of her navel, enjoying the music of Carly's soft moans while she writhed beneath him. She was so sweet, his Carly, Gideon thought as he tasted her, sweeter even than her scent had promised. He licked lower, swirling his tongue over the warm satin of her skin until he reached the thong. And still, he didn't remove it, kissing over it, inhaling the sweet, exotic scent of her until he reached the damp material stretched over the swollen heat of her.

God, she was wet for him. Carly pushed up against his mouth with a ragged moan, and Gideon suddenly wanted nothing more than to give her this, to see her come apart while he tasted the rich honey of her. He slipped a finger under the edge of her panties, his own breath quickening when he felt how damp she was for him, how ready. He slipped one finger, then another into her tight sheath, at first thrusting gently, then more forcefully as Carly demanded it, clenching her small hands in the sheets at her sides and begging for *more, harder.* All the while his tongue remained against thin satin, teasing the swollen bud of her sex, flicking his tongue against it, pausing to suck at it. Her hips pulsed against him of their own accord, faster and faster as she rushed toward her climax, toward the inevitable edge. Gideon paused, then pushed her over.

He slammed his fingers up into her and rubbed his tongue hard against her. Carly cried out over and over, his name, her whole body arching off the bed with the force of her orgasm. Gideon heard his own guttural groan, watching with primal satisfaction what he had done to her … needing more.

The wolf snapped again. And this time, the tether snapped along with it.

Carly lay immobile, barely hearing the rustle of material as Gideon moved to shove off his jeans. She hadn't known you could have a full-body orgasm, but that's exactly what this felt like. Like her blood was full of lightning, filling every inch of her with surging, pulsing waves of sensation. She didn't know what was next, couldn't believe that there could possibly be anything more than this that he could do to her, that he could make her feel.

Except she had a sneaking suspicion that Gideon did know, and he was about to show her. She watched him rise above her, like some rough pagan god. He simply took her breath away; he always did. Every inch of his skin was dusky bronze and covered rock-hard muscle. There was a sprinkle of black, curling hair across his chest, tapering down to his hard, rippling stomach, and the thick, hard length of him, big enough that Carly wasn't exactly sure what kind of a fit they'd make.

She was suddenly consumed with the desire to find out.

She loved seeing what she'd done to him, loved seeing that he was as affected as she was. Gideon's breathing was ragged, the thick waves of his hair tousled around his face, and his eyes ... Carly could see now that he watched her through the eyes not of a human, but of a wolf, yellow, hungry.

And all hers.

She rose up on her elbows, spread wide for him, her heart beating wildly, her short breaths matching his. "Now," she hissed.

He pounced, entering her in one smooth stroke that filled her completely, and she knew she cried out against his mouth as it crushed against hers, sucking, biting, tongues mating even as he pumped rhythmically into her. They rolled like animals across the bed, snarling as nails raked tender flesh, as teeth scored across sensitive skin to blend pain with pleasure in a rush of pure, unbridled lust. Carly sank her teeth into Gideon's shoulder, savoring his grunt of satisfaction, rocking her hips against his as she continued to rush, once again, toward her peak.

"Turn over," he growled, his voice so rough she could barely understand. But she did as she was told, strangely excited by the change in him, by the half-wild, animalistic power of him. So she rolled to her belly, breasts pressed against the bed as Gideon hooked his fingers into her hips and dragged her up against him, entering her in one hard thrust that had her giving a small scream as he filled every inch of her with throbbing, rigid heat.

He wasn't gentle. Carly no longer wanted him to be. Her hands clutched the covers in front of her as he hung on to her, slamming into her in quick, hard strokes that rocked the bed with their force. Gideon's rough breathing, rushing out in rhythmic pants, was driving her crazy. She was so wet, so tight around him, tensing with hot, aching need every time he filled her. She was so close...

He growled, loudly, helplessly, his thrusts wilder as he came undone. Carly felt her own body tightening, instinctively responding to Gideon's need. Teetering on the edge, she felt Gideon's thumb press hard against her. She gasped, arched, and pressed back into Gideon as she felt the slow, sensory implosion of her orgasm begin to rocket through her, flexing in tight pulses around him. Carly tossed her head back, riding the wave of shimmering sensation, blind with pleasure. She had never known it could be like this.

Gideon's guttural cry of release came right after her own as he gave one last hard thrust, holding her tight against him as he came in a hot rush. They stayed frozen that way for a minute that seemed to spin out into an eternity while Gideon spent himself, then, finally, withdrew from her, letting her sink slowly down into the softness of her mattress and curl onto her side. Boneless. Weightless. Perfect.

She felt Gideon fit himself against her back, felt the wild hammering of his heart that matched her own, and smiled lazily, her eyes at half mast. He might have been out-of-this-world amazing in bed, but she'd done a hell of a job keeping up, if that was any indication.

She heard a long, contented sigh behind her. Gideon slid his hand around to rest across the flat of her stomach, their skin a study in contrasts, dark over light.

"Gideon," she murmured softly, not a question, not even an invitation to conversation. Just his name, infused with the beauty of everything he'd just made her feel. She was gone over him. And there was no turning back now, not that she'd ever want to, come what may.

A gift, she thought, drifting slowly towards sleep wrapped in his arms, marveling sleepily at the way she seemed made to fit into him. For the first time in perhaps her whole life, Carly felt truly, deeply content, with a lovely stillness inside. Tonight there was nothing, and no one, but the two of them.

He really was amazing, Carly mused. Amazing, and gorgeous, and strong.

And snoring.

At least it was quiet. But Gideon was awfully lucky he was as far in her good graces as he was, because she had never voluntarily spent the night with a man snoring, however quietly, into her ear.

She snuggled more deeply into his warmth, neither needing nor wanting the comforter. Before letting sleep take her completely, she whispered the words that filled her, the ones that now seemed forever etched on her heart.

"I love you, Gideon."

And then she slept, never knowing that Gideon's eyes opened just as hers slipped shut, full of longing, and sadness.

And the love he couldn't help but return.

In the bitter winter darkness, a lone gray wolf crouched. It listened to the contented sighs of two new lovers drifting off to sleep, and bared its teeth in horrific pleasure.

It was nearly time. And then, there would be so much beautiful pain, real screams to silence the ones that never seemed to cease within his mind.

He could hardly wait to begin.

Chapter Eleven

SHE WOKE UP JUST BEFORE THE ALARM, AS WAS HER habit. But this morning, unlike every other morning of her life, Carly felt almost no incentive to get out of bed whatsoever. She reached over to hit the button that would cancel this morning's scheduled round of obnoxious beeping, then reluctantly flicked the ringer on the phone back on. She couldn't stay disconnected to the outside world forever, after all, tempting though the idea might be.

For these few moments, though, Carly could pretend. She lay there quietly, enjoying the feeling of waking up with Gideon wrapped around her.

Her limbs were deliciously tired, her skin feeling like it had been sprinkled with fairy dust. It was, she knew, although not from any experience she'd ever had before, the feeling that one only got from being well used by one's lover. She grinned sleepily to herself. She had a *lover*. Who would have thought? A big, handsome werewolf lover with, as he'd demonstrated three more times last night, stamina to burn. And he was so ... inventive. She was pretty sure her mother, father, brothers, and the entire Italian Catholic community of northern New York would be horrified beyond words.

Life was sweet.

"You're thinking awfully loudly this morning." Gideon's voice was a sleepy rumble behind her. Possibly, she decided, she might let Gideon demonstrate a little more of his stamina before she had to head off to work. Carly rolled over as Gideon nuzzled at her hair.

"Strangely, I think I'm starting to like the fact that you're sniffing at me all the time. And I'm not really thinking. Just enjoying."

"Ah, well. You can do that as loudly as you want." His mouth curved up into a sexy smile, and though she hadn't thought it possible, Carly found it even more ridiculously appealing than before. Probably because she'd had a very thorough demonstration of how multi-talented that mouth happened to be last night. She blushed at the memories. She couldn't help it.

Gideon brushed her hair back over her shoulder, letting his fingers trace a path over her collarbone. His amber eyes were warm with humor when he cocked his head at her. "Come now, you aren't going to be embarrassed, are you? Not after the wild thing you were last night."

She snorted. "I'm not a wild *anything*."

"Hmm. Must have been some other woman that gave me these scratches, then." He rolled just enough onto his stomach for Carly to see the bright red lines that sliced across his broad shoulders, as well as down the length of his back. Carly's eyes widened. God, had she done that? Gideon was still smiling, but she was completely mortified.

"Oh, God, Gideon, I'm so sorry! I didn't mean to *hurt* you!" The words tumbled from her lips in an embarrassed rush, not stopping even when Gideon laughed.

"If I hadn't enjoyed it, you'd know. Believe me, you can hurt me like that any time you like."

Gideon leaned forward to rub his nose against hers, and Carly sighed with helpless amusement. She was glad he was pleased, even if she wasn't exactly sure how she felt about her new status as "sexual animal." Gideon had certainly brought out an interesting side of her, though, no matter how she decided to feel about it. She'd think about it later. Maybe after exploring that new side in a little more depth.

"So, anytime, like, mmm, now?"

The lack of anything covering the two of them left Carly in no doubt as to Gideon's feelings on that. He laughed, a husky roll that had her ready to pounce immediately.

"I think I've created a monster."

"Damn right, Dr. Wolfenstein. And your new creation is hungry." She grinned wickedly as she reached down and wrapped her hand around the hot length of him, eliciting a laughing groan from Gideon.

"Never let it be said that I've shirked my duty." He rolled to pin her beneath him, nibbling at her neck with small, tickling bites that had Carly giggling. He was just starting to work his way downwards when the phone erupted into loud, jarring rings. This time Carly groaned, and it wasn't with pleasure.

"It's not even seven." She heaved a gusty, irritated sigh and flopped her head back onto the pillows. "I don't think anyone is obligated to answer the phone before at least eight."

"It could be my brother. Did you happen to check the messages last night?"

Carly lifted her head back up, blew a strand of hair out of her eyes as she was rolling them. "Somehow, I seem to remember being a little busy for that."

The ringing abruptly stopped.

"It didn't ring for long. Couldn't have been very ..."

Gideon just shook his head. "Wait." As if on cue, the phone erupted anew. He sighed. "It's Gabriel. He won't be happy I haven't called." Gideon slid off the bed and padded around to pick up the phone, leaving Carly to admire him in all his glory.

She wrinkled her nose. Looked like admiring was all she was going to get to do for the moment. Well, she shouldn't be the only one suffering.

"Hi, Gabe," Gideon said as soon as he picked up the phone, and then winced at whatever the reply was. Carly couldn't quite make it out, but it was loud. She got up and stretched languorously, arms above her head, enjoying the heat that put into Gideon's eyes.

"I'll just go put the coffee on," she said with a sweet smile.

Gideon nodded, placed a hand over the mouthpiece. "I think I saw your pajamas crumpled up in the corner over there."

Carly shook her head, fluffing her fingers through her hair. "I didn't say anything about putting on pajamas. Just coffee." She turned to sashay out the door and down the hallway, feeling wonderfully decadent prancing around naked in her own house, especially under the appreciative eye of the equally naked hunk in her bedroom. Just outside the door, she turned her head back to give Gideon a saucy grin, laughing when she saw that his gaze was now fixed on what he'd rather charmingly termed her "delicious wee round bottom."

"I'll be in the kitchen when you're ... *hungry.*" The pained expression on his face was priceless as she turned and walked away, sure it wouldn't be too long before he'd be out to join her for some sort of naked breakfast. Among other things.

She'd never been comfortable enough with men to tease them like this, Carly marveled as she moved down the hallway, feeling his eyes on her every step of the way. But with Gideon, she felt powerful. When she would normally shrink back, he pushed her forward. When she started to get shy with him, he emboldened her. He'd all but worshiped her body, making her feel cherished, beautiful, and refreshingly wanton.

Powerful. Carly turned the word over in her head as she got out a filter, measured the coffee. She grinned over the forgotten cartons of Chinese food he'd obviously ordered in lieu of actually cooking anything last night.

It wasn't a word she would have ever thought to use to describe herself, but with Gideon, somehow it applied. That was just how he made her feel. Powerful, and very, very female. So she smiled to herself, sang a little Aerosmith as she started the coffee maker ... what better way to wake up than with a little "Love in an Elevator?" ... and danced naked in her little kitchen to celebrate the beginning of another day.

Sometimes, she decided, it was awesome just being a girl.

"Damn it, Gideon, I'm not going to waste all of my best curses on you if you're not even going to pay attention."

Gabriel's voice barely registered in Gideon's ear as he watched Carly saunter away from him down the hallway and around the corner, adding a bit of wiggle to her walk, he was certain, just to drive him completely and utterly out of his mind. Sadly, at this point in his little adventure, it wasn't likely to be a long trip. It might help, he decided, if he could just rid himself of the constant and overwhelming desire to nibble on every last inch of smooth, creamy curve that had just pranced away from him. Would giving in do it, Gideon wondered? It couldn't hurt to try. Several times, if need be.

"Hmm?"

Gabriel's sigh was gusty. "Exactly. I've been trying to get ahold of your sorry hide for twenty-four bloody hours now, to tell you that Malachi and his lovely mum want a piece of us so badly that you ought to get yourself and your little friend out of there and back *here* as soon as possible, and …" He paused in his diatribe, and as understanding dawned, amusement flooded his voice. "Oh. *Oh.*"

With Carly now out of sight, Gideon's attention returned fully to the conversation, and as his luck would have it, he didn't care a bit for what he heard in his brother's voice.

"Don't," he growled. As was his wont, however, Gabriel blithely ignored the warning.

"I do believe I've just discovered what's been keeping you away from the phone."

"Gabriel."

"I *also,*" Gabriel continued, his deep voice brimming with the delight Gideon was sure he was feeling at having caught his eternally responsible older brother in such a compromising situation, "am now quite sure I know why you're so happy to hear from me."

"*Gabriel.*" What could he say? At this point, any sort of denial was useless, both because he didn't much care to lie about it, and even more because Gabriel was so thrilled with his conclusion that there was no way in hell he was going to let it go. Best to just be done with it and move on. Of course, that was easier said than done.

"So when do I get to meet her?"

"You don't."

"Like hell. Unless your brain was completely disengaged during the earlier bit of our conversation, you'll recall I said you need to bring yourself *and* your new girlfriend back here, and as quickly as possible. I had the distinct displeasure of lunching with Auntie Mo and her darling boy yesterday."

Gideon frowned, waiting for it. It would have been inaudible to anyone else, but the undercurrent of worry beneath Gabriel's good humor rang out clear as a bell to him. "And?"

"Oh, no dramatic monologue of admission or anything." He chuckled, then modulated his voice into an uncanny impression of their aunt's sharp snarl. "*You foul, disgusting creatures ... you shall never stop me from returning you to the excrement from which you sprang!*"

"We may well hear that before long, you know." Gideon's mouth twisted into an unwilling grin. Leave it to Gabriel to bring levity to any and all situations, particularly those that least called for it.

Gabriel's voice sobered. "I wouldn't doubt it. The woman, as you know, hates me at the best of times, but yesterday … she removed herself from the restaurant, I believe, to restrain herself from simply tearing my throat out right then and there. Not that she would have beaten me to the draw, you know, but still. She's losing what small handle she keeps on that violent temper of hers."

Gideon moved to the rumpled bed, sat down. "And Malachi?"

"He's in a state. Looks like he hasn't slept in a week, and something about his eyes … he was never stable, but I'd say he's going as mad as his mum. Twitchy, angry, lots of blathering on about how we have no class …"

"Not unusual, for him."

"No, and yes. There's something up, for sure, Gid, something eating at them both. I'm worried, and you know I hate to admit it. Not just for you, but for Dad."

"You've told him, have you?"

Gabriel responded with a sharp snort. "Oh yes, and gotten a bloody earful about how he can take care of himself, how there must be some other explanation. God love him, he just doesn't want to believe his baby sister wants to kill him, little as he likes her. And also, he'd like me to tell you to get your ass home so this can be sorted out on our own territory."

Gideon rolled his eyes back into his head and leaned back into the pillows. "Typical." For some reason,

Duncan MacInnes saved the tiny part of his nature that was forgiving all for his damned psychotic sister, no matter how condescending, nasty, or outright unbalanced she became. It was, Gideon had always thought, part of the reason he hadn't come down harder on Malachi when Gideon had nearly lost his eye. He thought the pair of them troubled, but his all-consuming family loyalty wouldn't, without concrete proof, allow him to believe in the true, violent nature of either.

It might already have cost him, and dearly, if his sons hadn't possessed a healthy dose of the suspicion Duncan lacked in that area.

"He's nothing if not predictable," Gabriel agreed. "On the one count, though, and much as it kills me to do it, I'm afraid I agree. You're at a disadvantage there, on several levels. Get your ass home."

Not feeling particularly accommodating, Gideon rolled to one side and inhaled the scents of freshly made coffee and sizzling bacon wafting from the kitchen. His rumbling stomach didn't do much to diffuse his annoyance with his brother's comment. "At what levels do you think I'm at such a disadvantage, may I ask?"

"Oh, are we going there now, then?" Gabriel's voice indicated his temper could snap to just as quickly as Gideon's. Gideon smirked. Good. It was useless being angry without reciprocation anyway.

"I'm afraid so."

"Fine." His voice was impatient, clipped. "For one thing, you're sitting in some snowy, woodsy nowhere of a town in a completely different country, not to mention on another bloody continent. Where you're being hunted, I might add, by a couple of unfamiliar were-wolves who appear to have been given their marching orders to tear you limb from limb."

"Brilliant. What else have you got?"

"You're isolated, an ocean away from the Hunting Grounds, and let's face it, Gid. You're distracted. Normally, I'd be the first to congratulate you on finally finding someone who'll put up with you, but you getting yourself all wrapped up in some woman right now is one of the worst things that could happen. Hell, you would have known about this yesterday otherwise! Go on, now. Tell me I'm wrong. I'd love to hear the reasoning."

Gideon gritted his teeth. There were moments when Gabriel sounded uncannily like their father, and it never failed to get his back up. That, and the fact that, in this instance, Gabriel had a point. He *had* been a bit distracted trying to get himself back into Carly's good graces. But then, what else was he to do? And if they'd both gotten a bit … carried away … with one another in the process, it was still no one's business but theirs. He hadn't let his guard down. Gabriel needed to know it.

"Gabriel," he said, keeping his voice even, "I may have been unavailable, but I'm far from distracted." He was hard pressed to ignore the disbelieving snort on the other end of the line, but he continued. "My being here has put Carly in danger. I won't ignore my responsibility for that. I can't, and you know it. You'd do the same. But beyond that, she's not a part of this."

"Isn't she?"

"Sod off."

Gabriel's voice turned reasonable, and somehow, it was just as irritating as when he'd sounded angry. "Look, Gideon. I'm not disagreeing with you that you need to keep your … Carly, did you say her name was? Lovely, that … safe. Especially since it sounds like she's my only chance at having nieces and nephews to spoil with candy and obnoxious toys. So that's why I'm saying, bring yourself, and her, home. You've got family to watch your back here, and hers. When the Pack is threatened, we stand together."

"I'm not bringing her anywhere. I'm going to kill whoever Malachi's sent, and *then* I will be coming home. Alone."

Gabriel huffed out an exasperated breath. "Still playing the martyr, are we then? It's getting tiresome, Gideon."

Gideon felt his hand tighten around the phone, and it took all of his willpower not to clench and crush it. He'd had about enough of his brother's lectures. "Not nearly as tiresome as this conversation. I've got to go."

"Have it your way, as usual. But now that they know we suspect them, things may happen quickly. Be careful. And if you get a moment, try and pull your head out of your ass, too. At this point, I'm beginning to worry you'll never get it out."

Gideon hung up, glared at the phone, then tossed it beside him onto the bed and shoved his hands into his hair. He was utterly disgusted, but he'd be a fool if he tried to insist it was with anyone but himself. It was getting too damned complicated, too *close* being here. How was a man supposed to think? Here, his senses were so full of Carly he could barely breathe, much less form any sort of workable strategy to get her out of danger so he could leave and deal with the source of the problem. And then there were her feelings to consider, the words she'd whispered to him when she'd thought he was asleep.

How could he keep touching her, Gideon wondered with a sick, sinking feeling. And yet how the hell could he stop? God knew he'd tried. He gritted his teeth. Bloodydamn impossible situation, and it wasn't fair to either of them. He was already doomed to a lifetime of wanting only her. Condemning Carly to the same fate was needlessly cruel, even if the thought of her with any other man made his stomach clench, made him want to draw blood.

He knew that when he left her here, he would never be able to return.

And for all that he loved them, the images he carried within his memory that had always brought warmth … the moonlight glittering on the waters of the loch, the mist that rolled in over the hills to turn the Highlands into a playground for the Fae … left him cold, cold, cold.

Gideon stayed there, slumped slightly, lost in thought for a few minutes before he took a deep breath, straightened, and stood to go out into the kitchen where the woman of his dreams was making him breakfast in the nude. He smiled, but it was bitter. He had no business losing himself in this pretty fantasy any longer, not when he knew in his heart what sort of reality was waiting just out of sight to come crashing down on the both of them. Not when entertaining impossible things might very well cost him not only Carly, but his family, his home … everything.

Gideon closed his eyes, braced himself. Loving him would bring Carly Silver nothing but misery and death in the long run. He couldn't stop wanting her, but maybe he could make her stop wanting him. It was high time she was told. Everything.

But later, Gideon decided, pushing away the black thoughts for just a little while longer. After they had this one last, lovely morning.

Then Carly's high-pitched shriek echoed from the kitchen, and all coherent thought fled his mind.

Protect thy mate.

He broke into a run, dashing down the hallway and around the corner, barely registering it when Carly streaked past him and back into the bedroom, where she slammed the door. *Good,* he thought. *She'll be safer there …*

But though he arrived charged with vicious energy, ready to attack, there were no bloodthirsty Wolves to be found in the kitchen.

Gideon stopped short, momentarily bewildered by the sight of the lone figure glaring at him from the edge of the kitchen. *Hairy, but no Wolf,* Gideon thought, trying to absorb the meaning of the short, dark-haired, stocky creature who, upon seeing him, pointed one meaty finger at him and wrinkled his snub nose.

And when he spoke, Gideon wondered if God had decided to put a curse on him, just for the hell of it. Because it was either that, or the Almighty had taken up drinking.

The man lowered his square head like a bull about to charge.

"What are you doing touching my sister, you son of a bitch?"

"Oh God, oh God, oh God …"

Carly dug frantically in her closet for her frayed terry cloth robe, pulling it on hurriedly when she found it. She knotted the belt as quickly as she could with her shaking hands before throwing open the door. She was heading back out into a bloodbath, if experience was any indication. And Carly honestly didn't know who to be more afraid for: the overprotective brother whose bellicose reputation had effectively ended her high school dating career, or the legendary monster she was sleeping with whose every movement screamed "predator." Luigi Silver versus The Wolfman.

They were going to kill each other.

"Oh *God,*" she groaned again as she got her first look at the natural enemies getting ready to face off in her living room. Luigi was spouting the usual invective upwards into a silent Gideon's face, whose intense stillness alone should have sent her brother screaming out into the street if he'd known what was good for him. Which, Carly had to admit, he never had. They would have been nose to nose if Gideon hadn't towered over Luigi, but that didn't seem to be deterring her brother. God, no, Carly thought as her brows drew together.

Heaven forbid that any sister of Luigi Silver should do something as untoward as get laid.

Gideon, to his credit, had wrapped the red throw she usually kept on the couch around his waist and appeared to be trying, at least, not to chew Luigi up and spit him out. He was just silent. Deadly silent. As pissed off as she was at Luigi, Carly knew she'd never forgive herself if she let her brother get hurt. Probably. And, of course, Luigi picked that moment to put both hands against Gideon's broad chest and shove. Gideon didn't move a muscle, but the murder flashing in his eyes had Carly stepping right between them, pushing Luigi backwards. And she *was* just the right height to get in his face, which she did with no qualms whatsoever.

"Oh no, you don't," she informed Luigi, finger planted squarely in the middle of his chest and thoroughly enjoying the shocked raise of his eyebrows. "Not this time."

"Carly," Luigi started, "what the *hell?*"

"Weege, this is none of your business. For once in your life, butt out."

Luigi sputtered for a moment before he managed to get actual words out. "You … you're running around the house with some … some naked Irish guy, and I'm supposed to butt out?"

Out of the corner of her eye, Carly could see Gideon, who'd stepped back a little in order to give her better access to her brother, still unsmiling but looking suspiciously amused. For the moment, she ignored him. She had mouthier fish to fry. Calmly, she folded both arms across her chest and glared at Luigi.

"He's a naked *Scottish* guy, Weege. And since it's my house we're running around naked in, yeah, I expect it to not be any of your business."

Luigi looked at her, then at Gideon, then back at her. It wasn't hard to see what he thought of the situation, and her attitude about it.

"Carly," he began in a warning tone, beginning what she was pretty sure was some variation on the canned All-Boys-Are-Bad speech of her youth, "you don't know about guys …"

"No, Luigi," she said flatly, resenting the hell out of the way he was spoiling her morning, "I know plenty about guys. Especially the kind of guys who take great pleasure in trying to run off their sister's dates for fear that she might someday start having 'the sex' and, holy shit, *maybe even liking it!* Which, I gotta tell you, was a dream that died like ten years ago in the backseat of Derek Overton's Tercel. Deal with it."

Gideon might have been the werewolf, but it was Luigi's eyes that seemed to change color from brown to murderous red at that point. "Overton? You let that little … I think I need to have a few words with him, about respecting women who happen to be my sister …"

Carly rolled her eyes so far back that she thought they might just fall into her head. "For the love of … he was perfectly respectful about it. And I think his wife and baby daughter might have something to say about your sudden need to 'converse' with him. Don't be a jackass, Luigi."

"But you're my sister!"

"Yes," she replied, seeing his affront and not much caring. This was a talk that was long past due. "And you're my brother. And although I'm assuming, at the ripe old age of thirty-one, that you have had sex once or twice, somehow I can't remember ever having had a kitten about it. Have I?"

"Jesus, Carly." Luigi reddened and stuffed his hands in his pockets.

"*Have* I?"

"I. Um. No." And despite her irritation, Carly had to fight back a smile. Her big brother was beginning to look as sheepish as he did when their mother went after him. Obviously, she'd picked up a thing or two over the years. She was going to have to remember to thank her mom.

"Then I have a right to the same courtesy. I'm a grown woman, Weege," she said, more softly now, letting her affection for him show through. "I love you dearly. I always will. But seriously. Back off."

Luigi stared at her as though he were truly seeing her for the first time. Or maybe, Carly thought ruefully, as though she'd just grown an extra head. She turned slightly to peek over at Gideon, who had remained perfectly quiet and immobile throughout her little confrontation, and blushed a little when he dropped a lazy, approving wink at her. Had she really just all but shouted that thing about Derek's Tercel? Well. Holy shit.

Still, it was high time to blow a hole in the old family dynamic. It might have been a handy excuse for preferring to curl up in her various hidey-holes over nerve-racking encounters with datable men for a long time now, but that was all bull. And now Luigi knew it. As did the mostly naked Scotsman wearing her throw blanket.

As did, finally, she.

Confrontational nude psychoanalysis. This was bound to be a riot to chew on later. Probably along with a pint of Ben and Jerry's.

"So," Luigi finally said, drawing her attention back to the situation at hand as he puffed himself back up a little, trying to regain some of his former swagger. He jerked his head at Gideon, who merely raised one dark brow. "You, ah … you like this guy?"

Despite herself, Carly did let herself smile, just a little. Luigi was now doing an almost pitch-perfect Joe Pesci in every mob movie ever made, whether or not he realized it (and sometimes, she thought he might). She'd swear he had to restrain himself from saying *youse* instead of *you*. Well, two could play at that game. She moved her hands to her hips and jerked her chin up, her best mob moll affectation.

"Yeah. I like this guy."

Luigi, however, seemed to have lost his sense of humor for the moment, simply sighing softly as he eyed Gideon speculatively. Finally, seeming to come to a decision, he stuck his hand out toward Gideon, calling an abrupt end to the hostilities. "Sorry man," he shrugged. "You know how it is."

Carly felt nothing but relief when Gideon readily shook it, releasing a breath she hadn't even been aware she'd been holding.

"Actually, no, thank God," Gideon replied, a trace of humor in his voice. "I've only got a brother to deal with. Gideon MacInnes."

"Luigi Silver. So," he said, returning his gaze to his sister and instantly becoming nothing but her adorable, frustrating yet lovable, freeloading brother again, "was that leftover Chinese I saw out there?"

Carly blew an errant lock of hair out of her face and sighed. Some things never changed.

And some things did. She planted both hands against her brother's broad back and steered him right back towards the door he'd come in.

"So Gid," Luigi called over his shoulder as Carly herded him out, addressing a rapidly retreating Gideon who, Carly was pretty sure, was on his way to pull on some pants. "What line of work you in?"

"It's Gideon," came the reply. "And I help run my family's estate. Bed and breakfast. That sort of thing. Not as interesting as my brother's pub, but I enjoy it."

At the mention of the word "pub," Carly could swear she saw Luigi's eyes actually light up. Smelling a stall tactic, she shoved harder. Still, she knew that, whether he wanted it or not, Gideon had just made a friend for life.

"Your brother owns a *bar?* Man, are you and me gonna get along. Beer is one of my favorite subjects."

Family, thought Carly as she happily let the door hit her brother in the ass on his way out. Can't live with 'em, can't shoot 'em. And with one more ruefully affectionate glance at her retreating brother, she headed for her bedroom. This was her breakfast, dammit. And this morning, no pants were required.

Chapter Twelve

DESPITE HER RENEWED THREATS TO PUT HIM BACK TO work, Carly and Gideon had finally agreed that simply dropping her off and picking her up (*early,* he'd demanded, and, after a great deal of bluster, she'd conceded) constituted perfectly adequate protection for the daylight hours in Kinnik's Harbor. Though in the end, he'd called her bluff and offered to continue his expert reorganization of her stockroom.

"Well … I think maybe one day of having your services available to the women of the Harbor was about all they should be expected to handle," Carly had laughed after he'd broached the subject, a twinkle in her blue eyes. "You don't want to be responsible for turning a sleepy little town into a hotbed of lust, do you?"

At which point, Gideon recalled now as he pulled on his coat (and he never thought he'd be so happy just to get into his own well-worn clothes again) for the second time that morning, he'd made some comment about how turning her little house into the local *shaque d'amour* would have to sustain him. And then, of course, kissed her thoroughly for looking so damned adorable in her work clothes. Well, and then removing them, making her a bit late to work after all.

Gideon frowned, sighed. So much for getting around to warning her off. Currently, he blamed her dimples.

And, he'd already decided, whenever that started to seem a bit ludicrous, he had at least two dozen other beautiful and mind-scrambling body parts to divide the blame between.

So he'd somehow managed to fold himself into the woman's miniature automobile and dropped her off. He'd done a fair job of concentrating well enough to get out to the inn and back to pick up his things. Perhaps he could even manage to fully re-engage his brain for the short while the only company he was keeping was his own.

He'd sensed a bit of relief on Carly's part, he thought, that she'd be having her workday to herself. He was still trying to tamp it down, but knowing how his presence distracted and flustered her gave him a rush of pure male satisfaction. That, and the knowledge that she didn't want to share him. Gideon didn't particularly want to share her, either. In fact, he was fairly sure that, if he saw another man touching her, he was going to have to remove the offending limb from whatever interloper was stupid enough to trespass on his territory.

His territory? Christ, had he really just thought those words? Gideon gritted his teeth and stomped out the front door, turning and locking it before heading down the front path he'd so industriously shoveled out this morning. He'd also shoveled out the driveway and Carly's car before they'd left, no small feat for a scant hour's work. Well, he amended, not for a normal man, it wouldn't have been, anyway. For him, it had been more like a nice, physically exerting break from thinking for a bit, because he'd certainly been doing more than his share of that lately, at least about some subjects.

Hence today's project, which involved less thinking, more doing. Oh, and a self-guided tour of some of the more remote camps and cottages along the water. After he checked in on his charge, of course. Just because he'd decided not to haunt her all day didn't mean Gideon was ready to trust that all would be hunky-dory as long as the sun shone. There were always lulls in a day's business, particularly in a snowy lake town in winter, and it would, Gideon knew, take very little to overpower a sleepy bookshop's diminutive owner.

And he didn't want to, couldn't, think about that right now. *Proactive,* he thought determinedly, and made his way out to the road, eschewing the car for a bit more mind-numbing physical exertion.

The day, despite the sun's ducking in and out from behind the clouds to bathe the snow-covered town in intermittent bursts of light, was blustery. The wind kicked up stinging mists of snow that Gideon squinted against as he slogged across the nonexistent walkway to get to the plowed and hard-packed surface of the road. The storm, at least, was over, according to the weatherman Gideon had watched this morning, moving on to dissipate somewhere over the lonely Atlantic. Just the first in what was looking to be a long and cold winter, from all reports. And Gideon couldn't help but be amused by the casual nonchalance the locals exhibited toward the unexpected burst of weather. Just a shrug, and perhaps that interesting noise of affirmation that was particular, he'd noticed, to New Englanders; a noise that sounded something like "ayuh."

As a Highlander, he had to appreciate inborn hardiness, and these people certainly had it in spades. Even, he supposed with some reluctance, recalling her indifferent reaction to the truly awful weather on their first morning together, Carly Silver herself. Weather was one thing, though. And finding it boring was hardly an indicator of inner strength. Gideon sighed, shrugged up his shoulders as he started down the road. He passed occasional industrious souls trying to remedy their own particular sidewalk/driveway situations, the muffled *crunch, crunch* of his boots on the snow the only noise in the still, freezing air except for the occasional rumble of a slowly passing car.

He knew so little about her, really. Oh, he already knew her sweetness, her quick sense of humor. But they'd only had three short days together, though that scant time had been, to him, fuller and more momentous than most of the years that had preceded them. Three days. And though he'd seen flashes of both bravery and strength, he had no way to take their measure. No way of knowing how deeply those things, the things that for his kind determined a lasting match, ran. How would she feel, he wondered, if she knew how very close he'd been, during the ecstasy of their lovemaking, to sinking his teeth into her? To claiming her the way his nature said he must, consequences be damned?

Would she shrink from him in horror? Or worse … knowing what he wanted, would she accept it, or even, Gideon thought with a sudden shudder, ask it of him?

His mother had asked for the bite, and she had died in his father's arms. It was a history he didn't care to repeat.

And though Gideon knew that his apparent inability to keep any kind of distance between himself and Carly Silver would only make things more difficult and painful in the long run, that he would eventually distance himself permanently was still, for him, non-negotiable. Given the choices, he had no idea which one she'd make. But the decision was his. And her life, her precious, beautiful life, was not something he would ever be willing to risk.

The world, Gideon was sure, would be a much darker place without Carly in it.

Gideon's long stride quickly ate up the distance between the house and the quaint little downtown. He inhaled deeply, enjoying the crisp scent of the air, letting his gaze wander over the cheery decorations people had begun to put out for Christmas as he crossed the road that led in and out of town. He turned right, grinning over the fairly audacious inflated, light-up display that was being erected in the yard of the stately blue colonial directly in front of him. He took the next left onto Main Street, which dipped on a gentle incline for about a quarter of a mile before flattening out and ending at the historic battlefield and Lake Ontario.

Gideon slowed slightly to examine the jumble of shops and restaurants on either side of him as he walked, liking the picture postcard they made when viewed in all their wintry glory. Might as well snap a shot, title it *A New England Holiday,* and be done with it, he thought with an appreciative smile.

And there it was, a red velvet bow on the door as though it contained a present intended just for him.

Carly's disconcertingly female bookshop/gift shop/ overpriced bauble repository loomed on his right just ahead, and Gideon felt an uncomfortably teenage sensation of nervous embarrassment. Would he be intruding if he poked his head into her little kingdom? Would she mind his lurking about? Would *he* mind if she minded?

"Good Lord. I'm apparently still thirteen," he muttered, and shoved the odd flutter in his abdomen aside as he pushed open the door, eliciting a bright jingle from the bell overhead. He felt an inadvertent smile curve his lips as the slight figure behind the counter turned to greet him.

And felt it freeze in place when the woman who returned that smile, damn it all, was most certainly *not* Carly.

"Hi," chirped the willowy young brunette whose presence had, for the moment, disconcerted him into surprised silence. "Can I, um," her voice slowed thoughtfully as her eyes swept down, and then back up, the length of him, "help you with anything?"

The conversation that had been bubbling between two forty-ish women perusing the shelves stopped abruptly as all eyes in the shop fixed on him with decidedly more interest than made him comfortable.

"I'm looking for Carly," he managed, sweeping an uncomfortable hand through his hair. "Ah, is she around here? Somewhere?"

"'Fraid not, at the moment." A knowing twinkle appeared in her gaze. "You wouldn't be Gideon, would you?"

"'Fraid so," he returned, thinking that the young woman, who he guessed was the Jemma Carly sometimes talked about, didn't look particularly unhappy about being the one he'd found in Carly's place. After a stretched-out moment in which he waited for a bit more information and got nothing but a decidedly flirtatious smile, Gideon asked, "Do you know where she went, by any chance?"

"Um. Oh!" It took a minute, but Jemma's eyes finally cleared. "Yeah. She went to lunch with Regan. And she said to tell *you*," she grinned, "that you don't need to check up on her in the middle of the day and she's fine." She paused, considering. "You are, however, welcome to check up on *me* as many times as you like."

Gideon couldn't help but chuckle. Jemma was very cute, *very* not more than twenty, and obviously not shy. When she got a bit older, he doubted any man she decided to pursue would have much of a chance. He, however, was decidedly occupied … preoccupied, even … with her beautiful blond employer.

"I'll keep that in mind." Gideon backed rapidly toward the door, and freedom. "Just tell her I came by then, I suppose."

"Oh, we will," chirped one of the women who'd been listening attentively to the conversation. Gideon looked more closely, recognized the one smiling and giving him a fingertip wave as one of the more egregious ass grabbers from the day before, and increased his speed. He didn't particularly want to test her self-control level today.

"Thanks," he said with a curt nod and hurried out the door, catching a burst of feminine laughter as the door swung shut behind him. He shook his head faintly as he continued down the street, making the left at the end of it that would take him down along the lake. He wasn't sure what he was looking for, exactly: a scent, a print, hell, even just a *feeling*. But Gideon felt like doing something, even without much direction, was better than nothing.

Where are you? he thought.

Tight-packed homes gave way gradually to spaced-out cottages nestled among towering pine trees and long driveways that disappeared down around shadowy bends. Gideon walked in silence, hands shoved deep in his pockets, his head down against the wind that blew stronger now that there was less to block it. Drifts formed in odd places on the road, parts of which disappeared with a hiss as Gideon kicked through them. An occasional car passed him, but he barely noticed, mind carefully blank but senses open. Just as he'd been taught.

He was hunting.

Then the watery sun ducked behind another cloud. A low, growling voice seemed to rise up from the woods themselves, surrounding him in a menacing echo that had no source, no substance. Nothing but a feeling of pure malice that dripped from it like blood.

"She'll die first, you know."

Gideon's head snapped up, and all of his senses kicked into preternatural alertness, searching for the almost-conversational yet decidedly inhuman voice that echoed around him. But there was nothing ... how could there be nothing? The wind carried no scent to him, and the woods were still and dark and silent. An unfamiliar sensation crawled down Gideon's spine like ice water. Again he was struck by that feeling of unfamiliarity, by the unshakable impression that what he was dealing with was not only not Pack, but no werewolf at all. Gideon managed to quash the odd thoughts clouding his mind and headed for the trees to his right, taking it slow, watching the movement of every shadow.

"You'll never have her. Or me, for that matter." He kept his voice even, though it took all of his effort. "Though you're welcome to try for me. Show yourself, coward."

The laugh that greeted this was a dry as the hiss of the snow along the ground. *"I'm afraid not. I have plans. This would be much less fun."*

"If you believe what your master tells you, you're a fool." Gideon moved quickly, silently into the trees. To his frustration, though the voice became louder, it still seemed to be *everywhere. The Gray,* he thought, his eyes blazing. And yet how could any Wolf have this kind of power? A clever trick. It had to be. Not that it would save him. Gideon was of Alpha blood. The Gray was no match for him without the advantage of surprise. And so he hid. *Bloody coward.*

"Really?" The voice remained pleasant, though Gideon could now hear the undercurrent of madness in it. *"I think not. My master has powers beyond your comprehension. I think you'll be quite surprised. No, I will drink her blood, Guardian. Hers, then yours. You've both been promised to me, you see. You're mine."*

Though he fought them, the images that rose in Gideon's mind at those words caused him to break out in a panicked sweat. His insides roiled. His Carly, writhing in pain, being feasted upon by some sick monster … the terror she would feel … the *pain* … and to lose her …

Gideon snarled and lunged blindly through the trees, desperate to silence the voice, to kill this beast that hunted them and be done with it. "Where are you, you bastard? Show yourself! I'm here now! Come and fight me, if you dare! I'll rip you to pieces!" *I need to Change,* he thought frantically, wanting the strength, the speed, the power he had in his other form. But a Change in the light was risky, not to mention physically difficult without the moon to ease and facilitate it. And he had no time, for the wretched voice was already fading away.

"Mine …"

Gasping, growling in frustration and anger, Gideon pressed on through deepening snow, fighting for more speed even as the wind hurled taunting whips of stinging snow into his eyes. Still, he tried to follow the invisible until at last he knew, with sinking certainty, that he was alone once again. Unable to bear it any longer, Gideon dropped to his knees and roared. He cursed his senses that for the first time had inexplicably failed him, cursed his bloody cousin for instigating this madness. He even cursed Saint Columba for having brought his people out of the wilds in the first place.

He did not want this. But he could not change what he was, or what was his to protect. And it was time, Gideon knew, to purge this place of what had come for him and go home to finish it.

Ignoring the painful throb somewhere in the vicinity of his heart as he turned back, Gideon tried to take solace in what he had always held dear, what he had always known to be true. *I am a MacInnes Wolf, son of Duncan MacInnes, Guardian of the Lia Fáil. I am of the strongest, the fastest, the cleverest. And I will prevail.*

But somehow, nothing could warm the chill that had settled, it seemed, into his very soul.

"Tell me again why Regan hung up on you when you invited her to come along?"

Carly paused halfway up the freshly shoveled steps that led to Jonathan and Maria Silver's well-lit front porch, turning her head to smirk at him. "She's determined that I only invite her to family dinners because my brothers are so busy lusting after her that they forget to pick on me. And just for the record, she didn't exactly *hang up* on me. She definitely mumbled something that sounded like a goodbye after she said that thing about not being the one who got caught running around my house naked."

"And?"

Carly widened her eyes. "I would never stoop to tactics like that!"

Gideon raised an eyebrow at her innocent expression, trying to enjoy Carly's good humor despite the darkness that had settled over his mood. He'd wanted to talk to her right when she'd arrived home from work. Truly, he had. No more secrets, he'd decided, and he still had every intention of telling her what had happened this afternoon. But when she'd practically bounded through the door to see him, and the way her eyes had lit up at the sight of him … God help him, he hadn't had the heart to say anything.

It was probably a stroke of luck that the infamous Luigi had called and all but demanded the two of them come along to the family's weekly dinner, he knew. It got Carly where he wanted her, and once they had their talk, well, chances were she wasn't going to want to follow him anywhere after that. He'd tried to act like nothing was wrong, though he'd caught Carly giving him curious glances once or twice when she didn't think he'd been looking. And it was better this way, Gideon knew. The truth, and then a clean break. Better for both of them, easier in the long run.

Still, no matter what his rational mind knew to be true, the sick feeling in the pit of his stomach refused to dissipate. And with each look he stole at her, he felt as though he were trying to drink in all he could of her in the time he had left, a man dying of thirst, for whom no amount of water would ever be enough.

And nothing was going to change, Gideon told himself firmly, dragging his thoughts back to the present. Carly was still smiling up at him, backlit by the warm glow from the house. Several of the snowflakes drifting lazily down from the inky sky glittered where they had caught in the pale glory of her hair. That, coupled with the way she was all bundled up in her coat, ridiculously furry boots, and scarf, made her appear almost childlike, a small, mischievous angel. Unable to resist, Gideon leaned down to brush his mouth against hers in a soft, undemanding kiss.

He chuckled at Carly's bemused expression when he pulled back.

"What was that for?"

"For being such a charming liar."

She considered him for a moment. "If I tell a bigger one, what does that get me?"

"Hmm," Gideon rumbled, pretending to give the matter serious thought. He caught her gloved hands in his and dropped back a couple of steps to put them on more even footing. "Well, I suppose I might start with something like this."

He caught a glimpse of Carly's smile right before he pulled her against him and brought his mouth against hers in a lazy, thorough kiss, angling his head to slide his tongue against hers in a slow, provocative rhythm. This was perfection, he thought with hazy pleasure, savoring the way every curve of their bodies seemed tailored to fit together just so. He'd heard it said that the best things came in small packages, and Carly Silver was certainly an affirmation of that. In spite of the temperature, just being with her warmed him in places he wasn't even aware had grown cold. Strange, that such trouble could have presented him with such a rare gift. Singular pleasure. Singular pain.

All thought of pain, however, was swept from Gideon's mind as Carly wound her fingers in his hair, tugging him more firmly against her in a silent demand to deepen the kiss. He gave a rough chuckle as he finally pulled his head back to look at her, pleased by the sparkle in Carly's eyes, the flush their kiss had put into her cheeks.

"You're going to get me kicked out of your family's house before I even get in, if we keep this up," he informed her.

Carly leaned in to nip his bottom lip with a wicked grin that did nothing to cool him off. "You started it. But now that you mention it, getting kicked out and going back to bed isn't such a bad idea."

Gideon groaned in mock protest, forcing a smile even as the thought flitted through his head that there would be no more tumbling this luscious little creature into bed. Ever. That would be for some other man from now on. Stroking her responsive little body. Receiving her sweet kisses. Making her laugh. Making her moan.

Gideon's smile suddenly felt like nothing more than bared teeth.

Carly eyed him with a mixture of curiosity and apprehension. "Are you all right, Gideon?"

"Fine. Why?"

"You just look … sort of funny."

"Funny ha-ha?"

Carly shook her head a little, frowning faintly. "No. Funny like you just caught a whiff of raw sewage."

Perhaps he ought to just tell her now, Gideon thought. Perhaps he should at least give her some sort of warning of what was coming.

"Carly. I need to …"

But he never got the chance. Just as he opened his mouth, the door to the house opened and bathed his and Carly's entwined forms in a beam of bright light. Whatever he might have said was cut off forever by a loud, masculine, and now-familiar voice bellowing into the night.

"Ma! They're not late, they're just making out on the front steps!"

"Luigi, you ass." Carly pulled away from Gideon with an apologetic look, apparently tabling their conversation for later as she caught one of his hands in hers and pulled him behind her toward the front door. Thankful for the distraction, not to mention intrigued beyond all comprehension, Gideon allowed himself to be dragged along. It was, after all, an almost sacred Silver family tradition to eat together once a week, at least according to Carly.

"If you don't show up, you'd better be either dead or thinking about it," she'd told him earlier. And truly, from the tone of Luigi's voice when he'd "invited" him, Gideon had been hard-pressed to refuse, *Sopranos*-esque visions of getting whacked dancing through his head. He'd told himself that his agreement for the most part involved not wanting to get Carly in more trouble than she was already in, but truth be told, after meeting her brother, Gideon was extremely curious about the rest of Carly's family.

And so here they were, in all their glory, apparently as interested in meeting him as he was in meeting them. The instant Gideon stepped into the Silvers' comfortable foyer, he found himself surrounded by a rush of chatter and movement, enveloped by a close family dynamic in which he found himself surprisingly at home. He was reminded, with sweet nostalgia, of every Pack gathering he'd attended while growing up, the rough hugs and pats, the humorous and borderline-inappropriate questions asked at top volume, and most of all, the warm feeling associated with being surrounded by those who loved you.

It was a sensation he'd never expected to feel outside of Scotland. But then, Scotland didn't have Carly Silver.

Gideon watched with a smile as Carly was picked up and spun around by a slightly older, slightly taller, and if it were at all possible, slightly hairier version of Luigi. Mario, of course. The original Luigi (and though, God help him, he liked the man, thank the heavens there was only one) appeared at Gideon's side to give his hand a firm shake and clap him on the shoulder as hard as he could manage. Gideon fought back the urge to return the favor and send him flying into the nearest wall with a friendly pat. He somehow doubted that Luigi's outsized ego would ever fully recover from the blow.

"Nice to see you again, Gid. Glad to see you, ah, dressed for the occasion." The tone was innocent, but the twinkle in the eyes was one Gideon had seen before ... right before a certain short female had guilted him into being her slave for the day. Apparently, for entertainment purposes, the tale of their meeting hadn't made it to Carly's parents. Yet. But knowing that Carly had endured years of imaginative torment at the hands of her two brothers didn't do much to ease Gideon's mind on that subject. He wasn't at all sure he was up for being the object of the Silver brothers' evening amusement.

Neither, apparently, was Carly. "Mario," she said flatly as she wagged one small, elegant finger in the face of the brother who had thus far refused to put her down, "if you say one more thing, I swear to God, I will start bringing the pain right at the damned dinner table. And you *know* I know things."

Mario, unimpressed, snorted. "Yeah, right, Carlotta."

"One word, Mario. *Magazines.*"

Mario continued to dangle her a couple of inches off the ground, but his eyes narrowed. "What do you know about …"

"Loose board, left-hand side, three from the wall in your old room." Carly's look was smug as she was immediately lowered back to the ground by a suddenly pale Mario.

"Blackmail. I'm impressed," Gideon murmured into her ear as she returned to his side. Carly simply shrugged.

"The necessary weaponry of a baby sister. And actually, I'm sort of indebted to the two of them. Without those magazines, it would have taken me a lot longer to figure out what exactly the bad kids at the back of the bus were talking about. Instead, I got to be," she grinned, "*worldly.*"

"Hmm. Then perhaps *I* should thank them," Gideon laughed, earning him a smart smack to his midsection.

"So! This is the boy you've been hiding from us!" Gideon turned at the bright, clear voice behind him to find his face grabbed by two plump, bejeweled hands and pulled down over a foot to be kissed, hard, on each cheek. Completely immobilized in his surprise, Gideon had his cheeks pinched, patted, then released before he could do more than widen his eyes at the woman who was now looking up at him with smiling approval.

Maria Silver, apart from her short stature, was about as far from her daughter in looks as night was from day. Gideon could see right away that she'd been beautiful as a young woman, with her almond-eyed, olive-skinned Mediterranean looks. She was attractive still despite the fact that she'd grown decidedly thick around the middle during the ensuing years. Her hair, black without so much as a thread of gray, was clipped back in a sleek chignon with a glittering marcasite clip, revealing the thin lines etched around her mouth and eyes that told him this was a woman who laughed often. But then, Gideon supposed, to have survived raising this particular brood she'd have to have had a sense of humor.

"Gideon MacInnes. Nice to meet you, Mrs. Silver," Gideon said by way of introduction, returning her smile. He noted, suddenly, that she'd taken care to dress up a bit before meeting him. She was casually elegant in a loosely flowing tunic top and wide-legged slacks, both in a rich shade of green that brought out, he was sure she knew, the warm hazel of her eyes. That she would take the trouble for a man she'd never met simply because her daughter had brought him home charmed him immensely.

"Nice to meet you, too, Gideon. It's good to finally meet someone smart enough to catch our Carlotta. Lucky for you, I'm predisposed to liking people with such good taste. And call me Maria. Mrs. Silver is my mother-in-law, as far as I'm concerned."

He laughed. "I'll remember that."

Carly just groaned, her cheeks as pink as the clouds at sunrise. "*Mama.*"

"Come on in, you two," Maria continued, ignoring Carly's obvious embarrassment and looping her arm through Gideon's after giving her daughter a quick kiss. "I made enough lasagna to feed an army, so I hope you brought your appetites." She looked up to eye Gideon speculatively. "I never expected Carly to bring home someone so *tall*. I hope you're careful with her, you know. She's awfully delicate."

Carly's cheeks were now more volcano than sunrise. "Oh, for the love of …"

Gideon simply slid his free arm behind her back, ignoring the snickers of her two brothers and earning an approving nod from the tall, mostly silent man who trailed them. He was identifiable by his fair looks and fine features as Carly's father. That, and a certain something about the ghost of a smile that played around his lips and the intelligent humor that glittered in his eyes.

Seeing the warmth between Carly and her family, the strength of that bond, Gideon realized that the Silver family's approval meant a great deal to him. He reveled in it, even as it twisted sharply into his gut. He would take this approval, this trust … and betray it utterly by breaking their precious daughter's heart. Still, better a broken heart than a broken body, Gideon tried to tell himself. The heart, at least, would heal. He was sure of this. *Almost.*

Swept along into a comfortable dining room and to a table covered in food that smelled like heaven itself, Gideon realized with a pang of conscience that not only was he being introduced, he was being welcomed with open arms. They so obviously wanted the best for Carly, and if he was who she had chosen, they were prepared to make him a part of their family. It was humbling. And as he watched her laugh with them, watched the graceful way she did things as simple as smooth back her hair, and as he enjoyed the long, slow looks she gave him from the corner of her eye, Gideon realized how very badly he wanted to stay.

He'd thought, after all his traveling, that he'd been looking for home. As it turned out, home was Carly. And everything in him tightened up in excruciating pain when he thought of what he had to do, and the life he would leave her to have without him.

Seeming to sense something was wrong, Carly tilted her head at him, a questioning look in her eyes, as the warm chatter continued around them. A phone rang somewhere in the direction of the kitchen, and after a brief battle of wills and name-calling between him and his brother, Mario jogged off to answer it.

"What is it?" she asked softly enough so the others wouldn't hear. Gideon could only smile thinly and shake his head. He was uncertain of how to express what he was feeling. And he was completely certain that he didn't want the rest of the Silvers, who were trying to listen without appearing to be listening and doing only a middling job at it, to know anyway.

Carly, to her credit, didn't attempt to push. She just slipped her small hand into his beneath the table, gave it a squeeze, and left it there as she turned back to answer a question Luigi had asked her.

"Gideon?" Maria Silver poked her head out of the doorway to the kitchen, a frown on her handsome face, jerking him out of his unpleasant thoughts. "There's a Gabriel on the phone for you...he says he's your brother?"

A fresh set of dark thoughts burst into bloom as Gideon rose quickly to take the phone from her. He managed a short "thanks" before disappearing into the empty kitchen, ignoring the questions on Carly's face. He hadn't told Gabriel where he was going tonight. This couldn't be good.

"Gabe? How did you find me?"

Gabriel's voice, usually loud and full of humor, sounded thin and hoarse on the other end of the connection. "Gideon. Thank Christ. I got online ... you're lucky there aren't many Silvers in that area code, because I just started dialing. I hoped someone could at least tell me where you were."

"What's wrong?"

"It's bad, Gid."

"Bad?"

"Dad's gone."

Gideon stood stock still, floored, as he absorbed this, tried to let it sink in. "Gone," he repeated slowly, hoping for clarity and finding none.

"Yes, *gone,* Gideon," Gabriel replied with a flash of irritation. "I thought I'd go and spend the weekend at home for once. Good way to keep an eye out, and I knew he'd tolerate it since I don't get back all that often, even if he didn't like the why of it. But when I got there ..." Gabriel's voice trailed off for a moment before he continued. "It was madness, Gideon. Furniture broken, blood everywhere. Ian and Malcolm are doing the best they can, and they haven't let it out to the Pack yet," he said, referring to Duncan's two trusted lieutenants, "but it's only a matter of time. And poor Harriet. She's just beside herself. Can't stop crying. Malcolm finally gave her something to make her sleep." He sighed hollowly. "Lucky for us it's off-season. The one couple we had staying here left not twenty-four hours ago."

"One small blessing, I suppose," Gideon murmured, feeling the numb cloak of shock settle over him, staring

blankly at the surroundings that had, only moments
before, filled him with warmth and comfort. Now, he felt
only apart, empty. And once again, alone.

"The only one," Gabriel replied, sounding more tired
than Gideon thought he'd ever heard him. "We have to
find him, Gid. Even with everything else, I never thought
they'd get to *him,* not really. He's so strong, and you
know what a clever old bastard he is. But the *blood* …"
He drew in a shuddering breath. "It's my fault, you
know. I provoked them that day in Edinburgh. Poked at
their tempers, said more than I ought, stupid git that I
am. And now look, look what I've done."

"No," Gideon said firmly, inwardly distressed at how
close his brother seemed to be to losing it completely. A
playboy he might be, but one who was strong and annoyingly self-assured nonetheless. For him to sound like
this, Gideon knew with a sinking feeling, the scene
would have to be bad. Worse, probably, than he could yet
imagine. He thought of the taunting voice in the woods,
and numbness began to be replaced by a seething black
rage, the likes of which he had never experienced before.
He'd been baited, distracted. Misled. His focus had been
on himself and Carly, their safety. Their bond. Had it
been deliberate, he wondered? Or had their adversaries
simply seen a better opening? Regardless, he had helped
this to happen, albeit with the best intentions. And now
he would have to own the part of it that was his, and
make the best that he could of what was to come.

"I asked that of you, Gabriel. If either of us bears
fault, then it's mine for ever leaving in the first place,
thinking I might escape from who we are, and what I'm

meant to do." Gabriel started to protest, but Gideon silenced him quickly. "No, Gabe. It's true. But even with that, I think we both know where to lay the blame of this. We'll make them pay for it, you and I. And we're going to get him back."

The façade of strength seemed to bolster Gabriel a little. "Well, then. I need you here, Gid. How soon can you come home?"

It was, Gideon realized, the first time he could remember that Gabriel, whom he knew to be quite self-contained and independent despite his outwardly gregarious nature, had ever told him he needed him. He found himself surprised and, despite the situation, touched.

"I'll leave first thing in the morning. What good's the family money if we don't throw it around once in a while, eh?"

Gabriel's voice remained sober. "They'll keep him alive long enough to be able to access the Stone. What are they about, Gideon? What do they think it can do? I'll be honest, I never really thought of it as more than a … a priceless artifact, you know? Something we guarded because of a tradition. I never quite bought into the reverence Dad accorded it, never bothered to ask him *why*. The secrecy, the ritual … a show, I thought. Hell, Gideon, I don't even know where the damned thing is!" Frustration welled in Gabriel's voice. "If it's so bloody important, why didn't he tell us?"

"He was going to," Gideon growled, battling his own frustration, along with the dull misery of chances lost, opportunities missed. *I should have been there,* he thought. "When I got back, he was going to tell me everything. I told him I was finally ready. And now it's too late, and I know as little as you, I'm afraid."

"You mean, he never told you? You next in line to lead, and he never told you?"

"The full knowledge is never passed until the old Alpha is ready to hand over the reins to the new one. Tradition, remember?"

"Tradition," Gabriel spat. "Always bloody tradition. Lot of good it's done us here. What if he'd kicked off before now, accidentally? Then where would we be? Bloody wonder the whole thing hasn't fallen to pieces before now."

"I'm beginning to think bits of the truth *have* gone missing in the past, or someone might have seen this coming. Ian and Malcolm know more, I think. Enough, at least, to keep us going … and to get you and me started."

Gabriel snorted. "That's reassuring. How long do you think we have, Gideon? How long before Malachi and that evil bitch manage whatever they're trying to do? Because for them to do this, they've discovered something I don't even think I want to speculate on."

His thoughts exactly, Gideon silently agreed. He'd heard the myths, the legends surrounding the *Lia Fáil,* had grown up on them. But it seemed that he too had always regarded it as more powerful in its symbolism and age than as a force to be reckoned with in its own right. A power that could actually be *used.* Or exploited. Well, it seemed that he, and the rest of the Pack, were slated to pay for their incuriosity if he and Gabriel didn't move quickly. He needed to get home. He needed a plan.

"Talk to Ian and Malcolm. We'll need all that they know. I'll be there as soon as I possibly can."

"And your Carly? Will she be safe, if you leave her?"

Carly. She, and all the promise she carried with her, seemed an ocean away from him already. Here was the only path that could ever be his, laid out for him in the starkest light. He would forge ahead like Duncan; with honor, duty. Alone. And she would be safe. Especially from him.

"The moon is nearly full. No, I think, with me gone, there's little chance she'll be harmed. They've too little time left to bother now. I'll suggest she stay with her family, though, until this is over. One way or another."

"So ... you'll be going back for her, then?"

Gideon closed his eyes, allowing, just for a moment, the warm music of Carly's voice, drifting from the other room, to fill him up one last time. "No."

And for once, Gabriel appeared to accept this at face value, and let it be.

"Whatever you think is best, Gid. This is certainly no place for a human right now. Just hurry home."

Hurry home, Gideon thought with a bitter twist of his lips as he replaced the phone in its cradle.

He'd been a fool in many ways, but in one, he thought, above all others.

For he'd begun to let himself think, if only for a moment, that he was already there.

Chapter Thirteen

"YOU'RE JUST ... LEAVING? AND THAT'S IT?"

He'd wanted her to stay. But she'd had to follow. And now Carly stood in the doorway of her bedroom, watching Gideon hurriedly stuff what few things were his into a duffel bag. One large suitcase, apparently the only other piece of luggage he'd been traveling with all this time, already sat neatly by the front door, ready to go.

Just like he was.

She should have known it was coming when his brother had called her parents' house. She should have *known*. But then, Carly reasoned, she hadn't wanted to believe he was ever going to go at all, had she? Despite the fact that he'd never uttered so much as a word to that effect. Despite the fact that she'd given herself to him, body and soul, like the lovesick idiot she'd turned out to be, all I'm-an-independent-career-woman bullshit aside. Three short days together, but because they'd felt like a lifetime to her, she hadn't been able to imagine it would be so easy for him to walk away from her.

Maybe she could have tried to understand if he'd been up-front with her, if he'd come right out and explained why he had to go like the hounds of hell were right at his heels. But after he'd politely excused himself from dinner, he had not so politely tried to get her to stay put. To let him go, just like that.

"There's trouble at home. You'll be safer here, until this is over. I'll let you know. But I have to go," he'd told her as she stood shivering on the front porch, searching his beautiful face for any hint of the warmth that it had always held for her. But all she saw was blank shock, weariness, and seething, bubbling rage beneath it all. There was nothing there of the man she'd come to know as Gideon. And though he didn't bother to protest when she'd simply come with him, it soon became obvious to Carly that there was to be no further explanation. He had closed himself off from her as neatly as though no bond, strange and intense though it might have been, had ever existed between them.

In this moment, as he quietly gathered his things in preparation to leave her life, Gideon MacInnes was as much a stranger to her as he had been the night she'd found him. It hurt, more than it should have, more than she'd thought possible. But what was killing her, what twisted like a knife in her heart was that it was so cold, so clinical. So intentional.

When he answered her, Gideon barely spared her a glance. "I have to go, Carly. I was always going to have to go, sooner or later. I never pretended otherwise. But for what it's worth, I am sorry."

"You're *sorry?*" she asked incredulously, and the deliberately cool tone of his voice, that rich, deep voice that had called her *sweetheart* and *love,* burned right through her. Angry tears that she absolutely, unequivocally refused to shed in front of him stung her eyes. *Sorry.* Well, so was she. If only she hadn't told him she loved him. Oh, he'd been asleep when she'd said the words, but it shamed her that they'd even passed her lips. More, that she'd allowed them to be true.

In love, with this stranger, Carly thought as she glared at Gideon's broad back with a toxic mixture of anger and abject misery. A bitter laugh welled up in her throat, nearly choking her. This whole thing was a mockery.

And yet who could say she didn't deserve it?

But now he turned and looked at her, and there was something in his eyes, something almost like sadness, though Carly refused to believe its sincerity. "I am, Carly. More than I can say. But it's better this way."

Carly fought back the urge to grab the nearest object and hurl it at him. "Oh, yeah," she snapped instead. "Running back to Europe with no explanation, shutting me out. It's great this way, thanks."

Gideon sighed and shook his head at her before turning away as, Carly thought with rising anger, a parent would from a petulant child. "I know you're upset. I don't expect you to understand."

"No," she replied mockingly, "you wouldn't, would you? You don't seem to expect much from me at all, as a matter of fact. But then, I am just an inferior *human.* Good for a quick fuck and some giggles, but that's about it, huh?"

Vicious joy surged through her when his head snapped back around and his brows lowered threateningly. This was so painful … she wanted him to feel it too. Wanted him to feel *something.*

"Don't do this, Carly."

"Oh, I wouldn't dream of it," Carly gasped in mock horror. "Making a *scene,* that is. I mean, I'm so grateful that you even bothered with me at all!"

Gideon grabbed one last shirt from the end of the bed, stuffed it into his bag with a force that Carly was surprised didn't rip a hole right through the bottom of it. "You're making this harder than it has to be," he muttered under his breath. Carly smiled thinly and folded her hands across her chest. She was getting to him, then. *Good.*

"No," she said. "I think this needs to be hard, actually. Because normally, when someone saves your sorry ass from complete destruction, it merits more than a quick screw and an even quicker exit. You want walking away from me to be easy, after all of that pretending to give a shit? Well, tough."

Gideon stood there glowering at her, clutching his bag in one hand, the other clenched at his side, and Carly could see that his civilization, what polish he had, had worn dangerously thin. With frustration pumping off of him in palpable waves and his eyes burning like two live coals, Carly could see the beast within him as clear as day, an ancient and wild thing. A beast she should run from while she could.

But though she tried to hate him, even managed it to some small degree, the potent emotion that flowed through her rising temper was a love she'd never thought existed. The heady, intense connection between them, far from being snapped, pulled at her more strongly than ever. They were bound, the two of them. She didn't understand it. Hell, she didn't even know if she wanted it. But she'd be damned if she'd let him go without a fight.

"I *do* care, Carly," Gideon growled through gritted teeth. "Quite a bit more than I should. Which is why I'm leaving you now. Any longer, and we would both wind up regretting it."

"I'm glad you feel so fit to judge for both of us," she snapped back. "But all things considered, I think I deserve to know exactly what I would wind up regretting. And why."

Gideon hissed out a breath, shoved his hair back from his face. "It's pointless."

"No, what that is, is a cop-out. I let you in, Gideon," she said firmly, never letting her gaze drop from his. "Not just into my home, but into my life. *In,*" she pressed a hand against her heart, feeling it beating surprisingly steady and true beneath her hand, "here. And I got to you too, or you wouldn't be doing this, not this way. What are you afraid of, Gideon? What have you got to lose by laying it out for me now, before you leave me here to pick up the pieces?" He looked stricken, but she pressed on, knowing that if they didn't do this now, if she just let him go quietly, she would regret it for the rest of her life. "I deserve a reason, Gideon. I deserve at least that. Because even though you're walking away, it doesn't change the fact that I've fallen in love with you."

And that arrow, Carly saw, had struck its mark. The abused duffel hung from his hand, forgotten. He simply stood there, stock still, his eyes now brimming with some indefinable emotion that drove that knife into her heart so deeply that it nearly brought her to her knees. And she knew then that though he might never say it, that she would probably, in fact, never see him again after tonight, those feelings weren't just hers alone.

Gideon loved her too.

She knew it with every fiber of her being. And she promised herself that, whatever happened, she would try to make that knowledge be enough.

Improbably, impossibly, those simple words seemed to have finally broken through the shield Gideon had put up. He left the bag on the floor and came to her, moving across the room and into her arms in only two of his long, quick strides. Carly's heart lifted and sang as she opened her arms to pull him against her.

And then shattered when he kept himself apart, holding back from her embrace but cupping her face tenderly in his big, calloused hands. Hands that Carly knew to be far more gentle than anyone might ever guess. His eyes, soft, full of longing and regret, finally undid her. One rogue, unwanted tear finally escaped and slipped down her cheek. He rubbed it away with his thumb.

"I need you to go to your parents' house and stay there once I'm gone."

"Gideon …"

"No," he said, and his tone was gentle but insistent. "I *need* you to do that for me. I need to know that you're safe. My father has been taken."

Her eyes widened. "God, Gideon."

"I don't know what's going to happen anymore. I don't know whether he's dead or alive. But I have to find him. And then I have to kill the ones responsible for hurting him."

Carly wanted to flinch, so matter-of-fact he was, almost casual, about the murder he was planning to commit. But she didn't. Still, he must have seen it in her eyes.

"Ah, you start to see now, love. Our worlds, our laws ... our people ... are really very far apart. I'm capable of killing, Carly. And I'm capable of enjoying it, if the one I'm killing deserves it. You deserve a life without any violence or fear. Without some rough beast who can barely keep from sinking his teeth into you."

Carly drew a shuddering breath. Gideon's tone hadn't changed, but there was a ferocity running beneath it that was slightly frightening. "If that's the price for being with you ..."

She stopped short as Gideon's eyes flamed, as his lips peeled back in an angry snarl and he gripped her shoulders to shake her roughly. "The price for being with me is *death,* Carly. If I bite you, *it will kill you.* My own father killed my mother in just that way, for *love.* She wanted all of what he was, to be what he was. But she was so damned soft, and sweet. So *human.* And the Wolf he unleashed in her blood devoured her. Just as it would you."

"But," Carly protested frantically, "you wouldn't have to ... you don't have to!"

"Perhaps, for a time. But I'm not strong enough, Carly. There would come a day when you would ask. It's simply the way of things. And the Wolf in me wants you. So much I can barely stand it." His hands tightened painfully on her upper arms, and Carly knew there would be bruises there tomorrow. Still, looking into the face of what most would consider a monster, she couldn't be afraid.

"You're hurting me," she said softly, but he didn't seem to hear her.

"Do you want to die, Carly? Am I worth so much to you, to give up everything?"

And he was pleading, Carly knew, for her to send him away, to free him, and herself, from the bleak future he'd just described. *Loving him meant death.* He had to be exaggerating. Didn't he? Wasn't love always supposed to find a way? She wanted to say this to him, to soothe him, to convince him that they could work it out. But with his words, and the bite of his hands into her flesh, a little pain now to warn her of unimaginable pain in the future, there was suddenly the faintest hint of doubt.

Carly hesitated.

And that, it seemed, was the answer he'd been looking for all along.

Gideon released her, closed his eyes as though girding himself in the final moments before a battle, and nodded once. "Stay safe for me, Carly, until I send word." He turned from her then, seeming to take no more than an instant to retrieve his bag from the floor and move past her into the hallway.

All the things Carly wanted to say seemed caught in her throat, unable to escape, unlike the hot tears that now poured freely down her cheeks. She was watching him go, the one man she'd ever loved. The only man, she was sure, she would ever love like this. And all she could do was to stand there, paralyzed except for her tears, and let him leave, *death* an insidious, whispered echo that rang in her ears.

What kind of a choice did she have, if that was really all there was?

He turned once to look back at her, his anger gone, sadness hanging over him like a mantle. "Whatever you may think of me, Carly, please know …" He seemed to struggle with it for a moment. Carly felt the words she so desperately needed to hear hanging just out of her reach, nearly spoken. But in the end, whatever he'd thought to tell her, the words remained unsaid. Instead he simply gave her a lingering, broken look. And turned away.

Carly could only watch mutely, unable to give voice to any of the thousands of things she wanted to say to him. So she said nothing at all, only closed her eyes against the sight of him leaving. Seconds later, she heard the door open. Carly waited for it, the sound that signaled the end of their brief relationship, of the door closing on a future she had only just begun to imagine. She waited … but there was only silence, stretching out until she had to open her eyes again. A wild hope rose in her. Had he changed his mind, after all? Her feet moved with a will of their own to get her to the point where Gideon had all but decreed he was walking out of her life forever. Where he now stood with his back to her, door wide open, staring silent and still out into the darkness.

"Gideon," she began, "I …"

She searched for something, anything to say that would hold him where he was, that would keep him from taking those final few steps out of her life. But the words died in her throat before she could begin to form them, strangled by an odd and thickening silence that had descended. She drew her arms around herself, trying to ward off the strange sense of foreboding that crackled up her spine.

It was still, so unnaturally silent and still, Carly thought with a shiver. She felt as though she'd walked into a scene frozen in time, she and Gideon bugs eternally trapped in amber. The tiny hairs rose along the back of her neck as the moments spun out, some primitive part of her alerting her to a danger she couldn't begin to imagine.

Didn't want to imagine.

Carly forced herself to speak again, desperately wanting Gideon to look at her, to reassure her that nothing was wrong. Except she knew damn well that wasn't true. Everything was wrong. Her voice, when it came, was hardly more than a whisper.

"Gideon?"

Nothing, not a movement. And then it reached her, carried on a breath of arctic wind that was heavy with a wild and unfamiliar scent that had all of her instincts screaming *run*. It started low, a barely audible rumble that swelled and deepened until it seemed to fill up every corner of the night, drowning out even the increasingly panicked drumbeat of her own heart.

Growling.

Whether or not Gideon had heard her, it appeared that something lurking out in the blackness had.

Carly knew she must have made a sound then, some soft, choked sound as she struggled to make her body do what her brain cried out she must. Because Gideon finally spoke to her, his voice soft, low. Deadly. And instead of bringing her comfort, it sliced her to the bone.

"Shh," he instructed softly, never turning. "Go back to your room, Carly. Shut the door and lock it behind you. Do you understand? No matter what, keep it locked. And if anything happens to me, go out the window. And run."

A chill that had nothing to do with the frigid breeze blowing in from the night worked its way through her veins like ice water, freezing her in place. What was out there, waiting? What did he see?

"Do you understand?" he asked again, more forcefully this time, and Carly realized that something was happening to him, the bones beneath his skin shifting as the skin stretched over them began to ripple, to sprout fur. It was horrifying ... and fascinating. Carly found herself unable to look away as claws sprouted from the tips of his fingers, as the force of what was happening to him began to rend his clothing in two and forced him, quickly, on all fours.

Her own voice was unfamiliar to her. "I ... I understand. But Gideon ..."

It was what she saw when he whipped his head back to face her, eyes that blazed a supernatural yellow above features that were no longer recognizably human, that finally shocked her into action. She managed one step back, then two as her mind grappled with the reality of what she was seeing.

"Run!" The word broke from his lips with an inhuman snarl just as a huge, brown *something* leaped through the door, pistoning into Gideon's chest and sending both of them crashing to the floor. It spun quickly, eyes glowing with madness, a hunger like none she'd ever seen ... and a terrible, terrible cunning.

Eyes that were now fixed on her.

Carly fled blindly down the hallway. She heard, rather than saw, the huge black beast that Gideon had become tear into his adversary with viciously long claws, slamming the other werewolf to the floor as he took the advantage with a triumphant snarl. Carly was nearly sobbing with terror by the time she slammed the door to her bedroom, a short sprint that seemed to have taken years. The door, the only barrier now between her and the living nightmare happening in her home, now seemed all too thin and breakable in the face of that … that *thing* that had come in from the night. She locked it, then looked frantically around for something, anything to place in front of it. She tried to block out the sounds coming from beyond it, the crashing and cracking of her furniture, her things, shattering. The unearthly snarling and roaring of the two beasts locked in battle. The thudding of their bodies against the floors, the walls, that seemed to shake the house to its very foundations.

Carly struggled with the overstuffed rocker she kept in the corner, dragging it past the bed, cursing when it caught on the leg of her dresser. "Shit," she panted. "Come on, damn it!" She looked quickly at her window, easy enough to climb out of if she had to. Except … what if there was another one waiting outside? Waiting for her to do just such a thing? It would tear her apart, she thought, shoving the chair as hard as she could against the door. It would … *it* …

Carly searched frantically for something else to put against the rocker, trying to block out the sounds of two creatures trying to tear one another apart mere feet from where she stood. *Creatures.* And Gideon was one of them.

The walls shook as something slammed into her china cabinet, its contents raining to her floor, shattering. There was an enraged bellow, a sharp crack as wood splintered. *Her table? Oh God, her house ... her life ...*

She put her hand against her mouth to muffle the scream that bubbled up in her throat as the thudding bodies, the chaos, moved steadily closer to where she stood. This was what she'd wanted, what she'd been all but dying inside for? *This?*

Carly shuddered as the vision of Gideon's face, the lengthening snout, the knifelike teeth, the blazing eyes, swam before her. She knew she would never forget it, the barely contained violence that had radiated off of him. In that moment, he had been beautiful. And terrible. And completely inhuman.

God help her, she loved him. But the snarling, slavering creature that had torn in out of the night after him was still closer to him, in both form and understanding, than she could ever be.

The walls shook again, harder this time, close enough that she wondered wildly when the two of them would come crashing through her door. And then a snarl, though she couldn't tell whose, rose into a deafening scream that could only mean one thing: *death.* It was ear-splitting, endless. Until it finally faded into nothing, leaving only oppressive silence.

Carly waited, blood pounding in her ears as she stared at the door, wondering what might come through it if she stayed. It could be Gideon. He could be hurt; he could need her. Or he could be dead already. Carly closed her eyes for a moment, steeling herself. She had to get out, she knew. It might not be too late to save herself, to save them both, but she had to go, and *now*.

She heard it then, the soft *whoosh* of the window sliding up behind her. And just like that, she knew it was over. Carly barely had time to tremble. It was too late, after all.

"Evening, darling."

A hot growl against her ear, claws sliding over her mouth to silence her scream. Teeth like razors, meeting no resistance as they slid into tender flesh. *Biting me,* she thought frantically even as her consciousness began to desert her. *It's biting me, oh God, no, where is Gideon, I need …*

And then there was only silent, blessed darkness.

Gideon stood panting over his attacker, his naked body, human once again, now covered in blood. Most of it, thankfully, was not his own. The Wolf at his feet, blood still pooling beneath it, would never take the human form again. It had attacked him as an animal, and an animal it would stay.

Foul, unnatural beast. Gideon's lips peeled back in a disgusted snarl as he gave the carcass one final kick, sending it skidding away from him, before turning his attention back to the door. The other, the Gray, lurked somewhere beyond it … waiting, he was sure, to strike.

He'd scented them as soon as he'd opened the door, sensed them lurking just beyond the ring of light that the illuminated house cast. And they'd wanted him to. He had known it with the full force of the heightened senses of his kind, tasted the tang of their excitement on the night breeze, felt the electric crackle of their blood lust. This Wolf, smaller and quick but no real match for him, had come first. But the other, the Gray who haunted him, had been there too.

And now it was time to finish it. The moon, so nearly full, coursed through him in all her glory. Gideon stood invigorated, ready for the kill.

Yet though the door hung open and he waited, there was no movement, no sound from the darkness beyond. The Gray hadn't run this time, Gideon was sure of it. This was the endgame for the two of them, time to kill or be killed. But as the minutes stretched out in the stillness, Gideon was filled with a creeping dread that he'd missed something, that some fatal mistake had been made.

I will drink her blood, Guardian.

"Carly," he whispered hoarsely, a split-second before he flew in lightning-quick strides to her door. She'd tried to block it. That registered as he flung it open, sending her chair flying into the wall as though it were nothing more than a pillow. Carly had tried to block herself in; she'd done as he'd told her. And the window that might have been her escape had let a nightmare in to her instead.

It was the Gray. Except, Gideon thought with dawning horror as he stopped short just inside the room, this creature who held Carly in its arms, cradling her limp form close to its chest as though she were a sleeping child, was no longer Wolf … nor was it even remotely human. It was both, and neither. And it stared back at Gideon with eyes red and full of hellish joy.

"I told you I would drink her blood, Guardian," he crooned almost lovingly as he stroked one long, dagger-sharp claw down Carly's pale cheek, those hideous red eyes never leaving Gideon's. He stood like a man, but slightly hunched, as though uncomfortable in this skin, caught as he seemed somewhere between human and beast. His body was covered in fine silver fur, though the wiry contours of his sinewy musculature were clearly evident just beneath. Sharply pointed ears swept back away from his face, which, while somewhat like a man's, held the slight protrusion of a snout, and a grinning maw of knifelike teeth. Long, deadly claws curved from the tips of his fingertips, from the toes on his oddly lengthened feet, warning Gideon off of moving too fast, too soon.

And that strange amulet, glinting dully in the light, still hung from the creature's neck. The sight of it filled Gideon with a dread that seemed bone-deep, though he couldn't say why.

What in the name of God are you? he wanted to ask. But he held his tongue, waiting for any chance he might have to snatch Carly away, for any opening there might be to send this thing back to whatever hell it had come from. Gideon chanced a quick glance at Carly's chest, feeling a faint kindling of hope when he saw its shallow rise and fall.

His interest in her condition did not escape her captor.

"Oh, your pretty is still with us, Guardian. Never fear. I've only had a small taste, you see?" The creature shifted slightly, allowing Carly's weight to drop just enough to the side so that the tender flesh between her neck and shoulder was exposed.

Gideon sucked in a sharp breath, unable to conceal his horror at the sight of the red, oozing slashes where she had obviously been bitten.

"Yessssss," the Gray hissed, running his tongue over his dagger-like teeth in hungry pleasure. "Just a small taste. But I assure you … she's quite delicious. Perhaps you'd like me to share?" His smile was mocking, and Gideon got the unnerving impression that the Gray was feeding off of Gideon's own barely contained rage.

"Put her down," Gideon growled roughly, determined not to give away any more of the pain he had felt, was still in. Carly's fate, no matter what might come, was now sealed. "You've come for me, haven't you? And here I am. Let her go."

"Mmm. You'd like that, wouldn't you? Not that you can save her." He stroked Carly's cheek again, the tone of his voice lilting, gentle … and utterly mad. Whatever this beast was, Gideon knew with certainty, his mind was broken beyond any hope of redemption. He wondered if even his murderous cousin knew exactly what he'd unleashed … if he was naive enough to think that anything so malevolent as this could ever be completely controlled. Gideon watched the creature caress her as an unspeakable despair welled up within him. Carly, the only mate he would ever want and the one he had fully intended to deny himself. So many mistakes, he thought. Foolish decisions, wasted time. And he vowed that if he got her back, he would make sure, with every ounce of his strength, that she knew what was in his heart. He would give her that.

It was all he had left to give.

For the moon rose full two nights hence, and then, Gideon was all but certain, the power of the Wolf would not only claim Carly's body for its own, it would devour her whole.

If this horror had his way, though, the two of them might never make it that far.

"What I would *like*," Gideon replied softly, "is for you to stop hiding behind cowards and cheap tricks and face me like a man. Or a Wolf."

"Oh, but I am neither, Guardian. Or hadn't you noticed?" The Gray curled his mouth into some hideous imitation of a smile, drawing Carly more tightly to him again. "I am what your people might have been, had you the strength to wield such power. I am your past, and your future. Your future *master,* that is. Does your blood not recognize mine? I am Drakkyn."

"An odd sort of strength," Gideon hissed, "to hide behind a woman." All his questions were lost in a gathering haze of rage as this intruder, this cowardly assassin continued to touch, to hold what was not his. Instinct began to override reason. *His mate was threatened … protect thy mate …*

The insult hit its mark. "Fool," sneered the Gray, blood-colored eyes narrowing in anger. "I might have let you watch her die. Now that pleasure will be mine alone." He tossed Carly's unconscious body aside then, as carelessly and roughly as one might discard an unwanted doll. Carly gave a soft moan of pain as she hit the floor, though she did not, even then, stir. It was a sound that shot directly to Gideon's heart.

"You'll pay," he snarled, intense emotion shifting his shape and form almost instantly, his Wolf form seeming somehow larger, charged with an energy he had never before experienced. And in his singular focus on the destruction of the beast before him, he did not care.

There was a flicker of something like uneasiness in the Gray's eyes for a split second before his bravado reasserted itself. He took a wide-legged stance, claws at the ready, arms beckoning. "You learn quickly, Guardian. Unfortunate, then, that it's too little, too late. Come. You'll only add to my feast."

Power shuddered through Gideon as he launched himself at his enemy, slamming into him with such force that their two bodies, now entwined in a deadly, bloody embrace of claws and teeth, nearly went through the wall altogether. He fought like a true animal. There was no thought for the hot flashes of pain he earned as he tore with his hands, his feet, at the one who had robbed him of Carly, his one chance at love, his *mate,* forever.

After all he had seen, he was still surprised at the strength of this un-Wolf who called himself a Drakkyn, a word Gideon had never before heard uttered and yet somehow resonated in him with a dull fury. Whatever he was, the Gray had muscles like stone, flesh that refused to yield to claw under any but the most punishing blows while lashing out with incredible speed and power of his own. Still, Gideon fought with more fire than he'd known he had in him. It would be small comfort to them both, eventually, Gideon supposed. But this was to him no less than the most important Honor Battles that had ever been fought by his kind, because the honor at stake was not just his own, but Carly's as well.

The Gray lashed upwards from beneath him, striking deep into Gideon's underbelly. Strangely, it was this blow, one that Gideon could feel had come a breath away from doing mortal damage, that gave him the last punch of strength he needed. The expression of hideous glee at the wound he'd just inflicted froze on the Drakkyn's face as Gideon reared back with a deafening roar and ripped his claws through bone and muscle. The force was such that the Gray's head came off of his body before either one of them had time to understand what was happening. Gideon felt a surge of relief as the creature's crystal amulet shattered against the far wall. The shards steamed and hissed for a split second before simply evaporating into thin air. The body beneath him jerked once, twice. And then was still.

Gideon remained frozen atop the carcass as reality swam slowly back in, the red haze of his blood lust dissipating like mist in the morning sun. *It was over.*

All at once the adrenaline pumping through his system could no longer mask the toll the night's fighting had taken on his body. Gideon collapsed to his side, shaking uncontrollably as his system struggled to shift back into human form and rid itself of what was left of the huge well of inner energy he had somehow tapped into. There were long, deep wounds across his belly, his back, still oozing as they started the long, slow healing process. But he felt nothing, noticed nothing except the glitter of pale gold where Carly still lay motionless in a limp heap beside her dresser.

Through his tremors, the warm and welcoming darkness beckoned him into its healing depths to rest, to sleep. Still, Gideon somehow dragged himself, bloodied, battered, to Carly's side to coil protectively around her.

"Stay with me," he whispered as he nuzzled at her neck, into her hair, inhaling her sweet essence. He licked at the angry red of the Gray's bite in the futile hope that the healing agent in his saliva would do more than just soothe her broken skin, banishing as well the wild poison that would even now be infecting her system, changing it … *claiming* it.

"Stay with me."

But in his own personal darkness, Gideon was alone.

Chapter Fourteen

WHEN CARLY FINALLY SURFACED, IT WAS WITH ONLY one thought in mind: she *hurt*.

It was like swimming up from the depths of the ocean after a long, cool dive. Except the closer Carly got to breaking through the surface of the water, the less she was sure she wanted to. She was lying down. She felt this now, and that she was between fresh, comfortable sheets that might have been cool but for the fact that, somehow, she was baking, and from the inside out.

She heard her own frustrated moan as she kicked at her coverings, trying to get away from the thousands of excruciating pinpricks of heat flickering under every inch of her skin. She wanted to shout, to cry out for someone, *anyone* to call for a doctor, she was sick, someone needed to *fix this*. But her tongue felt thick and dry. It was as though someone had stuffed a wad of cotton into her mouth that had subsequently sucked every blessed drop of moisture from not just her mouth, but her entire body.

As if in answer to her fevered prayers, a cold, wet cloth was pressed to her head, her mouth. Tiny droplets of moisture cascaded like liquid heaven down the desert of her throat.

"Hush, love. Not too fast, I've got more for you. I'm here. Hush …"

It was the sound of that voice, like the rough scrape of nails against softest velvet, that had Carly's eyes flickering open, though it took some effort. They felt like they'd been glued shut.

"Gideon?" It took her seconds to focus properly, and when she did, her head began pounding with a dull, nauseating intensity. The light in the small room was dim, at least, the glow coming from a small, antique-looking hurricane lamp perched on the night stand beside her. The light it cast was just enough for her to make out the foot of the wrought-iron bed she lay in, the soft quilt in muted browns and greens that covered her, the large, comfortably worn dresser and mirror that took up most of the wall opposite her. All this, and the fact that the dark and faded blue sky outside the one window indicated it was either dusk or dawn.

Carly shivered in spite of the intense heat that seemed to be radiating outward from her very core. She had no idea where she was, *when* it was … and the longer she kept her eyes open, the more the unwanted bits of memory kept emerging. Each provided her with a flash of illuminated misery before joining another, the pieces arranging themselves to form a more and more coherent whole, like a jigsaw puzzle from hell.

They had fought … Gideon had left … but then … but then …

At the nasty twinge in her right shoulder, Carly remembered it all, and what it meant. Her vision began to darken and waver, and it was almost a relief. She would rather not know any more, she decided. She would rather just drift away and wrap herself in sleep so she wouldn't have to be involved in what was happening to her.

But again, his voice drew her back, low and hypnotic, a beacon in the encroaching darkness. She couldn't help but heed it.

"No, Carly, love. Stay with me."

Those words … had he spoken them before? There was something about them, something to do with what had happened after all of the awfulness. But her thoughts seemed mired in jelly. And if she were being honest with herself, there was nothing about any of that that she wanted to remember. If only she could forget.

The cool cloth bathed her forehead again, and this time Carly found the strength to turn her head slightly toward the hand that held it. Her tired eyes traced the large, familiar outline of it, up the muscular forearm sprinkled with dark hair, and finally came to rest on the only face, at this moment, she really wanted to see.

"You're … you're here," she rasped, hating the raw feeling in her throat, the scratchy quality of her voice. She knew what was wrong with her, had perfect recall when it came to the teeth, neatly and precisely sunk into her shoulder. The bite had been, in an odd sort of way, gentle … and Carly knew that had been by design. It had wanted to watch her suffer. *It* … she'd gotten a look at it, the last solid memory she had, as a matter of fact, before waking up in this room. The thing that had bitten her hadn't been like Gideon, or the werewolf that had initially attacked. It had been something else, like a man caught between animal and human at the exact halfway point, but also more. Something demonic. And whatever ran through its veins to make it what it was, was now in hers.

Not wanting to think about it, about what all of that meant, Carly focused on Gideon's presence. There was a nearly overwhelming rush of emotion that flooded her overtaxed senses when she locked eyes with him.

"Of course I'm here," he said with a small half smile, betrayed by the worry reflected in the dark honey of his gaze. "Not going to throw me out, are you?"

As if. Carly was fairly sure she was no longer possessed of the sort of wherewithal it would take to banish Gideon MacInnes from any aspect of her existence, even if he hadn't looked as exhausted as he did. And he looked, actually, like he'd been through hell. It made Carly wonder just exactly what she'd missed since she'd succumbed to the comparatively pleasant oblivion of unconsciousness. There were shadows under his eyes, dark and haunted. His hair, even for Gideon, with his constant mussing of it, was a mess. It looked as though he'd shoved his hands through it so many times that it had finally just decided to stand up in odd directions permanently. *For her?* she thought, a faint hope kindling within her before she ruthlessly shoved it aside. He'd said that his father had been taken. There were bigger things going on in Gideon's life than her. He'd made that abundantly clear on his way out the door.

Yet even now, after all that had happened, she was entirely focused on his presence, hungry for it no matter how much she commanded herself to shut it off, to let it go. His weariness should have showcased *some* sort of flaw, at least, something she could console herself with as a token of his imperfection. Instead, though, Gideon seemed even more impossibly perfect than before, the wear stamped on his features only enhancing the rough masculine beauty of him. Even more appealing than a pagan god, Carly decided resignedly, was a pagan god fallen to earth and in need of saving. She thought morosely of exactly how she must be looking right about now and suppressed a sigh.

"I wouldn't even know where to throw you out of," she rasped. "So no, lucky for you, I think that portion of our program is over with."

Gideon's smile deepened slightly. Probably, Carly reflected, because she at least still had strength enough to banter, even if she wasn't at all sure if her legs would hold her if she tried to stand.

"That's a relief, then. I'd hate to be thrown out of my own house."

Though she wouldn't have thought it possible, the heat licking at her bones suddenly became secondary to utter confusion. Carly frowned.

"Your house?" When he said nothing, a gnawing, unpleasant suspicion began to work on her. It wasn't possible. Was it? "Please tell me you own a place somewhere in the continental United States."

His eyes crinkled up at the corners. "No."

"So … I'm at your house in …"

"Scotland."

"Ah." Carly paused, looking expectantly at him, waiting for more information. When none seemed immediately forthcoming, she prodded him. Did he not realize that her nerves were worn so thin at this point that she would just as soon black out again to escape? "I feel like death warmed over, Gideon," she began, trying (and failing, she was fairly sure) to keep her testiness out of her voice. "I'm not really in the mood for a guessing game right now, so probably you should just tell me how I got here. After last night …"

Gideon abruptly silenced her then, when he leaned over to take her hand, rubbing a soothing circular pattern against her palm with his thumb. What was *this,* she thought, confused, distracted by the tenderness in Gideon's eyes, his actions. Hadn't he been the one who was walking away from *her?* The one who'd insisted it would be better for them both if they never saw one another again? It came out of pity, maybe, or guilt, Carly decided. She was probably owed both. She wanted neither.

"It wasn't last night, Carly," Gideon said, interrupting her stewing. "It was two days ago." When she just looked at him, stunned into silence, he nodded. "After the … well, *after,* I must have passed out. I was holding you. Do you remember any of this?"

"No." Except there was something, Carly thought, searching for any shred of memory past that horrifying face. Something about his words that rang true, some vague and lingering impression of sudden warmth and security in a once-terrifying darkness, allowing her to slip deeply into comforting oblivion. "That creature. Is he…dead?"

Gideon nodded, his voice grim. "He was strong, like nothing I've ever seen. But he's been sent back to whatever dark pit he came from." He shook his head slightly, eyes closing briefly, as though trying to clear his mind of unwanted and disturbing memories. "When I awoke, it was some hours later. The ... your shoulder," he said, obviously not wanting to call her wound what it was, as though not naming it might somehow change the nature of it, "was beginning to fester, and you were feverish, unconscious."

Carly raised an eyebrow, uncomfortable now with Gideon's obvious concern for her. She wanted desperately to lighten the dark, oppressive sensation that seemed to surround them, pressing in on them from all sides. Though most of all, she wanted this to just not be happening.

"So, you thought you could cure me with the miracle of transatlantic flight?" she quipped. And the humor might have gotten through, she thought ruefully, if her body hadn't suddenly decided to do a complete one-eighty and shoot straight from burning heat to ice-cold chills. Concern darkened Gideon's eyes anew as he tucked her covers more firmly around her shivering form. The gentle way he was handling her had Carly struggling again with her own raw nerves and emotions. Tears, frustration, possibly even a good, loud screaming fit, were all worryingly close to the surface, and she wasn't at all sure how either one of them would handle it if anything broke through. It seemed like their footing had fundamentally changed since Gideon had saved her life. But until she figured out how, Carly was going to have to stay bottled up.

She was no drama queen, but she didn't relish the prospect of restraining herself right now. Every girl had her limits, emotionally, and she was right about at hers.

"I carried you," he said softly. "I cleaned your wound as best I could, locked up your little house, and carried you. To the car, into the airport, on the plane."

A thought struck her then, and the worry it caused nearly took her breath away. She was in *Scotland*. And she'd been here for two days, leaving behind a crime scene of a house, and her parents …

But before she could speak, Gideon headed her off, immediately seeking to assuage the fears he must have seen written plainly across her face. "Don't worry, love. You've a fine friend in your Regan. She's looking after your shop, placating your parents with a tale of how I whisked you away for a weekend trip."

"That won't make my parents happy," Carly sighed morosely. "Or my brothers. They'll be laying for you." *If they see you again,* she added silently, and hated herself for it.

"She even knew where your passport was. Apparently you got them together, planning on going to …"

"London. We were going to go next summer." Those plans, so innocent, seemed like they were made in another lifetime.

"Well." He paused awkwardly, as though unsure of whether to address her comment, the diminished possibility of those plans ever happening. Then he continued on smoothly. "I owe Regan a huge debt, Carly. If I hadn't been able to find your passport, there likely would have been a massacre at the airport."

She hated the shaky, uncertain sound of her own laugh. "Oh, I doubt they would have shot you."

"Maybe not. But I would have done quite a bit of damage to anyone who tried to prevent me from getting you on that plane. Because there was no way I was leaving you behind."

His gaze was so direct and intense that Carly had to look away. She had hoped for, longed for, everything that was in his eyes right now. And now it was there, but for all the wrong reasons.

"I'm so sorry," she said in a voice she barely recognized as her own. "I know this was the last thing you wanted." Way to go, Carly, she thought miserably. If she'd only been paying attention, she might have seen what was happening before it was too late, might have been able to call for help, at the very least. Instead, not only did Gideon have to worry about his missing father, but he'd found himself nursing her through the effects of a werewolf bite.

It was one hell of a way to be strong and show him she didn't need him.

"You're wrong," Gideon replied, bringing Carly's startled gaze back up to his. "You're *exactly* what I want, Carly Silver." He continued to stroke her hand, his touch amazingly gentle, a direct contrast to the intensity with which he looked at her.

"Don't," she said softly. "Don't feel like you have to do this."

"Carly, I *need* to do this," he insisted. "This is my fault. I should have realized walking away from you was never going to work. I should have told you."

Carly sighed, closed her eyes. She knew there was a pained expression on her face, but she couldn't help it. He was trying to be kind, and she appreciated it. But instead of comforting her, all he was doing was hurting her worse.

"Look," she interrupted him. "I know you feel responsible. I know how I must look to you, lying here, and I can appreciate the fact that you feel like you need to take care of me until …" she swallowed hard, not sure how to phrase it, then settling for " … until whatever happens, happens. But don't you dare try to tell me how much you care about me now, Gideon. Don't you dare. Because if I hadn't been bitten, we would be on different sides of the ocean by now, and that's the way it would have stayed."

She was surprised by the heat in her voice when she spoke, surprised by how desperately she did *not* want to hear him say those words now, where before she would have given almost anything to hear them fall from his lips. Because now, she couldn't see how they would ever feel like anything but a lie.

No matter what had actually happened, he would have left her. And although it surprised her, understanding her own nature as she did, it turned out that was something she couldn't forgive. Something she would never be able to forget.

"I would have come back for you."

She opened her eyes, forced herself to look directly at him. *This is better for both of us,* she told him silently, not wanting to think about how those words so perfectly echoed the ones that had cut her so deeply when they'd come from Gideon.

"You'll never be sure, Gideon. Not really." She shuddered again, feeling as though she were sitting in a vat of ice water instead of beneath a heavy quilt. "And neither will I. So let's just leave it."

"I can't leave it," he said roughly, his hand tightening on hers until it was almost painful. "I was wrong, Carly. It's not an easy thing for me to say, so you'll hear me out when I say it. When I saw you in his arms, bleeding, I thought I'd lost you. I thought you were dead, that I would never see your smile again, or hear you give me hell for kicking around your bloody boxes, or feel you against me. And I wanted to die too."

"Gideon," she pleaded, shaking worse now, and not only from the chills. Everything was too raw, too fresh. She wasn't sure how much more she could handle before she simply shook apart.

He loosened his grip on her, moving his hand up to stroke her cheek. To Carly, trapped in the cold, it was like being touched by the sun. "Have you not wondered why the bond between us was so strong, right from the first? It was because, for my kind, there is only ever one love, one mate. We know it instantly, feel it deeply. And once that connection is made, there is no turning back, no matter how we might wish it. You're mine, Carly. My only love. My life mate."

Carly just looked back at him, wishing she'd known, wishing he'd explained before it didn't matter anymore. Because no matter what he said now, the throbbing, insistent pain in her shoulder spoke louder. It was all too late. "So you would have wished that, I guess," she replied, trying to keep her voice from breaking. "Wished we'd never met. Then you would still be free."

"No, damn it," Gideon snapped, raking an angry hand through his hair. "I only wish I'd accepted my feelings. That I'd told you the truth so that you could have understood your own." He leaned forward, and Carly was unable to look away from the burning, roiling emotion in his eyes. "I wish I hadn't wasted what little time we've had trying not to love you."

She tried to jerk away from him then, shaking her head. "Well, I don't love you," she told him, but even to her, her protest sounded weak and unconvincing. "Whatever this is, it isn't love. I don't."

"I heard you, the night we made love." He nodded at her shocked, embarrassed expression. "You gave me the words, Carly, and I heard them. You may not want to love me. God knows, I wouldn't. But you do. Because just as you belong to me, I belong to you."

"I don't *want* to love you," she snapped, suddenly feeling very, very close to the edge of her restraint. She wanted to lash out, to hurt him for hurting her, for waiting until now, when she was *dying,* to open up to her. Violent emotion welled up like a tidal wave within her, and despite the weakness of her body, Carly felt her hands curling into claws. She fought the urge to bare her teeth at him in warning.

"I don't want *you!*"

She registered the change in Gideon's expression, something very like surprise, although her rejection of what he was telling her couldn't have surprised him so utterly. The anger she was cruising on, however, left her incurious as to its source. He wanted to bare his soul to her? Well, there were a few things he needed to hear from her, too.

"You think that I'm just going to fall all over you, that all is forgiven because you're telling me this now? On my damn *deathbed?* Nothing has changed, Gideon. I've never pretended to be anything with you that I'm not. I have kept nothing of myself from you. You, on the other hand, have done nothing *but* hold back. For every step forward I've tried to take, you've taken two back away from me. How is that love? How is that anything but the side effects of … of some unnatural, unwanted physical reaction?" She was snarling at him now, and she knew it. But to her surprise, Gideon was silent, letting her say her piece. *Good.* She wanted him to let her. But then she wanted him to tell her to shut up, to make her believe that he loved her the way she loved him.

Because he was right, of course. She did. God help her, but she did.

"I may love you, Gideon MacInnes," she finally hissed, "but I hope you understand, it's only because I can't help it." She collapsed back against her pillows, completely drained now. She was so tired of the push-pull between her common sense and her heart, neither of which seemed to be able to decide whether they wanted Gideon to stay or to get the hell away from her and let her die in peace.

Carly turned her head from him, staring at the wall. Minutes passed in silence, Gideon neither speaking nor leaving. She stayed motionless, not wanting to ask him to do either. Her anger had gone as quickly as it had come on, leaving her empty and exhausted. There was more light in the room now, leading her to believe that it had been just before dawn when she'd awakened. Her head ached worse than before now, and Carly closed her eyes against it, glad that at least her current level of exhaustion would allow her to escape into sleep. Still, before she could do that, there was at least one question she needed answered.

"How long do I have?"

Though he couldn't have mistaken her meaning, Gideon waited a moment before answering. When he did, his voice was soft, his tone guarded. Carly had no idea what he was thinking, and barely had the energy to care.

"The moon rises full tonight."

Carly said nothing. What else was there to say? She wished, futilely, for her family, for their warm comfort. She should call them later, let them know she was all right, for now. *Later.* She didn't want to say anything more, but there was one thing, one last thing, she needed to hear from him. There was something Gideon owed her that she did seem to want, after all.

"I don't want to be alone. When it happens."

"I'll be with you," he said gently, his voice the caress he didn't give her with his hands, and then she did hear him stir, pushing his chair back as he rose. "I'll stay with you. Don't lose hope, Carly. It isn't certain …"

She shook her head weakly, twisting her mouth into a small, unhappy smile. "I'm more of a bunny than a wolf, Gideon. I understand what that means, and so do you. Just come back later. I'm so tired …" And she felt herself slipping back into darkness, even as she heard Gideon open the door and pause just before he left.

"I'll be right here if you need me. And Carly … you're just what I would have wished for. I only might have wished that my loving you wouldn't have hurt you so."

"Mmm," was her only reply, as she took his sweet words down with her, something to hang onto in the darkness, the place where she waited for whatever padded silently behind her now, dogging her every step with excruciating patience. Waiting, she felt with every fiber of her being now, to claim her. It was from that darkness that she heard Gideon's parting words echoing to her, though whether they were real or imagined, she couldn't be sure.

"If you think you know nothing else of me, know this; I do love you, Carly Silver. Until the day I die, nothing will change that truth. Sleep, love. Save your strength. For me."

And real or not, Gideon's words flickered to life within her like hope.

Hope, however faint, that she really did have within her what it would take to make it through the night.

To take an ending, and make it a beginning.

Gideon shut the door quietly and padded down the narrow back stairs of his cottage. He'd had plenty of time to think on the long flight home, and at this point he'd decided that going minute to minute was as much as he could reasonably handle, thought-wise. He'd never felt so close to physical and mental collapse. It was sheer stubbornness that kept him going, Gideon decided, thankful that he'd had the good fortune to be sired by one of the most stubborn old goats he'd ever encountered. With that thought, of course, came a pang. Where was Duncan now? And was he all right? He could only hope that Duncan's legendary intractability was still serving him in keeping him alive.

It had been like walking into the aftermath of an explosion, Gideon reflected. There had been a car waiting for him at the airport, as he'd requested when he'd called Gabriel to let him know of his plans. It had been a long, silent drive from Edinburgh to Fort William and the Corran Ferry, with Carly either asleep or unconscious beside him, occasionally surfacing in a groggy confusion she obviously no longer remembered. It was just as well. Two miles past the tiny village of Lochaline, down a winding, single-lane road, he'd finally reached *Iargail*. And with it, the complete evaporation of the warmth he'd once felt at seeing the rolling hills, their tops dusted with snow that had not been there when he'd left them. *Iargail* had only just begun to don the cold beauty of her winter, from the bare and gnarled branches of the oaks that Gideon knew would be transformed each time it snowed, to the still gray waters of Loch Aline reflecting the brooding sky. Whatever the season, it had always been Duncan's domain, full of the raucous spirit and energy of that man. In his absence, there was only a mournful emptiness that hung about the bare grounds and sleeping gardens. The warm brick of the main house, the once-playful blending of medieval towers and fussy Victorian architecture held no charm. Gideon might never have believed it could be so, but so it was.

It hadn't helped that those still there looked more like the walking dead than anything else. Cousin Harriet, normally a robust woman full of good humor, seemed a pale shadow of herself. She'd soaked his shirt through with her tears before retiring to her room, overwhelmed and tired. Malcolm and Ian, on the other hand, had stood waiting, wan but erect, like the soldiers they were. Then there was the face Gideon had been happiest to see, that of his brother. He gave them all such credit, for despite their obvious need for some rest, all three had sat up with him most of that night. They'd heard what Gideon had to say, offering up what knowledge they had and tossing out any and all ideas for where and how they might prevent whatever Malachi and Moriah had planned … and get Duncan back.

Carly, whom he had settled on a couch in one of the sitting rooms for the duration of their discussion, had their sympathy, Gideon knew. But he also knew their main concern was Duncan, and who could blame them? They didn't know Carly as he did. He himself, however, was torn each time he had to leave her side, though up until just now, she hadn't seemed to have any inkling he was there. Now, he wasn't sure what was worse, the waiting for her to open her eyes, or seeing what was in them once she had.

Gideon swung to the left when he reached the bottom of the stairs, seeking comfort in the familiarity of his home. Once, when he'd first taken what had originally been the Factor's house for his own, this set of stairs had come out into a tiny, cramped kitchen, not much different from a series of other dark and cramped rooms that comprised the choppy floor plan of the nineteenth-century house. He hadn't cared, though. Hadn't been interested in what was, only what he could make it into. And he had— sometimes with help, often alone—transformed the stone cottage's old-fashioned and impractical interior into an open and welcoming modern retreat. Walls had come down, and then had come hardwood floors, granite counters in a rich burgundy that perfectly complemented the warm colors he'd chosen for the walls, the furniture.

Gideon had found he liked clean lines, and an uncluttered feel to his space. When he walked in his front door now, that was exactly what he saw. It had been Gideon's vision, and this place, the blending of the old and the new, had brought him peace. He'd been going to start on the upstairs when he came back, he thought with a touch of regret, remembering the joy he'd taken in the planning of it, the options he'd thoroughly enjoyed mulling over.

Now, unless his final vision included Carly to share it with, children to clutter up the expanded bedrooms, his father to crash about like a bull in a china shop, irritating Gideon with his overstepping and delighting those children with what would no doubt be incredible spoiling … there would be neither peace nor joy in any future Gideon might have in this house.

Gideon grabbed a heavy ceramic mug from a cupboard of his shadowy kitchen, pouring himself some of the coffee that sat warming in the pot of his coffee maker. Gabriel hadn't indulged himself, opting instead for tea, Gideon noted, from the looks of the still-steaming teapot on his stove. He might have done the same himself, on a normal day, Gideon reflected. But today was anything but normal, and he needed something stronger.

He lingered a moment before heading out into the living area and over to where Gabriel lay sprawled half on, half off his couch. His brother had obviously dozed off waiting for him to return from tending to Carly. His sleep was light, though, Gideon saw as Gabriel started, then straightened at his approach. They were all on edge, and none of them wanted to let his guard down for fear of who or what might be waiting for just that to happen.

"How is she?" Gabriel asked, his voice rough with sleep. Gideon had to smile, unable to help noticing the rumpled copy of *Maxim* still resting across his brother's broad chest, the shirt buttoned wrong and just as rumpled as the magazine. Gabriel's obstinately messy boyishness had irritated him plenty at different times over the years, but at this moment, everything about Gabriel's presence was a comfort. Particularly, Gideon thought with a rush of affection, Gabriel's firm and unwavering conviction that together, there was nothing the MacInnes brothers couldn't set to rights.

He needed to borrow some of that faith.

"Sleeping again," Gideon answered, sinking into the overstuffed chair opposite his brother with an audible groan. "She did wake, though. For a few minutes." He shook his head at Gabriel's questioning look. "She's already started the Change."

Gabriel's eyebrows shot up. "So early? I thought she'd have until nightfall before it really started in earnest. That's how it always was for us, after all, before we could control it."

"We weren't bitten. And certainly not by what got at her." Gideon gritted his teeth against the memory and took a large swallow of his coffee. "No, she, ah … lost her temper with me, a bit. And her eyes changed." He stared into his cup, remembering. "I don't think the teeth were far behind. She looked like she wanted to take a good-sized chunk out of my hide."

"Did she know?" His expression was unreadable, but Gideon had a feeling there was a fair amount of hope hiding behind it. He hated to quash it, but hope, in this case, was fairly pointless.

"No." Gideon took another swig of the strong, black liquid in his mug before setting it on the long, heavy coffee table in front of him. "No. Just that short moment took so much out of her that she needed to rest again." He stared into space, thinking of the way Carly's beautiful blue eyes had gone to feral yellow in the space of a heartbeat, startling him into silence as she raged at him. He'd watched, assessed ... and when she'd continued to cruise on the first small rush of that new power, he'd almost dared to consider the possibility ...

Then she'd all but collapsed, and Gideon had started to prepare himself for the inevitable. *I don't want to be alone,* she'd told him. And with all that was in him, he'd be damned if he broke his word on that.

"Well." Gabriel looked as deflated as Gideon felt. "Well, we still won't know until we know, I suppose."

Gideon put the heels of his palms to his eyes and pressed, hard. He knew his fatigue would lessen as the day wore on, as the moon began to pulse in his veins like a heartbeat. Normally, that thought would have comforted him. But now, knowing what the night held in store for Carly, he was hard-pressed to wish the day away.

"No," he finally allowed, though the words sounded false to him as he spoke them, "I suppose we won't."

Gabriel sighed and unfolded his long, lanky frame from the couch. Gideon was surprised when he walked over to clap him roughly on the shoulder. "If she can still give you hell, she's a fighter, Gid. She'll make it. Don't think she won't."

Gabriel's eyes were serious, dark, and Gideon could only give him a sharp nod. It was good that Gabriel was there to bolster his flagging spirits. Especially when Gideon contemplated that, no matter how much he tried to gird himself for what was to come, simply speaking of a world without Carly might break him apart.

A quick knock at the door had them both turning their heads then. Gabriel ambled toward it.

"Must be the rest of our merry crew," he quipped, and indeed, when he opened the door to the cold, gray morning, Gideon could make out Malcolm's brush of russet hair just outside.

"Come on in, Mal," Gideon called, straightening in his chair and downing the rest of the bitter contents of his mug. "Join the party."

Malcolm MacDonald, a tall, whipcord-thin man of fifty-eight whose slight build concealed a wiry strength that Gideon had been on the receiving end of many a time, moved quickly into the room. In one long-fingered hand, he clutched what looked to be a moldering bit of parchment, and his chocolate-brown eyes were ablaze with urgency.

"I've found something," he stated in his usual clipped way, getting right to the point. "After we spoke last night, I got to thinking about what your creature said, your Drakkyn, as he called himself. It rang a bell, somehow, but I couldn't think where. So I got to rummaging in the cellars."

"Musty old place, that," Gabriel interjected, wrinkling his nose. "Gideon and I must have ruined half of what was down there, all those old books and bits of paper, playing at pirates."

Malcolm looked down his long blade of a nose at him, and Gideon bit back a smile. Some things, it seemed, never changed. "Fortunately for you, you missed a few things," he said. "Including this." He handed the crumbling document to Gideon.

"It's a copy of the Dictates," he said after scanning it quickly. "Quite old, from the looks of it." He raised his questioning eyes to Malcolm's expectant ones, wondering what he was missing. The Dictates were hardly full of deep inner meaning. Saint Columba had written them as simply and directly as possible, he knew, for a rough group of men completely devoid of most of the trappings of civilization. So that they could *understand*. And anyway, he'd been raised on the damned things. He needed no tutorial. He wished Malcolm would just spit out what he was getting at. But he'd learned, through the years, that he would be led to the answer in Mal's sweet time, and that was all there was to it.

So when Malcolm simply continued to look at him, Gideon reached a little further. "I actually think this is the oldest copy I've seen."

Malcolm nodded, pleased. "Exactly. The oldest I've seen, as well. Possibly the oldest we have, as the wording is a bit off of what we've come to use." He kept his gaze locked with Gideon's. "Have a look."

Gideon frowned and looked more closely. The ink was faded on the small square of parchment, but he could still make out the writing. Gaelic, it was, but his rough knowledge of the language, as well as his familiarity with the Sacred Dictates themselves, enabled him to make out the words easily enough.

"First, no harm against thy brother wolf," he read aloud.

"Not that one, no," Malcolm interrupted, obviously impatient.

"Break no faith with the Pack, nor thy mate, but guard them well."

"No, no, nor that."

Gideon glared up at Malcolm, feeling suddenly as though he were back receiving lessons, he the ignorant student, Malcolm the omnipotent instructor. And the old man always had been a bit of a show-off in that area.

Malcolm's eyes gleamed. "Continue."

Gideon sighed, not bothering to conceal his exasperation. "Hold to the path of light, whether moon or sun. Fall not back on the ways of darkness …"

"Ah," Malcolm said with a flash of triumph. "That's how we know this particular Dictate *now*. But that's not quite what this says. Read it again."

Gideon squinted at the paper, then read again, his voice fading in shock as he saw what was actually written on this ancient scrap of paper.

"Fall not back on the ways of the Drakkyn," he recited softly, then lowered the parchment to his lap to look up at his companions. Malcolm looked pleased, Gabriel stunned. "But … what can this mean, then? How was this lost?"

"Simple," Malcolm replied, plucking the paper from Gideon's hands and moving to settle himself in another chair. "The wording was changed because we, as a group, forgot what these Drakkyn, and their ways, even were. Lost in the passage of time. Or, more likely, I think, forgotten purposely."

"Why? I mean, are you certain that isn't simply an archaic way of saying 'darkness'? Because what is a bloody Drakkyn?" Gabriel sounded incensed—not surprising since he and Malcolm had been at odds for years. It was a function of pitting sense without humor, Gideon had always thought, against humor without much sense.

Malcolm gave him a stony glare before dismissing him with a turn of his head. "Your father, Ian, and I have had many discussions," he said, "about the origins of our Pack, of the werewolf in general, and all of us agree that there are some interesting discrepancies in the story we've all come to accept."

Gideon sat back, intrigued. It was true. He'd never thought to question the history he'd been taught as a boy, had never, he had to admit, been interested in questioning it. He'd just accepted. Fortunately, it seemed, not everyone had been the same. "Such as?"

"Well," Malcolm began, obviously relishing slipping back into his role as teacher, "for one thing, we were supposedly brought out of the wilds of Scotland, before this was even Scotland. But then, why is there not a whisper of the man-wolf in the oral history of the Picts, from whom we would have come? You'd think we might have caused a stir, being as we are."

"If not from there, then where, though?" Gideon asked, frowning.

"Where, indeed?" Malcolm tented his fingers beneath his chin and leaned forward. "I asked myself this many times, and then I began to wonder ... our history begins, for all intents and purposes, at the Stone of Destiny. Were we brought forth from the wilderness to guard it? Or did Saint Columba and the rest not realize what they had ... until we sprang forth *from* it?"

"Madness," Gabriel snapped, throwing himself back onto the couch. "Utter rot. You and Dad drank a lot when you were discussing this, didn't you? Werewolves from a stone. Genius." He crossed his arms and glowered at Malcolm, who was now pointedly ignoring him.

"It does sound a bit ... far-fetched," Gideon allowed, not wanting to hurt Malcolm's feelings. Fortunately, Malcolm simply raised a sharply arched brow at him.

"As far-fetched as a tribe of moon-sensitive shape-shifters guarding a hunk of rock in the Scottish Highlands?"

"Ah. Well." Gideon looked to Gabriel for help, but even he could only shrug.

"So," Malcolm continued placidly, though his chin was raised a bit in defiance. "We have an ornate piece of stone, brought forth, if the story is true, from Egypt, and a culture that is still shrouded in magic and mystery. A stone with a history of inducing visions, if you will, of heretofore unimagined places. It supposedly served as a pedestal of power, for the ark of the covenant, then for the kings of Scotland. But I believe, and your father and Ian agree with me, that the *Lia Fáil*, whether all or none of the things I have just stated is true, is a power unto itself. A power with a nature that ancient man would not have understood and that Saint Columba had the sense and foresight to keep, essentially, secret."

"You think it wasn't meant as a throne," Gideon murmured, only beginning to understand.

"Not so much a throne," Malcolm nodded, "as a door."

"A door to where?" Gabriel snorted, still looking incredulous. "Toontown? Bimini?"

"There are more things in Heaven and Earth, Horatio," Malcolm shot back at him. "And better uses for historical documents than making paper hats."

"So you think that this is all linked," Gideon said, a bit overwhelmed by what Malcolm was implying but still, through the surface impossibility of it, seeing the sense behind it. "That Malachi is trying to get at the Stone because he knows what it is, knows how to use it."

"*Thinks* he knows how to use it," Malcolm said, now looking troubled. "I have very serious doubts that Malachi has any inkling of what he's really doing. I also doubt that he is, at the core, behind this. Whether or not he knows it, I'm quite certain our cousin could only be facilitating something, some*one,* a great deal more powerful than himself."

"One of these…these Drakkyn? Whatever that, or it, is?"

"It's only a guess," Malcolm replied, spreading his hands before him. Then he shot a look at Gabriel. "A *well-educated* guess. But it isn't such a stretch, if you begin to think about it, that these Drakkyn comprise the missing part of our history. That they are, in fact, what we come from."

"What we escaped from." The memory of the hellish creature that had bitten Carly surfaced in Gideon's mind, just for a moment. Gideon blew out a long breath and looked at his brother, who no longer seemed quite so disbelieving. "Fall not back on the ways of the Drakkyn. Well. I suppose it does make a twisted sort of sense, considering."

"No, not twisted. It makes *perfect* sense," Malcolm insisted. "Perhaps we were exiled here. Perhaps we fled. But in allowing us to guard the Stone of Destiny, a thing which humans regard as a symbol of power without even knowing how much it actually has, Saint Columba left it in the hands of the only beings who, at the time, understood it. Who, if I'm correct, could even wield it, and who could protect it …"

"… from one another." It was Gabriel who spoke now, softly but in a voice devoid of mockery. "Christ, Mal. This is a lot to digest."

"Digest it later," Malcolm replied flatly. "Our cousin appears to have captured the interest of someone with an eye for conquest."

"And the keys to the kingdom." Gideon thought of his father, of the way he was being used as nothing but a tool by those he had spent his life protecting, and welcomed the blaze of righteous anger that kindled to life inside of him. Perhaps he couldn't save Carly, but he could ensure that the pain she'd been caused counted for something greater than the megalomaniacal dreams of his cousin … a Wolf who had sealed his fate, Gideon thought with little satisfaction, no matter which way the tide might turn.

"How do we stop this?" Gabriel asked Malcolm. "If what we came from was so bad that our people erased it from our history, then how can we even begin to stop it?"

"I'm afraid," Malcolm replied, shaking his head, "that we'll have to go on all our predecessors saw fit to leave us with."

"Blind faith," Gideon growled, raking his hand through his hair. "I'm sure God will forgive me for wishing I had a bit more."

"Saint Columba believed in us," Malcolm said, rising and giving Gideon a fatherly pat on the cheek. "Let's hope we can remember why."

"Does Ian know all of this?" Gideon frowned, just now realizing how conspicuous the other old lieutenant's absence was.

Malcolm frowned. "That's the other thing I wanted to tell you, though it pains me. Ian's been acting a bit ... odd, since your father's abduction. Twitchy, jumping at shadows. I don't know for certain, but I worry that he's gotten himself involved. That he's been convinced, somehow, that he was on the wrong side." He looked pointedly at both of them. "And so I would ask that we keep what we've said between just the three of us, for the time being."

Gideon looked at Gabriel, who grimly nodded his agreement. "All right. Though it sounds as though he knows most of it already."

"So now we wait, I suppose," Gabriel intoned, his voice impatient. "Twiddle our thumbs until they turn to paws and then run off to save the world."

"I'm afraid so." And Gabriel's morose humor finally had Malcolm's thin lips twisting into a reluctant smile. "Until then, I suggest rest. We'll all need it." He looked at Gideon, who realized with a jolt that for the time being, *he* was the Pack's Alpha, Guardian of the Stone ... and Malcolm was treating him as such.

"I'll return shortly before moonrise. As I've told you, the Stone is only active at the full moon. Whatever is afoot, that's when it will happen."

"Moonrise." Gideon nodded, but a voice in his mind whispered to him, keeping him from letting Malcolm go.

I don't want to be alone.

"Wait," he said in a voice that had Malcolm turning back to him, a question in his eyes. "I promised Carly I wouldn't leave her. She'll likely not survive the Change. And if I go, she'll be alone."

"I'm sorry for the loss of your mate," Malcolm replied solemnly, again surprising Gideon with his quick acknowledgment of what he saw as fact. "But this is bigger than us all. I'll see you tonight."

Gideon could only watch, his gut churning at what he knew to be the truth, as Malcolm turned on his heel and strode quickly, purposefully out into the day. Though he knew Carly would urge him to do what needed to be done, the thought of leaving her at the mercy of the beast that had been let loose in her blood made him ill. Especially since when he left her, he likely was saying goodbye for the last time.

The clink of glass in the kitchen had him turning, distracted for a blessed moment at the sight of Gabriel rummaging in the cupboards to emerge, at last, with a glass bottle half-full of amber liquid.

At the question so plainly written across his brother's face, Gabriel only raised his glass in toast. "I may have agreed to go to hell in a handbasket with you," he informed him, "but no one said I had to do it sober."

At that, he drained his glass.

And after a moment, Gideon joined him.

Chapter Fifteen

CARLY, LOVE … STAY WITH ME …

"Gideon? Gideon …"

Carly opened her eyes to the dimly lit bedroom, seeing everything in unnervingly sharp relief. Every object seemed illuminated from within, things as minuscule as a speck of dust all but leaping out at her. Horrified, she slammed them shut again.

She was delirious, and she knew it.

The heat slithering beneath her skin had returned with a vengeance, snakelike in its movement and reach. Try as she might, Carly could no longer escape it. The pain was now too great to allow her any more reprieve in the darkness of her dreams. Gideon had been there. She'd felt him, had clung to his presence like a drowning woman thrown a lifeline. He'd just been there, was there still … wasn't he? She'd heard him …

"Gideon?" she croaked again, daring to crack one eye slightly open to look for him. But he was nowhere to be seen, the wooden chair beside her empty. Carly swallowed, hard, trying to remember. He had promised he'd stay with her. He'd *promised*. But there was something …

A cool kiss on her burning forehead, on her parched lips. "I'll return as soon as I can. Hang on for me, love. Remember I love you … I love you …"

Gone. Gone to fight. And she was left to fight alone, here in this prison of shimmering insanity.

Carly turned her eyes to the window and the rapidly fading light. Though the sky was turning to the deep, lit-from-within blue of twilight, a sight she had seen many times before, whatever had happened to her eyes changed it, magnified it. An early star flickered like a candle. The encroaching darkness seemed to beat with a pulse all its own. Carly could feel it, suddenly, rising in her chest. Gideon's voice whispered from the depths of her memory, and she could hear it as though he were still with her.

It pulls at me ... the moon ...

When it hit her, it did so with a vengeance. Carly gasped as searing pain, like a white-hot ball of fire, ripped through her from head to foot. Unable even to scream, her body arched up off the bed, rigid with silent agony. Her hands clenched in the sheets at her sides as she sought something to cling to, holding on until slowly, the pain began to ebb. Carly lowered herself gently back to the bed, barely aware of the tears that had begun to stream down her face.

She waited for relief, but there was none. Instead of fire, there was now a steadily increasing, suffocating pressure. Carly sobbed out a short breath, tearing at the quilt, the sheets that covered her now as though they each weighed hundreds of pounds.

Hang on ...

"Gideon ... I can't breathe. I can't ..."

The pressure lessened a little as Carly finally freed herself from the bedcovers. Someone had taken her clothes, had replaced them with a large tee-shirt that covered her to her knees. Carly gritted her teeth, scrabbled at it with her fingernails. *Who the hell would do this to her?* It felt like it was made of sandpaper, chafing her skin so badly she was certain there were bloody scratches on her chest, her back. With a cry of triumph, Carly ripped it away, unaware of her lengthening nails, her self-inflicted scratches as she shredded the thin shirt directly down the middle.

She tried to get up, thinking that somehow movement might help, might allow her to get away. But as she swung her legs over the side, as her feet hit the cold wood floor, Carly realized a second too late that they were not going to hold her.

And then she did scream as she collapsed, first in frustration, then in horror as another bolt of flaming agony all but lifted her off the floor. This time, when it passed, she lay motionless, panting in a gathering pool of intense, silvery light beneath the window. She needed it, wanted to drink in that light with every pore. Instinct had her dragging herself fully into that light, stopping only when it bathed every inch of her small form. Carly's pupils dilated. She inhaled deeply, all of her senses hungry for this, just this. It was beautiful.

It burned.

Carly moaned, writhing in pain as her skin seemed to slowly catch fire. She waited for smoke, for flames to simply erupt from within and consume her whole. Instead, her eyes widened as she watched the skin on her forearm ripple, begin to sprout hair … to Change.

And this time her screaming, once it began, didn't stop.

Moonrise.

Malachi stood before the Stone of Destiny in the small circular chamber that had held it since it had come into the care of the Pack, some fifteen hundred years before. He could feel it vibrate gently, as though it sensed it was about to gain a new master. One who would wield, rather than suppress, its power.

It was even more beautiful than he'd imagined, Malachi thought, glancing up only briefly at his mother. Changed already, she was finishing the feast she had made of the old lieutenant who'd been fool enough to believe her lies, to forget the teeth that lurked within her kisses. *Soon,* he thought as everything within him rose, responding to the moon that now rode the night sky. Soon she would join her latest fool in Hell. And he would be the one to send her there.

Moriah MacInnes had served out her usefulness. And it was true, she'd been more useful than Malachi might have expected. Her cunning in luring Duncan into a position where he could be taken, drugged, *used,* had been their salvation. The old man truly hadn't believed she meant him ill. And now, thank God, what was left of the old Guardian's sorry life belonged to them. To him.

Jonas, whom he'd once considered indispensable, was dead. Malachi knew it now, and though it appeared his wretched cousin had saved him the trouble of having to do it himself, it was still a bit of a shame. But Gideon, his woman, the entire wretched Pack … none of them mattered anymore. Moriah had, for the first time, surprised him. And in doing so, she had netted him the keys to the kingdom.

Stupid bitch. She still thought parking his ass on the top of a singing stone would magically make him Alpha. Of course, he might have had something to do with that, Malachi thought with a smirk. Magic, she would see plenty of. But Moriah might have wondered if her only son hadn't learned a thing or two about lying after watching her all these years.

Fortunately, she would never assign him so much credit. Malachi had no illusions about the fact that he had never been quite good enough for his mother. It would be sweet to see her expression when she discovered, in the last moments of her wretched life, that a being such as Mordred Andrakkar would choose *him,* her weakling bastard brat, to control this new conquest. That their new master would laugh as Malachi spilled her blood. A fitting beginning, Malachi thought, to his rule over this place the Drakkyn lord called *Urth.*

"Sing," Malachi growled softly as he felt his form go liquid, watched the hand that stroked the jet black surface of the Stone reshape itself into a large, deadly paw. He closed his eyes with pleasure as the human form he had come to despise, in a way, was shed. Until nothing was left but the perfect beast that lurked within an imperfect shell.

Candlelight from a huge wrought-iron chandelier that hung suspended from the center of the low, domed ceiling played over the shifting figures of their small group, shadows seeming to dance and move about the chamber. Suddenly the candles dimmed, and the golden hieroglyphs etched deep into the *Lia Fáil* brightened until they seemed to burn. A beautiful, unearthly song began to rise from the Stone itself, strengthening until the very air pulsed with it. It was a song at once hopeful and heartbreaking, and if there had been a shred of humanity left in him, it might have moved Malachi to tears.

But there was no human. There never really had been, just the illusion of it. In the beginning, they had been Drakkyn. Now that he knew it, could embrace it, he was Drakkyn once again. It was their heritage, their stolen birthright. Their power.

And it was cold.

Malachi padded around to the massive creature that slumped before the Stone of Destiny, its large form deathly still. But it wasn't dead, Malachi knew. Not yet.

Moriah, the fur of her streamlined form gleaming red in the dim light, pranced excitedly nearby. Her yellow eyes gleamed, her tongue lolling out hungrily from a muzzle already smeared with blood. Behind her, a squat, muscular Wolf waited, still, subservient.

Malachi bared his teeth at both of them. *Mine.* This kill was to be his, and his alone. He had not wanted Marcus here. In the end, though, he supposed it wouldn't matter.

"Guardian," Malachi growled, his attempt at speech nearly unintelligible. But he wanted Duncan to awaken from the stupor they had kept him in, to see the face of the one who had discovered the truth. To know who had brought an end to his failed dynasty.

To his pleasure, the huge Wolf stirred with a thick moan. Cloudy amber eyes rolled up to meet his steel-colored gaze. As recognition dawned, the haze cleared, just a little, and Malachi saw those things he'd wanted, yearned to inflict on this man and his heirs since he was almost too young to understand what they were. Anger. Humiliation. Fear. And above all, a terrible comprehension of what was happening. The Alpha curled his lip and struggled weakly in an attempt to stand.

Malachi grinned, teeth gleaming skeletal white. Once more, he spoke, a halting, snarling speech. The main thing, the last thing, Duncan needed to know.

"Your blood," he ground out, watching Duncan's eyes widen as he fought to get up, to stand against him. Malachi simply inclined his head toward the Stone, lit with moonlight from within and ringing with song. "The door."

Duncan tried to push himself back, away, but the drugs he'd been given made his movements sluggish. Futile. Malachi reared back and ripped into Duncan's flank, striking deep with his front claws. Duncan roared in pain as tender flesh was rent open, as blood began to flow freely over the stone floor. The old Guardian crashed back down and lay, unmoving, at Malachi's feet in a spreading pool of crimson.

There was an excited yip at Malachi's shoulder as Moriah danced up, thrilled at what had been done.

Slowly, calmly, Malachi turned to regard her, secure in the knowledge that his new master, the Andrakkar, would be well pleased. He had followed the instructions given him. The blood of the Guardian was on his hands, spilled at the rise of the full moon. The key.

Now all he had to do was unlock the door.

Malachi watched through narrowed eyes as his mother and Marcus frolicked in their excitement, rolling in a frenzy of bloodlust and joy. He gritted his teeth as Marcus moved behind her ... as she *allowed* it ... and the last gossamer thread of his sanity snapped neatly in two.

Malachi cast a quick glance at the pool of blood beneath Duncan's prone body, cocked his head to listen for his cousins, undoubtedly on their way.

Plenty for later, he thought, decision made, claws lengthening as he advanced upon the entwined Wolves. *This won't take long, my lord. Only a moment.*

But oh, how he would enjoy it.

They padded in silence toward the ruins of the old chapel, the tall, lean Wolf that was Malcolm leading through the eerie half-light. The moon had just risen, and while their forms had shifted, their purpose had only intensified.

Gideon fought to stay focused, pace steady, hot breath misting in the cold night air. And yet his mind was full of her, despite his best efforts.

Protect thy mate.

But he hadn't. He had left his mate. He had left her to be consumed from within, going against every instinct. To save them all, Malcolm had told him. One final broken promise. But in losing her, Gideon wondered what there would be left of him worth saving.

Gideon paused once, turning to look back in the direction of the house. How could he go forward to fight when every fiber of his being screamed out against it? Wanted only to go back? Gabriel, sensing his brother's wavering resolve, turned back, nudged him along. His eyes, a darker gold than Gideon's own, their cast faintly green in the night, were full of sympathy.

That, and urgency.

Gideon started forward again, but slowly. Knowing it was right didn't make it any easier.

The chapel, little more than one crumbling wall and an overgrown foundation now, rose before them. Behind them, the lights of the mansion house twinkled merrily in the bitter cold. Mockingly. They spoke of a warmth Gideon doubted he would ever feel again.

Because there was more afoot tonight than he could yet understand. Beneath everything else, the scents of those he hunted, of the night itself, there was something even more ominous. Tonight, he scented blood.

It was not unthinkable that it might be his own.

One by one, Malcolm, Gabriel, then Gideon stepped over broken stone, moss, and vine into what had once been the inside of the holy place. Malcolm went a few paces, then stopped, issued a warning growl. Gideon moved quickly to his side, and immediately saw what had prompted that reaction; a passageway beneath the far wall, once obviously well-hidden, now gaped open beside a haphazard pile of wood and rock. Instead of blackness, the opening revealed a faint glow. From far beneath them, a thrumming, hypnotic song began to rise, growing louder and more intensely beautiful with each breath they took.

The three Wolves stood still, caught in the web cast by the unearthly music, like nothing Gideon had ever even dreamed before. He closed his eyes and inhaled deeply, wanting to drink it in like water, like air.

Then an animal's roar of pain ripped through his trance, rending that fleeting sense of peace in two. Gideon shot forward then, pushing past Malcolm to lead the way down the ancient and narrow steps into God-knew-what. Racing, hoping he was not already too late.

He knew that voice, even through the distortion of its pain.

Dad.

Just as he knew that the blood he'd smelled, sensed, permeating the night, had already begun to flow.

Gideon moved like lightning, that odd sense of becoming bigger, stronger, somehow *more* with him again, just as it had been the night Carly was bitten. The stairway curved endlessly downward, into cool, dark earth. Gideon could sense Gabriel and Malcolm fast at his heels, though they made no sound. The song that had so enchanted him grew louder still, but some barely perceptible change had occurred. Instead of hope, it was now colored with deep and aching sorrow.

There was another shriek, closer to them now, and then another.

Not Dad. Not that time.

It was small comfort, but Gideon clung to it. It was all the hope he had left.

Suddenly, and without warning, the steps ended. A heavy wooden door stood open, a blessing at his current speed, and Gideon shot through the opening into a cacophony of light, sound.

And blood.

Gideon barely registered the fiercely glowing *Lia Fáil* before him, the thing he had sworn to protect with his life, the reason for his Pack's existence. It was the rest of the scene that washed over him in a blinding flash, only pieces catching in his mind to register.

His father, in a pool of blood, sprawled before the Stone.

Ian … Good Christ, Ian …

Two Wolves, one of them Moriah, mutilated, nearly ripped apart.

Malachi, eyes gleaming madness, paws dripping red, atop the Stone itself.

The last, Gideon finally fixed upon, snarling his rage as black fury flooded him, eclipsing everything in his soul but an outright lust for revenge.

"Traitor!"

Malachi only grinned at him, tongue lolling, and at Malcolm and Gabriel, who now flanked him. His teeth were bared, ready to strike. And Gideon saw that his cousin's mind, after all the years raised on a diet of hate and fear, had at last broken. It was time to end this. After all of Malcolm's worries, here was only Malachi. It seemed it was time to put the beast out of his misery.

Gideon started forward, giving a nod to the others.

Strike now. End this.

He had seen Duncan's chest rise and fall, however weakly. It might be that there was still time.

Until Malachi did the thing that had all three of them stopping in their tracks, unable to do anything but watch in horror. In a voice surprisingly clear, unnervingly strong,

Malachi ended fifteen hundred years of embracing the light.

And let in the darkness.

As the ground beneath their feet began to tremble, Gideon reached out with his mind to the woman who carried his heart, hoping she could sense him, that she was still holding on.

God keep you, my love. I will come for you.

The others fought for the Pack. In his heart, Gideon fought for her.

"In the name of the Drakkyn, I command thee open!"

Malcolm had been right. The Stone of Destiny was a door.

And it was open.

Chapter Sixteen

CARLY LAY ON THE FLOOR IN THE DARKNESS, FLICKERING in and out of consciousness. With every wracking convulsion of her body, she could feel herself slipping a little further away.

Tired ... so tired.

She understood now, understood everything. It was little wonder that Gideon had tried to run away from her, if this was what happened when werewolves and humans tried to get together. And what was in him ... oh, it was so far from human. Carly felt as though she were being devoured alive, fighting to hold on to herself with slipping fingers as she dangled above some awful abyss. What was down there, in the blackness? She didn't know, but it had sharp, sharp teeth. And it was hungry.

She couldn't handle it, couldn't control it. Her fingernails lengthened, then retracted. Fur began to burst painfully through her skin, only to disappear, then reappear again. The pain and struggle had gone on for so long now that she was just barely conscious, and too weak to move. Carly didn't want to die. But she knew, with a sort of dull certainty, that she was losing the battle.

It would soon be time to raise the white flag and be done with it.

If only Gideon had stayed with her, Carly thought wistfully. Maybe she could have tried to battle just a little longer. Maybe not. But at least she wouldn't be here alone, with only the indifferent moon to watch her final struggles.

Then, as though she had summoned him with a thought, she heard Gideon in her mind, as loud as though he were right beside her.

"God keep you, my love. I will come for you."

And with his voice, she was where he was, felt what he felt in a sudden rush that dissipated as quickly as it came upon her. *In the air, the pungent tang of anger, fear. A rush of adrenaline. Horror and wonder as the door opened ... the door ...*

"Door? What door?" Carly scrabbled at the edge of the feeling, trying to catch it, to see more, but it was gone. She would have wept with frustration, if she'd had any energy left. She had touched him, somehow. She knew it. And the scent of him, the exotic, singular scent he carried with him, surrounded her still. Carly drank it in greedily, surprised to find that it bolstered her, even that hint of his presence.

There was trouble. She wished she could get up, to go to him, help if she could. On her small burst of energy, Carly gingerly began to draw herself up to a sitting position. She was so close.

A growl tore from her throat as some unseen force slammed her back down, hard, against the floor. And she paid for her effort, because the pain returned in full force, trying, she felt, to tear her in half. Carly arched and clawed at the floor.

She was at war with her own body. How was that something she could ever win?

Desperate, defeated, she pushed her mind towards Gideon's, searching blindly. She needed to make him understand. She needed to say goodbye.

Gideon, I'm so sorry, babe ... I can't ...

It ripped into her this time, the snarling, tearing claws in her leg, a sensation like a fist to her gut. And the coppery scent of blood, filling her nostrils, choking her.

Carly gagged as it left her again, though this time, she had *seen*. A doorway suspended above a beautiful black stone, the land behind it straight out of one of her nightmares. It was full of lightning in a violet sky, craggy mountains in the distance that seemed to absorb all light, blacker than Gideon's Stone, black as pitch.

And surprisingly, blessedly, Gideon's face. It wasn't the face he'd worn when he'd left her. Rather, it was the face she'd been drawn to, had stroked, the night she'd found him. Covered in midnight fur, yes, but with the same honey-colored eyes that burned, it seemed, just for her. Two faces, but always her one Gideon. And she would know him, love him, no matter which he wore. Because in essence, there was no difference. None at all.

The realization, so simple, left her shocked and breathless nonetheless.

Was that the key? Could it possibly be just that simple?

She'd been fighting so hard, struggling to stay alive against the thing all instinct insisted was killing her. It would go against everything she knew, all she'd learned, to stop pushing back. But she was fighting herself, her own blood … and in doing so, killing herself right along with it.

It was all in her. Different blood. Same Carly.

It was a theory, the last she had. And something told her she was right. Although, she consoled herself, if she wasn't, there would at least be no one around to point that out.

Carly closed her eyes, took a deep breath.

Summoned the beast.

Come to me.

As the burning beneath her skin became an inferno, invisible knives stabbing at every inch of her, she saw only Gideon's lopsided smile, his eternally tousled hair. His silken fur, his gleaming teeth.

He'd said she would be his only love.

So she would belong to him. Forever.

Incredible pressure built within her, pushing and squeezing, *tearing* as her body began to rearrange itself. To Change.

For you. Because I love you. I love you …

When the fur broke through, when the claws and fangs emerged from tender flesh, Carly started on one final, agonized scream.

And ended on a bone-chilling howl.

Carly staggered to her feet, panting, aching. And *free.* She was alive, had never felt so completely alive. She had not lost herself. But still … she was more.

And there was no time to even try to understand. Her hackles rose at the oppressive weight in the air, an odd, almost electrical charge that had all of her senses screaming *danger.* Carly's ears pricked forward. There was music in the night, a trembling beneath the ground.

Gideon.

She had seen his eyes. He didn't think he was going to make it.

A wildness rose in her breast, intense. Deadly. Instinct took over.

Protect thy mate.

The Wolf that was Carly raced out into the moon-bright night, all she felt, all she was, focused on one thing.

I can feel you. I'm coming. Hang on.

Gideon watched, paralyzed, as Malachi leaped from the Stone and a beam of brilliant light erupted from the top of it. The song emanating from it swelled to near-deafening volume, then ceased, leaving his ears ringing in the abrupt silence.

Gabriel whined, ears pinned back, but to his credit did not retreat. Malcolm also stood firm, though his fur was raised almost on end. The scene was static, the four Wolves, even Malachi, transfixed as the light shifted, widened, cleared. And became a door.

Lightning raced through a bruised violet sky. Ominous black mountains stood sentinel in the distance. Across the pale, dusty landscape, oddly bright against the darkness of the rest of the scene, two figures approached. They moved with feline grace, slim, dark silhouettes wearing long cloaks that swirled about them in some otherworldly wind. Though their features were obscured by both distance and the dim light, Gideon could see that their eyes burned as violet as the sky above them.

Drakkyn. His blood knew them, and Gideon's blood rose in greeting, in anger, in kinship as though he had always understood who and what they were. There was a sharp crack and the acrid whiff of ozone as first one, then the other stepped through the door. Then, with long-limbed elegance, they alighted on the floor in the chamber of the *Lia Fáil.* Now Gideon did move. He took one step. Forward. And the soft growl that reverberated through the chamber was his own.

Gideon shot a quick glance at his father, left thankfully ignored before the Stone, stepped over as though he were no more than an inanimate object. *Still breathing.* But for how long?

"Excellent work, Malachi. Others may have doubted, but I was certain you would come through." The taller of the two gave his companion a sidelong glance full of barely repressed hostility, then reached down to stroke the head of the Wolf who sat patiently at his feet, adoring.

They looked like men ... almost. Gideon had expected creatures like Jonas, odd hybrids of man and beast. But these Drakkyn could pass for human. One was obviously older than the other, his hair a short, sleek crop of gleaming silver. But there was a marked resemblance; pale skin, sharp-boned features, tall, thin figures swathed in severe black cassock-like clothing shot through with gleaming thread of vibrant purple. Despite the rebuke, the younger Drakkyn, his own jet-black cap of hair accentuating his fair skin, looked fixedly into the distance, unmoved.

It was the eyes, so intensely violet, that marked them. These beings were no more human than he, Gideon knew. And quite possibly less.

Uncertain, he waited.

It was not long before the one Gideon knew was the leader turned those intense eyes onto him. The intelligence in them, the cunning … the malice … hit him like a fist.

"Well, well," he said in a smooth voice, soft, but commanding. "I hadn't thought to see so many remnants of the last age here to greet us." He bowed slightly, eyes never leaving him. "Well met … Gideon, isn't it? Hmm. Perhaps I placed a bit too much faith in your kinsman, after all."

At his feet, Malachi whined placatingly, even as his eyes sparked with hatred at Gideon. The Drakkyn, however, only shrugged elegantly. "Ah, well, no matter. Jonas, who I'm certain you met, was stripped of his powers for a reason. His banishment into the Tunnels could not have proven more useful, to be sure, but … he was possessed of an unforgivable weakness. He used what meager powers your kind still possesses as best he could, but still, he never ceased to disappoint me." Again, the disdainful glance at his companion. "My lot in life, it seems."

Gideon stared. *Your kind?* Were they not all one and the same, after all?

The man continued as though he'd read Gideon's mind. It gave Gideon a shudder to think that perhaps he had. "But forgive me. I'm rambling when I don't really have the time. You low Drakkyn obviously don't remember your own banishment, and as it's been years since the House of Andrakkar has used an *arukhin* High Guard, I've no interest in anything but removing you from my way." He looked around him at the carnage, then back down at Malachi, a small, cold smile playing about his lips. "As for you, I can only hope you will serve my son as … enthusiastically … as you have me thus far."

From the way Malachi's head jerked up at this, it was obvious that the idea of serving this man's son was one he hadn't heard before.

"Ah, yes. I suppose an introduction is in order. My son, Lucien. After some thought, I decided that the rule of this *Urth* would be better placed in more …" his eyes swept the bloodied room, " … *stable* hands. But you will of course have the reward of your continued existence. That is, as long as you do what you're told. Remember, for the *arukhin* of old, service was its own reward. Let it not be said that Mordred Andrakkar is not a fair master."

Malachi slunk back, all of the hatred in his gaze now focused on the one called Lucien. The man Gideon assumed was Mordred watched this, seeming to enjoy it. His heir apparent was more concerned with Malachi's warning growl, though in truth he looked as though he found the entire situation beyond distasteful.

Odd, thought Gideon. And irrelevant. The Drakkyn were distracted. Gideon wasn't sure what they were up against, but if there was a time to move, it was now. He looked at Gabriel, at Malcolm, who he saw had been waiting, just as he had, for the right moment. A breath, and they surged forward as one, catching only a split second of shocked surprise on the faces of their targets before the battle was engaged.

Gabriel plowed into Lucien with a snarl, knocking him backwards toward the Stone. Seeing an opportunity to exact revenge, Malachi piled on, though his target was no longer his cousin. Lucien's enraged howl was evidence enough of that. Malcolm and Gideon headed for Mordred. Gideon saw the surprise, sensed his advantage, and leaped.

Only to be thrown backwards through the air by a blast of sizzling blue light. He crashed into the far wall, heard a bone snap with the force of it as pain rocketed up his left front leg. Seconds later, Malcolm came skidding towards him as well, stopping at the wall with a loud thud. Gideon struggled to his feet, adjusting his weight as much as he could to accommodate the wounded leg. Malcolm, however, lay still, knocked unconscious.

Lucien, he saw, kept trying to rise, but was under vicious attack from two sides. Gabriel gave a sharp yelp of pain, and there was the smell of singed fur and flesh. And Malachi …

God in Heaven, Malachi was on fire. As Mordred advanced on him, his calm expression now twisted into a mask of rage, Gideon both braced himself and watched as Malachi and Lucien struggled. Lucien staggered backwards, trying to keep the burning, thrashing animal from locking onto his throat. They fell, together, back through the doorway and into that strange pale dust of the land that was suspended above the Stone of Destiny.

"Fools," Mordred snarled, and now Gideon could see his handsome face was only a mask, worn loosely over something ancient and terrible. "Had you done the thing your ancestors failed to do and bowed to me, I might have let you live to serve us again. But I see you are as weak as you ever were. You shun power and favor for your weakling charges, these *humans* of *Urth*. They are only suited to be the slaves and playthings of ones such as we are, and yet you protect them."

Light began to pulse at Mordred's fingertips, red, angry light. He spat at Gideon's feet, and the spittle sizzled as if it were boiling.

"You will all bow to the Andrakkar before you die, miserable *arukhin,* shame of the Drakkyn. *Urth* is ripe for conquest. And you have forgotten how to fight your masters. A shame," he hissed with a smile that showed elongated, wicked teeth, "but one, I think, I will recover from."

Gideon felt, rather than saw, Gabriel at his side, standing with him to the last. And this would be the last, Gideon had no doubt, though he would try to face it without fear.

Mordred's form began to shift into something Gideon had never before seen, something he had never *wanted* to see, a massive red thing all dagger edges and biting teeth, horns dripping venomous green liquid that smoked when it hit the stone.

And then he heard it, a high, chilling howl echoing through the night above them. It was a voice sweet and clear, and it reverberated with some intense emotion that carried it to him, here down below. It twined around the heartbreaking song of the *Lia Fáil,* became a part of it. Until it *was* the song. He knew that voice, somehow.

That voice.

Carly?

The howl came again, nearer, then faded into silence. Even the thing that had been Mordred turned its vile head to consider the noise, head cocked toward the entryway.

It was Carly. *She had made it.* Gideon knew it the instant he thought it, and his heart swelled first with unspeakable joy … then terror. She was coming to him, but she had no idea what would be waiting for her at the door. This Drakkyn *thing* would enjoy showing her, no doubt.

So Gideon centered himself, focused on the sensation he'd encountered the terrible night Carly had been bitten. Of being a Wolf, but then *more.* Looked within, at the strength he had always prided himself on, at the new love that added to it … and reached out for the *Lia Fáil.*

His birthright.

Their strength.

Immediately he felt the pain in his leg fade, felt his ebbing energy return in spades. Felt the rhythm of the Stone's song rise within him, driving him, filling him with what felt like the light of the pure moon. This Mordred Andrakkar had spat upon his kind, and upon the humans he and his Pack kept safe. Whom they had loved, and loved still.

You do not remember how to fight your masters.

But perhaps, something in him did.

Gideon gathered all that was in him, all that made him what this creature hated, and focused it at the monstrosity before him. When the light erupted from him, throwing Mordred backwards, it did so with a roar like all the voices

of the Pack raised as one. He stood, and fought for his
kind. And the power of that slammed his enemy to the
ground. Seizing the advantage, Gideon fell upon him,
sinking his teeth into foul-tasting flesh that burned his
mouth on contact. There was a louder roaring now, full of
pain and fury, and it came from what bucked beneath
him. But Gideon hung on, teeth sinking ever deeper,
whatever vile-tasting fluid that ran through this beast's
veins trickling through them to drip onto the ground.

Only when the thrashing had stilled did he release
his grip. Mordred, form melting fluidly back into the
one in which he had first appeared, lay gasping before
him, thick, dark liquid bubbling from the gashes in his
neck. He grasped it, pushing himself backwards with
his heels. Gideon simply watched, unmoving, imper-
vious to the black hatred that was reflected at him
through burning violet eyes. There had been enough
bloodshed here tonight.

But this scum would, God willing, bear the marks
Gideon had given him forever as a reminder to him and
his kind.

Wherever his people had come from, this was their
world, this magic stone theirs to protect. Its doorway
theirs to keep shut.

"*Go,*" Gideon growled, jerking his great, shaggy head
at the glowing entryway. Malachi and Lucien had disappeared from view. He found he didn't care what had
happened, so long as they stayed gone.

Mordred made it to his feet, fell. Rose again to
fumble, wound in his cloak, back to the Stone, all the
while clutching his neck as that viscous black liquid

flowed faster, harder. He paused before it, glowing eyes
full of humiliated rage … and death. "This is not the end,
Guardian. Your *arukhin* remnants cannot hold this place
from me and mine. The warrior caste is dead. And this is
not the only door."

Mordred stumbled up onto the Stone. The second he
lurched through the glowing entryway back into that
foreboding, desert-like place, the light flashed, then
shrank into nothing but a pinpoint of churning violet
night. And was gone, with a wind that snuffed even the
candles, and left the chamber in darkness.

The only sound in the silence that followed was heavy,
agitated breathing. It took him a full minute to realize it
was coming not only from Gabriel, but from himself.

As though sensing all was now safe, Duncan stirred
weakly where he lay, while a thick moan behind Gideon
told him that Malcolm was also still, miraculously, with
them. He swayed slightly on his feet, and immediately felt
Gabriel's muscular shoulder dig in to prop him up. Though
Gideon suspected Gabriel was holding himself up by
doing this as well, he accepted the help without qualm.

For the first time in his life he thanked, truly thanked,
the moon that still rode high in the night sky above.
Because he knew that at this point, the only strength he
had left, flowing like liquid silver in his veins, came
from its luminescent pull.

A flash of white caught his eye then, appearing in the
doorway like a wandering spirit. But instead of simply
vanishing like so many wisps of smoke, it only hesitated,
then approached him, eyes glowing the rare and beautiful blue of the sky at daybreak.

Gideon waited for her, his magnificent white Wolf. The love of his life, his mate now in every way she could be.

His Carly.

And as she reached him in the carnage of the chamber, sparing a look for nothing but him, putting her head to his, Gideon realized that his restlessness, his doubt, had vanished. All there was now, no matter what came next, was peace.

In love, at last, he'd found contentment. The Wolf had given him strength.

But Carly had made him whole.

The house was quiet when she awakened.

Carly opened her eyes to the first faint rays of dawn, burrowed beneath the covers, protected from the cold outside by the creaking, popping coziness of Gideon's home. Her memories of the night before were a blur, from her own difficult transformation, to the horrible scene beneath the chapel ruins, to collapsing, exhausted, into bed after seeing that Gideon's father and friend were settled and mending. It was probably a blessing, to have so few clear memories of such chaos.

An added blessing that with this dawn came sanity.

She smiled at the weight of Gideon's hand across her stomach, the feel of his body curled so tightly behind her. He hadn't wanted to let her go, even in sleep. He'd stayed by her side all night, touching her, looking at her, as though constantly needing to prove to himself that she was real.

She turned over to look at him, to admire the strong features she loved so dearly relaxed in sleep. *Mine,* she thought with satisfaction. And she'd only had to turn into a werewolf to get him. Still had the aches and pains to prove it, Carly thought with a wince as her abused muscles protested at her movement.

One golden eye opened as she shifted, regarding her with wry humor as she wiggled to get comfortable.

"Enjoying the view?"

She laughed, and was rewarded with that heart-stopping grin.

"Not going to punch me in the head this time, I hope?" His voice, always deep, was husky from sleep, a sensual rumble that immediately wiped all awareness of her sore muscles from her mind.

"Oh," she said lightly as she slid up against him, as he cupped her backside with his strong, rough hands. "I can think of a few better uses for you than that, I think. Although you *do* still owe me a pet."

She squealed as he flipped her in one smooth motion, pinning her beneath him. Gideon grinned wickedly down at her through the curtain of his sleep-tousled hair.

"I'm much better than a pet," he growled, sliding smoothly into her. Stopping her laughter with a gasp.

"Well," Carly admitted breathlessly as he began to move in her in slow, languorous strokes, "I'll give you this … you know much better tricks."

"You don't know the half of it," Gideon murmured, his breath fanning her face before he claimed her in a hot, demanding kiss.

And as he brought her quickly to the edge, as she cried out his name when wave after wave of pleasure crashed over her, she was forced to concede the point.

"I suppose," she panted, still trembling from the aftershocks even as Gideon nipped at her neck, her mouth, the incessant rhythm of his hips starting her on the climb once again, "I could keep you around to find out."

"Mmm," Gideon groaned, his eyes closing as the pleasure began to sweep him along with it. "Just you try and get rid of me now, Miss Silver."

"Gideon," she whispered against his neck, realizing she hadn't yet given him the words that were in her heart. Words she desperately needed him to hear. A truth she needed him to know. "I'm never getting rid of you. Because I love you."

When he stopped, looking down at her with his heart in his eyes, and then cupped her face to pull her into a lingering kiss, Carly realized that no matter how much she'd needed to say the words, Gideon had needed to hear them even more.

"And I love you," he told her, as she arched up to him, tangled her fingers in his wild, soft hair, joined to him heart and soul.

"Always."

Epilogue

Christmas Day, Iargail Estate

"FLASH IT AT ME AGAIN. COME ON, YOU KNOW YOU want to."

Carly obligingly held out her hand and waggled the glittering diamond and sapphire ring that had, as of last night, taken up permanent residence on her left hand. Regan had teased her for admitting she hadn't even taken it off to shower that morning.

Of course, Carly thought with a catlike smile of satisfaction, her company in the shower hadn't seemed to mind at all.

"His mother's, you said?" Regan asked, her dark eyes glinting in the light from the enormous tree Duncan and his sons had wrestled into submission and forcibly decorated some two weeks before. Regan twisted Carly's hand back and forth, admiring the way the ring caught the light from where the two of them relaxed on a couch in the massive foyer.

Carly nodded, still pleased beyond words that Gideon had insisted upon flying the people that mattered most to her to Scotland for the holiday. Her family had arrived three days ago in a jumble of loud voices, hugs, and well wishes, not to mention opinions on everything from wedding plans (Maria already had a folder going, to Carly's amused dismay) to an ETA for their first grandchild.

Gideon had done well with the onslaught, but that last one had sent him nearly running on some forgotten errand to the kitchen. Not that she blamed him.

"Yeah. One of the many reasons I cried when he gave it to me."

"*I* cried when he gave it to you," Regan laughed, dropping Carly's hand and picking up her glass of wine. "Not that, thank God, anyone noticed."

"Nope. Too busy crying." Carly took one more look at the ring, an emerald-cut diamond flanked by two sapphire baguettes and set in white gold, before forcing herself to stop mooning over it for that moment in time. Regan had a high tolerance for happiness, but she was pretty sure making goo-goo eyes at her engagement ring for hours on end would eventually make her best friend nauseous.

"I love that he wanted everyone to be here when he formally proposed," Regan sighed. "I always thought heavy-duty romance grossed me out, but not that."

Carly had to agree. While their engagement had been a foregone conclusion after all that had happened, Gideon had still insisted on a measure of formality about it. He'd won her father's undying affection by asking him for her hand. And her mother's for putting the ring on Carly's finger and professing his love in her presence.

That it had happened on Christmas Eve at a mansion in the Scottish Highlands by candlelight probably hadn't hurt her mother's opinion about the whole thing either, Carly thought with a grin.

Or her own, for that matter.

"You just don't like romance when it involves men in period dress wielding swords," Carly pointed out. "I always knew you'd like a contemporary. You just don't listen."

Regan snorted and relaxed into the pillows. "Speaking of, when do I get to stop babysitting the shop for you? Jemma's doing fine … though she does seem to take a sort of sadistic pleasure in running Chris around … but I would like to get back to being a simple baker. I'm not, as they say, management material."

Carly raised an eyebrow. "I never really saw you as Simple Simon, either."

"Well, I'm no Carly Silver, apparently. Sugar and flour don't ask silly questions about release dates and continuing plotlines, and that's just fine with me."

Carly tucked her knees up in front of her and smiled. Regan had proven herself more of a sister than a friend in the last few weeks, calming her worried parents at her abrupt departure, looking after Bodice Rippers for her, and generally holding together all the loose ends back home until Carly could get back to tie them up herself. She didn't know what she would have done without Regan, and had told her so.

Regan, of course, had agreed.

"Soon," Carly replied, tucking a loose wave of hair back behind her ear. "I've been handling a lot over the phone and online, but it's not really a substitute for being right there. We're thinking right after New Year's."

A burst of hearty male laughter echoed out from the kitchen, turning both women's heads toward the rich sound.

"What about Gideon?" Regan asked. "Doesn't he have to stay here?"

"Duncan's decided he's not quite as ready to throw in the towel as Alpha as he thought he was." Carly shook her head, rolling her eyes. "MacInnes men, I am learning, on top of being astoundingly hard-headed, also thrive on stress. It's like air to them. So we'll spend some time here, more there, for the time being."

And it was true, Carly thought with wonder. Rather than making him back down, the new twist to the *Lia Fáil* with the belligerent and mysterious Drakkyn had invigorated Duncan. He and Malcolm were constantly plotting, discussing strategy, and as far as she could see, enjoying the hell out of every minute of it. There were already plans for a massive Pack gathering for New Year's, a prospect Carly both looked forward to and dreaded. The MacInnes werewolves were to have a new purpose, one they would undoubtedly, from what Gideon had said, embrace.

That she was *one* of those werewolves was still something Carly was adjusting to, though with Gideon's patient instruction and the unexpected joy she found in her other form, that was getting easier all the time.

Regan smiled. "Good. Just don't get too bogged down in your marital bliss. Otherwise, who'll I bitch to about my sucky love life?"

"I bet Gabriel would let you cry on his shoulder."

Regan's eyes narrowed as her gaze returned to her friend. "Don't think about it," she said flatly. "I have enough jerk problems without adding the supernatural element to the mix." She sipped at her wine, stared into the glass morosely. "No pun intended, babe, but I think you got the pick of the litter. Gabriel MacInnes is very obviously in love … with himself. Plus, I caught him sneaking a bite off of my Bûche de Noël earlier. Jackass."

Carly didn't exactly agree, but she kept that to herself. "I'm sure he could be reformed."

Regan uncoiled herself from the couch, slim and striking as always in the burgundy cashmere sweater Carly had gotten her as a gift. "If you had about a hundred years. Which I don't. I do, however, have an empty glass and a grumbling stomach. Wanna see if the menfolk have charred the turkey yet?"

"Nah, go ahead," Carly said with a soft laugh. "I'm more interested in my mom's traditional Christmas spaghetti, anyway."

"You mean we can only have one?" Regan quirked a smile back at her, started to go, then turned back, suddenly serious. "Hey, I hope you know … you guys are my family, Carly. Being here means a lot to me. So …"

Carly held up her hands to ward her off, even though her eyes were already starting to water. "Regan, damn it. If you go all After School Special on me right now and get me going again, you're going to get it. And by the way, I love you too."

Then it was Regan who laughed, squeezing Carly in a quick hug and giving her an exaggerated smooch on the cheek before wandering off to the kitchen in search of food.

Carly reclined, resting her head on the striped silk

pillows and closing her eyes, enjoying the relative quiet, the faint sounds of continuing chatter and laughter coming from the back of the house, and the delicious smells she'd always associated with the holidays.

Well, except for burned turkey. That would be a new one.

Later, she and Gideon would walk back to his house … *their* house, she corrected herself, though it was hard even now to wrap her brain around that … and curl up together in bed, making their own warmth in the cold winter night. And though she loved the bustle of her family, right now she looked forward to that the most.

As though she'd summoned him with a thought, Carly suddenly found herself lifted, then settled into Gideon's lap as he gave her a sweet, tender kiss and nuzzled at her hair.

"Mmm," he breathed.

"I love the yummy noises you make when you *sniff* at me, Gideon."

"Get used to it," he chuckled, shifting her so she could rest her head against his shoulder. "You're missing all the fun. Dad's somehow burned that bloody turkey he insisted he knew how to cook, and your mother and Harriet have banded together to throw him out of the kitchen. I'm pretty sure they're about to start beating him with wooden spoons."

She opened one eye to make sure he was serious. He was.

"Not the spoons."

"Not to mention that Regan just threatened to shove her lovely cake into various orifices of my brother's that

I'd rather not think about."

"Hmm," she sighed contentedly, relaxing into him. "No, I think I'll stay right where I am. I like this better."

"You're not sorry, are you?"

Carly opened both eyes this time, puzzled at the worry in Gideon's voice, on his face. "Sorry? For what?"

"Sorry about what happened. That you're never going to be as you were."

"Gideon." She placed a hand on each of his cheeks, stroking them, enjoying the rough feel of a face that always seemed to be in need of a shave. "I wouldn't want to go back. My life was okay before. But this is so much better. Because I have you."

He cracked a faint smile, but the honeyed depths of his eyes were still unsettled. "Me. And a bit more than that."

"Yes. And to be perfectly honest, I like that too." She grinned. "Not that I plan on sharing it with my mother anytime soon. She's said enough Hail Marys on my behalf."

Gideon looked at her intently, searching. "You're sure?"

Carly thought about the handful of times she'd Changed since that first horrible night, the purity of emotion, of thought, when she could roam as a Wolf. The care that Gideon took with her as she adjusted to what she'd become, guiding her, coaxing her, occasionally now even playing with her like a rough-and-tumble puppy. And she was sure.

"It's like when I'm with you. I've never felt so free."

Gideon let out a relieved breath that warmed Carly to her toes. That her happiness could mean so much to this big, beautiful man was something she intended to cherish every day for the rest of her life.

"Good. Because tonight I want to show you some of my favorite places. I want you to run with me."

Carly imagined it, running like a breath of wind along the shore under the Highland stars, exploring all the hidden and moonlit glens tucked deep into this place Gideon's kind, *her* kind, called home. She found she was already looking forward to it.

But there was one thing she needed to ask him, something she'd been afraid to ask since they'd emerged from the chamber of the Stone of Destiny. Since he'd nearly lost his father, and buried a man he'd called friend.

"Gideon … the Drakkyn. Do you think they'll come back?"

His voice was soft, and sober, when he replied. "If they do, we'll stand together. All of us. There'll be no more secrets in the Pack from now on. After all, we're not just protecting the Stone anymore."

Carly turned to kiss him, thought of the way he'd looked that night when she'd found him, noble, brave. A leader. And she was so proud to call him hers.

"A bunch of werewolves protecting humankind. Nobody would believe it."

He smiled, eyes crinkling at the corners. "Nobody has to, as long as we do it well." He stood, drawing her to her feet and leading her away from the couch with her hand in his.

"Don't worry, love. It's Christmas. And you and I have all the time in the world."

Carly kissed him once more, then walked with him into the welcoming warmth of family and friends, ready to begin their future together.

And hoping, with all her heart, that he was right.

In the violet darkness of another night, a door swung open.

And Mordred Andrakkar smiled.

About the Author

Kendra Leigh Castle started out stealing her mother's romance novels and eventually progressed to writing her own. She brings her love of all things both spooky and steamy to her writing, and firmly believes that creatures of the night deserve happily ever afters too. When not curled up with her laptop and yet another cup of coffee, Kendra keeps busy in California with her husband, three children, and menagerie of high-maintenance pets. For news of upcoming novels, or just to drop her a note (she loves to hear from readers!), visit her online at www.kendraleighcastle.com.